"Between the sway of lush palm trees and the steely core of its protagonist, *Hawai'i Calls* is a novel that delivers a gripping paradox in paradise. . . . As a debut novelist, author Marjorie Matthews displays a remarkable mastery of storytelling, particularly in the way she intersperses chapters from Sadira's point of view with narration by her sensitive young son, Lionel. This dual perspective moves the story along apace, but also provides a layered look into the complex natures of both mother and son, and how easy it is for good intentions to be misunderstood and resentment to foment. . . . A must read."

–Joni B. Cole, author of *Good Naked: How to Write More, Write Better, and Be Happier*

"A compelling story of family, heartache, and transformation told in prose as intoxicating as the 1930s and '40s Honolulu that is its indelible backdrop."

–Meg Lukens Noonan, author of *The Coat Route*

"*Hawai'i Calls* is the quintessential American story: a sweeping family saga of movement, change, reinvention, and transformation, while the forces of history shape events and the characters' own haunted pasts lurk in the shadows. Told through two voices—that of the ambitious Sadira, who dreams of a life that offers more than being a housewife and enabler for her feckless alcoholic husband, and that of her young son Lionel, who sees the world through a markedly different lens—*Hawai'i Calls* reminds us that every family story has multiple narratives. Matthews presents Sadira, Lionel, and the large cast of other characters with depth and empathy; there are no bit parts in this richly woven, fast-paced novel."

–William Mark Habeeb, author of *Venice Beach*

HAWAI'I CALLS

Marjorie Nelson Matthews

HAWAI'I CALLS

Marjorie Nelson Matthews

Rootstock Publishing
Montpelier, VT

First Printing: June 2022

Hawai'i Calls, Copyright © 2022 by Marjorie Matthews

Release Date: June 21, 2022

Softcover ISBN: 978-1-57869-091-6
eBook ISBN: 978-1-57869-093-0

Library of Congress Control Number: 2022900434

Published by Rootstock Publishing
an imprint of Multicultural Media, Inc.
27 Main Street, Suite 6
Montpelier, VT 05602 USA

www.rootstockpublishing.com

info@rootstockpublishing.com

Interior and cover design by Eddie Vincent, ENC Graphic Services (ed.vincent@encirclepub.com)

Cover art by: Richard L. Nelson: *Sunrise Kula*, watercolor, 22" x 15", ©1997; photographed by Geoff Hansen.

Author photo credit: Geoff Hansen

For permissions or to schedule an author interview, contact the author at: marjoriematthews@me.com.

Printed in the USA

For my uncle, William Carlisle Nelson, and all the truth tellers.

Prologue

1918

Sadira

Alice and Daddy were gone. It took three men with handkerchiefs tied around their faces to manage the stretchers and the opening and closing of the doors, the how-to of navigating the stairs, the "turn a smidgen left, now lower it slightly, good, you've got it, you're clear now." First Daddy and then Alice. Elma, my mother, watched from the sides, as silent as Daddy and Alice, not quarreling with the men as I wished she would, not telling them to wait, that surely if they only waited, Daddy would waken. I could feel him still there in the house. Not Alice. She was gone. I'd felt the chill of her departure as I washed her body and combed her hair. At Elma's direction, I dressed her in her Sunday best and laced her boots tight. Elma saw to Daddy, placing him in his black suit, his favorite silk tie around his neck.

When Alice was out the door, the last man to leave removed the black sash hanging beneath the quarantine sign. We had no more bodies in need of collection.

Once the men were gone and the front door was shut and locked again, we stripped the mattresses, washed the bedding in scalding water from the stove, and scrubbed down every object, doorknob, and frame. Only when we had scoured the floors and bathed ourselves did Elma say, "That is enough for now. I need to rest. Go eat. Sleep if you can."

I left her curled on the bed she and Daddy had shared, the fresh linens and quilts pulled up to her chin, the scrubbed shades pulled down to the sill. "I'm sorry," I whispered as I closed her door, knowing she couldn't hear me but needing to say the words. It should have been me, not Alice. Alice was the quiet, obedient one.

I was her opposite, the bane of Elma's existence, the child who, at six, declared she hated mommies and from then on called her mother Elma. "A savage in need of taming," was how Father Cridge put it when I refused to say the Apostle's Creed and walked out of confirmation class. "Only twelve and she's already willful and outspoken," he told Elma and Daddy the evening he called at our house.

Once Cridge was out the door, Daddy declared him a man in need of a brain, a soul, and a heart and never entered Carlisle's Episcopal Church again. Elma chose to rise above. She suffered the congregation's glances and whispers and did what she could to mend me. And now, despite her solid Christian living, Elma had lost the two easy loves of her life and was left with only me.

As Elma slept, I sat at the kitchen table, my face to the fading afternoon light. I closed my eyes and rested in it, my feet planted on the floor, my arms flat on the table. The hall clock ticked away the seconds, steady as a heartbeat grounding me in the room, reminding me I was warm and alive. I waited for the thing that came next. Surely there would be tears. I would feel suddenly and forever shattered, or perhaps it would be more like a piercing, an arrow to the heart, a lance in the side. Something would wander into the room and lead me into grief. I welcomed that grief, wanted its release. But nothing happened except the fading of the light, the sun sinking behind the roofline of the Baxters' house next door, and the onset of hunger. Beside me on the table were cookies and cake and fresh bread. In the icebox, a platter of chicken, a bowl of shelled peas. All of it from my grandparents.

The day before, Grandad had dropped off a bounty of prepared foods and produce from their farm. He'd risked violating the quarantine, snuck in the back kitchen door so the neighbors wouldn't see, even hauled in a giant block of fresh ice for the icebox. We watched from the hallway.

"Thank you," Elma said, and he nodded.

The sadness hung so heavy on him he couldn't speak, could only unload first the ice, then the milk and the eggs, the platters of food.

"Any improvement?" he finally asked, his arms empty, his hand on the doorknob, his son upstairs near death.

Elma shook her head. "I don't expect they'll make it through the night."

Grandad nodded, said no word of protest, simply left. I hated her for killing his hope.

She started a flame beneath the kettle on the stove. "We should make ginger and lemon tea with lots of sugar. They need liquids and nourishment." She filled a large pitcher at the sink and handed it to me. "You can start bathing Alice with cool cloths. We need to get their fevers down."

For the rest of that day and all of the night we sat vigil, setting cool compresses on their faces and chests, lifting their heads so they could sip teas and broths, lifting them to sitting when the coughing fits came, until finally there was nothing more we could do except prepare them for the mortician's men.

When the kitchen finally darkened, I lit a lamp and made a plate of chicken and potato salad, along with a large slice of Grannie's apple pie, thick with fruit. I ate slowly, though I was hungry. All urgency had dissolved.

This is how it is to be alone, I thought. This is how it is to sit in the dark with no one to say a word of comfort. I bit into a piece of chicken, and felt Daddy's hand on my shoulder. I set down the food, wanting no distraction from his presence. I wanted to sense Alice as well, but she was nowhere, not outside on the swing, not asleep on the floor beside the cat.

I did not lean back into Daddy for warmth, though the day's heat rose and drifted away, for I knew he hadn't that to give me.

I picked up my piece of chicken, realizing that at least for Grannie and Grandad, Alice and Daddy were still alive. They must be notified, word must be sent to them and all the family, but for that moment and a while longer they were spared the knowing.

"How can you be so heartless?" I'd said to Elma when she sent Grandad off in despair. I'd held my fists tight at my side so I wouldn't bash them into the walls or sweep the glass lamp off its table. In her usual calm, matter-of-fact voice, she answered, "Like it or not, life will wound you, Sadira. You might as well learn that now. The only choice you have is how you respond when it does. You can let it defeat you, or you can face it straight on and keep going."

I finished my supper, washed up my dishes, and then, lamp in hand, I climbed the dark stairwell. Daddy didn't follow.

Chapter One

December 1935 to January 1936

Sadira

First came the jangle of bells, then the young voices clear in the frigid night. *Joy to the world, the Lord is come.* I pulled the sleeves of my robe over my hands to warm them. The candle's flame, the lone light source, shimmied in the drafty kitchen.

The bells rang again, then came the soft tapping of feet on the stairs and across the floorboards. Kenny's stockinged feet appeared in the circle of light.

"How come it's so dark?"

"Can you keep a secret?"

"Yup."

"I'm hiding. I don't want anyone to know we're here."

"How come?" He climbed onto my lap and I wrapped my robe around him.

"'Cause it's too cold and I'm too tired to make my hellos." A lie. Lying to the kids about Archie had become the norm.

Hooves passed, sleigh bells jangled then faded into a safe silence.

Kenny put a finger to his lips. "Sh."

I nodded and tucked his head beneath my chin.

* * *

The ringing pulled me from a deep sleep. I stumbled to the bedroom door before realizing it was only the phone, not one of the boys or someone at the door, only that miserable black instrument that set my heart to racing.

I climbed back into bed and pulled the covers over me. No sense breaking my neck racing down the stairs. The ringing would stop before I got there. Besides, I knew who was calling and why. The police could keep him for the night.

"Mom?"

Of course. Lionel.

I pushed my stockinged feet out from under the covers, slid them into slippers, and grabbed my wool robe. I stopped myself from flipping on the hall switch. I didn't want my mother-in-law, Prudence, to see the light. She would be keeping vigil at her window across the street, watching for Archie to come stumbling down the sidewalk or for a police car to drop him off.

"Did the phone wake you, puddin'?" I whispered, not wanting to rouse Kenny in the bed opposite.

"No. It's the Bible men. They're outside. I can hear them breathing."

A familiar terror, thanks to Sunday school.

I perched beside him on the bed, smoothed back his hair, and tried to be patient. I'd been horrid with him earlier that evening, letting my anger with Archie color my behavior. Lord knows, Lionel wasn't easy, but even as the words left my mouth, I'd regretted them. After all, it was only an open window.

"We've talked about this. Remember there are no Bible men out there. No spears. Even if there were still people from the Bible alive—and there aren't—and even if they lived in Carlisle—which they never did—no human being is tall enough to look in your windows." Reason should have appealed to him. Facts pleased him the way candy and comics delight most kids. But once something infected his imagination, there was no defeating it.

Lionel reached a hand from under the thick pile of blankets and grasped mine, his face pinched with distress. I kissed his palm.

"Tell you what, how about I check at the window and make sure no Bible men are out there?"

Prudence's light still burned across the street. I pantomimed a careful scanning from each window.

"No Bible men, only a whole lot of cold."

"Is Dad home?"

"Not yet. He had a lot of work tonight. Sleep now, mister."

"Wait." He grabbed my hand. "I'm sorry about the window. I just wanted to hear the carolers. I didn't mean to fall asleep and leave it open."

"I know, lamb. I know."

Lionel, age 7

In my world, people don't change the rules. If you give cookies to carolers every year for all the years you ever lived, you don't one day stop. Especially if you already made the cookies and someday are going to ride in that very same wagon and be one of the ones singing. In my world, you would walk out on the front porch and listen and hand out the cookies, never mind if your dad didn't make it home. But in our house, Mom breaks the rules all the time. Like the way she yells at me for no good reason. Yelling isn't allowed.

On carolers' night I only opened our bedroom window so the music could get in. That's all. I wasn't trying to freeze us to death, but soon as Mom came in our room, her voice got loud and she said, "What were you thinking, Lionel, opening a window in the dead of winter. You'll be the death of us." There's no way we would have froze to death that fast. Besides, I was going to close the window soon as the carolers stopped singing. I didn't mean to fall asleep before they came. I only shut my eyes a second and next thing Mom was exploding like a bomb.

After she slammed shut the window, she got even more boiled up inside and acted like it was my fault Kenny couldn't find his bunny. He was the one what went and lost it. She wouldn't even let me turn on the light to see better. "No lights, Lionel!" she yelled, so we had to feel around in the dark space under his bed. "I don't want some monster biting my hands off," I said, and she said, "Don't be ridiculous," and then Kenny started crying and saying he didn't want no monsters eating him up.

One day I'm going to be like those guys who jump on trains and ride away. I won't have to listen anymore to people talking loud at me or making me eat squishy foods or telling me to look people in the eye. I will be all by myself with all my own rules and no one sighing and saying, "What am I going to do with you, Lionel?" I don't want to make Mom so unhappy. All I want is for her to tell me it's all going to be OK and make the scared feeling go away.

Sometimes, if Dad isn't home, I walk all the thirty-three steps between my room and Mom and Dad's and climb up on Dad's side and sleep there, especially if the Bible men in their long robes come. Some nights they surround our house and hold spears. I know they aren't real—Mom says my overactive imagination makes them up—but they feel real, so real I can hear them breathing through the walls. They are tall as giants and reach high as Kenny's and my bedroom so they can see us through the windows. That's why I pull the shades down before I go to bed at night. Only sometimes Kenny goes and pulls down so hard they pop back up into the roll. If it's summer, he even opens up the windows high as they'll go. All those Bible men would have to do is cut the screen and climb right in.

Mom says even if the Bible men were outside my walls, they shouldn't scare me 'cause they're good men. But even good Bible men are scary. John the Baptist's got a bloody cut-off head and Jesus has nails stuck in his hands and feet. I don't want to see Jesus coming through my window with all that blood. Mom says I'm too old now to go down to their room during the night, so I lie in my bed and close my eyes and try to be brave as I can be, and only call for help if I'm really, really sure the Bible men are coming for me, but it only makes Mom mad.

Counting steps is something that makes my heart stop jumping and my brain gallop less. I know how many steps it is to almost every place that matters to me in our town. If it's not winter and there are no snow piles in the way, it takes about 173 steps to reach Grandpa and Grandma Doyle's house across the street. I lose track when I try to count the steps to my school where I am in Miss Gaston's third-grade class. I know how many steps it is to my Gran Schaeffer's house, but sometimes it changes. Sometimes I have to move out of the way and let people pass, which adds a step or even two, and sometimes I have to walk up to people's porches and make my hellos because they call to me and say, "Hey, Lionel, where are you headed on a day so fine as this," and then I have to do what Mom and Gran Schaeffer tell me I must always do with adults. I have to be polite and go up to their porch and say, "Good afternoon, Mrs. Hamilton or Mr. Fucci. This is fine weather we are having." Unless it's not fine weather and then I'm supposed to say, "Terrible rain or terrible snow or can you believe this humidity." But usually, if I don't get interrupted, it's 1,609 steps from my kitchen step, starting with my right foot right from the door, to Gran Schaeffer's kitchen door. I don't count the going-in part, just the getting to her door.

Sadira

I was never prepared for the toxic brew of grief and rage. It clung to the mortuary's drapes and carpets, seeped from the walls, swept a foul, suffocating wind through the open spaces. On my first visit to Tucker's Mortuary, the day Elma and I selected a casket for her mother, I tried to flee. Elma took me by the shoulders and marched me forward. Even as a grown woman, I had to steel myself to the battering spirits. My sensitivity to the preternatural can be more curse than gift.

Floyd and Archie were, of course, oblivious to the spirits, which is why they could work in that swamp, yet they weren't immune to its poison. Unaware perhaps, but corroded all the same. Thus the booze. Floyd was as apt as Arch to end a night on the floor of Clive's bar.

I was so furious the morning after Arch missed the carolers that I barreled through the emotional sludge and straight into Floyd's office, ready for battle. The huge leather chair he prized nearly swallowed him. His spindly arms rested on a desk meant for a man of substance. It was always too easy with Floyd, such a flutter of the bird in his eyes, though I'd seen the pellets of meanness there. Put a few in him and he was an ugly drunk, the sort who slaps around his wife and kids.

"I had no choice, Sadie. I had to fire him," Floyd said, studying the letter opener in his hand, worrying it into the desk blotter, as if there were weeds there that needed pulling. "One thing to be drunk on his own time. He can't be falling down around the customers."

"I didn't know you could fire your own partner. Especially the partner who saved you from going under." I was calm as can be, as if we were discussing the weather or the price of gasoline. I liked that about talking to Floyd. I didn't feel so much as a blush of nerves. He was that insubstantial. How could I fear a man who called Arch's mother to notify us Arch was fired rather than call me or walk over to the jail and tell Arch in person? Prudence was in pig heaven when she called me that morning with the news. Nothing she liked more than another example of how I'd ruined her angelic son.

"Sit down, Sadie. Please. Let's discuss this like two civil people. No one's tossing Arch out the door. Least not without a life jacket."

I didn't sit down. I didn't so much as take off my gloves. I wanted Floyd to have to look up at me. I wanted him to stay scared.

"Describe this life jacket."

Floyd could hand back Arch's share of the business, but it wouldn't make anything OK. That money wasn't Arch's to take back. Prudence and Ben had floated it, and anything Floyd returned would go to them. Without the mortuary, Arch was back to where he was five years before when he lost the pharmacy—no job, no income, no way for us to survive.

"I'll give Prudence and Ben their money," Floyd said, then added quickly, "but there's something else." He slid open the desk drawer and drew out a Western Union envelope, tissue thin. "There's a job. A good job that pays real well. They're desperate."

I laughed at that. Anyone paying real well for mortician work had to be in some place no one wanted to be. Floyd wasn't dumping us in some hellhole.

"Let me guess. This is one of those godforsaken towns out west. Where is it? Nevada? Arizona?"

"Hawai'i." His eyebrows relaxed and he sat back in his chair. "Paradise," he added, a smug little piggy, pleased with himself. I turned away for a moment, stared out through the gauzy drapes covering his window, as if there were something there to see. I needed to collect myself. No reason for Floyd to know what Hawai'i meant to me.

One Saturday night, I'd heard Queen Lili'uokalani's "Aloha 'Oe" for the first time. I was alone in the front room listening to the new radio show *Hawai'i Calls*. They actually broadcast it from Hawai'i, thousands of miles away. I could hear the waves touching shore, the strum of the ukuleles, practically smell the sea salt and feel the trade winds at my back. The yearning in the queen's melody stirred me, connected me to that distant island, as if it were calling me home. Ever since, I'd dreamed of escaping our dead-end town and starting over fresh in a place of beauty and romance. And I wasn't just being selfish. I knew in my bones it would give Arch the chance he needed to start over.

I took the telegram from Floyd. "Who says they'd even want him?"

"I'll make sure they do. And I'll negotiate a good deal. Travel costs for all of you. A better starting pay than he makes here."

"And the bonus for you is, we leave town. No nasty reminders of what a sad excuse of a friend and partner you are."

Floyd took offense at this, actually got out of his chair and stood tall as he could, which is to say, not very, since even on his tippy toes he barely reached my chin.

"I'm being more than fair, Sadie, and you know it. Blame me all you want, but we both know Arch brought this on himself."

I waved him back down. "This telegram makes it OK." I reached a hand across the desk. "You've got a deal, Floyd."

"And you'll tell Arch about the Hawai'i deal? And Prudence?"

I tossed him a bone. "Sure. I'll let them all know. Prudence won't like it. Hell, Arch may not like it, but that's neither here nor there." I certainly knew better than either of those two what was good for me and the boys, and yes, even what was good for Arch himself.

The last time, I thought as I strode out of his office and through the foyer. Last time that space would smother me. Last time I'd see those caskets yawning on their display shelves. I was about to begin a whole series of "last times" as I escaped Carlisle, a town that had never been home to me.

The church bells began the count to noon. Time to collect Archie from the police station.

Lionel

Even though I'm just a kid, Dad sometimes takes me to Clive's bar with him, especially if Mom says, "Arch, how about you take Lionel along?" and I think maybe Dad doesn't really want to, but he's too good a guy to say so. He'd never want to make me feel bad. I like going along 'cause I get to learn all about being a grown-up man, plus Clive's got lots of great stuff in his bar.

He collects license plates and hangs them on the back wall. He's got lots from New York, but he's got some from Ohio and Pennsylvania, and even one from New Hampshire. Used to be he'd give kids a penny for finding them, till he found out that Jeb and Carson were stealing them off cars passing through. I know exactly where each one of those licenses belongs on the wall. Sometimes, Clive plays a joke on me and switches the order just to see if I notice, but when me and Dad went to his bar the other day, they were all exactly where they were supposed to be. That's 'cause Clive wasn't expecting me to show up.

"Good to see you, Lionel, my friend," he called to me. "Kinda early, ain't ya, Arch?" he said to my dad, 'cause usually we don't show up there till after Dad gets done work at five, only that day Dad didn't go to work at all and around four o'clock he stood up and said he was heading out. Mom said, "Take Lionel along," in her no-ifs-ands-or-buts voice.

The place was empty, and I was going to go sit in my regular place in the back, but Clive said, "Come sit up at the bar, little man. Keep us company."

Dad pulled a marble out of his pocket and kept running it over the bar top with his fingers, pushing down so hard I thought maybe he was going to bust it.

"Usual?" Clive asked me, meaning did I want a root beer, and when I nodded, Dad said, "Make that two," which he never does. He always wants a beer and I expected Clive to say, "What are you talking about, Arch?" only he didn't, he just poured two root beers into mugs so cold they frosted right up.

Dad didn't say much the whole time we were there, and Clive acted like he was real busy even when there was no one else in the place. Once guys started showing up around quitting time, Clive left us alone and it seemed like all the guys were grumpy 'cause none of them came by to clap Dad on the back or give me a hard time the way they usually do. Most of the time when I'm hanging around the bar, they tease me something awful. "Breaking all the girls' hearts?" they ask me, or they want me to name all the presidents or the states' capitals and they laugh and laugh and say, "Kid's a regular little machine," unless Dad's right there 'cause they know he'll tell them to cut it out, tell them I'm not some "goddamn monkey," which I don't think is what they mean at all, but he gets funny about their talking to me sometimes. Maybe he doesn't think I'm grown-up enough to talk to men in a bar, but I don't mind showing them how smart I am, since I know more than most of them. I usually go sit in the back and try to be as small as I can when Dad gets worked up like a fiery red storm cloud and the guys back away and say, "Calm down, Archie, calm down. Nothing wrong with a little harmless fun."

"Seen my humdinger of a watch?" Dad asked Clive after we'd been sitting awhile. Dad had taken off his new watch, the one Floyd gave him the day before, and was digging his thumb into the back of it. "Bet I can scratch the gold right off this cheap thing."

"Looks nice enough to me."

"Gift from my buddy Floyd. A parting gift. Like he was my boss or something."

Clive didn't answer my dad. He just kept taking orders and filling mugs.

The longer Dad dug a nail into that watch, the angrier he looked. His face got as red as when he's had three or four beers, and his eyebrows were pulled in so tight, they almost touched.

"Sadie tell you not to serve me?" he asked when Clive came down our way again. The way he said it, his voice all small and hard like the marble in his fist, made me want to go sit at the back table.

"Haven't talked to Sadie in ages, Arch."

Dad laughed at that. Not a happy laugh. The kind of laugh he makes when he thinks someone's a real numbskull.

"Heard we're moving to Hawai'i? The gossip mill get ahold of that one yet?"

That was news to me. No one had said nothing about us moving anywhere.

"What are you talking about, Dad?" I asked, which I knew right away was the wrong thing to do 'cause I'm not supposed to ever interrupt a grown-up, especially not my dad and especially not if he's talking to another grown-up. He didn't answer me, but he sure did give me a look.

"I heard something," Clive answered. "Sounds like a pretty sweet deal, if you ask me."

"Right. You probably helped Floyd and Sadie cook that one up."

Clive put down the mug in his hand and rested both hands on the bar in front of my dad.

"Look, Arch. Nobody's out to get you. All Sadie wants is the best for you. Hell, that's all anybody wants for you." Clive glanced at me after he said that and added, "Pardon my language, Lionel."

He went back to pulling on the handle and held the mug so the beer wouldn't foam. I could see my dad studying that beer, the way it turned the glass gold with a bunch of white bubbles at the top. I knew he wanted one, only I didn't dare ask how come he was drinking root beer instead.

Dad slid the watch across the bar to Clive. "Merry Christmas, Clive," he said, only he didn't sound much like he meant it, and I couldn't see what Clive did or said that made him act so mean like, but I could tell Dad wasn't happy with Clive. It made no sense, his giving him the watch.

"Come on, Lionel," Dad said to me. "Let's head home to the dragon lady." I hate when he calls Mom that, 'cause it makes her sound like fire comes out of her mouth, and she's not really a dragon, not most of the time anyway, only when Dad stays too long at Clive's or has so many beers I have trouble helping him get up the steps to our front porch.

"Tell your mom Merry Christmas from me, OK, Lionel?" Clive said as I swung round in my stool and hopped down.

"Sure thing," I told him. "You have a Merry Christmas, yourself."

As we walked past my dad's chums at the bar, I started wishing them a good Christmas, too, only no one seemed very glad to see me, and Dad said, "Come on, Lionel, get a move on," and before I knew it we were standing outside and people were rushing by us.

"You doing OK, Dad?" I asked, but it was like he couldn't hear me. He just headed for home, his hands in his pockets and his head down low, like he was dodging snowflakes except it wasn't snowing. I had to run to keep up with him.

When we got to our place, he stood at the base of the steps looking up. I could see our Christmas tree in the front window, and Mom had lit some candles at the other windows. "Home sweet home," he said, not sounding like he meant it or like he was happy at all.

I started up the steps, but he didn't follow me. "Aren't you coming?" I called to him and he looked like maybe he was going to say no, like maybe he wasn't going to come in the house. A door squeaked open across the street. I knew it was my Grandma Doyle coming out onto her front porch. In a second she'd be yelling, "Archie? Archie Doyle?" As if she couldn't see that it was my dad standing right there lit up by the streetlamp. Her voice could make a guy shrivel up and want to run for the hills.

Before she could even call out his name, my dad ran up those steps so fast you'd have thought there was a rabid fox coming down the street. I hightailed it up after him. Whatever had him feeling so low and miserable, it wasn't so bad as having to cross the street to face my Grandma Doyle.

"I can do this, champ, I can do this," he said to me as he turned the doorknob.

"Sure you can, Dad," I said, not knowing what it was he could do, except I could see from the way his eyes looked that he needed someone to believe he could.

Sadira

The kitchen was steamy from the day's cooking, and my face as damp as the dishtowel in my hand. I was content. Our Christmas had been blissfully calm. Arch's parents stayed away, punishing us for the decision to move; Elma joined us for presents and dinner; and the boys amused themselves without fuss. Best of all, Arch stayed sober.

Arch pushed the kitchen door open with his foot, a generous pile of logs in his arms.

I held the door wide and enjoyed the blast of cool air. I felt a rare stirring of attraction as he set fresh logs on the fire. "My hero saves the day."

"Careful. You might have me believing you still feel something for me."

"Don't be ridiculous. Of course I do."

I tucked a wet hair strand behind my ear and returned to the sink. I could feel him studying me.

"What are you staring at? I must look like a drowned rat."

"I never tire of the view."

I fished for the last plate in the washbasin, the charm on my bracelet pinging against its metal side as my fingers searched the soapy dishwater. He wrapped me in a bear hug from behind.

"The dishes can wait."

A log burst into flame and I let the last dish slide back beneath the suds.

"See the effect I have." He untied my apron. "Things ignite spontaneously around me."

I woke shivering on the living room floor. Arch was asleep beside me, the fire burnt down to embers. A cat yowled outside. I wrapped myself in a shawl and added a log to the fire. The Christmas tree still shone in all its glory. I couldn't bear to unplug its lights, burned long past the safety point. I needed to savor the rare moment of peace and hope.

A blast of icy air cut through the moment. I found the kitchen door ajar. The black cat haunting our porch screeched from her perch on the railing and arched her back when I stepped out.

"Go on home." I shooed my hand at her. Her sagging belly suggested she'd given birth recently, and her healthy size said she was no stray. "Nothing for you here." It made no sense the way she hovered, complaining at such an hour. "You'll freeze out here."

At the end of the drive, beside the garage, a small gray mass leaned into a shovel and scooped snow.

"Lionel?" I called just loud enough to get his attention and motion him back, as if with the pulse of my hand I might reel him in. He set down the shovel and shuffled to the porch. Snow caked his slippers, robe, and pajama cuffs.

"What were you thinking? You'll catch your death dressed like that." I hauled him inside.

His face was damp with tears, his body shivering. I brushed off the snow, grabbed my wool coat from the rack and wrapped it around him, then pulled him onto my lap. He had grown too big for easy handling. His gangly legs and arms felt like tentacles around me. He buried his head against my chest and sobbed.

"You need to tell me what's going on."

"It died. I killed it."

"You're not making sense. Slow down and tell me what happened."

"I tried to save it. I even brought it milk, but it wouldn't drink."

The pieces snapped together. "You found a kitten."

"It was crawling out from under the porch. All by itself in the cold. I had to save it."

"Oh Lord."

I pulled my wool coat off him and slid on my boots. For all I knew, the kitten was still alive out there. By the time I reached the driveway, though, the mother cat was already carrying something by its nape. Dead or alive, the kitten was hers again.

Arch joined us as I hung up my coat. "What's going on?"

"Lionel took a kitten from its mother."

"I didn't mean to hurt it, Dad." Lionel started wailing again. "It was by itself. She left it alone under the porch."

"'Course you didn't, champ. I'm glad you tried to help the poor thing." Arch pulled him to his feet. "How about I make us a cup of hot chocolate. We'll get the fire burning strong, and you can show me those new baseball cards you got from Santa."

I unplugged the Christmas tree lights and glanced at the hall clock. Only 9:30. Still Christmas. Another one spoiled.

We were counting down the days. I'd shed our possessions as easily as a dog drops its fur in spring. No more musty antiques or winter garb for us, and I was not about to haul sentimental tchotchkes across two oceans. I wanted a clean slate.

I had one last column to write for the *Carlisle Bulletin* before I could pack up my typewriter. My options included the usual. Miss Melanie

Anderson, top of the week's list, was a column regular merely because, as the daughter of Carlisle's wealthiest resident, she shone a bit of glamour on our dull town.

"The last time I have to write about Prissy Miss Sourpuss," I said to Kenny as I fed paper into my typewriter. He lay on the floor behind me, sweeping a pencil over paper.

He laughed. "That's not her name."

"No, my love, it's not. But it suits her."

He drew the outline of the elm tree beyond our window. Give that boy a pencil and paper, and he was happy for hours.

"How's this sound—Prissy Miss Sourpuss and her most highly relieved parents today announced Miss Sourpuss's engagement to Mr. Pickleface of the Fifth Avenue Picklefaces."

"You're silly, Mommy."

"Hm. If only I were silly enough to put that in print."

I turned back to the typewriter and pounded out my copy.

> *Sources tell our gal about town that Melanie Anderson, newly betrothed to Albany's own Crawford Norton, was spotted this week sipping a double chocolate malted at Crane's Drugstore and sporting a cunning red felt hat recently acquired at Saks Fifth Avenue. Insiders say Miss Anderson most thoroughly enjoyed her shopping excursion to the big city, the highlight of which was luncheon at the Plaza with her mother and soon to be mother-in-law.*

Elma called from the kitchen. "Yoo-hoo."

"Finishing up. I'll be there in a few."

She was going to watch the boys so I could finish the packing and run some final errands.

I needed one last item for my column and my options were Elsbeth's new silk wallpaper or the addition of caramel tea rolls at Paulette's Patisserie. Since Elsbeth hadn't bragged to me about her decorating—I had overheard Judith Kimball raving about it at the church coffee hour—I decided to go with her story. Besides, Paulette rarely bothered advertising with the *Bulletin* and I saw no reason to give her free publicity.

> *Our sweet town is abuzz with news that the Winston Browns'*
> *dining room has been transformed into a salon to rival New*
> *York's finest, thanks to exquisite silk wallpaper shipped all the*
> *way from China. The Browns now dine cocooned in a delicate*
> *blush of pink with a dash of succulent green bamboo shoots.*
> *Bravo, Mrs. Elsbeth Brown, for elevating our dear town with*
> *your refined taste.*

I could think of a few women who'd be green with envy and indignant that such accolades went to modest Elsbeth. I wrapped up the column with my farewell message.

> *Now comes the sad moment, dear ones, when I must bid you*
> *adieu. This shall be my last missive from Carlisle as we begin*
> *our grand world adventure. I'm happy to announce that our*
> *esteemed publisher has asked me to continue my column from*
> *afar. When next you hear from me, I shall be in foreign lands,*
> *reporting on exotic sights and people. Until then, oh town of*
> *mine, aloha nui loa. Until we meet again, I remain Sadie,*
> *Your Gal About Town.*

I pulled the paper from the typewriter and stuffed it in an envelope to drop at the *Bulletin*.

"Time to put all that away," I told Kenny, and headed to the kitchen where Elma stood at the sink rinsing the morning dishes.

"I'll get to those, Elma." She couldn't help but remind me of my inadequacies.

"No time like the present." She scrubbed the brush hard against a plate. Sometimes it took all I had to remain civil with her. I dug my annoyance into my palms and switched my focus to two large shopping bags on the kitchen table. From one, I pulled out a large cookie tin, one of four.

"Cookies, Elma? I believe they'll feed us on the ship."

"But they won't have my gingersnaps. The boys are going to need something to spare them getting homesick."

From the other bag I drew a black satin evening gown wrapped in tissue and shook it out. It was another Elma masterpiece. The pairing of black satin with a white collar was startling, precisely the effect I liked best in my clothes.

"It's breathtaking."

"I saw it in *Vogue*. A new Chanel design. I thought it might prove useful for nights on the ship." There was yet another gown in the bag—a Madeleine Vionnet copy done in ice-blue silk with a back that dipped nearly to the waist.

"You must have been sewing day and night."

Elma's sewing skills and keen eye for design paid off well for me. I was definitely one of Carlisle's better-dressed women. Not even the women who shopped in the top New York City stores could boast a wardrobe equal to my couture-inspired gowns and dresses. The only problem was, in Carlisle I never had a place to wear them nor an audience that appreciated their worth. I was sure that would change once I boarded the ship and was in the company of true sophisticates.

I carefully rewrapped the tissue around the gowns. "They're lovely. Thank you, Elma." I hated the quiver in my voice. No cheap emotion allowed. "I'll run these up to my room."

"Please let Lionel know I'm here. I'll feed the boys lunch and then we'll make the rounds so they can say their goodbyes."

"Is that necessary? People can come to the train station."

"There are certain people to whom the boys must pay their respects. We should not presume their presence at the station." Rules. Always rules to follow, decorum to preserve. "I might also take them by the cemetery. Remind them who's who and whence they came."

I could not get out of town fast enough.

As directed, I headed upstairs to fetch Lionel. He was studying his book on railroad operations. He loved its intricate charts of signals and rules.

"Gran's fixing you boys lunch."

He didn't even look up.

Lionel

I don't like being a bad person. I try hard to be good, but the bad still pops out. Even when I try to do good stuff, bad stuff happens, like when I killed the kitty. Sometimes I get so angry at myself and other people I feel like I'm going to boil over. I feel boiling mad when Mom embarrasses me in front of other people by saying stuff like, "No, Lionel. That's not how you're supposed to do it." I don't see how come everything has to be done the same way by everybody and why I can't have my own set of rules. Someday I'll make my very own world where I'll write the rules. I'm scared I make God angry when I don't follow His rules, but I don't know how to stop being how I am.

There's a guy in our town, old George Marchand, who stands on the corner of the town green opposite the Catholic church. He yells as people go by, telling them to repent or be cast into hell. He says us Episcopalians and Catholics are heathens and followers of Satan. He gets extra loud on Sundays when people are pouring into church. I bet George makes his own rules, too, and doesn't care what people think of him.

I tried talking to George once. "Hey, George," I said, but he kept yelling at the people across the street, like he couldn't hear me. "Hey, George," I said a second time, and this time I tugged on his stinky coat that's too small for him. That time he stopped talking and looked at me.

"You ever try talking in a normal voice?" I asked him. "People might listen more. I know I don't like it much when people yell at me."

"Cry aloud, spare not, lift up thy voice like a trumpet, and shew my people their transgression, and the house of Jacob their sins," is all he said, but he said it quieter than his usual yelling voice and his eyes looked sad and watery. I don't know if he's crazy like people say, but I think maybe he's kind inside and just wants to save us all.

Some folks think the town should lock him up, but Mom says you can't lock somebody up for saying things you don't like. Even though she never thinks it's OK when I say things she doesn't like.

I don't mind Old George so much. He leaves me and the other kids alone, almost like he can't even see us, like he's so much inside his head he doesn't notice anything around him or hear what people say. I figure that's good 'cause if he did hear what people say, he'd be about the saddest man in the world.

Mom tells me what Old George says is nonsense and to pay him no mind. What he says sounds pretty much the same as what the preacher at Grandma Doyle's church says. Mom doesn't like us going to Grandma Doyle's church, but sometimes she says OK for Grandma Doyle's birthday 'cause Grandma says all she wants in the whole world is for her grandbabies to be there in church beside her. Dad comes along with us those times so he can tell us all the things we should put out of our heads after church. I try but it's not so easy to forget, especially the parts about sinners' flesh blistering in the fires of hell and sinners falling in the cracks or getting swept out to sea when the earthquakes and floods come. I sure don't want to fall into the center of the earth or land up in the Gulf of Mexico. I'm not sure why Jesus wants to make people suffer so much, but Grandma says that's just how it is. He gives us a way to be saved and that's all he can do. She wants me and Kenny to be baptized down at the river on Great-Grandpa and Great-Grandma's farm, but Mom says over her dead body. She says we boys are baptized good and sound and no ignorant Bible thumper's going to be holding her boys' heads underwater.

I say a prayer every night now for the kitty I killed, and ask God to forgive me. If it wasn't winter time, I'd go down to the river and walk right in over my head so I could be made clean and all my sins washed away. Someday when I'm bigger, I'll be able to eat the wafer and drink the wine once a month at church and maybe that will take care of all my past sins. It's a good thing we got people like George who want to help us repent 'cause sometimes I think I'm going to spend my whole entire life needing to be washed clean of everything inside of me.

My Gran Schaeffer's nothing like my Grandma Doyle. She may be just as no-nonsense, but she's not all the time angry and talking about the devil. She does nice things for me and Kenny, like make us cookies and take us to the cinema. Grandma Doyle hates us moving away, but Gran Schaeffer says it's going to be a great adventure for us all, maybe the greatest one of my whole life, and maybe someday she'll even take that long boat ride herself and visit us. She says I must be brave and strong and make the most of this opportunity. She also says I must never, ever forget my roots, which I think means her and all the old people in our family that came before her.

My ancestors on Gran Schaeffer's side are buried in the cemetery at the end of Orchard Street, right before the big apple orchard where you have to stop 'cause there's no more road. They have stones on top of them with their names and their birthdays and their death days carved in. Gran Schaeffer says my grandfather and aunt died young from the flu. Mom knew they were going to die before it happened. She knows stuff like that. Stuff people aren't supposed to know. She even knows if already dead people are around. I'm glad 'cause then she can tell me before she and Dad die and I will be ready for it, and if I die before her, she'll know it and can say goodbye before I kick the bucket.

Grandma Doyle says it's witchcraft to talk about spirits and knowing things from the other world. She tells Kenny and me we must shut our ears to things our mother says and "bind ourselves to the Lord." She tells us lots about the rules we have to obey if we don't want to go to hell. Mom says there's no such place as the kind of hell Grandma Doyle talks about and to ignore her 'cause that's the kind of talk that gives me nightmares about the Bible men. Gran Schaeffer says she doesn't pretend to know what it will be like after death, but she doesn't think we are supposed to spend our lives being afraid and miserable.

Before we leave Carlisle for good, Gran Schaeffer took us to the cemetery so Kenny and I would remember "the people we come from" and maybe someday come back and visit the little cemetery beside the apple trees. We are going so far away on a ship that I don't think we could ever be buried beside the people we come from. I hope it won't feel lonely being buried with strangers, but maybe it won't be all that different 'cause I don't think the people here really want me buried next to them. Nobody on the Doyle side likes me much, so why would they want me near them when I die? At least in Hawai'i, I will never be cold lying in the ground. And besides, Kenny and my parents are the only people I really want lying beside me forever and ever anyway.

Sadira

The day before we boarded the train to New York, I was on my knees scrubbing the oven's walls when Prudence rapped on the kitchen door. I hadn't seen her since Arch told her we were moving. I opened the door with sponge still in hand.

"Come on in. I'll let Arch know you're here." From the foot of the stairs, I called, "Arch, your mother's here."

Prudence waited by the door.

"Have a seat," I offered, soapy water now dripping from the sponge and running down my arm. "I'll wash up."

"Thank you, no. I won't be long."

Arch and the boys clattered down the stairs.

"Morning, Mom." Arch pecked her cheek and offered to take her coat, but she again insisted her stay would be brief.

"I come with terrible news."

"OK." Arch crossed his arms. "And what news is that?"

Prudence cried wolf so regularly, we both knew better than to react.

"It's your father. He didn't want you to know, but he's very ill. It's his heart. The doctor doesn't know how long he has." She paused as if to regain her composure, and I do believe there were tears in her eyes. "It could be he has only months. If you persist with this nonsense about moving, you're not likely to see him again."

Kenny burst into tears and buried his face in my skirt. Lionel drifted off to the front room. I could have wrung her neck.

With Kenny still clinging to me, I rinsed my hands and filled the teapot.

"I'm making myself tea, would either of you like some?"

"Have you no heart at all, Sadira Schaeffer?" Eleven years married to Arch, and I was still Schaeffer to Prudence. "After everything Ben and I have done for the two of you, you feel no affection, no compassion?"

I switched on the flame beneath the kettle and set a tea bag in one of our two remaining mugs. Kenny still clung to me.

"I wish no suffering on either of you." I managed to keep my voice calm. "This move is one of necessity."

"You don't fool me, Sadira. Nothing would please you more than to take Archie and the boys away from us forever."

"Stop blaming Sadie, Mom." I'd never seen Arch challenge Prudence directly. "I'm the one at fault. Look, I'm sorry if Dad's ill. I truly am, but the decision is made. We leave tomorrow. You're both welcome to see us off at the station."

"I will never understand the hold she has on you." Prudence's hand was already on the doorknob.

Chapter Two

January to February 1936

Sadira

I shed no tears for the town of Carlisle when our train pulled out at six on a frigid morning. I suppose that's a harsh way to feel about the place of my birth and home to generations of Schaeffers and Cunninghams, but I would miss nothing about it. Not the mean gossip shared over fences, nor the stench of dead fish that blew in off the lake. How could a spirit soar in a land where food was denied seasoning and every house was painted gray or white?

No one but Elma came to see us off, not a single neighbor, no one from church, none of my *Bulletin* colleagues, not a one of Arch's drinking buddies.

"You can't expect people to be here at dawn in the dead of winter," Elma said, as if their absence were about the cold and the dark. If it had been Elma setting off on a grand adventure, you can be sure half the town would have shown up.

"Good riddance to the lot of them," I muttered as Arch scooted the boys up the steps to our train car and Elma indulged me one last stiff embrace.

"Remember you have all the strength you need. Decide to do great things, and you will," she said with a firm if brief hug, then before the conductor called "All aboard!" she shooed me up the steps. "Now get a move on. Don't want you left behind."

"Go back inside the station," I called to her, but she stayed there on the platform, her shoulders bent, her head sunk into her coat. Arch lowered the window for the boys, who leaned out and waved until the train curved away and all was darkness.

Our departure made a lie of the copy I'd written the night before. Knowing I'd have no time to compose and mail something before we sailed, I imagined the send-off as it should be, wrote my column accordingly, and would post it at Grand Central Station.

> *Champagne corks flew, hugs and kisses were exchanged, and not a few tears shed, as yours truly, along with husband Archibald and sons Lionel and Kenneth, bid family and friends fond farewell at Carlisle's train station in the early morning hours this past Thursday. With a last toss of confetti and much waving of arms, we watched our beloved hometown and dear ones fade from view as the train picked up steam, bound for New York City. After a delightful if sooty day of travel, we disembarked in the great station that is Grand Central, hailed a Checker cab, and found ourselves deposited within minutes beside our ship. Stewards led us to cabins bedecked with massive bouquets and cheery bon voyage messages from loved ones near and far. Resolved to face the adventure ahead with verve and courage, we waved our final goodbyes to American shores. With a deep, deafening toot, the ship swung slowly out into the harbor and we gazed on the vast city, an enchanted castle of lit towers and turrets. Our hearts swelled as the ship sailed past the grand Lady Liberty, bound for the vast Atlantic Ocean and our first stop—Havana, Cuba. Though we bid farewell to our country and old, familiar life, we felt only joy and awe to be starting life anew. Your faithful reporter signs off now with the promise to keep you posted on all the events to*

come as we sail the high seas between New York and Hawai'i.
God bless you all and God bless our little town of Carlisle.

I admit that as I slid the envelope in the mail slot, I actually hoped champagne and flowers did await us in our cabin, but that tiny space was a further disappointment. No grand bouquets crowded our little table, no champagne chilled in buckets, not a single telegram rested on the desk. The world seemed not to care a whit about us or our departure.

My eyes teared as we passed the Statue of Liberty, and an unexpected wave of disquiet swept over me as the city receded and I gazed at the dark ocean ahead, a brutal wind whipping about us. I had not anticipated the primal fear the ocean's vastness would trigger. For a moment I doubted myself, wondered if this were all a vain, foolhardy endeavor. Perhaps I had devalued the stabilizing influence of home and land beneath my feet.

Kenny tugged at my arm.

"I'm cold, Mommy," he said, reminding me I hadn't the luxury of indulging doubt. I needed to shepherd my lambs to safe port.

"Sorry, love." I led him into the ship's warm interior.

Arch and Lionel remained on deck, seemingly invigorated by it all— the raw cold, the sea spray, even the heaving waves. The motion, the lifting and the dropping, reminded them of roller coasters, except, as Lionel put it, it was far grander than any roller coaster he'd ever been allowed to ride.

By our second day at sea, my motion sickness eased and I was able to venture from our cabin. I was determined to compose a missive before we reached Havana. I sent Archie off to explore the ship with the boys and set up shop in the library, empty at midafternoon. I fed a sheet of paper into the typewriter and considered my options. I could share first impressions of the ship, though I was still getting acquainted with its many parts. Profiles of the other passengers seemed a reasonable choice, as nearly anyone I described would read as exotic to Carlisle's residents.

If I focused on one passenger a column, I could easily compile a stream of reports to cover the long stretches between ports. For my first subject, I settled on Finnegan Rolfe, a distinguished cellist. As always happens when I write, time and place evaporated. A soft cough startled me as I pulled the sheet of paper from the roller.

"Any chance of bumming a smoke?" A stunning young blonde hovered by the door, as if she needed my permission to enter. "Left my cigs in the cabin and can't seem to scrounge up any."

If there had been men in the room, cigarette cases would have clicked open all around us.

"Sorry, not a smoker. Have you asked a steward?"

"Yeah. He was no help, but he promised me tea. Join me for a cup? Or would you rather be alone?"

Without waiting for an answer, she settled in the chair opposite mine at the table, stretched out her legs, and raised her arms overhead with her hands linked so that she was one long slender stretch of female perfection in wide silk pants and matching top. Creamy was the word that came to mind, and not just with regard to her complexion. Everything about her was luscious.

"Renee Manchester of New York," she said, her body recompressed, her hand out to me.

"Sadira Doyle."

"Jeepers, that's an exotic handle. I like it. Sadira." She took her time rolling out my name and motioned to the steward who came bearing a large tray with tea service—and a cigarette pack. "You're a peach," she said and shot him a smile sure to win her cigarettes the entire voyage.

"Where you bound for, Sadira?"

"Honolulu," I answered in as matter-of-fact a way as I could manage, as if traveling to distant places was routine for me. "And you?"

"Beats me. The idea was to sail to Shanghai, but who knows? I'll be glad if we make it to Frisco before Roger changes his mind." She handed me a cup. "You know how men are."

I had no knowledge of men like her Roger, a man of advanced years and great wealth, according to the ship's grapevine. Nor was I familiar with a world in which a person boarded a ship bound for a spot halfway round the world but was prepared to abandon the voyage at any port along the way.

"Your husband sounds intriguing."

"Hah!" She laughed. "Sweetie, Roger's many things, but my husband isn't one of them. It's no secret, and you'll catch whiff soon enough." She leaned closer and spoke as if we were longtime confidantes. "I'm Mr. Tarrington's 'special friend.' He's got a regular wife and family, but Mrs. Tarrington isn't keen to leave her Fifth Avenue townhouse. Lucky for me, I say, 'cause I get to be the one who sees the world." She squeezed a lemon wedge over her tea. "Have I shocked you?"

"Not at all." I laughed. "I suppose I should be, but it sounds rather fabulous to thumb your nose at convention. I especially admire your candor."

Renee squeezed my hand. "I just know you and I are going to be swell pals." She opened the small purse she carried, drew out a flask, and poured something into her tea. "Want a splash?"

This gave me pause. "Thanks, no," I said, fearing my distaste showed. "It doesn't agree with me."

"Pity." She raised her teacup in a bit of a salute.

Kenny chose that moment to burst in, his face flushed, his nose streaming from the fresh air. "I beat him, Mom. I beat Lionel. I'm the champ."

I passed him a tissue. "That's wonderful, love, but you're interrupting. I'm speaking with my friend, Miss Manchester."

He eyed Renee as he wiped his nose, then turned back to me. "Sorry to interrupt, but Dad took Lionel to the cabin 'cause he was being a sore loser. He told me to come get you. He told me to say he needs you right now."

"You can tell your father I am engaged in conversation. I will join you in the cabin when I am able."

"But Dad said come now."

"You're lucky you don't have kids," I said to Renee as I gathered up my things.

"Don't I know it. I plan to dodge that bullet. How about we meet up for drinks before dinner. I'll look for you in the lounge."

"Sounds lovely, and I apologize for taking off so abruptly."

"It's no skin off my nose. Besides, I've my trusted friend for company." She pulled a thick book from her bag and showed me the jacket—*Attributes of a Lady*. "Roger thinks there's room for improvement."

"Maybe Roger doesn't know a good thing when it's right in front of him."

Renee leapt up and pulled me into a tight hug. "I adore you. We're going to be the very best of chums."

As I headed back to the cabin with Kenny, I contemplated what life might be like as a close friend to Renee. Champagne brunches, afternoons sunbathing poolside, endless nights on the dance floor. Perhaps I would be seen as a scandalous woman, if only by association. And why not? I could create whatever version I wanted for myself. I checked my watch. Only five. I had plenty of time to get the boys cleaned up and to the café for the children's early supper. After that, they were the cabin steward's worry.

Even Lionel couldn't spoil my near-giddy mood. He lay facing the wall, refusing to talk to anyone.

"A little birdie told me a secret," I said. "Apparently, it's possible to order waffles and ice cream for supper. I don't suppose either of you would want that, right?"

"'Course I would," Kenny said. Nothing from Lionel.

"And maybe, just maybe, if you're nice to Mr. Young, he'll let you have some hot fudge and whipped cream on top."

"And a cherry?" Kenny said.

"I don't see why not. They're bound to have cherries tucked away somewhere."

"Grandma Doyle says lots of sugar's bad for you," Lionel said, his back still to us.

"Maybe so, but I think maybe no sugar's not so great for you either. We all need something now and then to make us smile."

Lionel rolled over. "Can I have mine with chocolate ice cream?"

"That's what I'd get if I were ordering."

I laid out their clothes for dinner.

"How's about a game of Old Maid before we go," Lionel said.

"Tell you what, how about you two get dressed and we can play till it's time for supper."

Archie looked up from his book when I entered our cabin. "Peace restored?"

"For now." No thanks to you, I thought, as I collected my clothes for the evening. Ignore it, I told myself, let it go. I was not going to let Archie and Lionel spoil my good mood and the chance of a glistening evening with Renee and Roger. I felt sure my grand life adventure had begun in earnest.

"Maybe Arch and I should settle here instead of Hawai'i."

Renee and I were parked poolside at the Hotel Nacional de Cuba. Havana's relaxed pace was so welcome and luxuriant, the hotel grounds so vast and lovely, I couldn't imagine ever rising from my chair. The evening before with Renee and Roger had gone so well, I suggested we tour Havana together. When we tired of the city's heat and congestion, we settled in for the afternoon at the hotel, hoping it would offer the boys a diversion and the rest of us relief from the oppressive heat.

Archie and Roger engaged the boys in a slow game of croquet as Renee and I sipped tea, the occasional click of mallet against ball our only disturbance.

"Um," Renee murmured. "I could be happy here. Beaches, rum, handsome men, sexy music." She jiggled her shoulders half-heartedly and added more rum to her cup. "Tonight we rumba."

I didn't know how she stayed awake, between the heat and the rum. But then, she was young. Still shy of twenty.

"We need something to wake us from this stupor." I forced myself to sit up straight.

"Don't even think of asking me to move," Renee said, her eyes closed. "This heat's drained me dry. Unless of course you want to jump in the pool. What a noodle I was to leave my bathing suit behind."

I tilted the umbrella so it shielded us more thoroughly.

"I've just the ticket. And you don't have to move a muscle. I'm going to read your tea leaves."

"Hah! You some kind of gypsy?"

I lifted the lid from the teapot, swirled the leaves in the cooled tea, and filled Renee's cup.

"Maybe not a gypsy, but they aren't the only ones with second sight." I pushed Renee's cup toward her. "Drink that up, then I'll tell you what your leaves say."

Renee sat up straighter, lifted her sunglasses, and stared hard at me. "You got some kind of con going?"

For all her bravado, the scared little girl sometimes broke through, wary of everyone.

"Not to worry. It's harmless fun, merely a way to pass long nights in upstate New York."

"Harmless till you start telling people they have to pay for it."

"That'll never happen. Besides, there's no telling if I'll even sense anything about you. Sometimes, not always, but sometimes the tea leaves convey a feeling, a glimmer of insight. I can't control it. I'm nothing more than a conduit. Now drain your tea and we'll see if the leaves have anything to say."

"You sound nuts, you know."

"You wouldn't be the first to think so." I directed her to flip her drained cup over on the saucer and turn it clockwise three times.

Concentration was difficult in the afternoon warmth, and I wished I had water to spray on my face. But sometimes concentration is the very thing that gets in the way of a clear reading.

I lifted Renee's drained cup and, holding it with both hands, peered into the damp swirl of swollen leaves. I closed my eyes to clear my head and an image appeared.

"You're going to be in some grand space, very posh, and you'll be luminous. But then you are always luminous."

"I'll take that."

I frowned. "But something's wrong. You're not happy. It feels like you're afraid."

"Of what?"

"I don't know. It's rarely very specific."

"Well that's convenient. Everyone's sad and afraid sometimes. How do you know this has anything to do with me?"

I ignored her and kept my eyes closed. The next image hit like a blow to the belly and I fell back against the chair cushion. The visions were rarely so visceral or as disturbing. I opened my eyes. I didn't want this, whatever it was.

"What's wrong? What happened?"

"I'm not sure. It's not that I see things happen. It's more that I feel emotions, especially when the emotions are strong ones. And there's no telling if it's something in your future or from your past."

"Well, there's no lack of misery in my past." She sat back in her chair. "Let me know if you ever actually know what's going to happen. Especially if it can help me avoid it. As for the past, you can keep it."

I made myself look again at the leaves, searching for something more positive. Most people want to hear that love and money are coming their way. Bad news, especially vague premonitions, never play well.

"Yours may not be a direct path to happiness, but I sense you'll find it eventually," I said, trying for a happy tone. I didn't add how long and crooked that path felt or that I sensed distress as the persistent tenor of Renee's life.

"Did you see me, Mom? I made a full circle before anyone else."

My head shot up. Lionel was beside me.

"You know better than to interrupt, Lionel. I'm in the middle of a reading."

I lifted the cup again and felt more than saw Lionel slink away. The powerful image and sensations present only moments before had vanished. All I saw was a slimy mess of tea leaves clinging to porcelain. All I felt was agitated and annoyed.

"I'm sorry. It's gone." I set the cup back down. Renee stared at me.

"So you're not putting me on? You really have some special sense?"

I shook my head, laughing it off as a silly game. There was nothing silly nor playful about the sensations I had received, but I knew to be wary of people's responses. The people who took me seriously were often the ones most frightened and threatened by my sight.

"Let me know if you ever pick up anything I should know about," Renee said as Archie and Roger headed our way. "A gal in my circumstances could use a heads-up now and then."

Lionel

This ship we are on is the most perfect place in the world. If Mom let me, I would live on a ship like this all the time. The beds are just right. They fit into the wall on three sides so I feel like I'm in a box. I can look out the porthole beside my bunk and see the water and sky, and on days like today when we are docked, I can see land.

We adopted a stowaway dog and named him Reggy. The crew was some surprised when Reggy showed up in the kitchen, begging for food, the first morning after our ship left New York City. They were going to kick him off in Havana, but they say that if we promise to take him ashore in Honolulu, they will let him stay on the ship for now, and the Chinaman who takes care of Kenny and me takes care of Reggy, too. Mom says OK, we can have Reggy 'cause no innocent animals should be put to sleep for no good reason. And she says I can't call the Chinaman a Chinaman, even if the other passengers do, and must call him Mr. Young. We get to walk Reggy around the deck anytime we want, which I like to do except that all the adults come and talk to us and I run out of nice things to say to all of them. Kenny says he won't "walk that dog and have to talk to a bunch of silly ladies," so I'm the one who has to do it. Mom says that shows how much I am growing up and becoming a man, but I think it shows how lazy Kenny is.

We got to go off the ship when we got to Havana. Dad hired a car and driver to take us and Mr. Tarrington and Miss Manchester sightseeing and out to a fancy hotel place with an outside restaurant and lawn where we could play croquet. Havana is not at all like home where people carry things around in trucks and cars. Here people put stuff on top of their heads, and their carts are pulled by horses instead of engines, like in the olden days. Mom says the sightseeing hacks remind her of pictures she's seen of carriages in Central Park, back in the gay nineties. She got very excited about all the bright-colored flowers everywhere and the big house where the president lives. It didn't look anything like the good old USA's White House.

I like Havana well enough except for having Mr. Tarrington and Miss Manchester come with us. They say mean things to one another and Mr. Tarrington kept telling me to hit more carefully when we played croquet. The sun is so hot in Cuba I thought I was going to melt like butter standing there trying to hit the ball, and then Kenny kept knocking my balls away, which may not be against the rules but it should be. I hated it when Mom got angry with me for interrupting her and Miss Manchester. I wanted to tell her how even with Kenny being a jerk and trying to make me lose, I still made the first loop before anyone else, only all she cared about was looking at Miss Manchester's tea leaves. Grandma Doyle says reading tea leaves is the work of the devil and Mom is inviting Satan into our lives every time she studies a teacup. I don't know why Satan cares about tea leaves or making guesses about what's going to happen in the future, but Grandma Doyle says spirits are best left alone. Mr. Young, the Chinaman steward who watches out for Kenny and me, says Mom has special powers like one of the cooks, an old man who can read people's future in their hands. He said maybe he'll take me and Kenny below deck sometime to meet that man and have our palms read.

Sadira

The heat on the packed dance floor was suffocating.

"I need to cool off," I told Arch when the orchestra took a break. I stepped off the terrace and onto the vast shaded lawn of Cuba's Sans Souci Club.

"This feels better." I opened my arms wide to the gentle breeze. "What an intoxicating place. And these stars. I've never seen a sky so brilliant. How can Hawai'i possibly compare?"

"Not to worry." Arch embraced me from behind, his body like a damp, heavy blanket draped over me. "Hawai'i will be as magical as you've dreamed."

I squirmed free. "Sorry. Too hot."

Even there in the most romantic of settings, after an evening of seductive dance and a bit of rum, I flinched at Arch's touch. I wanted to desire him the way I had Christmas night, but I had no easy access to those feelings. My very body was wary, braced for disappointment.

"I just need a minute to cool down," I told him, "then I promise we'll get back on the dance floor. You were sizzling out there." I took his hand. "The other women were green with envy." It wasn't even a lie.

He shook me off. "Don't patronize me, Sadie."

Just then Jasmine McConnell, a missionary bound for Shanghai, emerged from the darkness, her hair mussed and lipstick smeared. A puffing Roger Tarrington appeared behind her, his jacket off and tie askew. When Roger had suggested a group of us share cars for the eighteen-mile drive to the nightclub, we hadn't expected mousy Jasmine to join us.

"Come on, honey girl, don't ruin it. We've got a special connection, you and me." Spotting us, he called, "Arch! Sadie! Talk to this girl. Tell her Cuba's for lovers."

Roger reached out to grab Jasmine's arm and she batted him away. "Stop it. I told you I'm not interested."

"You worried about Renee?" Roger swayed as he spoke. "She's no problem. The two of us have an understanding."

Arch stepped between Roger and Jasmine. "It's a good thing we ran into you two. Sadie and I were about to start warning folks it's time we head back to the ship. Roger, let's you and I alert the drivers."

"But the night's still young."

Arch gripped Roger's shoulder and turned him away. "Not for us, my friend."

I linked an arm in Jasmine's. "Let's round up the others. But first, a visit to the powder room." I avoided our crowd of fellow passengers, noisy standouts in the club's main showroom, and ushered her down an empty corridor to the ladies' room. A dozen women crowded the spacious lounge with its long circle of mirrors and vanity tables. I led Jasmine to an empty row of sinks.

"I'm such a fool." She teared up and began shivering. "I believed he only wanted to show me the stars."

I wondered if she really was that naive or if some part of her had been curious or even flattered by Roger's attention. I shook out her silk stole and wrapped it around her.

"At least now, you know better than to go off alone with a stranger."

She squeezed my hand. "You're a lucky woman, Sadie. I hope someday I find a guy as decent as Archie. I'm so grateful to you both."

"You betcha." I wet my hanky and ran it around the edges of her lips, wiping away the lipstick stains. "Now chin up. We'll fix your hair and get you right as rain."

By the time the group assembled, Arch had Roger settled in one of the cars. Jasmine and I climbed in the other. Renee was the first to join us.

"Howdy do." She hopped in, her gown hitched nearly to her hips. "I am so ready for bed. My brain's gone all to mush." She squeezed in between Jasmine and me, then grabbed hold of our hands. "My two favorite women in the whole world."

I wondered if she even knew Jasmine's name.

Finnegan Rolfe leaned in. "Room for me?"

Renee clapped. "Oh goody, yes! We must have a handsome man to amuse us. If you promise to be nice, I'll even perch on your lap."

Others piled in. We weren't the only ones avoiding a ride with Roger. The sardine effect had been tolerable, even a little fun, for the ride out, but the stench of sweat, booze, and cigars made it unbearable now. I rolled down my window.

"Wasn't this just the most divine evening?" Renee asked no one in particular. She settled back against Finnegan and wrapped his arms around her waist. "I could have danced until the sun came up."

I nodded off.

Once shipside, Arch and I formed a barrier around Jasmine as we climbed the gangway.

"Wait for me!" Shoes dangling in one hand, Renee ran up the ramp after us. "I demand good-night kisses all around." Finnegan followed, clutching her purse and wrap.

The sound of retching drew our attention to Roger bent double at the rail.

"See you in the morning," I called back to Renee. Finnegan could provide her good-night kisses. I was done.

We opened our door to find our cabin's lights ablaze and Lionel seated cross-legged at the doorway connecting our room to the boys'.

"What are you doing up, champ?" Arch crouched down beside him.

"I was scared you'd miss the sailing." He wiped his eyes.

"We'd never let that happen. Not in a million years."

Not in a million sober years maybe, but Lionel knew as well as I the
value of Arch's promises.

"I'm sorry you were worried, lamb." I stepped out of my heels and
tugged off my earrings. "We're here now and we all need to get some
sleep. Be a good boy and get back to bed. Dad can tuck you in."

We'd be lucky to grab a couple hours' sleep, but the evening had been
worth it. The sheer beauty and sumptuousness of the nightclub exceeded
anything I'd imagined possible, and the rumba was a revelation. They'd
have hauled us off the dance floor if we'd tried those steamy moves back
in Carlisle. Even Roger couldn't erase the night's magic. As I wiped off
my makeup, I played with the description I wished I could send home.
Those other Carlisle women wasting away should know of the sensuality
in a Caribbean beat and the liberating effect of a mojito.

My Dear Ones,

*Champagne flowed and hips swayed into the morning hours
last night at Havana's San Souci nightclub, where yours truly
and husband Archie were seduced by the throbbing Latin
beat of this spicy Caribbean island. Hip to hip and lip to lip,
couples writhed across the open dance floor, all discretion and
decorum cast off in the sweltering night. More than a few vows
were broken and many fantasies realized in the deep shadows
of that world-famous club. Who could say which was more
enchanting, the deadly rum-laced drinks or the sizzling music,
but no one could dispute the hypnotic power of this tiny island
nation with its dashing men, exotic women, and decadent,
anything-goes attitude.*

*As we continue our voyage to new adventures, I bid you
hasta luego and remain Sadie, Your Gal About Town.*

All it needed was a reference to voodoo black magic, and Prudence
could feel vindicated in her belief that I embodied all that was corrupt in
this world. If only it were true. I wasn't even brave enough to write such

a column, let alone live up to its descriptions. Would I ever say goodbye to boring, good-girl Sadira and follow my heart? I stared at myself in the bathroom mirror, liking my flushed cheeks and bright eyes. To look at me, a person might think I was a wanton woman capable of great passions and excesses. I wondered if Arch was awake and waiting for me. I smiled recalling how well he'd handled Roger. Whatever his demons, Arch was at core a good man who could still, on his better days, play the hero.

I opened the bathroom door, pleased with the feel of my satin gown against my body, mindful of the way it clung to me. Arch lay on the cabin floor, asleep and snoring beside Lionel. I pulled the blanket off the top bunk and draped it over them, then switched off the cabin lights. I climbed into bed grateful I was too tired to think.

Lionel

Kenny and I nearly became orphans last night 'cause Mom and Dad went missing. The night started out like every other one on the ship. Mom came down from the grown-up dinner to tuck us in at nine so Mr. Young could go to bed himself.

"No monkey business and no leaving your room, understand?" she said, like she says every night. "And if you wake up, just go back to sleep."

"Got it," I said, and though I don't like sleeping when she and Dad aren't close by, it feels safe inside our cabin on the sea. Not like at home with so many windows that Bible men and vampires and monsters can peek in at us.

I woke up at midnight like I often wake up at midnight and opened the door to their cabin just a tiny bit to make sure they were there, only this time they weren't. I went all the way in their room and looked in the bathroom and in every corner in case they were playing hide-and-seek, but they were definitely not there. I was only a little bit worried 'cause sometimes back home, they stayed up late and played cards or sang songs with their friends till really late at night and I thought maybe they were upstairs having a grand old time. Mr. Young told me some grown-ups on the ships and in big cities watch movies and dance and listen to music so late at night that it's not really night anymore but almost morning when they go to bed.

I must have fallen back to sleep 'cause next thing I knew I woke up again but then it was two o'clock and they still weren't back.

I began to get scared that maybe they fell overboard or were kidnapped and smuggled off the ship and maybe Kenny and I were now orphans. Maybe at the next port the crew would sell us as slave boys to some rich Persian prince who'd make us wave giant fans to cool down him and his wives, or some Chinese empress would buy us to teach her American songs and dances and all the English slang so she could visit President Roosevelt and impress him.

I told myself to go back to sleep, that if I slept, I'd wake up and they'd be in their beds and everything would be hunky-dory again. I closed my eyes really, really tight, but hard as I tried I couldn't sleep. I was sure they'd fallen overboard. Maybe Mom's shawl blew off and she reached out to grab it and then started to fall over the railing. Dad tried to save her. He grabbed hold of her legs, only the wind was blowing really, really strong, and she kept reaching for her shawl and Dad tried so hard to save her he turned red in the face. Even though he says mean things about her and they yell at each other, I know they really love each other, and Dad would never let go. So instead of it only being Mom who drowned, they both went splat in the ocean right where the sharks circle waiting for someone to fall in so they can eat them up for supper. By three o'clock I was sure we were orphans.

I couldn't stop crying and that woke up Kenny.

"Why're you crying?" he asked, and I said, "I'm not crying, go back to sleep," but Kenny started to cry and say, "I want Mommy," and I said, "Mommy is dancing with Daddy, and will be here soon. Now you need to go to sleep before they get back or she will be mad at you," but he still cried and he still said he wanted Mommy, so I opened the cabin door and stuck my head out. I wanted to go looking for them only Mom always told me that when I'm alone with Kenny, I can never, ever leave him. It's my job to protect him from anything bad that could happen, and so I only stuck my head out and yelled, "Help," only not too loud 'cause people were sleeping and I didn't want anyone to be mad at me.

Kenny just cried louder 'cause I was crying "Help," so I closed the door and told him everything was OK and to stop being a baby. I told him, "Look at me, I'm not acting like a baby," and he said, "Yes, you are. You're crying, too," and I said, "I'm only crying 'cause you're crying." Finally he cried himself to sleep and it was only me awake and waiting.

It felt like I cried and worried for about a whole year that night, and finally sometime when it was nearly time for the sun to show up, they came back. Mom told me to go to my room, but Dad lay down beside me on the floor. He could feel how lonesome and scared I was. We all were so tired, we slept through the whole morning all the way to lunch.

"Another great day at sea, sport," Dad said the next day, like nothing ever happened and Mom said, "Be sure you two wash your hands real well before lunch." Maybe there's some reason grown-ups have to make kids suffer, but when I'm all grown up, I won't ever let my kids be so scared and alone.

Sadira

I couldn't resist resting a cheek against our table's cool marble top. After five hours of sightseeing in Los Angeles, I wanted only to close my eyes and rest my brain for a few minutes. Left to our own devices, the boys and I would have spent hours circling the city on a bus tour. Renee, gifted at amusing young boys, provided an entirely different kind of encounter with the City of Angels—amusement park rides, Foucault's Pendulum at the Griffith Park observatory, even a chance to compare handprints at Grauman's Theater. By midafternoon, we were starving and out of steam. Renee took us to Violette's Diner, choosing a table by the window.

"Best grilled sandwiches and banana splits in the world. Hot dogs aren't so bad either."

I was surprised by her choice. The humble diner was hardly the kind of place I pictured her frequenting.

"I have to run a quick errand, but go ahead and order whatever you want. It's on Roger. You can put me down for a hot fudge sundae."

"It's too much. This one's on us." I appreciated Renee's generosity, but I could certainly afford a meal from a diner.

"If Roger's going to desert me and steal your husband for a day of golf, the least he can do is pay for lunch."

I had no idea what "errand" she was up to and didn't ask. She'd kept me in a mixed state of bewilderment and amusement all day. When she reappeared, she hid her hands behind her back. "Guess what I have."

"A telescope?" Lionel guessed first.

Renee shook her head. "Not quite so snazzy." She nodded at Kenny. "Your turn, chum."

"A cowboy hat?"

"Nope. Even better than a cowboy hat." She held out two lizard masks. "What do you think?"

Kenny shrank into my side but Lionel grinned. "Keen! Monsters."

"Not monsters, lizards. Try one on." She passed one to him and handed me the other to slip over Kenny's face.

"I can't hardly breathe," Kenny said.

"Know why I got them for you?"

Just the question I had for her. I wasn't amused. I did not need scary masks giving the boys nightmares.

The boys shook their heads.

"Ever hear of the lizard people?"

Again, a shaking of heads.

"They're half people, half lizard and have a secret city underneath Los Angeles with more treasures than all the kings and pharaohs and emperors combined."

Kenny stared hard at the floor. "Do they eat people?"

I was ready to strangle her. There'd be no sleep for the boys that night, worrying over lizard people climbing out of the ground.

"No, silly-willy. Flies maybe, but never people. They're like us. Regular people, only they happen to look like lizards."

"How come they live underground?" Lionel wasn't biting.

"To hide all their money. They have so much gold and silver, they had to build a whole city of tunnels and caves to keep it safe. Besides, they don't like the sun."

"I thought lizards love the sun."

For once, I appreciated and was even proud of Lionel's skepticism and tenacity. He could drive me mad with his questions, but better that than a willingness to accept nonsense.

"You got me there, bud." Renee thought a moment. "Regular lizards do like the sun, but I think it's different with human ones 'cause they're only part lizard. They got the part of lizards that likes dark spaces."

"Do they ever come up here?" Kenny asked.

"Yup. All the time. I bet some of 'em are here right now."

The boys glanced about us. Even I reflexively scanned the people in the diner. No lizards so far as I could tell.

"Nobody here looks like a lizard." Lionel clearly wanted to believe her.

"With that mask on, you don't look much like a person. Don't you suppose the lizard people wear masks when they're out and about?"

I watched the doubts evaporate and his face ignite. Here was a curiosity he could grab hold of. Renee nudged him with her elbow and nodded at a man passing outside. He wore a long overcoat.

"To hide the tail," she whispered.

Lionel's eyes widened and Kenny leaned closer to me.

"When we finish eating, I'll take you to the park across the way where you can look for their portal. That's a fancy word for the place they come and go from. What say you?"

Lionel nodded, but Kenny looked hard at me, pleading.

"If you don't feel like hunting for lizard people, that's fine. I can push you on the swings," I assured him.

If Renee sensed my annoyance, she didn't show it. Her entire focus was now on the grand building across the street from us, an elegant, multistoried structure peppered with limousines at its porte cochere and parking lot.

"What is it?" I nodded in its direction. "Hotel? Apartment building?"

She shook her head and spoke softly. "I think the dressed-up name is 'gentleman's club.' Though gentlemen were in short supply when I was there." The waitress arrived with our sandwiches and ice cream concoctions. "I'll fill you in later." Renee picked up her long, thin spoon. "Dig in, boys, you're about to have the best hot fudge anywhere in America."

Once we reached the park and Kenny was convinced I could see him from the bench where Renee and I settled, the boys set out together in search of the secret portal. Renee found them each a long stick with which they probed bushes and the fenced perimeter for hidden holes.

"You sure know how to amuse boys," I said.

"Always been a natural talent of mine. Not much difference between men and boys. They all love a bit of danger and surprise."

"And when the boys are awake with nightmares thanks to that wild story you concocted, I'll be bringing them up to your suite."

"Hey." She held her hands up in protest. "I didn't make that up. I read about it in the *LA Times* back when I lived here. Some guy actually drilled a whole shaft deep into the ground trying to find the lost treasure. Why do you think they make those masks? People eat up that nonsense."

"And here I thought Carlisle was the home of fools. Folks there are hardly geniuses, but I can't think of a one who'd believe something that ridiculous."

"Welcome to Los Angeles."

"So fill me in." I nodded at the men's club. "You're saying that's one of those places where men sit in leather chairs and butlers serve them drinks?"

"Not exactly. Butlers serve the drinks, but the guys aren't there just to smoke cigars and read the paper. They're looking for a good time with the prettiest dolls in the city."

"It's a house of ill repute?"

Renee laughed. "Yup. The la-di-da version. It's all the same business, whatever you call it."

"And you've been inside?"

"Sweetie, I lived and worked there. It saved me. I took a bus here from South Dakota when I was fourteen and a country rube. No friends, no money, no street smarts. Ethel fixed me up good. She's got girls in there who could pass as Jean Harlow or Carole Lombard. She's even got one gal you'd swear was Garbo. Ethel's the one who matched me up with Roger. Knew he was my ticket to something better."

"But all those different men." I couldn't fathom how she could be so matter-of-fact about it all, as if it were just another job, like waitressing.

She shrugged. "There are harder ways to survive and worse men to be around. I got to meet a slew of Hollywood swells. Directors. Producers. Famous actors. All of them rich enough to give me tips so big, I built up a nice little nest egg. Plus I learned a lot about how the world works. More than any school ever taught me. If I hadn't found my way out here and landed with Ethel, I'd have gotten knocked up by some hick before I turned fifteen. I'd have churned out babies till I died in childbirth or froze to death getting to the barn during a blizzard. Roger's no insurance policy, but he's my ticket into a world where maybe I'll find someone who is. I know what a hard life looks like, and what I did in that place was not hard."

"So why are we here? You hoping to see Ethel?"

She laughed again. "Ethel and I aren't that kind of friends. We are here so I can check on Roger. He got lucky once at this place and might think he could do better the second time round."

If Roger might be there, I realized, so could Archie. "Arch would never go to a place like that."

She looked at me as she might an adorable puppy. "Oh, sweetie. It's every Joe's fantasy to go to a place like that, especially a high-class one with someone else paying. No guy turns down a gorgeous babe ready to make his every fantasy come true."

I didn't believe it. Not Archie. A drink might bring him to his knees, but not another woman.

One of the boys screeched. I stood and scanned the park but couldn't see either of them. A whimper followed, the kind that precedes tears. "I've got this," Renee said. "It was my idea to bring them here."

She took off in the direction of the sound, calling their names. I knew I should look around as well, but convinced myself it was better to stay there in the park's center where the boys expected me to be. It felt good to hand the worry off to someone else. Within seconds, Kenny emerged from a stand of bushes, galloping toward me.

"We saw one, Mom, we saw one. It stuck its head out between two giant branches and it was this big." He spread his arms as wide as he could.

"Oh my." I hadn't the energy to enthuse over this game of pretend.

"I wasn't afraid at all, but Lionel peed his pants."

Renee and Lionel appeared, strolling, hand in hand. Lionel now wore Renee's sweater wrapped like an apron around his waist.

"Lionel scared the bejesus out of some poor lizard man," Renee said, calm as can be, as if the boy beside her, a boy way too old to be having accidents, didn't have a massive wet stain on his pants. "I'm thinking maybe it's time to head back to the ship. What do you boys think?"

Our limousine sat curbside waiting for us. Renee spread a blanket across part of its back seat for Lionel, then climbed in and sat beside him.

"I think they give special awards to folks who scare off a lizard man," she continued. "I'm going to have to write the mayor and tell him what happened."

Kenny and I took the seat opposite them.

"I was the bravest one," Kenny said. "I didn't scream, cry, or pee my pants."

Lionel reached across and flicked Kenny's cheek with a finger.

"Enough." I pushed him back against his seat. "No teasing, no hitting."

"I didn't hit him," Lionel said.

"I wasn't teasing. I was telling the truth," Kenny said.

"Not another word from either of you. I have had it." Leave it to Lionel to turn a nearly magical day into a miserable one.

Renee had tuned us out. Her focus was now on the men's club. As the limousine passed its entrance, she inhaled sharply. "I think I steered you wrong, guys. That building back there may be the actual portal. Those clever lizards can try hiding behind a fancy human façade, but they'll never fool us."

Lionel

I changed my mind about Miss Manchester. Now I think she's about the most wonderful person in the whole entire world. She might be even better than President Roosevelt and his wife Eleanor who does all those good things for people even though some people like my Grandma Doyle say nasty things about her. Today Miss Manchester took Kenny, Mom, and me on the best adventure a guy could ever have. First we went to a carnival place with what I bet is the biggest roller coaster ride in the whole world. Even though I was too scared to ride the Cyclone 'cause it looked like I could fall out and drown in the ocean, I got to ride a carousel of wild animals and go in a building full of mirrors that made us fat and skinny and upside down. After that we saw the house where Will Rogers lived and did a whole bunch of other stuff like every tourist person who visits.

The best part of all was finding out about the lizard people who live in tunnels underneath the city. Those people scare me, but it isn't exactly a bad kind of scary. Sometimes scary things are also the best things 'cause they make your heart go fast and life feels so big you might just explode with how exciting it is.

The only part I didn't like was when we saw an actual real lizard person. That part was too scary. He was hiding behind a bush and had a whole pile of blankets and bags. When we found him, he jumped up and his coat was so big and he smelled so bad I knew he had to be a lizard man, so I screamed to scare him away. He sure did scare me, but I scared him, too, 'cause he ran away fast as lightning. I could tell Mom thought I acted like a big baby. I bet if a lizard man jumped up in front of her, she would scream herself blue in the face. Miss Manchester didn't mind I peed my pants. She understood 'cause she's got a big heart, and she's not like some grown-ups who lie to you and say stuff 'cause they think you're a stupid kid. She doesn't change her voice and she looks right at me, just like I'm nearly a grown-up man. Sometimes I don't like having to look at people's eyes the way Mom tells me to, but I can tell when I look back at Miss Manchester that she's interested in what I'm saying. She's not fake like most grown-ups.

I was angry when Mom said I couldn't go with Dad for the day. I didn't want to have to be stuck with the ladies like some little kid, but it turned out swell after all. Besides, Dad was with Mr. Tarrington, and I know I'd rather spend a day with Miss Manchester anytime rather than that mean guy.

One of the ship guys told me they got lots of little lizards in Hawai'i. I'm wondering if maybe that means there's lots of lizard people there, too. It's warm all the time like Los Angeles and they got plenty of caves where they can hide. One thing for sure, I am going to keep my eyes open once we get there. Who knows? Maybe I'll find some gold they buried way, way down under the ground. Then everyone would have to be nice to me.

Sadira

Arch was not on the ship when we returned and was still not back at nine when I met Renee as scheduled to leave for dinner at the Ambassador

Hotel's Cocoanut Grove. I had serious misgivings about going without the men, but Renee insisted we continue with our plans and brushed off my concerns.

"Why should we lose out just 'cause those two are so selfish they couldn't bother to get back in time? Besides, Roger already ordered the car, we're dressed and stunning, and I am not missing out on an evening at the Grove. I say we go and have the time of our lives."

She was right about her being stunning. Everything about her shimmered that night—the gold lamé gown caressing her body, the diamond choker around her neck, the diamond cuff on her wrist. Even her eyes sparkled with a mesmerizing brilliance, as if some internal flame illuminated them.

For all that, she was unusually quiet during the drive from ship to hotel. She stroked the buttery leather of the hired car, fixed her gaze out the window, and ignored me.

As we pulled up to the Ambassador's entry, her demeanor altered completely. She let the doorman come to the car rather than jump out as she usually did. When she swung her legs around and her right foot hit the ground, she was transformed. No longer merely a pretty nobody, she exited the limousine a star. There was no mistaking that she was the it girl of the night, a magnet for eyes and camera lenses.

Light bulbs flashed. Reporters surged forward and called out to her. "Who are you dining with?" "What's your next film?" "Remind me of your name, sweetheart." I trailed behind as she danced her way to and through the entrance.

The maître d' greeted her by name and, after exaggerated air kisses, ushered us into the grand showroom, her arm in his.

"We were thrilled when Mr. Whitney phoned to say you'd be joining him tonight," he said. "Such a pleasure after so long." I had no idea who this Mr. Whitney was or why we were his guests, but I followed along as best I could.

I thought nothing could match Cuba's Sans Souci, but I was wrong.

The Cocoanut Grove was spectacular beyond imagining, all of it an excess. We had entered a sultan's palace—hundreds of round tables, hundreds of diners and dancers in an immense space bedecked with palm trees, gold pillars, and crimson drapings. Stars twinkled overhead, so real it seemed the very roof had opened. Overloaded with visual stimulation, my eyes tried to absorb it all as the maître d' escorted us to a table front and center beside the dance floor. It was all as grand as Renee had promised, and I was glad I'd shrugged off my worries.

A balding, portly man rose as we approached, his face pink with pleasure, his arms wide. He thunderously recited Byron. "She walks in beauty, like the night of cloudless climes and starry skies; and all that's best of dark and bright meet in her aspect and her eyes."

"Oh, Max, you and your fancy Shakespeare talk." Renee blessed him with a radiant smile and pecks on both cheeks.

Another gentleman at the table pulled out a chair beside Max's. Renee's sable slid from her arms and was caught by the gentleman, who handed it off to an attentive waiter.

As the men settled back in their chairs, I remained standing. All eyes were on Renee. A waiter appeared beside me, a chair in hand, and I was squeezed between two men who, like every man at the table, seemed not to have registered my presence.

When Max hooked an arm around Renee's waist, she blushed and protested, "Oh, Max, you know I'm already taken," but she didn't remove his arm. When he led her to the dance floor and stroked her back and hips, and then even her buttocks, she moved closer to rest her head on his chest.

I sipped the club's signature cocktail, which Max had ordered for us, a pink mix of gin, lime juice, maraschino liqueur, and grenadine, nibbled on foods for which I had no names, and tried without success to engage the dinner companions to either side of me. When Renee settled onto Max's lap, her arms looped around his neck, and sighed, "I don't think I've ever been so happy as this," I picked up my purse.

"If you will all excuse me, I need to wash my hands. Will you join me, Renee?"

Of course, I fully expected her to stand and follow me to the ladies' room. Instead, she responded with the dreamy smile of a lovesick schoolgirl. "Sadie, love, I couldn't possibly move a muscle. I'm much too comfy right where I am."

I don't know what transpired after that because I collected my wrap and asked the doorman to summon our driver. I had no doubt Renee would get herself to wherever she was headed that night.

"How is it you're here and Archie isn't?"

I was angry. Archie had yet to appear and Roger was enjoying his breakfast in the dining room. I was frantic with worry that the ship would set sail without Arch, but I didn't dare let the boys see my fear.

"I've no idea what you're talking about. Archie and I boarded the ship together last night. It is Renee who never returned. She sent some goon of Max Whitney's to pack and haul away her things this morning." He waved a notecard at me. "This is all she sent by way of explanation. 'Dearest Roger,'" he read. "'It's been a swell time. Thanks for everything. Your dumpling, Renee.'" He tossed the note on the table. "I kept her in luxury, catered to her every whim, transformed her from a know-nothing hick into a classy gal, and she walks away, stupid enough to believe Max will make her a star. She always was more tinsel than gold."

His fist rested on the morning's paper with its huge, above-the-fold photograph of Renee on Max Whitney's arm.

"That doesn't sound like something Renee would do without cause."

"No?" He lifted the paper so I could have a closer look. "You think she didn't plan all of this, waiting for her chance at someone who could move her up the Hollywood food chain? Poor little Max. He fancies himself a collector of fine things. I bet he hasn't a clue she's the collector."

"Renee isn't conniving."

Roger laughed with gusto. "Now that's precious. Trust me, I get why you're attracted to her. I imagine she's everything you wish you could be. But I figured you were smart enough to see through her charade. No wonder she chose you as a friend. She knows a mark when she sees one." He dipped his spoon in the soft-boiled egg before him. A bit of yolk dribbled down his chin.

"Curious you're still standing here and not off looking for Archie. It's almost as if you care more about Renee, a girl you barely know, than your own husband. Or is there something else you're interested in? Perhaps something I can assist with?" He reached out and stroked my elbow, running a finger up and under my sleeve. I jerked my arm back.

"Leaving you was the smartest thing she ever did." Even to my own ears, I sounded like a petulant little girl. "You don't deserve her," I added, my face flaming. I was furious that I'd let him rattle me.

I returned to the boys, ordered their breakfasts, and set off in search of Archie, unsure who angered me most—Roger, Archie, or Renee.

Lionel

Kenny's too little a kid to know what was going on with Dad the day the ship left Los Angeles. Dad got lost for a whole night and when Mom found him sleeping in a deck chair, she was plenty mad, so mad she didn't want to talk to him or even be near him.

"You can take care of the boys today," she told him. "I've got work to do." And we didn't see her again all morning.

We tried to play shuffleboard, but Dad kept having to sit down, so we played checkers instead, only he didn't do so good with that either.

"Your move, Dad," Kenny told him during their game, and Dad raised his head off the table and blinked a few times like he couldn't figure out it was a checkerboard in front of him.

Kenny looked like he was getting grumpy and might say something stupid that would get Dad all riled up or, worse, make him feel bad and like he was a disappointment to us boys. I don't know what Kenny had to be so worked up about. He was beating Dad something awful. He had a whole big stack of Dad's black checker pieces in front of him. Dad had no reds, not a single one. I'm not sure Dad even knew he and Kenny were playing checkers. His eyes went really small when he looked at the board, like it hurt his head to use them. He drank a lot from the glass of water I got him, but when he tried to put the glass down, it shook in his hand so bad the water spilled everywhere.

Kenny got so cocky, he pushed back from the table and balanced on two legs of his chair, which is something we're never, ever supposed to do 'cause you can crack your head wide open if you fall backward. Dad's not going to like this, I thought. Dad's going to start yelling at him to stop. Only Dad didn't say a thing. He just let him stay there rocking back and forth, hanging on by his fingertips to the table's edge, like he wasn't doing anything wrong.

Then Dad made a stupid move. He slid a black piece to a space that let Kenny take three of his pieces.

"Hah!" Kenny yelled and he let his chair fall forward. He picked up his red piece and jumped over Dad's three, then looked over at me like he was so smart, only he's not so smart 'cause he couldn't even figure out that Dad wasn't even trying to win.

"You're beating the socks off me," Dad said, and that only made Kenny grin even bigger. "You're way too good for me, chum. I surrender."

Kenny looked like a balloon with a hole. All his bounce went away.

"I'll finish the game for you, Dad," I said, 'cause I thought that would help make things better, but Kenny said, "I don't want to play with you. I can play with you any old time," which made me real mad, especially when I was trying to do a nice thing.

"You OK, Dad?" I asked when I looked over and it seemed like Dad might start throwing up.

"Sure thing, chum. Just need to shut my eyes for a few. Your old dad's just fine." Dad closed his eyes, then he put his head on the table. Kenny pushed his chair away with a loud screech, but even that didn't wake up Dad.

"Don't be a grumpy Gus," I said. "Can't you see Dad doesn't feel good?"

"It's not fair," Kenny said and stomped off. I was stuck there beside Dad till it was a long time after lunch and a steward came in and said would I like help getting Dad to his cabin, and I said, "Sure" and "Thanks," and we helped get him down the stairs and into his bed. Mom went to dinner without him that night and she didn't even dress up. She just wore one of her regular old dresses and didn't even say good night to Kenny and me.

Sadira

The evening we set sail from San Francisco I stood hunched at the ship's rail, a blanket wrapped around me. I wanted a last glimpse of the city and land before we headed across the vast Pacific Ocean. Only after we glided beneath the Golden Gate and rounded the peninsula's head did I turn away from the humped hills, now barely visible in the darkening sky. This should have been a moment of immense anticipation, even exhilaration after a long and trying journey to realize my dream, but an untethered anxiety consumed me. What if I was wrong and only misery awaited us?

"I understand Roger Tarrington won't be continuing with us," Karen Mesrobian, the self-appointed grande dame of our voyage, announced as I swung open the heavy doors to the ship's lounge where we gathered for the cocktail hour. "Apparently, he's heading back, tail between his legs, to his wife's loving embrace."

Weeks of shared life aboard ship had softened the collective stiffness of our journey's start, but the group was subdued that night. We faced a long stretch at sea, with only one another for distraction.

"I don't blame Renee for casting him aside. He's a beast of a man," Jasmine said. She squeezed the juice of a lime wedge into her soda water.

"Love's a powerful force. It can make a man forget himself," Finnegan mumbled. He had his own wounds to lick.

"As if either of them ever loved anyone but themselves," I snapped, which was unfair to poor romantic Finnegan. My quarrel was not with him.

"My, such anger." Karen was enjoying herself. "Feeling bruised by your gal pal?"

The barb hit its mark. I did feel abandoned. It stung to be discarded, as if ours were a friendship of mere circumstance. All my days of worry since Los Angeles and no message of any kind from Renee.

Finnegan clicked his lighter on and off, never managing a flame, his cigarette limp between his fingers. "Renee must be so alone and frightened in that big city."

"Trust me. She's not alone." Karen spoke with great assurance. She must have seen the newspaper photo of Renee with Max. "Something tells me she'll come out of this just fine." For once I agreed.

I sank into a chair at the room's periphery and closed my eyes, trying to shut out the chatter. These final days crossing the Pacific would be tedious. My fling with glamour and excitement was over. I was once again merely ordinary, with no hope of magic piercing my world again.

Lionel

If you ask me, and no one ever does, I say good riddance to Roger Tarrington and hope he misses Renee so much his heart breaks in two. I won't say I hope he dies 'cause I know that would be an even worse sin than hoping he's suffering real bad, but Mr. Tarrington is not a nice man and Miss Manchester is just about the most beautiful woman in the whole world and maybe the nicest one, too, so I think she was right to leave him. I don't know what happened exactly 'cause the grown-ups stop talking soon as Kenny and I come around and then they make us leave the room, but Mom was boiling up angry when she found out Renee wasn't on the ship anymore and she wouldn't talk to Mr. Tarrington or even look at him after that. If we were walking down the promenade or going up the staircase and he went by us, it was like he didn't exist, like he was a ghost she couldn't see. Mom likes Renee almost as much as Kenny and I do. I don't think I ever knew a person who laughs as much as Renee, and when she does, it's like every single part of her is lit up like a Christmas tree. Mom says there's no such word as glowy, but I think that's exactly the word for what Renee is. Glowy and perfect in every way. And I'm not just saying that because she told us about the lizard people, though I think that's about the best fact anyone ever told me. Some of the grown-ups laugh when I talk about them, and Mom says, "I think Renee was having a little fun with you boys," 'cause she doesn't think the lizard people are real, but Miss Manchester wouldn't lie to me.

We are now really, truly on our way to Hawai'i. I was hoping we'd see the seals again once we got out of the harbor, but it was almost dark and Kenny and I were eating our supper when the ship sailed out of San Francisco. Now we look at nothing but ocean and ocean and more ocean until we come to those little islands in the middle of the Pacific. Kenny and I check the map every day to see how far we've gone. At least there are no icebergs so we won't go down like the *Titanic*, but I still worry about other stuff floating out there that could break the ship in two and send us to the bottom of the sea.

I keep telling Reggy it won't be much longer till he sees his new home. Then he'll be able to sleep in my room with me, not like on the ship where he has to stay in Mr. Young's room. One night after we left San Francisco, Mr. Young invited me and Kenny to visit Reggy and eat with the Chinese stewards in steerage. Mom said OK, but I could tell she was a little worried about it. Mr. Young said, "You come, too, missus," and I know she wanted to, but Dad said, "Let the boys have an adventure of their own," and so just me and Kenny got to go down with Mr. Young. Forty-two Chinese men came on board at Balboa, all heading back to China. They have their dinner at four o'clock along with the ship stewards. They eat early because the stewards have to wait on all of us passengers. They sit under a big tent set up on the deck, and while they wait for the food, the Chinese men gamble with ivory dominoes made out of real live elephant tusks. They don't have any forks, so we had to use chopsticks, and the only spoons are gigantic ones for drinking soup. The soup was my favorite. It had beaten eggs and chicken in it and then they gave us rice with shrimp and mushrooms. Kenny picked out all the mushrooms, but I ate mine 'cause I know you should be polite when someone invites you to dinner, and eat everything they offer whether you like it or not. The main dinner food was a big mix of all kinds of stuff like beef and pork and chicken with lots of vegetables. It was like someone took everything out of the vegetable drawer in the icebox, added in the leftover meat for a whole week, and tossed it all together. Reggy sat right beside my feet while I ate and I snuck him some pieces of meat. He loved that. He wagged his tail and licked my hand, he was so happy. He is my best friend, so I won't be lonely when we get to Hawai'i and have to go to school again and have no friends. I'll go home from school and there he'll be waiting for me, wagging his tail and licking my face to show how happy he is to see me.

Chapter Three

February to October 1936

Sadira

Only Daddy would have understood what the thin green line on the horizon meant to me the morning we approached Oʻahu, how much promise and hope rested in that sliver of land. Daddy understood what a grave Carlisle was. All that thick brick and those stark streets laid out precisely, unyielding, as if life must always run in straight lines and turn at sharp corners, never a curving bridge to desire and possibility.

Alone on the isolated deck, I leaned into the wind. The ship faithfully churned forward, its wake wide and white. No discernible structures yet on the island ahead, only the thickening line. I didn't mind the island's gradual reveal. I had all the days of my life ahead to learn its contours and elements. It was enough that I was in Hawaiʻi's waters. Warm waters. My voyage done. My destination in sight.

And then the engines quieted. The ship slowed. It stopped. The engines churned on again and the ship reversed.

"What's happening?" I called to a passing crew member, who must have thought me crazed, my untied kimono flapping open, my nightgown a billowing parachute in the brisk wind, my feet bare on the slick wood.

"We hit a whale. It's stuck in the propeller. They're trying to shake it loose."

Forward again and then back. Over and over, the water foaming pink, and then, at last, the torso bobbed to the surface, and we were underway again.

I refused to be cowed. This would be no harbinger of things to come. I chose to see it as a reminder that the human spirit welcomes a challenge and will triumph, if there's sufficient resolve. I stayed at the rail until we drew close enough to distinguish the curve of white beaches and the sharp outline of the Koʻolau mountains. Finally, I gave in to decorum, gathered my robe tight around me, and headed back to the cabin to dress for our first day in paradise.

Lionel was showered and ready, his suitcase beside the door. He sat beneath the porthole, its curtain pulled back to give him light enough to sew. He was stitching a piece of fabric onto the misshapen crazy quilt Elma had had him begin before we left Carlisle.

"You can collect bits of fabric everywhere you go on your journey," she told him. "And the quilt will become a record of your life."

She gave him a scrap from the curtains she'd made for his Carlisle bedroom and a bit of sackcloth dishtowel to remind him of her kitchen. She threw in other pieces from dresses she had sewn for me, and a swatch of his first baby blanket.

"The beauty of a crazy quilt," she added, "is you can sew pieces together in any way you want. It doesn't matter what designs or colors or shapes the pieces are. Parts of it can even be ugly, but at the end, it works and becomes something beautiful."

She was right about the ugly. It hurt my eyes to look at the hodgepodge mess of colors and patterns. Lionel had no instinct for harmony.

"Good for you for being ready. I'm glad someone listened to me."

"I didn't want to get left behind." His eyes didn't leave the quilt. "I thought maybe you already got off."

"Why would you think that? Honestly, Lionel, you do get the oddest ideas. I just went up to watch our approach. I'm going to get dressed and then we can have some breakfast."

He nodded, his eyes never leaving the quilt, as if the needle and fabric were some kind of anchor.

I jostled Kenny's shoulder. "Wake up, mister. We're nearly there."

I roused Arch before heading to the bathroom. He groaned and rolled over.

"Lord help me," I muttered as I pulled off my nightgown. How different it would be if I were starting over alone.

We made it on deck in time for the ship's entry into the harbor. Diamond Head, a jagged crater at the shore's edge, and Waikīkī Beach's crescent were easy to identify. The mountains' ragged ridges were sharply delineated against a brilliant blue, cloudless sky. Their muscular slopes, sweeping down to sand and sea, conjured the arms of a god stretched out in welcome.

I leaned at the railing, standing on tiptoe and craning to see more, to soak in every detail. As we approached Aloha Tower, I could hear the faint strains of "Aloha 'Oe," one of the songs I had played over and over again on the Victrola.

It seemed the entire island had turned out to greet us. This truly was paradise, a place where they not only welcomed all who came, they celebrated their arrival. It was so unlike Carlisle, where even friends and family didn't bother to wish a person well. People crowded the upper decks of the pier opposite us, leis draped over their arms, and tossed rolls of colorful paper streamers to us, binding boat to land. Young Hawaiian women in skirts of wide green leaves danced on the pier beside the Royal Hawaiian Band, wreaths of flowers in their hair. The yellow leis draped round their necks swayed with their movement. As the streamers swayed in the breeze, a quartet sang my favorite Hawaiian song, "Song of the Islands." Passengers began flinging coins into the murky harbor water, and smiling Hawaiian boys dove in after them, then stowed the coins in their mouths.

It was not until they were winding the giant ropes to secure the ship to the dock that I forced myself to return with Archie and the boys to our cabins to collect the suitcases we would carry off ourselves.

"Goodbye, old ocean home," Kenny said, a teddy bear in one arm and a small suitcase in the other.

We scanned the two rooms one last time to be sure we hadn't forgotten anything.

"I'll miss sleeping on you," Lionel said, bouncing on his mattress.

We were nearly out the door when Archie turned back. "Tell you what, boys." He pulled a pen from his pocket. "How about we leave a little something behind to say Lionel and Kenny were here? Let's find us a good spot, some place secret that no one will know about except us."

Leave it to Archie to delay us when both boys were ready to go.

The boys set down their things and began eyeballing the room.

"How's about here, Dad?" Lionel opened a drawer of the little built-in desk.

"Perfect."

Archie handed him the pen, pulled out the drawer, and turned it so the back wooden panel, the part no one would ever see, faced Lionel. Lionel slowly and precisely wrote his name as small as he could manage, then handed the pen to Kenny, who scrawled his name in large crooked letters.

Arch slid the drawer back into place. "Now your names will always be a part of this ship. Are we ready to collect Reggy from Mr. Young and get off this tub?"

"Aye, aye, sir!" Lionel saluted.

As planned, Mr. Young waited by the gangway with Reggy on a rope leash. Lionel solemnly shook hands and thanked him for taking such good care of the dog.

"You and Reggy go first, Lionel," Archie directed, and Lionel stepped up to the local customs official stationed beside a ship's officer.

"Hold up there, young fellow. You can't take that dog ashore."

Lionel froze and looked back at me.

"What's the problem, Officer?" I asked. "Surely you have dogs on the island?"

"Dogs, yes, but not rabies. All animals go into quarantine. You must hand the dog over to the agricultural officials. After four months you can pay the kennel fees and collect him."

"No!" Lionel yelled. "You can't take him. He's mine. He was promised to me."

He turned as if to run down the gangway, but Arch caught him by the shoulders, took the leash from his hands, and handed it to Mr. Young.

Lionel turned to me. "Mom, do something."

"Calm down, Lionel." I turned to the officer. "How much are the quarantine fees?"

"No, not that," Lionel said. "They can't lock him up by himself with nobody to love him. Four months is forever." Tears streamed down his face.

"Make up your mind. It's quarantine or the dog stays on the ship."

"If he stays, I stay. I'm not getting off this ship without him." Lionel grabbed the ship's rail and clung to it. "I'm not going. You can't make me."

"Take Kenny and go," Archie said to me. "I'll handle this."

Wanting nothing to do with the public spectacle, I grabbed Kenny by the hand and fled down the gangway, furious that once again Lionel had ruined what should have been one of the most joyous moments of my life.

I navigated the lengthy agricultural inspection of our bags, saw our jar of homegrown popcorn confiscated and my personal items pawed through. The inspection done, I found a porter to push the dolly loaded with our trunks and suitcases back to the foot of the gangway, where Kenny and I waited for Arch and Lionel to appear.

"That hurts, Mom." Kenny wiggled out of the grip I had on his shoulders.

"Sorry, love."

I'd chosen the wrong outfit for the day and was baking in my tight suit jacket and pencil skirt. My wet silk blouse stuck to my chest and back. Strands of hair clung to my cheeks. With one hand I dabbed a hanky against my face. With the other, I fanned myself with a limp brochure. I closed my eyes and remembered how the wind had felt on my face earlier as the ship churned into the harbor. How was it Lionel could send me so quickly from ecstatic to miserable?

For what seemed hours, Kenny stood silent beside me, not a word of complaint. Finally, a red-faced Lionel appeared at the top of the gangway, a tense Archie behind him.

I asked no questions. I didn't care what scene had transpired. I simply wanted to get out of there and on our way. We were a sad, bedraggled group—me with the boys in hand, Arch following behind with the dolly. We blinked as we stepped out of the terminal into the glare of the blazing Hawaiian sun.

Archie hailed a cab.

"You and the boys go ahead with this first load," he suggested once we loaded as much as we could in the taxi's trunk. "I'll get another cab for the rest of this."

"I want to ride with you." Lionel gripped Arch's pant leg.

Archie nodded for Kenny and me to go on ahead. In what I meant as a kind gesture, a thank you for his dealing with Lionel, I placed an arm on Arch's shoulder. He shook me off and stepped away, his arm raised for another cab.

"The Blaisdell Hotel," I told the driver and slipped onto the blistering back seat. I rolled my window down all the way, not caring if the wind whipped my hair into a ratty mess. The breeze did little to staunch the sweat streaming down my face and soaking even the back of my skirt. Paradise, it turned out, was hot as hell.

I woke to morning light streaming through the Venetian blinds of our new house, my satin nightgown damp against my skin, and the steady thump of what sounded like balls hitting the outside of our bedroom wall. Archie lay sprawled beside me. An unfamiliar scent, thick and sweet and cloying, drifted in through the window. I slipped into my robe, walked barefoot to the kitchen and across its gritty, uneven wood floor to the screened back door. An object whizzed past and landed with a splat against the house's deep-green exterior wall. The pink, seedy flesh of guavas smeared the planks, heavy yellow rinds piled below.

Kenny stood with his arm raised, guava in hand, ready to fire another.

"I told him not to." Lionel was crouched beneath a plumeria tree in the corner of the yard, digging at the dirt with a stick.

Kenny dropped the guava.

"There're a million of them, Mom." He gestured to the fruit-laden tree behind him. "And you can't eat them 'cause they got too many seeds."

"Like them or not, you are not to use them as missiles. Now grab the hose and wash this off. Have you two eaten yet?"

"Yup." Kenny struggled to haul the hose from where it lay neatly coiled.

"Give him a hand, Lionel." The way Lionel hid in the shadows set me on edge.

"Why do I have to? I didn't make the mess."

"You will help him because I told you to help him. And because he's too little to do it himself."

All I needed was for the boys to anger our landlady, Mrs. Fong. She scared us all. Few women rattle me, but Mrs. Fong was no ordinary woman. Archie's new boss, Vernon Hardwick, had arranged our rental of one of her cottages, assuring us we could find no better, more reasonably priced accommodations in a market with few houses to let. Ours was one of three on the property, hers being the largest.

The day before, she had stood stone-faced on the front porch, openly appraising us.

To Archie she said, "Rent check is due the last day of every month. Mow the grass around your place every week." She turned to the boys and added, "I want no *pilikia* from you two."

Kenny shot me a questioning look. I didn't know the word's precise meaning, but I understood her intent. "She means you must behave yourselves."

Mrs. Fong nodded and squinted at me. "What kind of work do you do?"

I bristled at the directness of the question. "I write."

"You get paid to write?"

"Of course. I am a journalist for a New York newspaper."

She grunted. I wasn't sure if I had failed or passed her test.

As the boys wrestled with the hose, I headed back indoors. Two cereal bowls full of milk sat on the kitchen table, the cereal gone. I hated such waste. Life on board ship had spoiled the boys.

"Party's over, guys," I mumbled as I washed the bowls. "It's back to reality for us."

I filled the coffee pot and could hear Archie stirring in the bedroom, the squeak of the springs as he sat up, the groan as his head adjusted to being vertical. I set the stove flame on high.

The clicking of a tiny lizard hugging the wall startled me. I dropped the pot so abruptly it nearly toppled over on the stove. None of my images of paradise included geckos running across our ceilings or giant cockroaches flying above me as I slept, their wings brushing my cheek.

"Sadie?" Archie called from the bedroom.

"Putting on the coffee, Arch."

Only seven thirty and I already felt there wouldn't be hours enough in this day. We had to enroll Lionel in school, see about buying a car so we could return the mortuary's, and shop for the long list of items we needed to make this house a home. And then drinks that night with the Hardwicks at the Moana Hotel.

I pulled a clean bowl from the cupboard and set out a spoon and the Grape-Nuts Archie liked.

"Hey, Mom." Kenny pulled open the back door. "A man wants to see you."

An Asian man with a broad-brimmed hat stood at the base of the steps, a huge basket of vegetables in hand. He bowed and lifted his basket so I could see its contents more easily. There were bananas, onions, a head of lettuce, cabbage, a few tomatoes, and carrots. All appeared freshly picked.

I chose one of the plump, flawless tomatoes and held it to my nose, inhaling the sweet scent. It was heavy in my hand, a good sign. I sorted through the rest of his basket, selecting a head of lettuce, a couple bananas, and some carrots. I'd expected to miss the fresh produce of Elma's summer garden, never imagining a place where a vendor brought fresh produce to the door in all seasons.

I set my bounty on the kitchen table where Archie now sat, sipping a cup of coffee. He raised an eyebrow.

"He brings them right to the house," I offered by way of explanation. "Flowers, too, apparently. He says he'll be back on Fridays with those."

"A regular Eden. Cost you an arm and a leg, I bet."

"Nope. No more than what I paid at home in the winter months." Which wasn't exactly true, but close enough.

I chalked Arch's sarcasm up to nerves over adjusting to so much that was new. He hadn't slipped since Los Angeles, but I knew we were headed into treacherous times. Life was simple on board ship, the biggest worry being what to order for dinner. Stress surrounded us now, and the temptation to ease it would be overwhelming. I wrapped my arms around him from behind.

"It's going to be a fine day, and you will be a smashing success with Vernon."

He shrugged me off with a grunt. "Don't get ahead of yourself, Sadie."

I resisted the impulse to point out his readiness to assume the worst of himself and life, to note how he sabotaged every promising situation with his negativity. He couldn't even embrace hope in this place ripe with possibilities.

"I'm going to jump in the shower. Boys are out back." You stew in your juices, I added silently, if that's what you need to do. Just keep it to yourself and spare me.

I could feel eyes on me as we crossed the Moana Hotel's grand lobby bound for the Banyan Court. As Arch and I passed a cluster of tourists, I caught the hint of a gasp.

"Told you," he said.

"I'm taking it as a compliment."

Archie, who rarely voiced an opinion about my wardrobe, didn't approve of my outfit that night.

"That's a lot of skin you're showing," he'd said when I appeared from the bedroom. "Vernon and Louise are pretty traditional folks. This could give them the wrong impression."

"Or maybe the right one." I had clipped on a pair of jade earrings, perfect compliments to the emerald green of my pantsuit. "Why should I care what they think? I like it. Besides, Renee said it was the perfect outfit for cocktails." Renee hadn't actually said that, but I was certain that would be her opinion.

What she had actually said was, "You must have this outfit. The color's all wrong for me, but you've just enough red in your hair for the green to work."

When I tried it on in her stateroom, I couldn't imagine ever having the courage to wear it, but I liked the way the bodice hugged my breasts and left my back exposed. The pants, cinched tight at the waist, were as voluminous as a skirt.

"Trust me," Renee had said, standing behind me as I stared into the full-length mirror. "All eyes will be on you. All you need is the nerve to pull it off."

I decided my first night out in Waikīkī was the perfect moment to exercise some courage. I had only one chance to make a first impression, and it might as well be a bold one. That evening I learned I liked people staring. My confidence grew as I strode through the lobby, the green silk billowing. I felt powerful, a woman confident enough to handle attention.

We descended the staircase to the courtyard, the very spot from which *Hawai'i Calls* was broadcast to the nation each Saturday. The ocean beyond sparkled shades of orange and pink, the last flecks of daylight. Tables and chairs circled a massive banyan tree.

"Archie! Sadira! *E komo mai.* Welcome." Vernon rose from his chair, his arms extended, his face shining.

He smothered me with a too-tight hug.

"So wonderful to have you here with us." He turned to the beaming woman beside him. "Louise, this is the exquisite Sadira." He spoke as if introducing a celebrity. I liked it. No one in Carlisle ever recognized me as exceptional.

"I'm so pleased to finally meet you, my dear. You've made quite the impression on Vernon."

Louise was a dumpling of a woman, the kind of comforting mother figure who exudes virtue. She no doubt delivered chicken soup to the ailing and Christmas baskets to the poor, but I sensed steel beneath the soft exterior. She smothered me with leis, then did the same to Archie.

"I'm practically drowning in blossoms." I shifted the leis so they weren't so heavy on my neck. The fragrances, while lovely, were overwhelming. My greater concern was what the damp blossoms might do to the silk fabric of my top. "Perhaps I can remove a few of these and save the others to wear tomorrow?"

"Of course, my dear, do whatever you must. You should know, though, that the flowers won't last past tonight."

"Well, we would certainly hate to see these go to waste, eh, Sadie?" Archie said. "I wouldn't think of removing a single one of mine."

"Nor would I." I forced a smile. "They are quite wonderful."

"Don't worry, dearie." Louise patted my arm. "You'll soon adjust to the exuberance of the islands. I know it can be overwhelming at first when you're accustomed to a restrained life back in the States. Though, judging from this adorable outfit you're wearing, I'm guessing you're hardly a puritan."

Score one for Arch. Louise definitely disapproved of my outfit.

"Speaking for Sadie and myself," Arch said in his most syrupy voice, "we certainly do feel welcomed, Louise. We couldn't ask for a more gracious hospitality committee."

"Four G and Ts, please, Jake," Vernon called to a passing waiter. I tried to catch Archie's eye, but he kept his focus on Vernon.

"A toast," Vernon said when the drinks arrived. "To a long, prosperous collaboration. *Ōkole maluna.*"

"Hawaiian for 'bottoms up,'" Louise whispered to me with a giggle.

I lifted my glass and watched Arch swallow nearly half his drink in a single swig. I wanted to swat the glass from his hand.

"The perfect drink for the tropics." Louise raised her glass in salute.

I swirled the ice cubes in my drink, took the tiniest of sips, then decided I should play nice. "It occurs to me you both know a great deal about us, and yet I know very little of you. What brought you two to the islands?"

It took no further coaching to get Louise and Vernon talking about her Massachusetts roots, Vernon's childhood on Maui, where his father was an undertaker, and their meet-up one summer in Boston. I smiled and nodded and discreetly studied the other patrons. A few were tourists, but many appeared to be local, judging from their attire and ethnicity. One group in particular drew my attention. A half dozen men, their ties loose or off, their jackets slung over the back of their chairs, were loudly discussing the opening of the Winter Games in Germany.

One of them, a particularly striking man, caught my eye and smiled and winked as if he knew precisely how bored I was. I smiled back, then felt a delicious panic when he rose and headed our way.

"Vern, Louise. We've missed you at the club." He buzzed Louise's cheek, shook Vernon's hand, and apparently delighted them with his attention.

"Why, Harrison. It's been forever," said a flustered Vernon. "Good to see you, as always." He turned to us. "Arch and Sadira, I'd like to introduce you to one of our most distinguished residents, Harrison Bellingham, publisher of our daily newspaper, the *Honolulu Chronicle*. Harrison, this is my new assistant, Archie Doyle, and his charming wife, Sadira."

Like Vernon, Archie stood and extended a hand to Bellingham. There had been a time when Arch conveyed a quiet male authority as potent as Bellingham's, but those occasions were rare now. That evening, he telegraphed only weakness with his flushed face and too enthused handshake.

When Bellingham turned to me, I offered him my hand and hoped I wasn't imagining that he held it longer than was quite proper.

"Welcome to the islands, Mrs. Doyle. May you come to love it here as much as we kama'āina do."

"I'm sure I will. I can't imagine a place more enchanting."

"Excellent. I look forward to seeing more of you both."

With a nod to the table, Bellingham retreated, and I forced myself to turn my focus to Louise, who prattled on about places to shop and activities to amuse the boys.

"You must take them for a ride on the train that runs out through the cane fields." She paused when the waiter placed a platter of creamy crab canapés on the table. "These divine things will be the death of me, I swear. You must try them." She piled two on a plate for me.

"Thank you, no. I fear I gained so much weight on board ship that I must practice some restraint."

"But I insist. Just a nibble, at least. Besides, as that tiny slip of an outfit makes very clear, you're nothing but skin and bones."

I took a small bite, declared them "yummy," and handed the plate off to Archie.

He gobbled one down. "Now that's delicious. Not like that poi you had me try, Vern."

"Aren't they simply the best?" Louise turned back to me. "I envy your self-control, but then I suppose when someone's as pretty as you are, my dear, maintaining your appearance is the focus of your life."

My cocktail glass, still nearly full, sat sweating on the table. I took a good swig. I could see why Vernon had such an appetite for gin.

"So tell me more about this train, Louise," Archie said. "Lionel's a real train buff, as am I."

"Well, the trains hardly measure up to what you're used to back home, but they have their own particular charm." Louise beamed and proceeded to describe in great detail the path the train took around the island. I wasn't sure which of them I admired more at that moment, Archie for his ability to anticipate my reaction and redirect the conversation or Louise for her ability to insult with a compliment.

I was nearing the limits of my capacity to tolerate any of them further, but I realized this new arrangement might work, provided Arch's ability to amuse and be amused by them was not dependent on alcohol. He was already on drink number three.

"Tell you what." Louise turned her attention back to me. "How about I pick you up tomorrow morning and introduce you to the people in town you should know?"

"There are people I should know?"

"Well, of course there are." The syrup was gone from her voice. "This might feel like a big city, but it's a very small town. Reputations matter. You want to get off on the right foot."

"Thank you for being mindful of my reputation, Louise. Unfortunately, my schedule is overbooked, what with setting up the house and getting Lionel started in school. But let's be sure to do that as soon as time permits." I pushed back my chair. "Speaking of things I should do as a newcomer, I simply must put my toes in the Pacific. I've been here three whole days and I haven't even felt Waikīkī sand, let alone Hawaiian waters."

I gathered up my skirt pants, slipped off my espadrilles, and crossed the short distance from our table to the still-warm, fine white sand. I knew I had not only the Hardwicks' and Archie's attention, but that of others in the courtyard. I hoped Harrison Bellingham was among them. I strode to the water's edge, the pants' fabric clutched in my fists, and let a wave lap my feet. The receding foam tickled and my feet sank in the wet sand. My first contact with the Pacific Ocean.

I held my stance, feet firmly planted and eyes on the horizon. The sun, already plunged into the sea, still lit the sky in that arresting shade between blue and black, with licks of orange and pink flame.

"Keep an eye on the waves," a voice behind me said.

One of the men from Harrison's table, the tall, wiry one in a shirt that looked like it had been rescued from a laundry heap, stood on the walkway behind me. He might have been attractive without his smirk. I figured him to be the guy in the room who counts everyone else a fool. The cool, cocky type who plays it safe on the sideline, observing and judging and risking nothing.

"The waves can take you by surprise. Look away and a big one will knock you flat," he added.

"Thanks for the warning."

I turned back to the water in time to see the surge but too late to dodge it. The water rose to my knees, soaking my pants and challenging my balance. "Point taken," I said, but he was already gone. His jacket slung over his shoulder, he was moving at a fast clip toward the Royal Hawaiian, the "Pink Palace," as they called it, the exotic neighboring structure done in a Moorish style.

Probably having a good laugh at my expense. I wrung out the bottoms of my pants, now gritty with sand. My wet feet caked in sand, my pants clinging to my legs, I headed back to the table. So much for being spectacular.

"Poor dear," Louise said as I approached. "I hope your outfit isn't ruined."

"The pants will dry up just fine. And if they don't, how can I complain? I've been baptized by the Pacific."

I took my seat and stretched out my legs as if utterly unbothered by the sagging wet fabric. If I didn't feel confident and impervious to what others thought, I could at least act as if I did.

Lionel, age 8

Dad says I should write a letter to the governor of Hawai'i and tell him how bad his policy is that takes dogs away from kids who love them. I was supposed to keep Reggy when we got to Hawai'i. That was the deal. I would help take care of him on the ship and then when we got here I was supposed to take him off the ship and he would live with us, only the people in charge in Hawai'i said he would have to stay locked up for four months to make sure he doesn't have rabies. Locking him up was not OK with me. Dad said, "I guess we need to let Reggy stay on the ship and have a home in some place like Manila or Singapore," only I don't think the ship captain will let him get that far 'cause before we even got to Havana they said if someone didn't say they'd be his owner, they would have to put him down (which means kill him and I don't know why they don't just say that), so no way they'd let him live as long as it takes to get to Manila. Dad said to stop being rude to the ship's officers and the customs man because they were only doing their jobs and obeying the law, but I think they deserve to be treated bad because the law is a stupid, mean law that hurts kids and dogs. I don't know why we had to move to a place with bad laws.

When I get worked up about how unfair things are here, Mom says, "Don't be a gloomy Gus. There's a nugget of gold in any situation, no matter how bad it seems."

So the bright-side things so far are that people here don't carry things on top of their heads like in Havana and there are no mosquitoes and almost no flies at all. Mom says we will never get bored here 'cause there are so many people from all over the world and it's a big city with lots going on and if we were back home, we would be cold and have to wear coats and boots, but here it's warm enough to swim during winter. Only I don't like to swim so I don't really care about that part and I get a funny feeling in my stomach when we are downtown and there are so many cars stopped at the intersections and so many people walking by that I never saw before in my whole life. A Hawaiian man in the middle of the intersection tells the people and cars when to go, and he always smiles and says hi, so that's a bright-side thing. And they make the milkshakes here with more ice cream than at Crane's drugstore so you have to use a spoon instead of a straw and Dad says the trip here was worth it just for the milkshakes.

I think Mom thinks the trip was worth it just to be able to dress up and go out all the time 'cause that's what she and Dad do almost every night, leaving me and Kenny alone with the geckos that make a clicking sound. She pays me five cents when they go out and I'm supposed to keep an eye on things and go tell the landlady Mrs. Fong if something goes wrong, and I have the phone number of whatever hotel they are going to, but I would rather not get the five cents and have them stay at home.

It gets scary when it's dark and the wind starts blowing hard and the blinds hit the windowsills with a bop-bop-bop sound, and Kenny says, "Those Bible men are knocking on the walls, Lionel. They're coming to get you."

Mom tells him to stop doing that and tells me to ignore him, but that doesn't stop him. He's always trying to scare me that way. Now if he does that, I say, "Uh-uh, it's just the *menehunes* creeping in the house to steal you away soon as you fall asleep."

That scares him good. He doesn't ever fall asleep now when Mom and Dad go out.

Sadira

I slid my hands over the fabric as Mrs. Miyagi pinned the hem of my dress. I loved the feel of the heavy silk and the delicacy of its design, pink jasmine blossoms set against a pale blue background.

Two weeks earlier, Louise Hardwick had placed the fabric in my arms, telling me it was a gift so that I might have my own cheongsam made.

Over dinner at Lau Yee Chai a few nights before, I had mentioned how much I liked the dresses and the way they flattered the female form. When I protested that the gift was too extravagant, Louise waved me off. "I've had this fabric in my closet forever. We both know you'll look fabulous in it." And I did. The style was flattering and the fabric's ice-blue shade a perfect complement to my auburn hair.

Admiring myself in Mrs. Miyagi's mirror, I resolved to try and find something to like about Louise.

"She's been nothing but generous to us all and says only good things of you," Archie said when I voiced discomfort with the obligation a gift imposed. "Are you so hard and cynical that nice people now repulse you?" I was not persuaded there was anything genuinely nice about Louise Hardwick, but I promised to work on hiding my distaste for the woman.

I turned to Kenny, who was sketching Mrs. Miyagi's Siamese cat perched on a window sill. His drawing, far better than any Lionel had drawn at age five, even resembled a cat.

"What do you think, puddin'?"

He studied me with serious deliberation. "You look like a princess."

"All *pau.*" Mrs. Miyagi tucked the last pin in place. Louise had recommended Mrs. Miyagi as not only her personal seamstress but also the best on the island. I could tell her sewing skills equaled Elma's. "Two days you pick up, OK?"

"*Hai,*" I said, nodding. "And *mahalo.*" I was slowly learning some of the local words thanks to the boys and Mrs. Fong.

After I latched the chain-link gate to Mrs. Miyagi's cottage, I took a moment to get my bearings. I had timed my appointment so we could meet Lionel when school let out and walk the short distance home with him. I knew how to go between our house and Mrs. Miyagi's, but getting to the school required some thought. At least there were the ever-visible mountains to orient me. Islanders used an entirely different directional system from our north, south, east, west method. *Ma uka* meant to go toward the mountains and *ma kai* meant to go toward the sea. So long as I could see the mountains, I could determine which direction I should go. *'Ewa* and Koko Head provided the equivalents for west and east.

"We'll head ma kai to Beretania," I told Kenny, taking his hand. "Then 'Ewa."

The street names themselves defied mainland norms. No boring Main Streets or Church Streets, none of the usual tree names—the Elms and Maples and Oaks of so many New England towns, and none of that ever-practical Yankee resourcefulness of naming streets for the towns to which they led you. Here streets were named for kings and queens and natural wonders, the names musical and delicious to the ear. Kapi'olani. Auahi. Kalākaua. Liholiho. Maunaloa. I loved most especially the ones like Ke'eaumoku and Pi'ikoi that required careful distinction on the double vowels. I was determined not be a mainland *haole* who mangled the Hawaiian language.

I was grateful for the wide-brimmed hat I'd learned to wear when in the sun, but I was still soaked with perspiration when we reached the stone elementary school. At least in Hawai'i, winds moderated the temperature so long as the trades were blowing.

Yellow shower and pink plumeria trees shaded the school's fenced playground. We settled ourselves on a bench beneath one, and Kenny resumed drawing as I returned to Agatha Christie's new novel, *Death in the Clouds*. The school's bell screeched and kids barreled out the door. Spotting Lionel's blond head was normally easy in a sea of dark-haired kids, but that day I couldn't find him.

"You see him, Kenny?"

Kenny jumped up on the bench for a better view. "Nope."

We waited as the river of kids thinned to a stream and then a trickle.

"Maybe he had to stay after to talk with the teacher."

I was worried Lionel had gotten himself in trouble. Again. I found his teacher, Miss Reynolds, in the classroom erasing the chalkboard.

"I'm so glad you stopped by," she said. "I was concerned. Is Lionel feeling any better? I didn't like sending him home alone, but there was no one available to escort him."

"What do you mean? Lionel's not here?"

"No." She set down her eraser. "He complained of stomach pains after lunch and asked to go home. Since you live so close by, it seemed best to send him there."

I could have slapped her.

"I've been out all afternoon. You sent him to a locked and empty house."

Hauling Kenny by the hand, I raced home, ticking through all the things Lionel might do when he found no one home. I was sure he feared Mrs. Fong too much to ask for help. As much as I hated most everything about Carlisle, most especially the nosiness of neighbors, at least there were always a dozen eyes watching at the windows. I could trust someone to take Lionel in if he were locked out and distressed. With no familiar neighbors, would he go looking for Arch and me? Try to find his way to the mortuary?

When I saw he wasn't at our front door, I headed to the back. The stoop was empty as well, but Mrs. Fong appeared at the screen door.

"Your boy's here."

Lionel was seated at the kitchen table, a chessboard in front of him.

"Mrs. Fong's teaching me chess," he said.

I leaned over the kitchen sink to catch my breath, then soaked and wrung out a dishtowel to cool my face. Mrs. Fong placed a glass of iced tea on the counter beside me.

"You sit," she told Kenny and poured him a glass of cold water from the fridge. To Lionel she said, "Time to put away the board. I'll teach you more tomorrow after school, but no more coming home early. You understand? Your mother has enough to worry about."

Lionel nodded.

"Thank you," I said.

"He means to be a good boy," she said. "He'll learn."

I wished I shared her confidence.

"So what am I to do with you, Lionel?" I sat across from him at the table. "Have you any idea how much you scared me?"

"I'm sorry."

His lip quivered and the geyser of tears began.

I handed him some tissues and willed myself to be patient as I waited for the sobbing to slow. "Now take some deep breaths and calm down. I want you to tell me what happened."

He managed to say, "I don't want to go back there," but I couldn't get any information out of him. "Am I in trouble?"

"I don't know, Lionel. I am at a loss as to what to do with you. Clearly you aren't sick, and you won't tell me why you told the teacher you were. For now, since you lied and said you were ill, you'll need to spend the rest of the day in your room. We'll talk more when your father gets home."

It hardly seemed a punishment, since being alone in his room was his favorite activity. I wasn't sure if punishment was even called for. I wouldn't tolerate deception, but I also suspected he was being bullied, as he was always bullied back home. He was too much a puzzle to decipher. Or maybe I just hadn't the energy left to keep trying.

"We can't send him back there." Arch grabbed a Primo beer from the icebox.

"Seriously, Arch? A couple kids call him names and you want to coddle him? He can't just run away when things get tough. Besides, school's not optional. He has to go."

I poured milk into the potatoes and beat them hard.

"Did he tell you Friday's something called 'kill haole day'?"

I set down my bowl. "Yes, and I think maybe that's a good thing. It means this isn't about him being the weird kid. He's just like the other haole kids. He only has to get through one day of hazing."

"There's that boys' school Vernon's talked about. Maunalani. Up in

Nu'uanu. They don't tolerate bullying of any kind. We wouldn't have to worry the way we did in Carlisle."

I turned back to the potatoes and switched off the flame beneath the peas.

"A boys' school with no bullying? That'd be a first. And how do you propose we pay for it?"

"I'll figure out a way. All I know is I'm not sending him back tomorrow."

The timer rang. Meatloaf was done.

"Kenny, would you pour the milk, then tell Lionel I'm serving up."

Kenny collected the milk bottle, set out the glasses, but paused before pouring.

"Will they kill me too when I go to school?"

"Nobody's killing anyone, love. It's only an expression."

"Besides, it's just me they hate," Lionel said from the doorway.

"Hey there, sport." Arch opened another beer. "Good to see you out of bed."

I plopped peas and potatoes onto plates and sliced the meatloaf.

"I know one way we could find some cash for private school." I stared at the bottle of beer in Arch's fist.

"Leave it alone, Sadie. This isn't the time." It was never the time for that conversation.

We ate in silence. Lionel picked at his food, then set down his fork. "OK, I'll go to school tomorrow, Mom. You won't have to be mad anymore."

"Your mom and I already settled it, kiddo," Archie said. "No more of that school for you. Tomorrow we check out a super-duper one for smart kids."

"Really, Dad? You mean it?" He hugged Arch. "You're the best dad in the whole world."

Which made me—thank you so much, Archie—once again the worst mom ever.

Lionel

First chance I get I'm going to leave this stupid island with its mean people who don't even wear shoes to school and don't know New York is a state and not just a city and never saw snow and don't know lakes turn to ice when it's cold. I'm going to sneak down to the water some night and jump on board one of the big freighters headed back to the mainland. I'll stow away and then Mom and Dad will be sorry they made me come to this awful place where the kids punch you in the arm if you tell the teacher on them for playing games with knives or laugh when they say the wrong answer in class. I don't care how much Mom cries or how angry Dad gets or how much Kenny says please. I am getting off this stupid island and going someplace with people who like encyclopedias and can't run fast. There has to be someplace with people like me.

At least I get to go to a new school where Dad says kids don't pick on other kids. It's an all-boys school, though, so I'm not sure Dad has it right. Girls are nicer than boys to me in school. They don't punch me or toss my lunch in the dirt. At this new school, I'll have to wear a uniform and go to chapel, and priests will tell us what to do. Dad says the priests will do a better job of making the boys be nice to one another.

Sometimes I wish I had a giant sword I could take to school. I'd show those kids how super strong I really am and make them sorry they were ever mean to me. Sometimes I wish I was never born, but mostly I wish Gran Schaeffer could come take me away to someplace better. If I lived with her, she would be home nights, not like Mom going out all the time or Dad getting so red-faced and angry at night. Everybody talks about Hawai'i being paradise, but I think there's no such place as paradise. Not in Carlisle and not in Hawai'i and probably not anywhere except a really special place where they only let in people who don't care about all the things that everybody else cares about. And where there are no Bible men staring in the windows at night and no cockroaches landing on your face when you sleep. Maybe I'll make my own kingdom just for me and the people I choose. All the others can say sorry all they want and beg me to let them in, but I won't care. My kingdom will be paradise 'cause it'll be me and people like me.

Sadira

My silk cheongsam, courtesy of Louise Hardwick, was narrow and tight at the knees. I waddled more than walked into the Royal Hawaiian Hotel the first night I wore it.

"They must make them like that so you have to take dainty steps," Archie said. Dainty was hardly the image I meant to convey.

I thrust back my shoulders, held my head high, and worked to make my slow, constricted stride appear deliberate, not demure.

As we entered the dining room, Vernon and Louise waved from their table at the opposite end and we continued our awkward, slow journey. I buzzed Louise's cheek and collapsed into a chair.

"That dress fits you like a glove. I knew those colors would be perfect on you." She made me stand again and turn so she could see the back.

"You definitely have an eye for colors, Louise. It's lovely. And far too generous a gift."

It wasn't until I turned to the waiter at my side, precisely at the moment when I felt my equilibrium returning, that I spotted Renee on the dance floor. Stunning as ever, apparently transported by whatever her dance partner was saying, she glided smooth as honey, her hair a pillow of blond. She glistened in a blue lamé gown I recognized from the voyage.

"Max must have tired of her quickly," Archie muttered.

The music ended and Renee's eyes connected with mine, but she registered no surprise, only delight. She left her companion and nearly ran to where we sat.

"I thought you'd never find me."

I didn't dare stand in the tight dress. In her effort to hug me, she practically tumbled onto my lap.

"You are a sight for sore eyes. Did you miss me terribly? Don't answer." She looked round for a chair and pulled one next to mine. "We've all the time in the world to catch up. For now, I just want to sit here beside you. You look positively delicious." She took one of my hands and held it between hers.

When a waiter appeared with my drink, she registered at last the presence of Archie and the others. "Archie, love. It's so good to see you." She planted a noisy kiss on his cheek. "And these must be new friends of yours."

Archie made the introductions, and Renee duly showered Louise and Vernon with her radiant smile. "How splendid to meet the friends of my two dearest, dearest loves in all the world." To Louise, she added, "Aren't we just the luckiest people ever to know this stunning woman?" Louise could find no words.

Her attention back on me, Renee asked, "Are you as divinely happy as you look? Tell me everything."

"I don't even know where to begin. I've so many questions."

"Oh, let's not do questions. Why risk spoiling the night? I forbid mention of anything ugly or dull." She picked up an unattended champagne glass and raised it. "Here's to spectacular times ahead and no looking back." As always, I found her energy and confidence intoxicating. She was irresistible, the spotlit star around which the rest of us orbited.

"Mrs. Doyle? Sadira?" Harrison Bellingham stood beside us, hands in his pockets, head cocked to the side, looking more shy schoolboy than powerful businessman.

"Mr. Bellingham. A pleasure to see you again." I extended my hand, realizing only then that Archie, Vernon, and Louise had drifted away. "This is my dear friend Renee Manchester. Renee, Harrison Bellingham, publisher of the *Honolulu Chronicle*."

Renee extended her hand. "Why, you are much too handsome to be so very important. It's a pleasure to meet you, Mr. Bellingham."

"Please, call me Harrison, and I assure you the pleasure is all mine."

Before I could invite him, Bellingham swung a chair around and set it between us, creating an intimate threesome.

"I apologize for intruding, but I have been watching you from a distance, Miss Manchester, ever since you arrived on the islands. I'm sure the people of Honolulu would be delighted to know something about the mysterious beauty who is the talk of the town. Unfortunately, we've no society columnist at the moment, but perhaps I can persuade you to speak with one of our reporters?" He nodded at a man in a business suit near the room's entrance. "His name's Jack O'Brien. For now, he's covering visiting celebrities, but only the most important ones."

I recognized O'Brien as the man from the Moana Hotel who warned me about the waves.

"I think I'd prefer having you interview me." Renee leaned closer to him.

Harrison reddened, even looked ruffled. "I haven't the skill to do you justice."

"Hm." Renee sat back in her chair. "I'll tell you what." She hitched up her gown hem as she crossed her knees. "I'll give you an interview, if you hire Sadira to write it. I'll tell her the story of my life and she'll juice it up with the details only a friend knows. And you'll pay her, of course." She smiled, her face animated, her eyes dancing. She ran a hand up Bellingham's arm then cupped her hand at his cheek, as if to admire his handsome face. "Better yet, hire her permanently, and you've got a deal." She placed her face close to his, as if poised to kiss him.

I started to protest, uncomfortable at being thrust into the center of this negotiation and uneasy about Renee's motives, but the tension between the two created a protective barrier. I had disappeared.

Harrison finally shifted his attention to me.

"You know anything about writing?"

I reminded myself I could be anyone I wanted to be in this new place.

"As it happens, I'm an experienced newspaper columnist."

"And you think you can handle this?"

"I know I can. I believe you have yourself a columnist." I stuck out my hand, hoping my arm wouldn't tremble, and kept my gaze fixed on Bellingham.

"Deal, but with one provision. You ladies begin tonight. I want a first draft on my desk by nine tomorrow. If the editor and I like what we see, you are the *Chronicle*'s new society columnist."

He stood and tucked his chair neatly beneath the table from which he'd borrowed it. "You do know where the newspaper is?" With a goodbye nod to us both, he left and joined O'Brien.

"I can't believe you did that," I said. "And that it worked."

"Come on. Let's get out of this joint. Where's your typewriter?"

I struggled to stand.

"What the hell is wrong with that dress?" Renee stared down at my skirt. "Did they sew you into it? Turn around." She turned me away from her.

"There are no slits in it. How the hell are you supposed to walk in that thing?"

"I assumed it was supposed to be like this."

Renee grabbed a steak knife from the table, stuck its tip in the skirt's side seam at the height of my knees and before I could protest, ripped the seam open down to the hem. Then she did the same on the other side. "There. That's how it's supposed to be. Now you can walk and show a little leg."

I glanced over at Louise dancing now with Archie. I wondered if this was Mrs. Miyagi's oversight, or if she'd been told to sew the dress that way.

"Definitely better. I do love being around you." I linked my arm in hers as we strolled across the room. *Take a good long look, everyone*, I wanted to shout. *This is the moment when Sadira Doyle stops being a nobody*. I made sure we passed next to Archie and Louise on the dance floor and scooped the car keys from his pocket.

"Harrison Bellingham just hired me as a columnist and I'm heading home to work. Sorry to miss out on dinner. Catch a cab home?"

We continued our trek across the room, hips swaying in unison, arms circled around one another's waists. We passed Jack O'Brien, a study in nonchalance, his back against a wall. He nodded.

I extended a hand. "Sadira Doyle, Mr. O'Brien. It seems we are now colleagues."

"Lucky me."

"And this is my friend Renee Manchester."

O'Brien nodded at Renee.

Such an annoying man. So unflappable and sure of himself. I would not be thrown by Jack O'Brien or Harrison Bellingham and certainly not by Louise Hardwick. I was on my way. A woman to be watched. A woman of consequence.

The train of Renee's gown swept over my kitchen floor as she paced the small room. I hated to think how much grime was clinging to the delicate fabric, but I'd stopped suggesting she sit down at the table. Being in my home seemed to agitate her.

She took a small cream pitcher off a kitchen shelf and studied it. "Looks like one we had, shamrocks and all. We never used it. My ma kept it in her dining room hutch. Wouldn't let us kids near it. She acted like it was some jewel too precious to touch."

She turned it over. "What does this seal mean?" She showed me the inscription.

"It shows who made it. Belleek is the company. It's in Ireland."

"You Irish?"

"Nope. German and English."

"Is it worth anything?"

"I think it's good quality, but I don't know how much it cost. It was a wedding gift."

Renee laughed. "That'd be something if all that stuff my ma fussed about was actually worth something. I always figured she was putting on airs over some cheap five-and-dime stuff."

I glanced at the clock. Ten. We'd been home nearly an hour and Renee had yet to say anything about how she ended up in Honolulu. I tried a more direct approach. "How about you tell me something about your life in the Dakotas."

"Not much to tell." She set down the creamer, crouched in front of one of the lower cabinets, and stared into it. She reached to the back and pulled out a paper sack. "Somebody's secret stash." She held up a Hershey's Mr. Goodbar. "Yours?"

"I wish. Probably Lionel's. Saving it for when no one's around so he doesn't have to share."

"Smart boy." She put the bag back, stretched, then took another cigarette from the silver case she'd placed on the table. She smiled as she lit it. "I have to say, you're being mighty patient. Ready to strangle me yet?"

"Getting close."

She plopped down in a chair. "OK, let's do this thing. What do you need to know?"

If I hadn't wanted the reporting job so much, I would have ended the whole effort right then. Renee looked more cornered animal than glamorous bon vivant, her usual creamy complexion splotchy under the harsh light overhead, her eyes darting. I suppressed my sympathy and pushed on.

"I want to play this as a miracle story. Small-town girl of humble means is poised to be America's next it girl. The camera loves you. America will love you. Despite your beauty, you are genuine and unblemished. Every high school girl will wear her hair like yours. Men will lust after you. Mothers will name their daughters Renee."

"Not Renee." She twirled the cream pitcher on the table.

"What do you mean?"

"That's not my celebrity name. Max says my celebrity name is Lucetta Chase."

So Max was still in the picture.

"What's wrong with Renee Manchester?"

"Max says it's not sexy."

"What exactly is Max's role in all of this? I didn't see him at the hotel tonight."

I doubted Max would keep a low profile if he were anywhere on the island.

"He's how I got here. He thought it best I lie low until he gets the ball rolling in Hollywood. He's going to make me a big movie star."

Her tone dared me to question Max's sincerity. She didn't need me to point out that he'd paid her off with a one-way ticket out of town.

"I'll be very careful to write this in a way that serves his plans for you. Do you think he wants to be the one to introduce Lucetta to the world?"

Renee shrugged. "I suppose so."

"OK then. You are still Renee Manchester, a rose risen from the Dakota plains and about to be plucked for stardom. I'll lay the groundwork for Hollywood's eventual discovery of you."

She nodded. "I like that. Max could use a kick in the ōkole to get things moving. He gave me enough to live on for a couple months and promised to set up screen tests and makeovers, only I haven't gotten a single letter since I left." She stared up at the ceiling and took deep breaths.

"Oh, Renee." I squeezed her hand.

"I'm fine." She shook me off. "Stupid nerves. That's all. He's a decent guy. Nothing like Roger."

"OK. We'll play this however you want. So tell me about that small town of yours and why you got on the bus to Hollywood."

By the time I finished typing the last line, Renee was asleep, her head atop her folded arms. I considered letting her stay there, but decided it best she was gone when the boys and Archie got up. Archie had come home in a cab shortly after midnight and gone straight to bed. He didn't so much as stick his head in the doorway to see how it was going or to say good night. I didn't want a scene with him in the morning. Best to get to the paper, drop off the article, then take Renee to her hotel.

I shook her gently. "Time to get a move on, sleepyhead. We've a story to deliver."

The early morning was quiet but for the trill of bufo toads scattered around the lawn.

"We've got the world to ourselves." I opened the passenger door and helped her in. "And I do believe it is our oyster."

"Then why don't I feel happier?" Renee barely opened her eyes.

"Because, like me, you always want more. I don't care what anyone says, that's not a bad thing. It's what drives us. It's why we'll never end up a pair of boring housewives."

I slid behind the wheel; switched on the headlights, illuminating the bungalow in a harsh, bright light; and eased the car onto the road. Despite the hour and the slumbering city, I felt energized. "You suppose everything's closed up for the night? I wouldn't mind getting some breakfast. I never ate any dinner."

"I know a place."

"Of course you do." I laughed. "It's good to have you back in my life, Renee."

"Geez, I should hope so. But don't go getting all mushy on me. We aren't that kind of gals."

"We do have that in common." I'd avoided the question all night, not wanting to spoil her mood and have her clam up on me, but I still needed to know. "You ever going to tell me what exactly happened back in LA?"

"What do you mean?"

"Don't pretend with me, Renee. Some switch got flipped. I watched you throw away your relationship with Roger. Why that night and why that way?"

"'Cause I saw something you didn't. Remember the ice cream parlor we visited by the park in LA and the big fancy building behind it? Roger and Archie were at that building that afternoon. I saw them get out of a car as we drove past."

"Why didn't you say something?"

"The boys were with us. And besides, no need for you to worry about Archie. He probably didn't even pair up with anyone. Roger was just dragging him along. But I had plenty to worry about. Roger and I had an arrangement. Other girls, ordinary girls, were fine. But whoever else he saw, I remained number one. I'm not a fool. There was only one reason Roger was walking into that place, and her name's Selena. He propositioned her long before he ever approached me, but she had bigger fish in mind. So I was the one he settled for. I knew he'd toss me out if she ever said yes. Those diamonds I wore to the Cocoanut Grove? The coat and the gown? Those were part of my safety net if anything happened and he dumped me. I made sure to walk out wearing what Roger promised was mine, in case I saw an opportunity. When things went well with Max that night, I saw my chance. No better insurance than stardom."

She rolled down her window and lit a cigarette. "What do you know about this Harrison Bellingham? He married?"

"I don't know much. I think there's a Mrs. Bellingham."

"That's a shame. I could get used to those eyes. I'm guessing he's got money to spare."

"I don't suppose Max would like that."

"No harm keeping some prospects in my back pocket just in case Max fails to deliver the goods."

I agreed with her about Bellingham. He was definitely a man who could make a fool of me.

I pulled up to the curb in front of the newspaper building on Kapiʻolani Boulevard.

"Want to come in?"

"No. I assume the publisher doesn't hang around the newsroom at this hour. Besides, Mr. Bellingham needs a little time to realize how much he liked meeting me and how much he'd like to see me again."

The building's lobby was unlit, as was the wide aproned staircase at its center, but light streamed from the newsroom on the second floor and typewriters clattered away. I slowly climbed the marble stairs, marveling at the massive domed ceiling above. I paused when I reached the landing and surveyed the huge open room of desks, its wall perimeter lined with offices. A half dozen reporters were bent over typewriters, the space cavernous around them. This was now my world. I was a reporter at a city paper. I would rub elbows with the most renowned, the most powerful, the most beautiful. I considered the article in my hand. Would it be good enough? Would it gain me admittance to this masculine club so smug with self-importance? I reminded myself I was good enough and marched in as if I'd done this a thousand times.

Harrison sat down beside me at the celebrity table, the spot in the Royal Hawaiian's dining room where visiting celebrities gathered to be seen and amused. Most nights, as the stars played, I watched and listened, recording their wit and describing their clothes, preferred drinks, and skill on the dance floor.

"Cheer up. Maybe someone will die," Harrison said.

"I should be so lucky." I was surprised my boredom was so apparent. "I don't know which is worse, the tycoon with sweaty hands"—I feared he had soiled my satin gown forever when we danced—"or the starlet who not only believes there are lizard people living beneath Los Angeles but is quite convinced she's seen them."

"Maybe she has. Go ahead and use it. There's your color for tomorrow's column." Harrison drained his martini and signaled a waiter. "You drinking?"

I shook my head.

"A drink might make the night more interesting."

"Or help me forget what little I've gleaned, and then I'd have nothing. I stay sober, they get drunk and careless, and sometimes I get lucky."

Later that night, I would weave the paltry bits into a breathless column meant to make celebrities and Honolulu's elite seem fabulous and enviable.

In these few short weeks, I'd come a long way from describing what

Carlisle's young ladies wore to the Fourth of July dance. I was not only meeting famous men and women, I was dining and dancing with them. The day before, I had enjoyed breakfast with Bing Crosby and his wife, Dixie Lee. A week before, I had taken a turn on the dance floor with Fred MacMurray.

In many ways, though, this job wasn't all that different from what I did in Carlisle. I wrote about people blessed to be more attractive or more powerful or richer than the average person. If I did my job well, I made them appear more glamorous than they actually were. Most were predictable and too often tedious company.

Harrison didn't usually show up at the hotels to take in the night scene, but if the visitor was powerful and of potential value to his business interests, he made an exception. The other exceptions seemed to be particularly beautiful women.

"What brings you here tonight?" I asked.

"Atkins." Harrison nodded in the direction of the tycoon, whose greasy hands were now wrapped around tiny Miss Kara Silver, an aspiring actress in town with her mother to promote her first big movie. "He's someone I can't afford to ignore."

I found that difficult to buy. If Atkins were that important, Jack O'Brien would be hovering nearby. His eyes on Kara, Harrison asked, "How'd the photo shoot go today?"

I'd spent much of my afternoon on the hotel's beach with Kara and one of the paper's photographers as Duke Kahanamoku taught the young woman how to ride a surfboard. I was there to interview Kara and, hopefully, beef up the news bit that would accompany the photo. As it was a Saturday, I took the boys along and they helped set Miss Silver at ease.

"You'll like the photos. Miss Silver has a way with a bathing suit."

Harrison grinned. "Not a surprise. And the story?"

I gave him a meaningful stare. He had to know there was no story with someone as vacant as Miss Silver.

"Right. Photograph dependent." He sipped from the fresh martini a waiter brought him. "But now you have the lizard people bit. All of Honolulu will be talking."

I smiled. "Where would we be without a free press to report the important news of the day." I glanced around the room, which was still going strong at eleven o'clock. I rarely made it home before midnight, and it had been a long week. At least working late nights meant I could have the boys fed and ready for bed before I left. All Archie had to do was stay home and sober.

"You're giving up on getting something juicy out of Atkins? His wife has retired for the night, as has Miss Silver's mother. He's blotto and Miss Silver's probably seeing double. The night could still get interesting."

I knew Harrison was joking. He'd never let me write about a sexual indiscretion—in explicit terms, anyway. But there were ways to write the dots and let the readers connect them.

Atkins returned Kara to the table and extended his hand to me. "Your turn, lovely lady."

If Harrison hadn't been seated beside me and if I already had something of merit to write about the man, I would have declined, made excuses about getting home to my family, but this was what Harrison paid me to do. Write the hype and imply the dirt.

Atkins placed his clammy right palm on my bare back.

"You're one cool cucumber." His breath reeked of bourbon and was warm against my cheek.

"What makes you say that?" I was determined to stay friendly and not let my irritation show.

He twirled me around the parquet floor, expertly leading me with the mere pressure of his hand at my back or with a nudge of the one holding mine.

"I may be drunk and I may be old, little lady, but I ain't blind. You haven't had a drop all night. You just sit there looking pretty, watching and writing it all down. And tomorrow you'll tell the whole world every juicy detail, real or imagined. Feel pretty good about yourself? Feel superior to the rest of us? I bet you get a real thrill destroying lives."

I stiffened as Atkins tightened his grip on me. I looked over to Harrison, who was now seated beside Kara, leaning close, an arm across the back of her chair.

"I'm working, that's why I'm not drinking. I'm not here to try and get any dirt on anyone."

"Like hell you ain't. And I suppose your friend over there isn't trying to get in that pretty little girl's panties." Atkins nodded toward Harrison.

"I think we're both done for the night." I broke free. All I wanted was to grab my purse and leave. Atkins wasn't going to give me anything I could use in my column, and I didn't want to confirm who might end up in Kara's bed that night.

"I'm bushed," I told Harrison. "Going to call it a day. Lovely to see you again, Kara."

"Bring your boys back to the beach tomorrow. They were simply adorable."

"They enjoyed themselves immensely. It was so sweet of you to play along with them about the lizard people." Let Harrison take a close look at the mind within that pretty little head.

"But you were there when the boys saw the lizard man," Kara said, puzzled. "You saw him, too, right? Trust me, they're everywhere in Los Angeles. I think my neighbor's gardener might even be one."

I smiled and nodded, not daring to look at Harrison or Atkins.

"I'm going to stay on a while longer," Harrison said, and I understood. The girl could be a vegetable, for all he cared. And he didn't appreciate me pointing it out.

As I headed for the door, I composed the column that would connect these dots.

> After a night spent dancing and conversing in that enchanting dining room beside Waikīkī Beach, the Chronicle's own Mr. Bellingham sadly bid good night to the assembled guests.

Only moments later the lovely Miss Silver did the same, as if
the clock had struck midnight and a spell had been broken.
Or perhaps cast? Love was in the air.

If only I could write that copy. The click of my heels echoed down the long, empty marble hallway. I found no joy in learning that Harrison was, like any other man, a fool for youth and beauty. I had imagined him a cut above the rest.

Lionel

I never expected the blood. I've seen a kid bleed before, but I'd never hit anyone, at least not enough to make him bleed. I didn't think I was strong enough to do that, but I sure did make the blood pour out of Howard. There was blood everywhere. All over him, all over me. Soon as I saw it I stopped hitting him, which was good 'cause that's about when Father Wilson showed up and it's a good thing I didn't have my fist in Howard's face right then. Father Wilson doesn't know me well enough yet to know it's always the other guys who hit me, but he seemed surprised Howard was the bloody one. Maybe even a little glad. Not that he said that exactly, only I think maybe he thinks Howard's a jerk who needed to be taught a lesson, only he can't ever say it since he's the principal and an Episcopal priest.

I didn't want to say how come I hit Howard when Father Wilson first asked me 'cause there was a big crowd of kids gathered round and I don't think most of them heard what Howard said to make me angry enough to hit him. I didn't want to have to say it out loud in front of everyone.

"You two boys come along with me," Father Wilson said. We left Howard at the nurse's office to get cleaned up, but Father Wilson told the nurse to be sure and send Howard straight to his office when she was done fixing him.

Even when we were in Father Wilson's office, I didn't want to tell him what Howard said, 'cause maybe he hadn't read the paper, but then I saw the *Honolulu Chronicle* sitting right there on his desk.

"Did Howard say something to upset you, son?" he asked. He calls us boys "son" even though he has a couple of sons himself and a daughter, too.

I only nodded at first, but then I started talking and I couldn't stop. It was like a river came pouring out of me. I told him what Howard said about Mom just because Renee is her friend and what he called Renee and how he said that his father thought Mom and Renee were loose women who gussied themselves up and were out dancing and drinking when they should be home taking care of a husband and kids. I told Father Wilson I didn't think anyone should be allowed to call my mom or Renee bad names because they aren't bad and besides that, Renee is the nicest lady in the whole entire world. I don't care what anyone says. I should know. Nobody else in our school ever met her. All a guy has to do is look at her face to know she's an angel.

Father Wilson interrupted me and said, "Take some deep breaths, Lionel, and try to calm down. You're getting yourself worked up."

He gave me a handkerchief to wipe my nose and eyes and just waited with his hands crossed on the desk in front of him until I was breathing normal and not gulping anymore.

"Feel better?" he asked, and I nodded.

"You going to call my mom, sir?"

I didn't want him calling my mom. I was afraid she'd come in and yell at him. She does that sometimes. Yells at the wrong person.

"No, Lionel. I'm not going to call your mom. But I am going to ask you to do me a favor. Think you can do something for me?"

"Depends on what it is," I said, and I know I should have said, yes, sir, and not even thought about it, but I didn't want to promise something I couldn't do.

"What I'd like is for you to trust me and try a different way of showing how angry you are."

I didn't answer him. I just waited for him to say what it was he wanted me to try.

"The next time one of the boys says or does something to upset you, I want you to try to be as calm as you possibly can be and come straight to my office. You don't have to tell me what happened if you don't want to, but you can sit here until you're feeling calm enough to be around the other boys again."

"How come I'm the one who has to come to your office, not the boys who say and do the bad things? Everyone knows that you're in trouble if you're sitting in the principal's office."

"I'm asking you to be the one who comes because I trust you. I don't know if the other boys could show that much self-control or be mature enough to act responsibly. I think you can do it. I think you have what it takes to make the tougher choice."

I thought about that a bit and decided he was right. I am smarter than most of the other guys and I do a good job keeping track of what's right and wrong. All I have to do instead of telling a guy he's the one who's wrong is go to Father Wilson's office and he'll know I'm right just 'cause I'm the one brave enough not to fight or run away.

"It's a deal," I told him and shook his hand.

"I'm going to ask you to do another favor for me. This one may be even more difficult."

That made me nervous. It sounded plenty hard enough just to walk to his office when someone's being mean to me.

"I want you to come out into the waiting room and apologize to Howard."

I definitely did not want to do that.

"He should not have said mean things about your mother and her friend, but that does not excuse your hitting him. Remember what Jesus said."

"Turn the other cheek?"

He nodded. "Yes. Think you can do that?"

"Does Howard have to turn his cheek?" It only seemed fair that Howard should have to act like Jesus, if I had to.

"I will certainly ask the same of him as I ask of you," Father Wilson said, so I said OK and we shook on it.

I haven't told Mom and Dad what happened 'cause I know it'll only make things worse. Dad's not too happy Mom has got a job and Renee is back. He says everyone's talking about it now and that people think Mom's wrong to go out at night with a racy woman. I sure don't know why anyone thinks there's anything wrong with Renee, especially Dad who knows her well enough to know better, but for now, it's probably best for me not to go stir things up any more than they're already stirred.

From now on, I'll keep my lips zipped, and if any of the kids start saying stupid stuff, I'll just go plop myself in a chair in Father Wilson's office and wait till he can talk to me. Then I'll give him a good earful about just how mean-hearted people can be. I'm not as angry now at Mom and Dad for making me come to this island. Thanks to Father Wilson, school's a whole lot better than it ever was in Carlisle.

Chapter Four

October 1936 to January 1937

Sadira

I followed the boys off the train, scooping up the stalk of untouched sugarcane Lionel had left on his seat. Kenny was still gnawing on his. I didn't understand Lionel's lack of interest. The entire train excursion had been meant to lift his spirits and yet all he'd done was sulk his way through the ride, refusing to speak to me or Kenny. He'd stared out the open window as the train cut through the fields hauling cane stalks to the island's mills. He had no reason to be angry with me. I had gone to great lengths to make that trip happen. I'd called in favors, got someone else to cover an afternoon tea, all because he loved trains. Back in Carlisle, he'd stood by the tracks every Saturday morning watching the freight cars barrel past. Honolulu had no big trains, just the tiny single-gauge workhorse, but it was better than nothing. Yet here he was, acting like I was forcing him to endure something miserable.

"Wait up for me, boys," I called as I climbed down the narrow steps to the small platform. Kenny paused, but Lionel ignored me and went straight to our car now powdered red with field dust. He was growing more insolent with each passing day, testing my patience.

Now that I was working nights and Archie put in crazy hours at the mortuary, the boys had to be more self-reliant. For this all to work, Lionel

was going to have to find a way to fit into this new lifestyle and let go of
his constant anger. I was doing the best I could.

"What do you say we try that shave ice treat everyone talks about?"
I said when I reached the car, hoping maybe that would break Lionel's
stormy mood.

Mrs. Fong had told me to be sure and ride the train on a Sunday, when
the Japanese plantation workers set up roadside stands and sold a treat
much like a snow cone, only locally they called it shave ice because it was,
quite literally, flakes shaved off a block of ice.

"Mrs. Fong says there's nothing better on a hot afternoon."

Lionel squeezed past me to reach the backseat, his face a study in rage.

"Do you suppose they'll have root beer?" Kenny said as he climbed in
after him.

"You betcha. How could you sell snow cones and not have root beer?"

"Maybe they'll have cockroach guts," Lionel snorted from his side of
the car.

I slammed the door.

"Or we could drop the idea of a treat and head straight home." I glared
at Lionel through the rearview mirror.

Kenny curled up in his corner of the backseat, his arms wrapped round
his legs. Lionel slumped down in the other corner, his cheek pressed
against the seat back.

I pulled the car onto the highway so fast the wheels squealed on the
asphalt. If I were a different kind of mother, I'd have deposited Lionel at
the side of the road and driven off, taught him a lesson.

"How about we sing something?" Desperate to break the tension, I
sang the first line of Lionel's current favorite. "You've gotta win a little,
lose a little, yes, and always have the blues a little, that's the story of, that's
the glory of love."

"Trains are what I do," he blurted out.

Uncertain I'd heard him right, I checked him in the rearview mirror.
He was a mess, tears streaming down his face. His whole body trembled.

"It's not fair. Trains are what I do."

I pulled off to the side of the road.

"You didn't want to share the train ride with us?"

"It's what I do." He wiped his forearm across his eyes.

I sank back in my seat. What I needed was a guidebook, some kind of dictionary to translate my son for me.

"I see." Only I didn't see. Not really. "I'm sorry. Next time you can ride by yourself." I didn't like the bite in my voice, but I couldn't help it. Nothing I did for him ever came out right.

He gulped for breath.

I headed back onto the highway, unsure now whether to bother stopping at the stand I'd spotted earlier. Why let Lionel ruin the day for Kenny, I decided. When we reached the three-sided shed beside the road, I eased the car into the parking area in a cloud of red dust. Miles and miles of cane, nearly flattened by the afternoon trades, encircled us. We were cocooned in a sea of green and dome of blue, something like the way I felt after a winter storm when the world went white but for a taut blue sky overhead.

"They do have root beer." I read to Kenny the list of flavors scrawled on a giant chalkboard. "How's about you, Lionel? Root beer or maybe orange?"

The woman at the counter smiled and nodded. A man behind her turned the wheel of an elaborate contraption, forcing a large block of ice over a sharp blade. Shavings settled in tender mounds.

When Lionel didn't answer, I ordered a root beer for Kenny and a vanilla for myself.

Lionel stepped up to the counter. "I'll have a pineapple, please."

I wrapped an arm around his shoulders and gave him a squeeze. "Good for you, buddy, trying something new."

His muscles tensed and I released him, but a moment later, he inched closer, leaned against me as he watched the man pack the fine ice shavings into white paper cones. I resisted the impulse to ruffle his hair or stroke his arm, unsure of the reception I'd get.

When the woman at the counter passed him his cone doused in a light yellow syrup, Lionel bowed slightly. "*Arigato gozaimasu*."

My cone was a clear mound of vanilla ice. I resolved that next time I would try something different, choose a local flavor, maybe even have them pack sweet azuki bean paste in the center.

"We should bring Dad here sometime," Lionel said as we headed to the car. Hard to believe that only minutes before he'd been in a fury.

He opened the car's back door but paused. "Can me and Kenny sit up front for the drive back?"

I stopped myself from correcting his grammar.

The rule was kids in the back, grown-ups in the front. A rule established by Archie for no particular reason except that was how his parents did it. That's how everyone's parents did it. If I had learned anything in these few months since leaving home, it was that rules were constructs, often arbitrary, sometimes mean, mostly ways to retain power. I could break them.

"Why not? It gets lonely being up front by myself."

The boys piled in next to me, Lionel opting to sit in the middle, allowing Kenny the window. I rested my arm on the window frame, felt my tension ease as we barreled through the fields.

"Look." I pointed to the Ko'olaus on our left. "That's something you'd never see back home."

Dark clouds shrouded the mountain peaks, and in each valley, a rainbow arched.

"That's why they call it paradise, Mom." Lionel's intonation suggested it was I who couldn't see what was smack-dab in front of me, as if I were the one who didn't understand.

Lionel

Mom thinks our landlady Mrs. Fong is OK, and I like her fine when she teaches me chess and how to say Chinese words. What I don't like is the angry way she sometimes looks at and talks to Dad. If Dad has a bad night, she comes storming over here, making a big deal about it.

Dad's just having a hard time getting used to Mom working. It confuses everything. Dad might have had a few beers more than was good for him the other night and maybe he was hollering kind of loud, but he wasn't doing anything wrong. Not really. Still, Mrs. Fong marched right up to the front door and called in through the screen at him.

"What are you thinking, Mr. Doyle, carrying on like that," she yelled. "You're going to scare the *keikis*," only I wasn't scared and I think I'm too old to be called a keiki.

She put her face right up against the screen like she couldn't see, but Dad had turned on every light in the house and everyone in the world could have seen what we were doing. Dad wasn't even in the living room when she came over. Just me and Kenny. We were sitting there on the couch. Kenny had covered his ears 'cause he doesn't like it when Dad starts making a racket. It's not like Dad would ever hurt us. He was just enjoying himself. He likes to sing and he has a good voice and he wasn't even singing about anything bad. He was singing that song about flying away. He must have knocked something over 'cause there was a big crash and Kenny jumped, but not me. I know better than to make a big deal over something that's no big deal.

When she heard that crash, Mrs. Fong didn't even wait for Dad to invite her in. She just swung open the screen door and told Kenny and me to go to our room, like she was our mom or teacher or something. We did what she said but it didn't seem right to me, her giving us orders like that. I could hear her slapping her hand against the door frame and yelling to Dad.

"Mr. Doyle!" she hollered. "Mr. Doyle! You come talk to me right now."

Dad's singing stopped when she started hollering.

"I'm not here to yell at you," she said, except it sure seemed like she was. "I only want to talk."

Dad must have gone out to the living room 'cause I heard him say, "What do you want?"

"I want you to come outside, please, Mr. Doyle. Come talk to me."

The voices went outside and I couldn't hear everything they said, so I went in the bathroom and stood next to the window.

"Shame on you, Mr. Doyle," she told him. "Shame on you. Is this how you want your boys seeing you? You want them scared of their own father? No more pilikia. You go inside now and sleep it off. Leave those boys be."

I thought for sure Dad would get real mad at her for talking to him like that, but he didn't say a word, just went back in the house, and I had to hightail it out of the bathroom so he didn't find me there and know I was listening.

Kenny must have gone back out to the living room 'cause he wasn't in our room and I heard Mrs. Fong say, "It's OK now. You can sleep. I'll keep watch from my front porch till your mother comes home. No need to worry anymore tonight."

I don't know why she thought she had to sit out there like Dad was dangerous or something, and I didn't like her tattling on Dad to Mom. Dad sure doesn't need Mom getting more mad at him. But the good part is Dad did listen to her and fell asleep on the living room floor, which was a good thing since he had to get up and go to work in the morning. I went to sleep, too. I slept so hard I never even heard Mom come home.

Sadira

I heard Renee's laugh before I saw her. That jeweled tone, rising and falling, suggested someone was with her, no doubt a man, a rich one, who had uttered something wickedly funny. She sat perched on a barstool, her short evening dress hitched up above her knees. It was nearly eleven and all the other women wore gowns. The men were in dinner jackets, their bow ties tossed off somewhere between Waikīkī and downtown. If the attire of the Young Hotel's crowd on a Saturday night was somewhat rumpled, it was still formal.

It was a perfect night for the rooftop lounge. No rain, not even clouds to threaten rain, so people crowded the open-air tables and dance floor. I lingered in the shadows by the hostess stand, the stand where Renee was supposed to position herself as the on-duty hostess for the night. She was, as always, too distracted to attend to guests. I figured it was just a matter of time before the manager had enough of her casual approach to her job, although, as Archie always pointed out, her presence didn't hurt business any.

"Looking for someone?" I turned to find Jack O'Brien at my side. "Never seen you hang back from the action."

"Just surveying the room."

While I wouldn't say we had become close friends exactly, Jack and I had established an unspoken truce. He never said so directly, but I sensed I'd earned a measure of his respect after the paper ran a few of my pieces. I knew I had a ways to go before he would see me as a true colleague—perhaps none of the men at the paper would ever accept me as an equal—but there was something less snide in the way he looked at me and less condescension in his tone.

"Anything of interest happening at the Pink Lady tonight?" He kept his eyes on the room, not me.

"Nope. Just some Midwest business yahoos with boring wives. I can't find anything to write about. You seen Archie around? I thought he was going to stop over once the boys were asleep."

I was trying to draw Archie out in the evenings in the hope he would drink less if with me. I trusted Mrs. Fong to manage any crisis that arose at home.

"Haven't seen him. But I just got here myself. Been covering a fire out in 'Aiea."

An elderly man in bed slippers and robe stumbled past.

"Evening, Charlie," we said in unison.

Charlie nodded but didn't break concentration in his beeline for the bar. A permanent resident of the hotel, Charlie's nightly ritual included two manhattans before bed. He could be counted on to weave his way through the crowd every Saturday night as the Kamanā Brothers sang haunting Hawaiian melodies and Julie Keanu danced. Right now the trio was playing Johnny Noble's new version of the "Hawaiian War Chant" and two other dancers had joined Julie for the spirited hula.

"Who's that with Renee?" Jack turned his focus to the end of the bar where Renee sat beside an older man.

I grinned and gave him a playful shove. "Why? Jealous?"

"Trust me. I am immune to Miss Manchester's powers."

"The guy's new to me, but I'm hoping he's important enough to write about tomorrow."

"Here's your chance to find out."

Renee had jumped off the barstool and was headed our way.

"Sadie, love." She approached with arms outstretched.

"Introduce me to the guy?" I asked as she enveloped me in a hug.

"Nice to see you, too. Sheesh. I'm beginning to be sorry I ever got you this reporter gig. You're all business and no fun."

"As if you ever needed me to have fun. You remember Jack O'Brien?"

"The reporter, right?" Renee barely looked at him. "Sorry to be a party pooper, dear, but I was just heading down to my room. I'm dead on my feet."

"And pretty feet they are. Those shoes are spectacular."

Renee's feet were wrapped in sparkling heels the same crimson shade as the tight silk dress she wore.

"Aren't they divine? A lovely friend bought them for me, right after he bought me this yummy dress." She planted a loud smooch on my cheek. "Night, night, sweets. Catch ya tomorrow? Brunch at the Halekulani?"

"Maybe. As always, it depends." No need explaining to her the uncertainties of my family life.

"Ring me. But not before ten!" And she was gone. In a flash, as always.

"She's a piece of work." Jack tossed his cigarette on the floor and ground it out with his foot.

"And she's my friend, so keep it to yourself. I'm going to go find out who she was talking to and see if I can dig up a story."

By the time I finished making my rounds, looking for something on which to hang the next day's column, Jack was settling his tab. My plan was to grab a cab, write my column from home, and call it in, but when he offered me a ride to the office, I took him up on it. It never hurt to put in an appearance at the newsroom.

Though I wasn't covering anything earth-shattering, I aimed to be as serious about what I wrote as the reporters covering the real stories. I refused to be apologetic about my reporting. As in Carlisle, there was a market for the stuff I wrote. Jack and the other reporters could sneer all they wanted, but I helped boost sales. I loved the sense of power that gave me, not only in dealing with Harrison and Ben Fox, the *Chronicle*'s editor, but in terms of interacting with the celebrities and society mavens I wrote about, most of whose fortunes depended on how the world saw them. Celebrities needed me to showcase their talent and charisma, executives needed me to showcase their power and smarts, and politicians needed me to describe all the ways they worked to help the community. Jack could kid me all he wanted about writing fluff, but I held real power. Or so I told myself.

I glanced over at him as he drove the deserted boulevard. He rested his right hand on the wheel and dangled his left out the window, a cigarette balanced between his fingers. He was the epitome of cool, could even be called good-looking when he wasn't frowning. Not handsome in Harrison's movie star way. More angular and weathered. He lived on a sailboat he kept anchored at Kewalo Basin, and the hours in the sun showed. I had yet to see him bring a woman to the reporters' late-night gatherings or for that matter even flirt with the beauties hovering about. I liked that he didn't indulge in off-color humor or rate women the way the other reporters did.

The only time I saw him drop his cool demeanor was when a reporter brought along a young Chinese woman from Shanghai who was headed to Mrs. Fong's alma mater, Mills College in Oakland. The other men at the table paid her little attention—she didn't register as a knockout—but Jack spoke to no one else that night once they established a mutual interest in Chiang Kai-shek.

Jack left me at a typewriter in the newsroom and headed off to see Ben. Moments later he passed by again, hat in hand.

"That was quick."

"Something came up. You OK with calling a cab?"

"Sure. That was my original plan. See ya later, alligator."

I waited for an "after a while, crocodile" that didn't come. The man hadn't a playful bone in his body.

"A bit on the thin side both in length and interest value," I said as Ben read through my copy. "No ships at the harbor, no celebrities around. It's a giant snore out there."

"I thought Harrison's wife was putting on some event?"

"That's tomorrow evening. Cocktail thing to raise money for their kids' school." I'd thought I was done covering the boring society stuff, but it seemed Honolulu's women wanted their parties and clothes written about, too.

"Be sure you cast it in a good light. I don't need Jacqueline blazing in here to read me the riot act."

"I'm on it."

"Good." He returned to marking up an article, my cue to leave.

I was surprised to see light shining from under Harrison's door. He was rarely in the office, particularly at night. I considered knocking and asking for tips on what to cover at the cocktail party, but decided only something important would bring him to the office that late. As I turned to go, something red caught my eye. Below the chair outside his door, a single red jeweled shoe lay on its side.

Of course. Renee never went to bed early.

"Best be careful, Renee, dear," I whispered. "Mrs. Bellingham has claws."

"Damn," I muttered as the cab pulled up to the curb beside our house. Our landlady, Mrs. Fong, was out on the walkway, broom in hand, sweeping. I checked my watch: 1 a.m. Did the woman never sleep?

I paid the driver, carefully gathered the back of my evening gown so it wouldn't wick up the evening dew, and commenced my walk to judgment. Mrs. Fong would have something to say about either Archie or the boys. And it was never something good. Either the boys had been fighting or Archie hadn't mown the lawn. I could tell by the way she strummed the sidewalk with her broom that Ying Fong had an earful for me that night.

She stopped sweeping and stood like a sentry before me. Not tonight, I wanted to say. Yell at me when the sun's up.

"Good evening, Mrs. Fong. You're up late."

"Your husband."

Of course. What now. "I apologize for whatever he did."

I could barely see the woman in the darkness. She was only outline and mass, but I sensed a softening in her grip on the broom and in her stance.

"He's a weak man."

"Yes." I was past pretending, especially with someone who saw Archie daily.

"Your sons are good boys. Smart boys."

"I think they're pretty special guys."

I was wary of where this was going, not sure I could trust this new version of my landlady. That she would compliment the boys' intelligence seemed meaningful. I knew the value she placed on intellect and education. Arch's boss Vernon told us she graduated from Punahou School, then went on to Mills. Her son and daughter, now grown, also

attended Punahou and mainland colleges. "One *akamai wahine*," is
what Vernon called her. Though she lived modestly, still residing in the
bungalow she'd grown up in, she was rumored to be one of Hawai'i's
wealthier women, with a fortune based in real estate. She managed most
of her business out of her home with the help of her son and daughter.

"You work hard and keep your boys in line. It's not easy raising good
boys."

I figured Ying knew something about raising children alone while
working full-time. No one spoke of a Mr. Fong. I assumed he was dead,
but it wouldn't have surprised me if a strong woman like Ying had shown
her husband the door.

"On the nights you work, you can tell your boys to come get me or to
yell 'Aunty' if there's trouble. I'll come help."

"That's generous. Thank you."

So what had happened to precipitate this change of attitude, I
wondered.

"I think everything is all right now inside your place. Mr. Doyle was
asleep by the time the haole man got here. Go see, then come back out.
We'll talk more."

"What haole man? What happened?"

"The man at the newspaper, the one who answered when I called."

Jack. That's why he left in such a hurry. I ran up the steps to our little
porch and pulled open the screen door. I nearly tripped over Archie
sprawled in the center of the living room, snoring in his usual trumpeting
way. His once lean, athletic frame now carried a giant belly that rose and
fell with each breath.

Light spilled from the kitchen beyond. I found Jack bent over his steno
pad at the kitchen table, pen in hand. I leaned against the door frame,
curiously comforted by his presence.

"I didn't have you pegged as the white knight type."

He finished the line he was writing, capped his pen, and closed the
notepad.

"I'm not. I never ignore a lead."

For a moment, I tensed, fearing he was serious, but his smirk gave him away.

"Right. How big a story is it?"

He gathered up his hat and jacket. "Nothing worth publishing. Kids are asleep. They'll probably all want to sleep a bit late tomorrow."

"Going to share any details?"

"I'm sure they will fill you in on whatever they think you should know. I was late to the show. Don't know all that much about what caused the ruckus."

Booze. That's what caused it. That's what always caused it. "Well, thank you for whatever it is you did."

I extended my hand and he shook it with an assurance that was curiously comforting. He really was a good guy. Not nearly so tough as he pretended.

I saw Jack off and checked on the kids, then paused a moment beside Archie. He looked so boyish and carefree. How had he misplaced that version of himself? I headed to Ying's bungalow, as directed. I could only just make out her shape on the porch.

"Here." She extended a cup to me.

I settled into the comfortable rattan rocker beside hers and took a sip, unable in the dark to see what it was. Tea. Green tea. Warm not hot. We sat in silence staring at the Ko'olaus' ridge, illuminated by the full moon. The silence between us was oddly easy and comfortable. I drained my cup and set it down on the table.

"Thank you. I need to go to bed now." I rose and added, "Thank you for the phone call."

Ying nodded.

As I headed down the steps to the walkway connecting our bungalows, she asked, "What year were you born?"

"1906."

"Horse. I thought so."

I was exhausted but curious. "In the Chinese calendar? What does it mean to be a horse?"

Ying rose and gathered up our cups. "Another time. Get some sleep now."

I locked up the house, turned off the kitchen light, and undressed. As I slipped between the sheets, I wondered about being born under the sign of the horse. According to Western astrology, I was a Leo. Horse and lion. Hooves and roars. I should be one formidable woman, I thought, as sleep overtook me, but I had still a long ways to go.

Lionel

Today was one of the best days of my whole life. My very favorite day might have been when we went up Round Top and watched the army pretend to drop bombs and fire rockets from Fort DeRussy. The pretend enemy planes looked like silver moths in the sky. I also really liked it when the fleet arrived last summer and we got to go on the USS *Maryland* and drink lemonade in the commander's quarters, but today was definitely almost as exciting as those two things. Since Mom had to write a newspaper story about it, we had tickets that got us onto Pearl Harbor base and we sat in the very front row of chairs set out on the grass. Everybody else, even the army's band, had to sit behind us. We could see all of Pearl Harbor, and there were lots and lots of boats in the water and lots of planes in the air doing fancy formations and turns. Bunches of photographers and even a Movietone camera recorded it all. Mom told me not to look up when stunt planes started doing tricks that made it look like they were going to crash and fall into the sea. I watched all the same and it made me feel sick inside to watch them, just like when the tightrope walkers start bouncing on the wire or the trapeze guy lets go of the bar.

The important people, even the head of the whole navy, arrived in a special boat and everyone clapped while the band played a song for them. Somebody yelled, "There she is," and we stared up in the sky out past

'Ewa way. Then I saw it, the Pan Am Clipper, a big silver bird with little ones flying beside it. The Clipper glided down onto the water perfectly, with hardly a splash, after making it all the way across the ocean from the mainland. I think if I had been on that plane for as long as the men inside it, I would have jumped right into the water and not waited for them to tow the plane to the pier. After they got everybody out, I got to talk to the radio operator and even got to meet Captain Musick, who smiled a lot and said maybe someday I'd get to fly in the Clipper myself, only I don't think I'd like that as well as going by ship. Even if the Clipper is still kind of a boat and can float OK, it would be scary to fall out of the sky and crash into the sea. Mom said not to worry about it, I won't be having to go anywhere for a long time, maybe not till I go away to college, which made me glad I won't have to go up in the air in a plane. But it made me sad too 'cause I'm not so sure I want to stay here and never go anywhere until I'm in college.

Sadira

From the newsroom's center, I assessed the Norfolk pine someone had brought in and decorated with seashells.

"I don't care what you say, that is no Christmas tree."

"Hate to break it to you, Doyle, but there's also not going to be any snow when you wake up Christmas morning. Welcome to paradise."

"Ah gee, O'Brien. There you go dashing a gal's dreams again. Here I was thinking we'd be sledding and drinking hot chocolate after we opened our presents."

With a drink in hand, his face flushed and his shirt sleeves rolled up, Jack O'Brien looked as if he'd been enjoying the office Christmas party for quite a while.

I didn't really mind that the usual rituals would be missing that Christmas. I actually liked the simplicity of the tree, but I had been feeling the distance from home since Thanksgiving. We'd celebrated that holiday with Ying Fong's family. She served up a fine feast with exotic offerings like shark fins and birds' nest soups, stuffed oysters and roast duck wrapped in a pancake. Kenny declared it better than turkey, and though I agreed the feast was grand, I missed the familiar menu, a fire crackling in the living room, and the windows sweating as the cold pressed against them.

"You'll get used to it," Jack said. "After a while, hanging out at the beach on Christmas Day doesn't seem all that strange. I usually spend the day sailing."

"I keep hearing about this boat of yours and yet I've never seen it. Ever take people for a ride?"

"You know anything about sailing?"

I shook my head. "Not a single thing."

"Then don't hold your breath."

"So how do these parties work?" I surveyed the crowd milling around the newsroom, some clustered by the improvised bar, others at the *pūpū* table, a few monitoring the Victrola. "This is my first office Christmas party."

"We eat, we drink. After everyone's had a few, things loosen up. Some couple begins the dancing. Bellingham gives us all an envelope with our yearly bonus, Ben makes a toast, reminds us of our responsibility in a free society et cetera, et cetera. At some point, Ben or Harrison decides we've had enough, they cut off the bar, and we go home."

"No singing Christmas carols around the tree?"

Jack eyed me over his glass. "You could always start a new tradition."

"I'm guessing you'd find that pretty funny, me trying to get people to sing Christmas songs."

I was beginning to wish I had a drink in my hand.

"Doyle, I find just about everything you do fairly amusing. So you just keep doing things your way, and we'll all be smiling."

"Laughing, you mean. I know you think I'm an idiot, Jack O'Brien."

"Then you know wrong. One thing I know for sure is you are no idiot."

Someone had switched albums on the Victrola, removing Fred Astaire's

"Cheek to Cheek" and swapping in Chick Webb's "Stompin' at the Savoy."

"That's more like it." Jack put down his glass and grabbed my hand. He led me out to the small area cleared for dancing. Other couples followed. Suddenly, the party came to life.

"Will wonders never cease!" I said as he twirled me away from him. In all the evenings I'd spent at the Young Hotel's rooftop lounge, I'd never once seen Jack on the dance floor.

To my surprise, he wasn't bad. Nothing fancy, but he had clearly paid attention all those evenings when he sat watching others show off their steps. Or he did his dancing elsewhere.

He pulled me in close for a moment, just long enough to say, "Merry Christmas, Sadira," then set me spinning away again at the song's conclusion.

"Merry Christmas," I said as he gave me a jaunty salute and headed back to where he left his drink.

Time to head home, I decided, surveying the crowd. Go before the light, celebratory tenor turned sloppy. Hard to believe this was my life. Me, a reporter at a major city paper, and our family celebrating Christmas in the tropics. Strange, the twists life takes, but how much better we all were for the twists in ours. The night before, Archie and I had taken the boys to 'Iolani Palace, where thousands of residents gathered before the palace's lit balconies and listened to Christmas music. The magic of those lights, the thrill of standing in so large a crowd, the miracle of singing carols without shivering—I loved it all. I squeezed Archie's hand and we grinned at one another like dumb, happy kids.

Lionel

Sometimes the worst days are the ones that are supposed to be the best. Like last Christmas when the kitten died or the time Dad took us all the way to Yankee Stadium for a baseball game and I ate so many hot dogs I threw up right in the stands and we had to leave before the fifth inning. I've learned not to get my hopes up about anything. That's why I told myself not to get excited about Christmas this year, especially 'cause it wouldn't be anything like the ones back home. No snow, no grandmas, no Santa Claus parade down Main Street, no carolers in a hay wagon.

Some good Christmas stuff happened before Christmas day. They lit up 'Iolani Palace so it looked like a fairy castle, and they had a Christmas pageant at St. Andrew's Cathedral that was bigger than back in Carlisle, but otherwise church was pretty much the same. That's what's good about Episcopalians, Mom says. Wherever you go, they'll be using the same prayers and the same hymns and you'll know exactly what to do and say.

We have no fireplace here for our stockings, so we put them on the kitchen table next to the cookies and milk and carrots Kenny put out for Santa and the reindeer. Santa Claus found us, just like Mom promised Kenny he would, and filled up our stockings then put them on our beds. It was pretty different waking up on a warm Christmas morning, I'll tell ya. We even thought about going swimming, it was so sunny and warm.

After we ate our breakfast and opened all our presents, Mom went and got Renee at the Young Hotel so Renee would have somebody to be with. "After all, it's Christmas, Arch, and it's not like she has anyone else," she said. "I know, I know," he said, "but she wouldn't be lonely if she chased after unmarried men," and Mom got red in the face and said, "Archie, the boys!" Dad was quiet after that and I don't know what it had to do with us, but they didn't talk about it anymore.

Mom and Renee put on their swimsuits and lay out on beach mats in the backyard even though there's no pool or ocean in our backyard. "Just to get some color," Mom said in her tired voice that means I need to leave her alone. They had a pile of silly magazines and a bowl of chips and a pitcher full of daiquiris. Mom didn't drink the daiquiris, but she helped herself to those chips and drank two bottles of Coke from the pack Dad gave her for Christmas, and the two of them were laughing and laughing like silly teenage girls, not grown-ups. Dad, Kenny, and me played a game of Monopoly while they burned themselves in the sun. After they came in to change and start making our Christmas dinner,

Dad said, "How's about you boys go see if there's anything interesting on the tree," and by tree he meant the Norfolk pine he brought home, which doesn't look anything at all like a real Christmas tree but had to do the job. "What are you talking about, Dad?" I said, 'cause we'd opened all our presents and there was nothing left anywhere near the tree, but sure enough, tied to one branch was a big red envelope that said *Kenny and Lionel* on it. Kenny tore it open and inside was a piece of paper that said, "I'm red as a cardinal with a bright yellow beak; women wear me to parties when it's a husband they seek. What am I?"

We were confused till Kenny figured out it must be part of a treasure hunt and we were supposed to figure out the clues. I kept trying to think of places where we'd find cardinals, but Kenny's the one who thought of women in Hawai'i wearing flowers behind their ears and that made us think of hibiscus 'cause they're the only red flowers we've got in the yard. Only the clue's not a good one 'cause married ladies wear flowers, too, they just put them behind a different ear from the not-married ones. "It's a game, Lionel. Just go look at the hibiscus bush," Dad said when I told him the clue didn't make sense. Sure enough there was another piece of paper tied to one of the hibiscus branches. That clue was even harder. "I've got frog eggs in my belly and a tender spot around my core; toss me in lemon, and you'll really have scored, what am I?"

It took some thinking but Kenny thought of papaya and sure enough, there was a red note stuck on one of the papaya trees, only I thought it was another pretty stupid clue 'cause there are no frog eggs in a papaya. Dad said, "They look like frog eggs, Lionel," but they don't, not really. They're big and black and don't have any jelly stuff holding them together.

There were three more clues that had us scrambling all over the yard and inside the house and some of them took a long time to figure out. But not the last one. I got that almost right away.

"I'm dark as a cave and filled up with junk; you can open and close me, but I don't move like a trunk." I knew right away it was a closet. We opened every closet till we got to the one in our bedroom and there it was—our main Christmas present—a real live kitten. Not just any old kitten, but a Persian one, already two months old so it was OK she was away from her mom. I was so excited I almost wet my pants. Mom said, "Oh, Arch," and I was scared she was going to say, "What have you done now," and make us give back the cat, but she said, "What a precious gift, you wonderful man," which made me wonder if she actually did drink some of Renee's daiquiris. I had to fight Mom for a chance to hold the kitten. She decided to call her Pele. When I said I thought she was supposed to belong to me and Kenny and we should name her, Dad said, "She's a gift for all of you," and I didn't want to make him feel bad by fighting about it, so I said OK. I still think we should have called her Sugarsnap 'cause of her color and how sweet she is. Mom had to go make the Christmas dinner and Kenny went outside to paint pictures with the paint set he got from Gran Schaeffer, so it ended up being just me petting Pele for a long time and I think that now she likes me best. Only I didn't say that to Kenny and Mom 'cause I didn't want to make them feel bad.

While Mom cooked, Renee let me help her set the table. She didn't leave it plain like usual. She turned it into a party table with pretty fruit and flowers and even some candles. Renee turns everything into something better. We had a chicken instead of a turkey or ham, and cranberries from a can, and Mom's apple and pumpkin pies had fillings from cans, but they still tasted OK. Instead of tiny sausages from a can for pūpūs, Mom put out a whole bowl of fresh boiled shrimp on a pile of ice. We dipped them in a spicy sauce and I showed Renee I wasn't afraid to try one, but I only had one 'cause they're kind of slimy. Kenny and I even got to sip some sparkling wine. All in all, I'd say it turned out to be a pretty swell Christmas. A couple days before, Mom had said, "Maybe we should just go eat Chinese for Christmas dinner," which is what we sort of did for Thanksgiving when we ate at Mrs. Fong's. That was OK, but I'm glad Mom decided to cook. It felt like a real Christmas sitting at our own kitchen table, the candles making it almost like at Gran Schaeffer's. I didn't even know to ask for a kitten, and maybe that's why it all turned out so good. I got something even better than my brain could imagine.

Sadira

As soon as we stepped off the elevator and into the Young Hotel's lounge, I knew I should have dropped Arch at home. The place was packed. It hadn't seemed right to suggest he stay home on New Year's Eve, but it proved a distraction to keep an eye on him while doing my job. The Young Hotel's event was our third of the night. We started at the Moana and from there went on to Lau Yee Chai, where we couldn't hear a thing above the roar of firecrackers. After the Young we would count down to midnight at the Royal and then head to the Wai'alae Country Club to watch Honolulu's elite celebrate. Not a bad gig, to party at all the hot spots and not pay a dime.

"About time you guys got here." Renee was manning the hostess stand, sedately attired in a simple black gown but crowned with a wildly colored paper hat, complete with small feathers.

"Interesting." I eyed the headgear.

"Here." Renee pulled two hats out of a box behind her. "You get to dress up, too."

Archie's looked like something a clown might wear and mine was much like Renee's, only with longer feathers that swooped down in front of my face, making it difficult to see.

"Do we have to?" I brushed a feather away.

"Yup. I've been making these all week. I heard they give out dolls at the Royal, so I figured we had to hand out something. Who wants a doll when you can have something as fun as these?"

Archie's was too small and kept sliding off. "Trade you for something bigger?"

Renee pulled out another lady's hat, much like the one she'd given me. "All I've got left." She put it on him. "But hey, don't you look adorable?" She pinched his cheek for emphasis. "Now come on. You owe me a dance, mister. Mind if I steal him?"

"He's all yours." I pulled out my notebook and began wending my way through the crowd to the roof's edge, where I could watch the party and enjoy the view of Honolulu. I couldn't see much that night. Heavy smoke from the firecrackers was settling over the city and the steady explosions made it seem more like a war zone than a partying town. "Just wait till midnight," someone had told me at Lau Yee Chai. "The roar is deafening." I wondered how the boys were doing. Ying had invited them over to her place for a family celebration. Better than leaving them alone on a night like this, but I worried they were out in the street setting off firecrackers with Ying's grandkids.

Focus, I reminded myself. I needed enough details to keep Ben and the Young Hotel's owners happy. I jotted down the names of those I recognized, the details of the more striking evening gowns and descriptions of the clownish hats. A photographer was what I needed. It was a night better captured in photos. I squeezed through the mob, bound for the front desk to call the paper and ask that they send someone over. I scanned the room for Archie and Renee. It was insanity to pack so many people into so small a space. As I reached the unattended hostess stand, a fresh group of revelers spilled from the elevator. No point trying to call from here, I realized. I would never be heard over the din.

So where've you gotten to, Arch? I wondered. As best I could tell he wasn't at the bar and he wasn't apt to still be on the dance floor.

"Over here, old girl." He sat hidden behind a potted palm in a dark corner of the entry area, twirling the sad hat with his finger.

"Why are you hiding back here?" I crouched down beside him. His eyes were clear, no blush to his cheeks.

"Being a good boy. Anything to make you happy."

I extended my hand. "Come on. Let's go welcome in the new year at the Royal. I've got what I need to write a glowing review."

"Can't wait." He groaned a bit as he rose. "After all, I hear they're giving out dolls at the Royal."

I laughed and linked my arm in his. "And us with no daughters to enjoy them. At least we've got these." I stuck his hat back on his head and nodded my head so the feathers bobbed. "It's all rather absurd, isn't it?"

To think that in past years I had envied those celebrating the new year at fancy hotel parties, parties made to sound romantic and thrilling by reporters like me.

"Not to worry about me." Archie settled in a chair at the periphery of the Royal's showroom. "I've a pack of smokes and I'm bound to run into some chums."

"You don't need to stay back here, Arch. We've got a reservation. There'll be room." I leaned closer. "It's New Year's. I want you beside me."

"Thanks, but no thanks, love. Sitting at a big table where no one knows me or wants to know me and having to make small talk with some movie star's wife is not my idea of a good time. I'll be fine. Scout's honor." He held up two fingers in salute.

The maître d' led me to the center table and seated me beside Isabelle Montgomery, a British woman rumored to be wealthy and vaguely aristocratic. We'd met earlier that week at a luncheon and Isabelle proved an easy subject. She loved to share details about her wardrobe.

"French?" I eyed her gown, as if I had any clue what would distinguish a Parisian gown from a New York one.

"But of course." Isabelle gleamed. "Clever girl to know fashion when you live so far from any real culture."

It was easy to manage the rich and the vain. Smile and flatter them and they bubbled over with information. "And those shoes! They're divine." I leaned closer to admire Isabelle's feet.

What a way to spend the last minutes of my year—recording the minutia of some woman's wardrobe. I made note of the carat count of Isabelle's diamond necklace, the designer who conceived her gown, and the name of the dinner dish she most fancied that evening.

Isabelle moved on to the dance floor with a much younger male companion, and before I could find another target, Jack O'Brien sat beside me. "How's it going, Doyle?"

I made a face. "Same old thing. Not exactly the grand time I imagined it would be. How about you?"

"The usual New Year's stories. A house caught fire in Kaimukī. Bad smashup of cars in Makiki. One driver dead."

"So why do they have you covering this when there's real news going on out there?"

He nodded at a general seated one table over. "Ben wants me to get a response on some news out of Japan."

"Lucky you. Sounds way more interesting than what's ahead for me."

Jack shrugged. "Not really. The general's not going to be pleased when I interrupt his evening and probably won't give me anything anyway, unless he's sloshed and slips up. I'm waiting for the countdown, then I'll give it a shot."

I checked my watch. "Oh geez. I lost track." I gathered up my things. "I've gotta find Arch and head over to the Wai'alae. Hope you get your guy."

I found Archie, but not before the new year. As the emcee led the crowd in counting from ten, I kept pressing forward, but at countdown's end, my way was blocked by couples embracing and I was alone. At least Archie wasn't mourning the moment. Engrossed in conversation with an elderly woman, he missed it entirely.

"Best thing you could ever do for your family," he was saying as I approached. "Oh there you are, love. I've been explaining to Mrs. Lawrence the advantages of prepaid cemetery plots and funerals."

"I'm done for the night," Archie said when we reached the Royal's portico. "I'll grab a cab."

"It hasn't been much of a night for you." I squeezed his hand. "I'm sorry." I was trying to be more patient since his sweet gesture of giving me a kitten for Christmas.

"Generous of you to notice."

It never failed. I made an effort and he spoiled it.

I let go his hand and held out my palm for the car keys.

I trudged up the drive to the Wai'alae clubhouse, disappointed with the whole evening. The previous New Year's Eve, Archie, the boys, and I had celebrated by lighting candles in ice lamps along the walkway to our front door, then gathered on the porch and toasted the year to come with sparkling cider.

"It looks like a land of magic," Lionel had whispered, and in its humble way, it did.

"Just wait till next year," I said, imagining myself just as I was—all dolled up and attending the most glamorous parties imaginable. Except it didn't feel magical at all.

I entered the club nervous but determined to get my best material of the night. The members of this elite club intimidated me more than any Waikīkī celebrity. These were people who wore their power and privilege discreetly yet with such quiet assurance, I lost all personal sense of ease.

"It's that New England reserve inherited from their missionary ancestors," Jack once told me. "Mixed with the kind of unspoken, subtle code only an isolated, island community can evolve. I think you have to be born into one of these families to get it."

As with all people, though, the façade sometimes slipped, and abundant alcohol helped. On a night like this the crowd was sure to be well sloshed, and that might mean a story for me.

I secured a club soda at the bar and made my way round the room, chatting with those who approached me, slipping into a corner to jot down notes about the usuals—who was there, what they were wearing, what the band was playing. I couldn't say later whether the band had actually stopped playing or if it only felt that way, but when Renee entered, I felt the room's attention swivel to the entrance. She had changed her gown since the Young Hotel. She now wore an exquisite, shimmering silver dress that plunged to her waist at both front and back. It sparkled nearly as much as her jewels and flowed like water around her. Renee knew how to make an entrance. The problem was, this was not the place for that kind of entrance or that kind of gown. I couldn't afford to fall on the wrong side of this crowd, and I hoped Renee would fasten herself to someone else.

I circled the room, covering my bases, and had almost made it to a safe corner when Renee appeared beside me, cocktail in hand.

"Don't worry. I know you're working, but you have to let me stand by you. These people give me the willies." She pulled me over to the wall.

I had never seen Renee visibly nervous in a public setting.

"I don't want to be here, but Harrison told me I had to come and I had to wear this gown he bought me."

I didn't want to know any more. The last thing I needed was to be pulled into a new Renee drama, especially a drama I couldn't write about and that could diminish my access to these players.

"You're welcome to stick by me, but I won't be here long."

"Got it." Renee looped her arm through mine.

I ached to lay my head down and close my eyes. Another woman at our table had done just that, though hers was an alcohol-induced slumber. The orchestra still played and couples swayed on the dance floor, but people's energy was flagging throughout the room.

Jack placed a drink in front of me. He'd followed his general to the club, dogging him till he got his quote. "Your ginger ale."

He handed Renee a flute of champagne.

"Thanks, Jack." Renee ran her hand down his arm and cupped his elbow with her palm. "You're a peach."

I wasn't sure which annoyed me more, that Renee had fastened herself to me and insisted I stay or that she was flirting with Jack. I glanced again at my watch. Nearly two. Renee no longer needed me there. She had gathered a circle of fawning young men and indifferent women. When she had approached this table of Hawai'i's powerfully connected young adults, I thought it a bad idea. This particular crowd could do worse than ignore her—they could toy with her, as I'd seen them do with others they considered their social inferiors. Yet it seemed I had underestimated Renee. Even Oliver Spence, who usually wore boredom as an accessory, was animated in her presence.

"May I?" Jack pulled out the chair beside me.

"Of course." It pleased me that he chose to sit by me rather than hover close to Renee.

A young woman, shoeless and with the skirt of her gown pulled up and tossed over one arm, planted a deck of cards in front of me.

"Ta-da," she trumpeted. "Told you I could dig up a pack."

Renee had suggested earlier that I read people's cards to liven things up, but no one had a deck and I thought I was off the hook.

"How delicious." Oliver's familiar demeanor returned, his eyelids back to half-mast. "Perhaps we'll find out about Renee's secret past."

For a moment so fleeting that I doubted anyone besides me noted it, Renee's face registered rage.

"Yes, you best be careful." Renee feigned playfulness as she clutched Oliver's arm and leaned against his shoulder. "You wouldn't want to upset me."

"So who's going to be *my* first victim?" I shuffled the cards.

The table quieted. Harrison had appeared behind Renee and placed his hands on her shoulders. Renee practically twitched beneath them. I couldn't discern if she was registering delight or fear as her face flushed and her fingers dug into the table's white linen cloth.

"I'll have a go," Jack offered when no one else spoke up. "I've always wanted to witness this supposed talent of yours, Doyle."

"Prepare to be amazed." I put the shuffled pack of cards in front of him. "Cut it into three separate piles, faceup."

"What do you see?" Renee leaned forward, a strap of her gown falling away to expose too much of her chest.

I closed my eyes. I needed to calm my mind, clear it of the night's clutter. An image of water came to me and the sensation of gentle rocking.

"You'll definitely be spending time on the water."

"Amazing. It's almost as if you knew I live on a boat."

"Hush. The cards won't speak if you mock them."

Jack raised his hands in surrender. "My apologies to the cards. Carry on."

I knew I didn't have the group's attention. No one there cared about Jack O'Brien's future. Their focus was on Harrison's hands sitting atop Renee's shoulders. A statement. I felt obliged to at least try and provide a distraction.

I shifted my attention to the first card on the table, the nine of spades, never a good one. Again I closed my eyes. A scene I felt sure was the one Jack experienced earlier that night in Makiki flashed through my mind. When I opened my eyes, Jacqueline Bellingham had joined the circle, standing directly opposite Renee and Harrison. I glanced at Jack, who studiously kept his focus on the cards.

"See anything?" He was the only person feigning interest.

"Harrison." Jacqueline's voice was slurred. She leaned forward, resting both hands on the table to steady herself.

"Yes, my darling." Harrison gently massaged Renee's neck.

"I see a terrible accident," I told Jack. "A big pileup of cars."

"It's time for your little friend to leave." Jacqueline spoke over me, but kept her voice level, her volume low.

Renee made a move to rise, but Harrison held her down.

"Miss Manchester is with me, Jacqueline. You are free to mingle elsewhere or leave if you prefer. But Miss Manchester is staying."

And here it comes, I thought, recalling the image I'd seen months ago when I read Renee's cards in Havana. At the time I hadn't known where or when or even with whom Renee would share an angry scene, only that she would. Jacqueline slowly circled the table to where Harrison stood, then slapped him hard across the face with her open palm. He didn't block the blow nor did he flinch.

"Feel better?" He redirected his attention to me. "I believe you were about to share Jack's future. I apologize for the interruption. Carry on, please."

I tried to steady my nerves and focus, not easy to do with such foul energy swirling around me. The whole room vibrated now. Distorted images flooded my mind. I couldn't distinguish any particular emotion or image as belonging to Jack's future. I would have to give a reading such as anyone might give, a literal translation of the cards visible on the table, nothing more.

"This three of hearts." I held up the card. "A good one. Love may be right around the corner for you, Jack."

"About time," Harrison said. "I'd like to meet the woman who can penetrate that heart of steel."

Jacqueline still stood beside Harrison, but he studiously ignored her, his hands remaining on Renee.

"This ace of clubs means you may come into money."

"Will you please shut up." Jacqueline turned on me, still careful not to actually raise her voice. "For God's sake, you're babbling like a crazed gypsy woman."

"Here's the thing, my dear," Harrison said. "You are the one acting crazed, not Sadira. You're making a scene. A scene none of us wish to be part of. Be a good girl and run on home. I promise we can do this tomorrow with all the drama you desire, but this is neither the time nor the place."

Jack pushed back his chair. "Tell you what. Much as I love having my future laid out for the world to see and mock, I think I'm done for the night. I'll give you a lift home, Jackie." He wrapped an arm around her and she slumped against him. As Jack led her away, I scooped up the cards.

"Do me now!" Every bit of Renee sparkled, her gown, her jewels, her eyes. She was a woman radiant.

"I'm afraid I must go as well, Renee. Remember, I'm on the job and have a column to write. Maybe someone else would like to give it a try." I passed the deck to Oliver. Afraid I might not manage to stand, let alone walk across the room without visibly shaking, I rose quickly, used the table for support, and with a nod to Harrison, took my leave, hoping I appeared what I was not, a woman unfazed.

It was nearly four before I pulled up to the curb in front of our house. By the time I had my column composed, the sky was lightening. I stood, phone in hand, reading my copy to the newspaper's stenographer, when Ying rapped on the kitchen door. I waved her in. One of our routines was to end the night sharing a cup of tea at the kitchen table. Sometimes I prattled on about my evening adventures, sometimes I confided my fears and disappointments, and sometimes she shared hers. Often we sat in silence, sharing a kind of companionship I hadn't known with any other woman friend.

Ying had brewed and poured the tea by the time I hung up the phone. She raised her cup.

"*Kung hee fat choy.*"

I raised mine.

"Happy New Year."

Chapter Five

January to December 1937

Sadira

I was dying for another cup of coffee, but it was already past nine. The boys and I needed to get going. Shirley Temple was in town, meaning there might be good material for my column if I played it right. I wanted to catch her on the beach before the *Hawai'i Calls* broadcast began at two.

The day before, the boys and I—along with most of Honolulu, it seemed—had turned out for the child star's arrival at the harbor. Thanks to my press pass, we were able to stand at the foot of the gangway. I armed the boys with leis and brought a newspaper photographer to capture the moment. As I described it in the paper,

> *The Royal Hawaiian Band played "On the Good Ship Lollipop" as the darling girl, all decked out in a cunning little yellow and white frock with a white naval cap over her tumble of curls, rode down the gangway on Duke Kahanamoku's shoulders. The poor child was practically smothered with leis. Your correspondent's brief interview with Shirley and her parents confirmed Shirley to be as unspoiled and polite as rumored, and her parents utterly without pretense.*

For the paper's front-page story, they used the shot of Shirley riding on Duke's shoulders, but for my column, they went with the one of Kenny and Lionel in the background, leis in hand, as Duke lowered the little girl to the ground.

Observing it all, I had felt the now-familiar surprise that this was my life. Only a year before, the boys and I had been gawking at the Temples' Beverly Hills house as Renee ushered us around LA. Imagine what that wide-eyed Sadie would have said if anyone had suggested she would soon be meeting the entire Temple family, or that Shirley would shake her hand and say, "Such a pleasure to meet you, Mrs. Doyle."

"Kenny, Lionel," I called from the kitchen door. "Time to head out."

I had dressed for the beach when I got up and had only to grab our beach gear and my work bag. The old brain will have to manage with limited caffeine, I decided as I downed a banana, then swiped peanut butter over a piece of bread. I ate standing beside the sink. Lionel scowled as he came in.

"How come we have to sit at the table when we eat, but you don't?"

"'Cause I'm the mom. Now go put on your swim trunks, you two, we're heading to Waikīkī. If I get lucky, you may get to swim with Miss Temple today."

Lionel sighed dramatically.

Lovely, I thought, rinsing my hands. I shut off the faucet with a hard thrust to each handle. All I needed was for Lionel to be in one of his funks. *Ignore him*, I told myself. *Don't indulge his theatrics.*

As the boys ran into the water, I scanned the beach between the Moana and Royal Hawaiian hotels, found a spot amid the tourists, and rolled out our straw beach mats. From my giant all-purpose bag, I dug out my notebook and pen. I'd learned I needed a special uniform for these trips to the beach. If I was after a male celebrity, it helped to walk the beach in my two-piece suit. If the prey were female or, as was the case today, a child, I was better off adding a cover-up. I always wore a large hat and dark glasses and protected my feet with rubber slippers or *tabis*. The boys' feet had grown so tough from running around barefoot all the time, they rarely noticed the sand's scorching heat.

I began as I always did by checking in with the beach boys. They often had tips for me about who was around, who had already done their swim for the day, who might be arriving later for a surfing lesson. The day's hot tip was that the Temples had requested an umbrella, lounge chairs, and a surfing lesson for 11 a.m. That was perfect. It would allow me enough time to talk to Shirley and clean up before the *Hawai'i Calls* broadcast. The show always provided a rich opportunity for celebrity watching, and Shirley wasn't the only big name in town, just the most recently arrived.

To kill time, I strolled along the Royal Hawaiian's beach to see if the Morgenthaus were about. Secretary of the Treasury Morgenthau, vacationing with his family, had taken a shine to me—despite, as he claimed, his aversion to all members of the press. He allowed me an interview of substantial length, from which I fashioned a rather dry but informative column. I didn't mind showing Ben I could do more than report on what people ate and wore.

"I'm going to walk the beach," I called to Lionel, who sat at the water's edge, covering his legs in wet sand. Kenny was paddling in the shallow waves. I could count on the lifeguards to keep a close watch.

As I headed up the waterline, I studied the tourists, looking for familiar faces. Several nodded and one called out, "Hey, beautiful, come join us!"

It was Johnny Felton, the rich young man from Boston who'd sailed in on his father's yacht along with an entourage of other attractive youngsters. I had met him and his group at a party Renee and Harrison hosted in his honor. Johnny's attention to Renee had Harrison fuming by evening's end, but I felt no sympathy for him. Perpetual worry about which handsome young man would snatch Renee from him was the bargain he'd made when he discarded Jackie for her.

I crossed to the group's encampment, a construction of three umbrellas anchored in the sand behind straw mats, with buckets of cooling champagne strategically placed beside them. I declined the champagne and a seat on the mats, laughed at Johnny's jokes and account of trying to ride a small motorcycle around the island, and kept an eye out for the Temples. When I spotted them bound for the sands, a gaggle of hotel personnel with umbrellas, towels, and mats trailing behind, I excused myself. Give me a curly-topped eight-year-old girl any day over a spoiled rich boy. I blew Johnny a goodbye kiss.

"Mrs. Doyle!" Shirley's mother called.

It was going to be a good day. They remembered me.

"So good to see you all again." I hoped it seemed I was simply out at the beach catching up with people and not looking specifically for them. "How is the visit going so far?"

"We are enchanted." Mrs. Temple beamed and settled herself in one of the chairs set up for them. "Join us? Shirley is about to have a surfing lesson with Mr. Kahanamoku."

"Wonderful! I bet you'll be brilliant at it."

Shirley sat demurely on a mat, a child clearly taught to be seen and not heard. "Thank you, Mrs. Doyle. I shall certainly do my best."

Kenny chose that moment to appear at my elbow. He looked as if he'd taken a good roll in the sand.

"I'm thirsty, Mom." He tugged at my skirt.

I felt my face flush.

"Kenny, it's not polite to interrupt. I am speaking with Miss Temple."

"Is he your son?" Shirley stood and extended a hand.

"Yes. My youngest, Kenneth. I apologize for his sandy appearance. You met him yesterday, but he looked a good bit tidier then."

"I like him just as he is. How do you do, Kenneth?"

Kenny dutifully shook her hand and mumbled his own version of "how do you do."

Mrs. Temple signaled for a waiter and had a glass of water brought for Kenny. Not good, I thought, to start off indebted to the people I wanted to charm. Duke Kahanamoku's arrival spared me further embarrassment.

"Mind if I watch your lesson?" I asked.

"That would be lovely." Shirley turned to Kenny. "You, too, Kenneth. But please don't laugh when I fall off the board."

"I wouldn't laugh at you." He seemed genuinely wounded that she could even imagine him capable of such unkindness.

I pulled off my cover-up, dropped my notebook beside it, and headed into the water beside Duke and Shirley, scanning the beach for the paper's photographer.

I could see Lionel out of the corner of my eye. Mostly I could feel him watching me, his eyes boring into me, willing me to leave the water and join him on our mats. I waved to him to join us, but he ducked his head as soon as I looked his way. Fine, I thought. Stew in the misery you create for yourself. I turned back to Shirley, who knelt on the surfboard with Duke beside her explaining how to paddle away from shore.

"You're doing swell," Kenny said as Shirley dipped first one and then the other hand in the water.

Oh, to have a camera. I cursed myself for forgetting my own little Brownie and scanned the beach again for Kimo, the paper's photographer, who often roamed Waikīkī collecting candids. The Temples were, of course, taking their own photos, but I could hardly ask them for copies.

For a few moments, Lionel slipped from my mind. We all cheered when Shirley propelled the board over a small cresting wave and clapped when she tried standing, as Duke steadied the giant board. When I turned back toward shore, I saw Lionel was now lying on his back, clutching his stomach and writhing.

"Want to try paddling to ride this next wave?" Duke asked Shirley. A small bump of a wave was headed their way.

Shirley nodded.

As the little girl paddled, Duke gave the board a helpful shove, but the jolt bounced Shirley into the water. Duke scooped her up.

"Your first fall. Now you're a real surfer," he told her.

I signaled to Kenny that it was time to go. *It's not as if something dramatic is going to happen*, I told myself. The surfing lesson would continue as all surfing lessons continued. I had my column item.

"Good luck, darling girl," I called to Shirley, and with a wave to Mr. and Mrs. Temple and a final, "Perhaps we'll see you at the broadcast," Kenny and I headed back to our mats and Lionel, who anyone watching would have been sure was at death's door.

Lionel

Of course Kenny got to meet Shirley Temple and stand in the water by her while Duke Kahanamoku showed her how to surf and no one thought to say, "Hey, Lionel, why don't ya come join us?" They forgot all about me. I hung out by our stuff so no one would take it, even though I was dying of thirst and hunger. Mom didn't bring anything for us to drink and I didn't have any money to go buy something. I knew her wallet was hidden in her bag and I could have dug down and found it and taken some money if I was the kind of kid who did that sort of thing. But I'm not.

When she and Kenny came back to the mat, they were laughing and happy and didn't even notice how miserable and in agony I was. Mom said, "Come on, boys, let's rinse off at the showers and make ourselves presentable," which means, dry off and put on some T-shirts and slippers but stay in our swim trunks. Most days she makes us go in the bathroom and change into shorts and unders, but that day she forgot the change of clothes 'cause she was in such a rush to get out the door.

At least she bought us burgers and Coca-Colas at the Banyan Court, so we could eat while we listened to the *Hawai'i Calls* broadcast. Mom is friends with Harry Owens who leads the orchestra, so we got to sit right up front, and Webley Edwards came over to talk to us before it all started. Mom was so busy talking to everybody she practically forgot all about her papaya and lime sitting on a white plate where the birds could come peck at it, so Kenny and I had to keep swatting them away. I worried through the whole thing that Shirley Temple would show up and steal the show, but she didn't. Mom said, "They should be so lucky as to get her on the show," as if Shirley Temple is the greatest person in the whole world, which she isn't. If you ask me, she'd get picked on at school if she had to go to one 'cause she's plump like a baby and her curls are such silly baby curls. No girls I know look like that.

Someday I'm going to sing on *Hawai'i Calls* only I haven't told anybody that yet. I don't know any Hawaiian songs, but I can learn some, and sometimes they have haoles singing and the choir director at church says I sing so good he's going to have me sing a solo for Christmas Eve. Dad got all wet in the eyes when the choir director said that. He patted me on the back and said, "That's my boy," 'cause he's got a good voice, too. I like it when the kids' choir sings with the grown-ups 'cause then I get to be near Dad and hear his voice above all the rest. I'm also training to be an acolyte and Father Wilson says I'm about the best acolyte he ever saw when I help at the school chapel. I remember everything I'm supposed to do in the right order and sometimes even have to remind Father Wilson and Father Horton, our church rector, of what comes next when they mess up and don't do things the right way. It helps that I made a cardboard set of all the church people. There's the priest and bishop, the dean and the canons, the acolytes and service assistants, the organist and choir leader. I even have a deacon, though we don't ever have any at our church. I made a set of vestments for each of them, and each week, I put them in the right colors. With Dad's help, I made it so they can stand up, and every Sunday I stand them up in a little church I made with no roof. There's the altar part and the nave with tiny benches and even a sacristy where the vestments are kept. On Saturday nights I practice putting the right clothes on everybody and then I do the whole service, which is why I know the order of everything forward and backward and won't ever get it wrong when I'm acolyting during a service.

Mom doesn't always make it to church 'cause she has to work till it's nearly morning and sometimes even till the sun comes up. "Leave me be," she'll say if Dad asks her. I wish sometimes that I could stay in bed till afternoon, too, but not so much now that I get to be an acolyte and sing in the choir. I bet Grandma Doyle would have lots to say about Mom not going to church regular and sleeping when the sun's shining.

Sadira

Two lines of kids facing one another looked to Archie for their next directions.

"OK, everybody on the 'Ewa side, take one giant step back."

The row of kids to his left stepped back. Archie walked down the line, moving them into place so all pairs were an equal distance apart. He blew his whistle.

"OK, toss the eggs."

The eight kids in the Diamond Head line gently pitched their eggs to their partners, all of whom managed the catch.

"And again," Archie called. "'Ewa side, take one big step back."

Eleanor Hitchcock surveyed the picnic table stacked with supplies for the various games. "We're short on potatoes," she said to me. "I'll collect some from the kitchen."

"I can do that. You stay put. Anything else we need while I'm there?"

"That should do us. Thanks, Sadie. You're a dear."

Eleanor, one of the matrons of the church, had always been friendlier than the other church women. We often ended up working together on church projects, and each encounter revealed some interesting new tidbit about Eleanor's past. Only the month before, I had learned she had a doctorate degree in botany from Syracuse University, which was practically around the corner from Carlisle. "Now those were cold winters," Eleanor told me when we compared notes. "Especially for a girl from Hawai'i." I'd never met a woman with a doctorate degree, let alone one who taught at a university. I especially liked Eleanor's lack of pretension, given she was a woman of means.

More people had shown up for that year's church picnic than any of us expected, nearly double the previous year's attendance. As with everything in Honolulu, the church was growing rapidly, filling with new parishioners as people streamed in from the mainland.

Families sat on blankets and straw mats spread out over the church's lawn, teenagers played a game of football at one end of the field, and toddlers splashed in a tin tub someone had set out in the grass. The ladies of the women's guild took turns manning the tables brimming with platters of deviled eggs, tuna and ham sandwiches, fried chicken, potato and coleslaw salads, and cookies and cakes of every kind. The menu of an Episcopal picnic lunch in Honolulu was not so very different from those I knew in Carlisle, except there were mangos instead of peaches, pineapple instead of apples.

I found the kitchen in disarray. In their haste to get the food out and onto tables after the morning service, the ladies had left empty baskets and containers strewn across the counter space, complicating my hunt for the potatoes. I had grabbed a bag from the countertop earlier and knew there was another, but it had disappeared. It occurred to me that perhaps Eleanor had tucked the second bag in the pantry. The pantry was nearly as much a mess as the counter surface. I was checking the cupboards when a group of women entered the main kitchen.

"Marilyn said there's more potato salad in her cooler. I'll grab that."

"Anyone know where the rest of the pies are?"

"I set them out on a table in the parish hall."

"Why were these cartons of eggs left sitting out?"

"For the relays. Eleanor made sure there were extras just in case."

"Of course she planned for that. She knows better than to trust Sadira to be on top of the details."

A knowing laughter followed.

"Poor Eleanor. She's such a dear to work with the Doyles. I swear she can put up with anyone." I recognized Margaret Cransten's voice.

"Sadie's not so bad as you all make out. You should give her a chance. She's really quite interesting." I couldn't place the soft, tentative voice of my defender.

"Thank you, no. I don't need her kind of interesting in my life. Since she took over writing that newspaper column, it's been nothing but trashy celebrity gossip. Not like the days when Madge Crawley wrote it. She had a sense of decorum."

"I heard Sarah Mason asked the paper to have someone cover the flower show's tea and Sadira refused to show up. Thought Mickey Rooney being in town was more important."

"All I can say is I feel sorry for those two kids. Imagine how embarrassing it must be to have a mother who's gallivanting about every night. I even feel a little sorry for poor old Archie. Barry says she henpecks him something awful. Why, today she's got him out there helping with the relays instead of letting him visit with the other men."

I imagined, in the silence that followed, an exchange of knowing looks and puckered lips. I was well past the point of being able to reveal my presence. There was nothing for it but to stay hidden and listen to their spiteful drivel.

"It's no wonder that older boy's so odd."

"You ask me, she's not only ruined the boy, she's ruined the husband. Archie's a sweet man. He wouldn't be a drunk if she were any kind of wife and mother."

"I hear she still associates with that woman who broke up the Bellingham's marriage."

"Father Horton wouldn't like us talking this way," the quiet voice offered.

"Oh, Lydie. You always try to see the good in people. Now give me a hand, hon, with these pies. I'm afraid I'll drop one." Lydie Jacobson. My defender. The mousy young woman whose timidity so irritated me.

"Sure thing. I'll grab these top ones. Anything else we need?"

"I think we're all set."

And then, as quickly as they'd come, they were gone. I leaned back against the shelves and unclenched my fists. No more, I decided. I was done with the church and its gossips. Apparently, Carlisle did not have a monopoly on small minds. Archie could attend services with the boys if he wanted, but I wouldn't set foot in that place again.

Lionel, age 9

Ever since we got here, Dad's been saying I should come to work with him sometime 'cause I'd see things that would "blow my socks off," except I hardly ever wear socks anymore. I think he was exaggerating. I wasn't so sure I wanted to go along to a funeral 'cause when Dad starts talking about what it takes to run a good one, he gets all red in the face and breathes hard, and Mom says, "There you go, Archie, talking yourself into a sinkhole of worry and distress." Mom thinks all a person has to do is decide to be happy and they will be, only I don't think she knows how really, really hard that can be for some people. Dad and I are alike that way. We can't think ourselves to happy the way Mom and Kenny can.

I finally did go to work with Dad on a day when there was no school and Mom had to interview an ambassador with a name I couldn't pronounce. Kenny went to his friend's house for the day and I went with Dad. It was my first Chinese funeral and just like Dad said, it was some different from how they do things back home. I can see how tough his job is, what with all the different people in Hawai'i doing things their own funny way. He says some funerals are just like back home. People wear black and sing hymns and the coffin gets put in the ground. But the Japanese and the Chinese and the Hawaiians and the Filipinos all have their own ways of doing things, and it's Dad's job to keep it all straight and give their loved ones a proper send-off and if something goes wrong, who knows? Maybe the loved one never makes it to heaven or wherever it is they're supposed to go and it'll all be Dad's fault. That's what happened at the Chinese one I went to. Some kid bounced a rubber ball down the mortuary steps and the worst thing possible happened and maybe all the evil spirits were set loose and now some poor guy might be doomed to walk the earth forever. Or something like that. I don't know exactly what the Chinese think happens when the body falls out of the coffin.

And it wasn't even Dad's fault. He didn't give the kid the rubber ball. Like Dad said, who gives a little kid a rubber ball to play with at a funeral? Everything had gone perfect up till then. He had the apartment next to the chapel all set up for the family the way it's supposed to be. There was a cook to feed everybody and make sure there was always food and hot tea by the dead guy. And when he and Hector, the guy who helps him, wheeled the coffin out of the apartment and into the chapel, they went really, really slow to make sure it didn't touch any part of the doorway. The priest made lots of noise on his horn to ward off the evil spirits, and the place was jammed full of people. Of course, it didn't help that there were so many people when it came time to leave the chapel, 'cause that's when the trouble started. The pallbearers were headed down the stairs that lead to the drive where the hearse was parked, and people were crowding out the two big doors. They all wanted to get out on the stairs to see them load up the coffin, and I don't know if the kid dropped the ball on purpose or because he got bumped or maybe he was just scared and let go of it without meaning to, but suddenly there was this red ball, the kind that bounces super high, bouncing off a step and hitting one of the pallbearers smack dab in the face. That scared him something awful and he dropped his grip on the casket and started falling, which made the guy below him trip, and then it was just like dominos falling and the casket was sliding down the steps with the guys still trying to hold on, but it flipped over and though the whole body didn't fall out when the locks popped open, an arm did fall out. It didn't come off the body, but it was hanging there so everybody close by could see it, and the widow screamed and other women started screaming and at least one lady fainted. Dad and Hector dove right for the coffin and got the arm back in so fast not that many people saw what happened, but it was enough 'cause the ones who saw were all the family people. The ones that weren't screaming and fainting helped get the coffin in the hearse real quick and then got all the family into the limousines, though lots of the family were some angry. The widow kept wailing and one of the sons was all red in the face and yelling at Dad and telling him that thanks to him, his father was cursed for all time. I wanted to say, "Don't blame him, blame the kid with the rubber ball and the pallbearer who didn't hang on," but I kept my trap shut 'cause I know that would have only made it worse. Dad says at times like that, people need someone to blame and that's his job—to be the one they blame. I can see why he sometimes hates his job.

People calmed down during the drive to the cemetery, or at least they were a lot quieter and stony-faced by the time they piled out of all the cars. I got to ride in the hearse between Hector and Dad. Dad tossed white confetti out the window the whole time we were driving there to help ward off the evil spirits, and he made sure to throw even more than usual just in case. I don't know if the family realized all he was doing to make sure the evil spirits wouldn't curse their loved one.

Once we were at the grave, he did exactly what he was supposed to do. He gave every guest a red paper envelope with a nickel in it, and every man got a cigar. The women and kids got pieces of candy. Dad even brought food and tea to put at the foot of the grave. An old woman was going to sit there till the gravediggers finished filling in the hole. When they were done, she'd give them the food and tea. I bet the gravediggers like the Chinese burials the best, what with the good food they get at the end, but I wouldn't like being the old lady who has to sit there after everyone's gone, just her and the dead guy in the ground.

"Think I'll have a job come Monday?" Dad asked Hector when we all piled back in the hearse.

Hector only shrugged. He doesn't say a lot. Dad doesn't know if that means he doesn't like Dad or if he just doesn't have an opinion.

Once Dad was done tidying things up back at the mortuary, we headed off to Stanley's Grill 'cause Dad needed a beer about as much as he'd ever needed one in his whole life. It took more than a few for him to be feeling better that night and he had to drive super slow all the way home to be sure he kept the car where it was supposed to be on the road.

"You kneel on the seat, Lionel," he told me, "and tell me if I'm steering wrong." So that's how we went home, with me leaning on the dashboard, watching for other cars and making sure Dad didn't drift into the other lane.

"Soon as your legs are long enough, I'll teach you to drive," he told me, "then you can take me home when I've had a few."

Mom was some angry when we got home 'cause Dad never called to tell her where we were or when we'd be home and no one was there to take care of Kenny, so he had to go stay with Mrs. Fong, and Mom came home early and didn't make all her usual rounds of the hotels.

Her voice was loud and her face nearly as red as Dad's. "I have a job, too, Arch," she said to Dad. "A job we need if we're going to pay for private school and to put food on the table."

Dad hates it when she says that. I think it makes him feel small and like he's not doing what he's supposed to do as the husband, and even though I know she's angry that he's screwed up again, I still feel bad for him. She talks as if he wakes up some days and decides to make her life miserable. I don't think it's like that. I think he drinks 'cause he hurts. He has a beer the way the rest of us might have an aspirin or a hot cocoa. When I get real sad or confused or worried, I want something to quiet my insides. That's all Dad's doing. Calming himself down. Only once he starts he can't stop and so he ends up making himself sadder, not happier. I wish I could wipe away the stuff that makes him hurt, so he wouldn't need that beer or that whiskey. Mom's like Grandma Prudence and the church ladies who think drinking's a sin and Dad's a sinner. I wish she could see all his good parts, then maybe he'd start believing in himself again. I try to tell him he's a good man and to not get down on himself, but when I say stuff like that, he just looks sadder and gets even more quiet. I know how bad it makes me feel when I do something I know isn't right. I bet sometimes after a bender, Dad wishes he could disappear and never have to face people again. Think how hard it is for him to go back to work, I tell Mom, but all she ever says is, "You're too young to understand, Lionel."

Sadira

I sat in a rocker on Ying's front porch, protected from the afternoon sun. The boys would be home from school soon. There would be the supervising of Lionel's homework and preparation of an early supper before I left for work, but I had a few moments to linger. That day, Ying had appeared at my kitchen door dangling a branch of lychees.

"Come try these," she said in a tone that was as much order as invitation. I obeyed, setting aside the letter I was writing to Elma.

I peeled away the crusty red shell of a lychee and tossed it in the cardboard box Ying set up as a discard pile, then bit into the sweet white flesh, separating it from the dark seed with my teeth.

"These are addictive."

"And 'ono for pūpūs. You stuff them with chutney or guava jelly and maybe a macadamia nut."

"I'll give that a try if I ever entertain again." I couldn't imagine squeezing people into our tiny space. Besides, we didn't exactly have a crowd of friends. "Next time Renee stops by, I'll be sure to serve her some. Which reminds me, she wants you to introduce her to a Chinese medicine doctor."

Ying smiled. "That wahine will try anything."

"Yesterday she introduced me to the 'real' downtown Honolulu. As if she's some kind of kama'āina now that she's with Harrison. One stop was a Buddhist temple, about the least likely place I could imagine her going. She was a regular mynah bird. Wouldn't shut up. She bombarded some poor woman with endless questions. 'Why do you clap three times? What are these beads for? What kinds of things can I pray for?' The woman was impeccably polite, but it was painful to watch."

"More painful for you, maybe, than the woman?"

I was on to Ying's pattern of conversation. I would complain. She would counter with some pithy insight meant to open my eyes.

"Maybe. I liked how quiet and peaceful it was there. A real retreat from the world. It's the one right next door to Auntie Malia's mu'umu'u shop. Even the sound of the sewing machines was calming. But I couldn't really enjoy it with Renee yakking at full volume."

Ying leaned in closer and placed a hand on my knee. "Be patient. She's akamai, that one. She pays attention and she's good for you. She'll keep your spirit light. You get so serious all the time."

I groaned. "If she doesn't wear me out. After that she took me to the park by the river. The one where the Chinese ladies do their exercises."

"Hah!" Ying was clearly pleased. "Did she join in?"

I nodded, confused. I'd thought Ying would disapprove. It seemed to me the height of rudeness for Renee to participate uninvited in another culture's customs, as disrespectful as the tourists taking hula lessons on the beach.

"You think that's OK?" I said. "You don't find it offensive?"

"Renee doing tai chi? How could that not be a good thing?"

As if for emphasis, Ying dug a nail into the skinned lychee she held, separated it from the seed in one swift motion, and popped it whole in her mouth. "You're the one who's all the time complaining about mainland haoles not trying local stuff."

"I know, but it's one thing to be curious about a culture and another to act as if you're a part of it. I was embarrassed watching her mimic their moves, as if she didn't have to bother learning to do it right." I threw another seed onto the pile. "Such arrogance."

Ying thought for a bit.

"Maybe it's like when I was in college. A roommate invited me to come stay at her house over spring break. Her parents lived in Sacramento, so it wasn't far to go from Oakland. I tried hard to fit in. I went along to their church and did everything they did: stood up, knelt down, sat still, read from the books in the pews. I was like a little monkey copying them, but I didn't understand why we were up and down so much or what it meant."

"Exactly. It becomes meaningless."

"All the same," she continued, "it was good I tried to fit in. They appreciated my effort. And it's good Renee tries. Better than the haoles who want everyone here to act like them 'cause they think their ways are better. You're not like that." She studied me. "You never say the mainland way is better. You never even talk about your mainland home."

"That's because Hawai'i is my true home. I knew even before we got here that this was where I belong."

"There's nothing you miss?"

I missed Elma. I didn't understand or like those feelings, but I felt her absence whenever life got scary and felt more than I could manage. I didn't miss anything else about the town, not the snow or ice or gossip.

"Crisp apples," I finally said. "The ones here are mushy. And berries. All kinds of berries. We picked them right off the bushes in our yard. But that's not enough reason to want to go back."

"When I was on the mainland, everything felt *kapakahi*," Ying said. "All the time, I had to stay alert otherwise I might mess up. Use the wrong fork at dinner, wear the wrong kind of clothes or say something local-style instead of talking standard English. My brain got tired. Your brain doesn't get tired like that?"

"I suppose it does sometimes. But it also feels like it's woken up. Knowing exactly what every day of the rest of your life will look like is deadening. Nothing surprising was ever going to happen there. Here most everything is new. Even if what happens is bad, it's still proof I'm alive and my life can change. It doesn't hurt that Hawai'i is the most beautiful place on the planet. When I think of Carlisle, all I picture is a faded, gray town full of sleepwalkers."

"Yet that town made you." Ying spoke softly, as if speaking to herself more than to me. "I think maybe you can't even see how much of it is inside you."

I groaned. "For someone who pretends she's so tough, you're sure romantic. The only influence Carlisle had was to make me want to leave." I stood. "Enough talking story. I have to get ready for the boys. Want me to dump all this debris in the trash?" I motioned at the pile of shells and seeds.

Ying waved me off. "No, you go. I'm not *pau* yet."

As I set the table for Archie and the boys' dinner, I thought about what she'd said.

"As if she knows me better than I know myself," I grumbled as I folded napkins. I was nothing like the other people in Carlisle.

A water rat, nearly cat-sized, scurried up the coconut tree outside the kitchen window. I shuddered as it disappeared into the canopy above. *Good try, Ying. Your water rats and monster cockroaches won't change my mind. I have found my paradise.*

I called out, "Supper's ready, guys," and began ladling stew over bowls of steaming rice.

Lionel

I jumped because I thought I could fly. The wind blows so hard at the Pali's top, I was sure it would lift me off my feet. The fields at the bottom are like velvet blankets and I wanted to glide all the way down to them. Everybody thinks I jumped 'cause I was sad and wanted to smash myself to smithereens. Sometimes I do want to stop hurting so much inside, but not that day. That day I wanted to fly like the birds do, zigzag back and forth and change direction just by turning my body until the wind dropped me on the ground. Dad knew as soon as I put out my arms what I wanted to do and he yelled, "No, no, Lionel. Don't," and I knew he was running at me, so instead of waiting for the wind to lift me up the way I thought it would, I helped it by running fast and jumping. It was blowing such a blast of air I thought it would pull my skin clear off my face, but I guess that still wasn't strong enough to make me fly. Instead of gliding down to the valley, I fell onto a part of the cliff below that sticks out. It wasn't super far, but it still hurt bad when I hit the rocks. And then I was right on the edge and it was so narrow I couldn't stand up, and straight down below me was the bottom of the cliff and lots of boulders and things that would have killed me for sure if I rolled off. That was the only time I got scared, when I looked down and there was just the cliff going straight down and the grass and bushes far, far away at the bottom. Kenny was crying and Dad was yelling, "Go get help, Sadie, go get help." I don't remember anything after that part until I woke up in the ambulance and Dad was beside me, holding my hand, and then I went back to sleep and woke up in Queen's Hospital, where I had to stay for a couple weeks and eat crummy food with no taste and practice using a crutch for my broken leg. They made me talk to a doctor who kept asking me why I jumped and if I want to die, and I knew if I told him sometimes I do want to die that he might make me stay there forever, so I lied and said no, I never wanted to die. I even told him I was happy and liked my new school and had lots of friends, which are big fat lies except I sort of do have a friend at the new school and I like it better there than at the old school. Jerry Takahashi lives one block away from us and he invites me to his house where we make fake teeth in his dad's shop 'cause his dad's a dentist, and his mom gives us cookies and guava juice and when it's time for me to leave, they say, "Come again any time, Lionel," so I do have one friend, but only one not lots. And I only kind of like him 'cause he isn't mean to me. He doesn't care anything about planes and ships and trains though. The kids at the new school leave Jerry and me alone pretty much 'cause Father Wilson keeps a close eye on the bullies and the cheaters. That's why it's better to be there than the old school. What would be best of all would be to fly off the Pali lookout and glide over Kailua all the way to the beach. But Mom and Dad and the doctor say that will never happen. I will always drop to the ground and die. Now when we drive over the Pali, Dad doesn't stop the car at the lookout, he just stays on the winding road that goes back and forth and back and forth along the mountain's side until we come to the bottom.

Sadira

A ranch hand swung wide the gate for the horses and we rode through, Noelani in the lead. Though a thin band of sunlight grew on the horizon, it was difficult to distinguish the dirt road from the open fields. The horses knew the way, but we took it slow.

Noelani said little before we set out, and it was clear from her manner that silence, or something near to it, was called for. The rush of the wind off the ocean and the steady clop of the horses' shoes striking packed dirt were our only accompaniment.

Arch opted out of joining us, not wanting to leave the boys alone in our small cabin tucked off by itself beneath a grove of eucalyptus trees. That was fine with me, as I preferred the chance to be alone with Noelani, even as I was unsure what to make of her. She had been polite in her welcome the afternoon before, showing us around the working ranch that doubled as an inn, but there was also a quality of reserve I rarely encountered in Hawaiʻi. I sensed she found me wanting, and I needed to figure out why. She was the reason we were staying at Kahawai Ranch and Lodgings.

"You'll learn from her," Ying told me when she suggested we book a weekend visit. "She knows the ancient Hawaiian ways." Ying implied Noelani would be open to teaching me, that she would sense I had an affinity with the spiritual world. A gift worth nurturing.

The trek to the ranch was a long one by Oʻahu standards. First the climb over the Pali and then the winding road through Kailua and Kāneʻohe, past Kahaluʻu and Waikāne to the valley tucked behind a wide swath of open shoreline. The ranch acreage stretched from beach to mountain, divided only by the coastal road. Its working buildings and lodge were sheltered up on the cooler slopes amid the eucalyptus forest. The main family house enjoyed a private section of beachfront. A separate stretch complete with pavilion provided lodgers a private oasis for sunning, swimming, sailing, or canoeing. It was one of Oʻahu's better-kept secrets. Most vacationers were locals.

Besides wanting a chance to connect with Noelani, I was eager for a dawn ride along the beach. Hawaiʻi's sunrises, as famed for their spectacular colors as its sunsets, eluded those of us on the leeward side.

A rustling in the tall grasses startled me. A large bird rose, its enormous wings falling and rising heavily. We pulled up and watched as it flew high, the underside of its wings a spot of white in the dim light. It circled as if in dance, then plunged to earth, sweeping over the fields, and then up again.

"*Pueo*," Noelani said, her voice soft as a prayer. "Owl," she translated. "Our sacred guide and protector. They nest in these grasses."

The owl circled wide again, dropped low as if taking aim, and flew straight at us. I ducked, arms over my head, but Noelani sat serene in her saddle, trusting it meant no harm. The great bird swept over us, circled once more, then disappeared into the cloud-shrouded mountains. We rode on in silence, my face hot with shame.

The sunrise was as spectacular as I'd imagined—an explosion of color across sky and sea, but I no longer cared. I shivered in the harsh wind blowing off the ocean as we followed the shoreline to the property's edge, turned, and retraced our steps, the horse's hooves sinking in the wet sand.

"Ying tells me you are one who can see what lies in the future," Noelani finally said. "Perhaps something like what we call a *kilo*."

"Sometimes. Not always," I answered, wary. "Nothing very specific, more a feeling of big emotions ahead. I'm surprised Ying mentioned it. She's not a fan of my reading tea leaves and cards."

The pinks and oranges streaking the sky had dissolved into a harsh white light that stung my eyes.

"Ying respects and honors the spirits too much to toy with them," she said.

Strike two. Clearly, nothing I said or did was going to earn this woman's respect or trust. I decided to be blunt.

"I'm confused, frankly, as to why Ying sent me to you. She said you possess great wisdom and knowledge of ancient Hawaiian practices. Wisdom you might be willing to share with me."

"Ying's a generous woman," was all she said, and I understood the door was closed. I was unworthy in some way.

The return ride was tedious. Where curiosity and anticipation had stirred me earlier, there was now only my indignation. We rode through clouds of dust, the morning sun harsh against my back. We parted in silence.

I headed straight to the lodge for breakfast, where I found the boys and Arch finishing their meal. Kenny was eager to get to the beach, and Lionel was trying to screw up his nerve to get on a horse.

"You can do this, buddy," Arch was saying. "Sitting up there, holding the reins, you'll feel just like Will Rogers or the Lone Ranger."

Lionel's face settled into what was becoming a familiar expression, the one he wore each morning as he headed off to school and any other time he faced a situation he feared. "The epitome of courage," was how Headmaster Wilson described it.

Courage wasn't the word I'd use. His expressions of suffering smacked of the histrionic, a tendency reinforced by Father Wilson and Archie's indulgence. He had scared the bejesus out of us with his attention-seeking stunt at the Pali lookout. Pure melodrama. I wasn't going to encourage any more of that behavior.

"How about me? You promised I could go swimming." Kenny kicked a leg of the table.

Through the large plate-glass window I watched Noelani calm a skittish mare.

"Tell you what, Kenny," Arch said. "If you stop whining, I bet Mom will take you down to the beach after she finishes her breakfast. Till then you can check out the horses with Lionel and me."

When Lionel protested, Arch put up his hand. "I know. You don't want to get on a horse. Let's at least go and meet them before we decide for sure, OK?"

Archie looked to me for confirmation. "Sure. I'll take you down to the beach, Kenny." Whatever made them all happy.

I spread the day's *Chronicle* before me and dug in to a stack of pancakes, but my attention continued to be drawn outside to Noelani and Lionel. She showed him how to stroke the horse's head, and though he was tentative, Lionel gave it a try. She then offered him her hand. Lionel had only ever allowed two people besides Archie and me to take his hand—Elma and Renee—but he took Noelani's without hesitation and together they led the horse back to the barn.

I turned my attention to breakfast and the paper, trying to focus on the morning's headlines as I ate, but the words jumped around and smeared. Chalky lumps of pancake caught in my throat. Not trusting my hand to raise the coffee cup to my lips, I placed both palms flat on the table surface and waited. I knew the internal storm would pass, as my storms always passed. It only required time and that capacity Lionel lacked—willpower.

By the time I finished my meal I had determined there was no reason to stay another night. By noon Lionel's ride would be done and Kenny would need a break from the sun. I set off to let the front desk and Archie know we would check out that afternoon. I would not stay where I was not welcome.

Chapter Six

September to December 1938

Sadira

"I wish for once you'd put me and the boys first. The world will not end if you aren't there to report what hotshot's dancing with what bimbo after midnight."

Archie slapped his palm against the kitchen table as if his red face and volume weren't sufficient punctuation. An orange rolled to the table's edge, wobbled, and fell to the floor. I nudged it with my big toe.

"Seriously?" I finally asked, raising my eyes to stare across the table at him. "You've the audacity to suggest I don't put you and the boys first?"

I watched Archie retreat before my eyes, as I knew he would. All I ever had to do was push back even a little and he caved immediately. So weak. I resisted screaming: *For once, be a man and stand by what you say. If you're angry, be angry. Fight whatever battle you need to wage.* I picked up the orange and began peeling it.

"I know, I know," he muttered. "It's just, it's just . . ."

"It's just what, Archie? Is it just that you want me here to fix your dinner? That you want me to make sure the boys do their homework, take their baths, brush their teeth? I would love to do all that, only I've got a job. If we're going to have food to eat and a place to live, I have to go out and earn a living."

He shriveled.

"And someone has to take care of things here. Unless you've got another plan, that leaves you to manage the home front."

Why not just shoot him, I thought, seeing the emptiness in his eyes, the slump in his shoulders. It would be more compassionate. And I resented him all the more for his effect on me, for letting me chip away at him until I was more monster than woman.

"I've got to dress." I tossed the skinned orange on the counter and headed to the bedroom.

It wasn't my fault Archie went and lost his job. Again. The first time he went on a tear and didn't show up to work for two days, Vernon canned him but caved two weeks later, rehiring him when the workload became untenable. Vernon might be a soft touch, but in the end, even he couldn't tolerate the drinking on the job. Arch couldn't even write a new script for the ways he failed. When Vernon called to let me know he'd fired Archie, he apologized.

"I hated doing it, Sadie. I love the guy and my heart aches for you all, but I can't risk it."

I couldn't summon any outrage on Archie's behalf. I didn't blame Vernon. He'd tolerated more than others before him.

"I promise to see what I can do," he said before hanging up. "I'll put in a good word with some of the guys downtown. I bet he'd be great at sales. You'll see. He'll land on his feet. It's all going to be OK."

I played nice with Vernon, gave him the reassurance he needed that he wasn't the bad guy here. "I appreciate all you've done, Vern. You've been a good friend to us all. And you're right. Arch will be fine. It will all be fine."

As I clipped on my earrings, I noted the way my eyelids drooped and how dark the circles were beneath them. "Not going to be turning any heads tonight, lady," I told my reflection. That was all right. The night ahead was all about the ladies. Only an Italian princess and an opera singer were in town. No male celebrities to flatter and charm. I plumped my hair, rubbed lipstick off my front tooth, and practiced my smile. "The show must go on."

My purse tucked under my arm, white gloves in hand, I slipped into the boys' room.

"I'm headed off to work, guys." I kissed Kenny on the forehead. "Night, love. Be good."

Lionel didn't look up from the book in his lap.

"Get a new one at the library?" Archie had taken the boys to the library that morning so I could sleep in.

Lionel showed me the cover. *The United States Navy in the Great War.* "It's got amazing pictures." He paged ahead and turned the book for me to see. "Even some of the planes."

"Pretty nifty." I checked my watch. "Lights out in half an hour, guys. Ying's home if you need anything."

"OK," Lionel answered without looking up.

At least he was doing better socially, now that he was excelling at school. At Maunalani the other boys respected academic success. In Carlisle and at the public school in Honolulu, he had been ridiculed for knowing the answers to the teachers' questions and for showing off what he knew. His natural interest and skill in acquiring information were serving him well in the more competitive private school, especially as he moved up in grade levels. The problem now was how to pay the tuition with only one paycheck coming in. It might be time to talk again with Ying. A few months back, she'd asked if I would write ad copy in my spare time. What spare time, I'd answered playfully. Perhaps, if Ying was still interested, I could find a way to squeeze in the time.

"I'm just dandy," I said. "Really."

"You don't look it." Ying filled a glass with iced tea and handed it to me.

"I've been working all day, woman. What do you expect?" I drank deeply from the glass. I'd spent the morning pruning back the honeysuckle and oleander bushes crowding our front porch and was drenched in sweat. I looked over at Ying, who was, as always, unruffled and cool as the glass I pressed to my face. "We haoles sweat."

"I've noticed."

I dipped my fingers in my tea and flung droplets in her direction. "It's not human to never perspire."

"Stop changing the subject. You need help. I have an idea."

"Of course you do."

"First thing, you need to hire a girl to help out. I know a university student who needs a place to live."

"Nice idea, but how are we supposed to squeeze in another person? The boys are sharing a room as it is."

Ying nodded toward the cottage adjacent to ours. "She could stay there."

"I suppose you'd want rent? We can't afford to rent two places."

"*Auwē*, let a woman finish." Ying took a long, deep swallow from her own glass of tea as I let the condensation from mine drip onto my chest. Even in the shade of Ying's back *lanai*, my body would not cool down. Thick, sweltering Kona air enveloped the island. "It's time you brought your mother here. She could share the cottage with the student. Maybe open up a sewing shop right there in the living room. She can help watch the boys."

Here were those tears again. With our circumstances so dicey, Ying's generosity unglued me. I felt the wet glass slipping in my fingers and set it on the table.

The week before I'd stood frozen before Liberty House's Christmas display. Beneath a midnight-blue ceiling with twinkling stars sat a white church steeple and tiny lit houses surrounded by cottony snow banks. Soap flakes fell as three golden Christmas bells on large gilded ropes swayed, chiming softly. When I stepped into the store, the unexpected, pungent odor of real pine overwhelmed me and, for a moment, the glistening balls of the store's towering tree blurred. I hadn't expected to ever miss home, let alone shed tears. I didn't like these signs of weak sentimentality.

"You would have two women to manage at home, so you could work even more. Plenty of money for rent."

"You saying I don't work hard enough?"

She shrugged, said, "Not too bad for a mainland haole," and smiled.

I knew Ying didn't think I was a slouch. She respected me for all I did to support my family. She was nothing like the busybodies at church and back home. But she set a high bar.

The very idea of having Elma next door, of having two others to help keep our home orderly and the boys safe, provided an unexpected flood of relief. I hadn't realized how much life weighed on me and how overwhelmed I felt. Even the news of Archie starting a new job hadn't eased my worry. He would be traveling to Maui, Kaua'i, Moloka'i, and the Big Island, leaving me with even less support. And odds were, he wouldn't last long at whatever he did.

I nodded. "That would help. How much is it going to cost me?" I expected no favors from Ying when it came to business.

"We'll figure something out until you can pay rent. Maybe the girl helps with my cleaning and your mother sews for me. Maybe you help me with my business. I promise—no charity."

I reached over and tried to hug her, but she stiffened.

"All the time, you have so little dignity." Ying dismissed me with a sweeping hand. "Go now and let me get some work done."

"You don't fool me for a second, Ying Fong. You're a soft touch under that iron façade."

I skipped down the porch steps and called back over my shoulder, "I owe you."

"You most certainly do."

Lionel, age 10

I betcha Gran Schaeffer's going to be some pleased when she gets Mom's letter asking her to come live with us. It's not like it'll be a total surprise 'cause they were talking about her coming even before we left Carlisle, but I don't think Gran was thinking about coming this soon. Back home, she told Mom, "Let's wait and see how you all settle in down there"—she was always talking like Hawai'i was at the bottom of the world. "See if you end up liking it enough to put down roots," is what she said, like we were some kind of plants. I guess Mom feels pretty rooted now 'cause she talks like she might never go back to Carlisle, not even just to visit and see old friends. I don't think she's missed one single thing about it, not like me and Dad who get pretty homesick for things like old Harker MacKenzie singing "Bye Bye Blackbird" at Clive's bar after he's had a few too many, or the smell of bread baking when you pass by the Sweet Treats Bakery in the morning.

But after Dad got fired from the mortuary, Mom got more and more jumpy, so jumpy she couldn't keep her hands still and she peeled the skin off her lips so much they bled sometimes. She was all the time writing lists for Dad, telling him what needed to get done, and he was all the time telling us to keep super quiet. "Not a peep," he'd say in the morning before we went to school, so Mom could sleep in. Now that he's going to be gone on the ferry to the other islands lots of the time, Mom needs someone else to keep us quiet.

"Don't be getting all excited," Mom said when she told me she was writing to Gran. "It's not like she's going to hop on the next boat that's headed this way." I know Gran'll have lots to do before she can even think of coming here. She has to sell the house, pack up all her belongings. Mom says it could be a year, maybe two or more, but I sure hope it doesn't take that long. We could use some help calming things down here right now. Gran is good at making things be the way they should be.

It's winter back in Carlisle now. I bet the day Gran gets Mom's letter it'll be snowing or sleeting and the ground will be so icy, she'll be worried about the mailman falling on the walkway. She'll tuck her sweater tight around her when she opens the door to get the mail and will get all glowy when she sees the thin blue letter from Mom. I know

Gran. She won't rip it open and read it right off. She'll go make herself a pot of tea and set the table as if she's having people over. She does that all the time, even if it's only her sitting there. "We don't have to live like savages just because we're alone," she used to tell me. "If I put out the china and linens for company, why wouldn't I do the same for myself?" She'll sit down at the kitchen table, her teapot with the painted pink roses set in front of her, and use a paring knife to slice the letter open. Then she'll open up the letter and spread it out all neat and flat in front of her, careful not to get it near the tea or the cookies. She won't even hurry reading through it. She'll take her time. Sip her tea, take a bite of her cookie, then read some of the letter. "No sense racing through life's moments," she told me. "Slow down and enjoy what you are doing." She'd say that when me or Kenny was too quick to crunch down on a lollipop instead of taking our time licking it.

She's going to be some happy when she reads the part of Mom's letter that asks her to think about coming out this way. At least I hope she'll be happy. She might be nervous about how different it is here, the same way I was worried it would be nothing like home. And it is nothing like home, but that's OK. It's good in its own way. Maybe I can write her my own letter and let her know that she's got nothing to worry about. There may be no trains passing through or snow for making forts, but you don't have to rake up leaves here and the sky gets so full of color in the mornings and nights that it makes my insides hurt. I betcha she'll like it just fine.

Sadira

My hands trembled when I reread the letter from Elma. I set it down, rolled two sheets of paper with carbon into the typewriter, and began my column for the Carlisle paper. These days it was a challenge to find time to write for the people back home given my schedule with the *Chronicle*, and truth was, my enthusiasm for the enterprise had waned considerably. Carlisle felt as far away as the moon and just as alien, but this was one column I had to write. The words came swift and easy.

Dear Ones,

We are having quite the laugh here in Honolulu after hearing from my poor mother of rumors flying all about Carlisle. Apparently Archie has left me and the boys high and dry in order to live the glamorous life of a gambler and playboy in Australia. If it were not for our loved ones back in Carlisle who must listen to these ridiculous stories, I would not dignify such malicious gossip with a response. I trust that all who know us will know these tales are utterly false. I assure you Archie is very much with us here in Honolulu, thriving and happy as we all are now that we have found our true home. As to the claim that Archie was fired, let me just say that if following the advice of Honolulu's top business leaders to map out a better life plan with guaranteed prosperity and prestige and choosing to leave a job neither respected nor well compensated by the people of this city is equivalent to being fired, well then, yes, indeed, Archie was fired. In actuality, he has made the huge leap to an exciting business opportunity with one of Honolulu's big five companies and is busy touring the islands as part of its merchandising team. As you might imagine, Archie is well suited for this sales work. I think of how Chester Osborne used to say Archie was so smooth, he could sell a case of whiskey to Carrie Nation. So, to Carlisle's expert female broadcaster who aired the news that Archie Doyle had been shown the door, let me just say, I hope you realize how terribly amateurish your efforts were and that you will sign off from spreading such hateful gossip in the future.

"Old biddy," I muttered, as I typed the last word. I suspected it was

Prudence spreading these horrid stories. Archie disagreed.

Whoever the gossip was, she'd confirmed how right we were to escape Carlisle.

I pulled the paper from the typewriter, folded and placed the first sheet in an envelope, then placed it in the pile of outgoing mail. Archie might be the bane of my existence, but I was damned if I was going to let anyone else speak ill of him.

"Why do we have to bother with calendars," Kenny whined.

I stood, pen in hand, beside the giant calendar hanging on a kitchen cupboard. I was mapping out the rest of the week with the boys.

"To make sure we keep track of our schedules." I looked over what was already written down for the coming week. "I don't know why you're complaining. You've got nothing but fun stuff up here so far."

Kenny lay his head on the kitchen table. "I don't care. There's still school and too many days till Dad's home."

I hadn't anticipated the boys missing Archie. He would only be gone for a week or two at a time, but I should have realized that for someone as young as Kenny, a week might as well be a month.

"It'll go by fast, lamb. Dad'll be home before you know it." I turned back to the calendar. "Now let's go over this day by day. Piano lesson tomorrow, Lionel."

Lionel nodded without looking up from the book he was reading while he ate his supper.

"And you've got your drawing class at the Academy on Wednesday, Kenny. You can walk over from school by yourself and then home afterward. I'll make sure Ying will be around when you get home. I've got an afternoon concert I need to cover that day."

I ran through the four remaining days and made a list of times to confirm with Ying that she would be home to keep an eye on things. In many ways I thought life might be easier with Archie away so much. Whatever worries I had about the boys getting into trouble were nothing compared to Archie's brand of nuisance. With careful planning, I could make this work.

"Tell you what. Let's wash up the dishes real quick and go see *Just Around the Corner*." I knew the boys were eager to see Shirley Temple in her latest film. Even Lionel had become a fan after meeting her, despite his professed disinterest when she was visiting.

"On a school night? Really?" Kenny jumped up and began clearing the table.

"Sure thing." It was good to see his dark mood lift. "How about you, mister?" I asked Lionel, whose eyes were still glued to his book.

He grunted and shrugged.

"Stay home then, gloomy Gus," I snapped and immediately regretted it.

"Fine. I will." He slammed his book shut and pushed his chair back so hard it squealed against the linoleum.

I knew I should make him clear his dishes, remind him to show some respect, but I couldn't face a battle. Not when I was trying to cheer them both up. I let him stomp off to his room. Just like his father. Would he spend his life swinging between highs and lows, one minute rapturous over some new passion and the next wallowing in rage and despair?

"Not fair. Why doesn't he have to clean up," Kenny muttered. He stood at the sink rinsing his own dishes.

"I know, I know." I gathered up Lionel's plate and glass. "Life's not fair, love. Soon enough you'll be the moody one wanting nothing to do with me, and we will all be tiptoeing around your storms."

"That'll never happen, Mom. Not ever."

I bumped a hip against him as I placed the dirty dishes in the sink. "OK, punkin'. I believe you. Now let's get these dishes done so we don't miss the music and news reels."

Lionel appeared in the doorway, his eyes avoiding mine. "I'll do my dishes, Mom."

"Terrific." I moved away from the sink. "Come with us to the movie, too?"

He shrugged. "I guess."

Eggshells, I thought, drying my hands on the dishtowel. My life is nothing but a landscape of broken eggshells.

Lionel

I don't think Dad's all that happy about his new job. He tells us it's great, but his eyes don't look happy when he says it. They look scared. I was scared the day he left for his first trip to the Big Island, scared of all kinds of things like would the ferry be OK going through the Moloka'i channel and would he be able to find his way around an island he didn't know with no familiar faces to help him?

We all went down to the dock to see him off. We don't do that anymore, now that he's gone on so many trips, but it was a big deal the first time. Mom made him a sack of food and Kenny and me even made him a couple leis. We didn't go on board, but we stayed to watch them load the car onto the ferry and then decided to stay and see the boat off. It made my heart hurt to stand on the pier and see Dad up above waving at us and then getting smaller and smaller as the ferry pulled away.

"Careful about that lounge," Mom had said to him as she gave him a goodbye hug, and he said, "I know, Sadie, I know," and I could tell he didn't like her reminding him what he already knew. Sometimes Mom acts like she thinks Dad hasn't noticed all the bum times he's had 'cause of drinking. This time's going to be different. He promised me and Kenny, no more drinking. "I'm going to straighten up and make you boys proud," he told us.

I told him he didn't have to worry about me 'cause I was making an extra special way of keeping track of where he is and when he's coming home. I drew pictures of the ferries and liners that come into Honolulu harbor, then I cut them out and pasted them on cardboard. While we were seeing Dad off, I picked up the schedules for all the ferries and all the liners. Back at home I made a big chart of when and where each one arrives and departs. It's posted on my bedroom wall, alongside a big map of all the islands. Every morning, I move the ferries and ships to the places they'll be that day. That way I can start my day saying, "Today, Dad will sail into Kahului," or, "Dad will spend tonight in Kona," or best of all, "Tomorrow Dad will be home." If it's a ship day and one of the big liners is due in, I put up a bright yellow flag on my bedpost and sometimes I can get Mom to take me down to the pier to watch them tow it in.

The night after Dad left the first time, Mom took us to the movies. I think she was trying to make us less sad or maybe she was trying to make herself less sad. We went to the Waikiki Theatre, which is one of my favorite places in the whole world. It has all those white steps that look like they lead up to a Greek or Roman temple and I like to pretend I'm Caesar or Nero when I get to the top and I pretend Cleopatra is coming or maybe the city is burning or maybe all the people down below want to worship me.

Mom stopped to talk to some friends and told me to go ahead by myself, so that night I pretended I was returning from battle and everyone was yelling, "Hail, Caesar!" as I passed by. I kept my shoulders super straight and my chin tipped up, like an emperor would.

A real Roman temple wouldn't have a water fountain like the one at the theater. Kenny likes the fountain best and would splash around in it if he could, only it's not like the one at the water supply where we used to go as little kids sometimes when it was hot. They don't mind if you take off your shoes and get in to splash around in that one, but you're not supposed to do that at the theater.

I really like it inside the theater, too. They've got pretend clouds in the ceiling and twinkling stars, so when you look up, it's like you're outside at night. There's a giant rainbow that goes over the top of the movie screen and they have coconut trees and banana trees and all kinds of other pretend plants along the sides, so you feel like you're sitting in a Hawaiian jungle. It's swell. I bet in the whole world, there's no movie theater as good.

Mom gave me and Kenny a whole dime each that night and said we could buy whatever we wanted. She never does that. Maybe a nickel each, but never a whole dime. It took us a long time to decide what to get, so long that we barely got to our seats before the lights went off. It was a night to remember, that's for sure.

Dad did OK, too, though I didn't tell him what a great time we had while he was gone. I didn't want him to feel bad.

"You woulda been proud of your old man," he told me when he got back from that first trip. "I didn't even go near the ferry's lounge on either passage, just hid away in my cabin and read my book."

"Good for you, Pop," I said, and I was real proud of him 'cause I know how much he likes to meet new people and share some stories. He must have been real lonesome down in his cabin.

"Piece of cake," is what he told Mom when she asked how the selling had gone. "Nothing to it. The store managers know what they want and most of them have their order sheets all ready for me. Most of the time, we were just talking story, getting to know one another."

"Well, no one talks story better than you, Arch," she said and kissed him on the top of his head where he has no hair. I could tell she was some glad to have him back home, even if he was going to leave again in a couple days.

"Someday I'm taking you all along with me," he said as he handed out the souvenirs he brought back with him—postcards plus napkins and matches from the hotel where he stayed. He held up one of the postcards that had a picture of the island's coastline. "The Hāmākua Coast," he said. "This card doesn't do it justice. Most beautiful thing I've ever seen. Not a cloud in the sky the morning we arrived. Looked like someone had dumped a can of pink paint over it all, it was so rosy in the early light. And waterfalls! My Lord, I couldn't count them all. Water rushing down those sheer green cliffs. It was something marvelous to behold. There's a train runs right along the coastline. Someday I'll take you all with me so we can ride that train."

"That'd be swell, Dad," I said, 'cause I knew he was saying that for me. I'm the one who does trains.

Chapter Seven

February 1939

Sadira

Judging from the photographs, I thought challenger Otis Cook was by far the handsomer of the two men, but the crowd gathered at Honolulu's Civic Auditorium wasn't there to pick the best-looking man. They were there to see heavyweight champ Micky Byrne annihilate the upstart.

I couldn't have cared less which man won. I was there, my thighs pinched by the slats of a wooden folding chair, only because Ben Fox had told me to be there. He wanted the human angle. "Anybody can report the fight details," he said, "but I need the stuff the women will read." Apparently, Byrne was more than a sports figure; he was a full-fledged celebrity, which plopped him in my territory.

Archie and the boys were thrilled to tag along, so I could at least make a family outing of it. With Archie away so much, there was little opportunity to do things as a family. From across the ring, I could see Jack O'Brien sizing up the crowd. I caught his eye and waved. Slowly, he made his way to us.

"You boys introducing your mom to the world of boxing?"

"Nah. She doesn't care anything at all about any of this," Lionel said without so much as a glance in Jack's direction. He wasn't about to risk missing a single detail. "Betcha she writes about the color of their trunks and the way they wave at the crowd and doesn't even mention how they throw a punch."

"She didn't even know how to spell Micky Byrne's name right," Kenny added.

"She better get that one figured out before she turns in her column. Good thing she's got you boys to keep things straight." Jack nodded in Archie's direction. "Hey, Arch. Been a while."

Archie smiled but quickly turned his attention back to the ring.

"Seriously. Do you have any idea what you're in for tonight?" Jack asked, crouching down beside me.

"You worried I'll faint at the sight of blood? Get the vapors when the sweat starts flying?"

Jack stood. "OK, tough lady. I forget you're made of iron. Have at it. We can compare notes later."

"Hey, before you go. What are you putting the crowd size at?"

Jack smirked. "My gallantry's been rebuffed. I'm done being Mr. Nice Guy. Find your own stats."

I shrugged. "Fine. But don't expect any help when you need to know who designed those fancy robes they wear."

A roar from the crowd drew my attention back to the center aisle and Cook's entrance. Flashbulbs popped and the crowd flanking the aisle stood and leaned in for a closer look as he pounded past. I shivered, perhaps in response to the frenzied emotion around me, or maybe it was the sense of impending violence. The crowd's raw energy excited rather than repulsed me. Cook himself added to the sense of danger, with his sheer mass and the way he taunted the fans with his swagger as he barreled toward the ring.

Another roar, and it was Micky Byrne strutting down the aisle, waving to the crowd, relaxed and confident. The roar for him was thunderous. The entire arena was on its feet. My own boys were jumping up and down and hooting. He had star power, I had to give him that. He reminded me of Renee in the way he seemed nearly luminous. I couldn't look away.

"That's the announcer, Mom," Kenny said, pointing to the small man in a dark suit who climbed into the ring and stood at its center, his hand grasping a microphone lowered from the ceiling. The boxers waved at the crowd from their corners opposite one another.

The announcer gave the fighters' weights and introduced the judges, timekeeper, and refs. Finally, Micky and Otis were alone in the center bumping gloves, their shiny robes off, their mouth guards in, and their feet dancing. Because I had asked for four seats rather than one, I had to settle for being quite a ways back. This was fine with me. I had no interest in a close-up of the violence, but the distance made it difficult to read the expression on each man's face. Was either of them afraid or showing a glimmer of doubt? The bell rang and they began swinging. Cook hadn't a chance. In less than a minute, he was flat on the floor and out cold.

"That's it?" I said to Kenny. "All this for a few seconds of action?" I didn't get it. How was this entertainment?

Kenny shrugged. "It was fast 'cause he's the champ, Mom. Nobody's got a chance against him."

I agreed with Kenny. There was something special about this Micky Byrne. I'd always thought the cartoons silly when they showed women swooning at the sight of strong men, but my pulse was racing. Micky Byrne might prove a Neanderthal and complete bore, but he left me agitated and even a little breathless.

"Well, sports," Arch said, standing, "I guess we're done here. You heading down to Waikīkī, Sadie? I was thinking maybe I'd tag along. Wouldn't mind meeting the champ in person."

I gathered up my purse and wrap. "Yup. I best make an appearance since I can't really claim the fight took up the whole night. We've time enough to drop the boys at home."

"If you see Micky Byrne, Mom, could you ask him something for me?" Kenny asked as we made our way through the river of people headed for the exits.

"Sure thing, noodle. What is it?"

"Ask him how many eggs I should eat every day to build up my muscles? I'm thinking I should start adding them to my milk."

That was all I needed. Kenny deciding to be a boxer. Might as well remove his brain right now.

"We'll see," I said and gripped his hand tight as we pushed through the crowd.

Dropping the boys at home took forever and not just because Archie had to switch into his tux. Usually, the boys barely registered our absences, but that night Lionel insisted I write down all the phone numbers of where we might be and then led me through the entire house checking the locks on the windows and doors.

"You can always get Ying if you need help," I reminded him. Elma would be with us as soon as she sold her house, and a girl Ying knew named Kaiyo Watanabe would move in when she entered the university in the fall, but for the time being, Ying was all I had.

I didn't have time or patience for Lionel's fears. I needed to get to the Royal while there was still a chance of getting a quote from Byrne.

"Maybe I should stay home with them," Archie said when we finally closed the front door behind us and Lionel bolted it on the other side.

"Twenty minutes ago would have been the time to make that choice." I climbed into the car. "They'll be fine."

It wasn't as if the boys would be any safer if Archie were with them.

The Royal was packed by the time Archie and I arrived. We faced a mob at the entrance, but I wasn't going to let that be a problem. I pushed through the crowd clogging the hallway to the dining room. The maître d' waved us in. Arch drifted off in search of a waiter.

"Losing your edge, Doyle? I've been here nearly an hour." Jack was in his usual post beside a yawning passage out to the hotel's terrace. He preferred the periphery and its easy exits.

"Sometimes it's good not to appear too eager."

"Thanks for the tip." He lit a cigarette as I scanned the room. "If you're looking for Byrne, they've got a table up next to the orchestra."

"Careful. Keep being nice and you'll have me thinking you've got a real human heart beating in that cynical body of yours."

"Any heart I ever had shriveled up years ago. I'm not being nice. It just amuses me to watch you in action. You're always so damned earnest."

"Why are you here anyway? Not exactly your turf."

"I'm not sharing all my secrets, Doyle."

I went in search of the fighters. As I squeezed by people, I came face-to-face with Louise Hardwick. There was no getting past her. Louise turned her head, pretending not to see me though I was inches from her. That was not how I was going to play the scene, not when she was on my turf. I reached out and embraced her.

"Louise, darling. It's been ages." I squeezed her tight. "Where's Vernon? Have you two been away? We seem never to run into you!"

Louise wiggled out of my grasp but forced herself to smile. "Busy. We've been very busy."

"Well, don't be a stranger, dear. We simply must have lunch one of these days."

Damned if I was going to play the role of injured party to her queen. I knew Louise had spread the word around town that Vernon let Archie go because of his drinking. Vernon had been more gracious, supporting Archie's story that he was overqualified for the work, that he needed something more challenging to engage him.

"Sadira!" Harrison Bellingham called from the table closest to the stage. Micky Byrne and Otis Cook sat on either side of him. Leave it to Harrison to be at the center of the action. Reflexively, I looked for Renee. She was, of course, right behind Byrne.

"You've got an admirer," Renee said as we applied lipstick in the ladies' room.

I put a finger to my lips and scanned under the stalls for signs of others.

The room was empty but for the attendant seated nearby who appeared engrossed in a copy of the *Daily Mirror*.

"Don't be ridiculous." I tossed the lipstick back in my bag, powdered my nose, and refreshed my perfume. "He's a charmer accustomed to the spotlight. Flirting is part of his job description. I bet he couldn't tell you my name."

"I bet it's not your name he's interested in." Renee leaned closer. "I can tell you, he sure wasn't checking me out. As the song says, he only has eyes for you."

"Don't worry, punkin." I grinned at her in the mirror. "He's just playing it cool. You will always be every man's dream girl."

"I'm done with that gig. I found my guy." She held up her left hand and flashed a giant diamond ring. "I can't believe you didn't even notice."

I felt bad for being surprised, but I was. I figured Renee was nothing more than a fling for Bellingham.

"Congratulations. I hope it works out for you."

"Geez. You could show a little enthusiasm. Have some faith, why don'tcha? There are happy endings. Even for folks like me."

"I'm sorry if it came out wrong. I just imagine it could be a little complicated, what with Jacqueline and his family and all."

I also wondered if Renee was capable of the lifestyle she was choosing. Could she think before acting, consider Harrison's interests as well as her own? For that matter could she really give herself to one man alone? I admired her ability to ignore other people's opinions and live the way she wanted, but Harrison did not seem the man to marry if she wasn't ready to adapt to social conventions.

As we headed back to the dining room, I wondered if Renee was right. Did Micky really have eyes only for me? I liked the idea, absurd though it was. I'd have to be someone very different from who I thought I was to turn the head of a man like Micky Byrne. I'd need real star quality— the kind of charisma Renee had in buckets. But if Renee's sparkle came from confidence as well as beauty, maybe I could sparkle, too. I'd given it a try our first evening in Waikīkī, and though it began as an act, the act had become reality, at least for a short while. As Renee and I entered the Royal's dining room, I told myself I was the most stunning, enticing woman in the room. Micky Byrne adored me. All men adored me. I was as much a star as Micky was. And it seemed to work. Eyes turned my way. I could feel them follow me. I told myself it was me, not Renee, who mesmerized them. In return I blessed them with my dazzling smile, gazed back with twinkling eyes. An enchanted Byrne rose when I reached the table and offered me his chair. Pulling up another beside it, he let his knee rest against mine and held his face so close, the warmth of his breath washed over me.

Two drinks and a half hour later, Renee jumped up. "Time to dance, everybody," she cried and hauled Harrison to his feet. "Enough with all this fight talk. You, too," she said to Micky. "On your feet."

He turned to me. "So, pretty lady, how about we take a turn on the dance floor?"

He hasn't a clue what my name is, I thought, as he led me into the mass of dancers and pulled me to him, his chest against mine, close enough for me to feel his heart beat. Or that my husband was sitting on the other side of me. He didn't need to know my name or my marital status: I melted into him all the same. His hand, cool, dry, and immense, swallowed mine. He smelled of expensive cologne. Fresh and crisp. I felt Honolulu's elite watching us, knew Archie was as well. Or he had been. As we swirled past the large table where I'd left him, I saw his chair was empty.

"How did someone with looks like yours wind up in such a forgotten corner of the world?" Micky whispered.

"Forgotten? Are you nuts?" I bumped my hip against him playfully. "You have arrived in paradise, my friend." I didn't pull away when he let his hand rest on the small of my back, didn't resist when he pulled me more tightly against him.

"No kidding." His breath tickled my neck. "And I may have found my Eve."

It was only a game. An experiment to see if I could play the role. Renee always said flirtation was a form of power. Something every woman needed to be good at.

It was also a game that felt good. It worked better than any drink to lift me out of myself. I wondered if booze was like that for Archie. Did it push away the loneliness and fear? This was better though than alcohol. Alcohol couldn't make a person feel special and desired. The way Micky looked at me, held my gaze too long, the way his eyes adored my every word, was intoxicating in a way that woke rather than sedated me. Dangerous stuff, I thought, looking up at his firm chin, so unlike Archie's fleshy one.

I had no patience for sentimental nonsense like true love and soul mates. A visiting starlet smitten with an older, married movie star had once assured me that when you find the one person God chose for you, you must obey no matter the circumstances. I counted her a silly goose. I was too clear-eyed to believe such hogwash, but as we moved around that dance floor, I understood for the first time how an otherwise sensible person could slip into a state of absurdity and contemplate unthinkable, even personally destructive choices. My desire for the man felt ferocious and primitive. And very unfamiliar.

I knew I should step away, have nothing more to do with Byrne, but by the end of the night, he felt essential to my survival. This was no ordinary attraction. I was sure I was at last experiencing the transcendent blend of physical and spiritual love poets and lyricists write of. Most people only yearn for it, but in an instant I was swept into bliss. If the universe was providing me a rare glimpse of the divine, I decided I had no choice but to accept.

I let my head slip into place beneath his jaw and rest on the lapel of his white dinner jacket, my eyes closed, my lips nearly touching his neck, my entire body melding with his. Who was I to deny the gods' will?

Lionel, age 11

Nobody knows how those giant stones got there. They've been on the ledge since before there were trucks or machines to carry something so big and heavy, and they're on a straight up and down cliff.

"It's a mystery," Mom says. "Some things just can't be explained."

When we started hiking into the valley that day, Mom wouldn't tell us what we were looking for. She just said, "There's something special at the end of this valley. Keep your eyes open," so Kenny and I had to be patient and hold our horses. We would run ahead of Mom and Micky, thinking maybe the good thing was just around the corner, but then we'd get so far ahead we couldn't see or hear them, so I'd say, "Hold up, Kenny. We got ahead of ourselves. We gotta wait for them to catch up." Then we'd plop down on the path or, if we were by the stream, we'd stick our feet in the water and cool off.

To see the stones, we had to go to the very end of the valley and then climb a winding trail that went back and forth and back and forth till we were near the end of the trail at the top of a steep cliff. I don't like looking down from high up. Ever since I fell off the Pali, I haven't liked high places. "What are we looking for?" I asked. Mom said, "Look up." I looked up, but I still didn't get what the big deal was. All I could see were four giant boulders balanced on top of one another. "They're sacred stones," Mom said. "And no one can figure out how the Hawaiians got them up there." She also said it's *kapu* to go near them, so we could only look at them from far off. I guess it was some kind of amazing that those boulders are up there on a rock shelf, but I'm not sure it's worth a long hike to look at them. Mrs. Fong probably told Mom about the stones. She's the one who knows the most about Hawai'i's mysteries and stuff that happened a long time ago.

Mom was acting real goofy that day. She was laughing a lot and all the time punching Micky in the arm or saying stuff that sounded mean except they would both laugh when she said it. It made no sense. I know Dad couldn't help being away on Maui that week, but I felt bad for him.

He got cheated out of spending time with the champ. I bet he was some jealous we were spending so much time with Micky.

Dad seemed pretty sad about it when he got home 'cause all he wanted was for me to tell him how it was with Micky and what we did and did Kenny and me like him a whole lot. I told him Micky was an OK guy, but not so great as he's cracked up to be. Sometimes when we were out with Mom and Micky, it seemed like he forgot Kenny and me were there, like he was just another one of those grown-ups who act like they really like you at first, but then it turns out they were just being nice to seem like a good Joe.

I was glad to have Dad back home even if all he wanted to do was practice my baseball skills and ask questions. He thinks if he practices throwing and catching and hitting a ball with me, I'll become a good ball player, only I don't think all the practice in the world is going to help. All the guys want Kenny on their team 'cause he's a natural, but no one ever picks me. Kenny can hit hard enough to get a homer and forget him ever missing or dropping a catch. He's the best. Not like me. I can barely throw the ball across the plate.

"Leave him be, Arch," Mom says when Dad says it's time to practice, but Dad tells her, "Lionel's no quitter, Sadie. It might take him a bit longer to learn the sport, but he'll get there," only it seems like I don't ever get any better. Not even a little bit.

Even he gave up the day after he got back from Maui and I couldn't catch a single ball. He finally said, "Tell you what, let's go to the hobby shop instead and get those supplies you want." He was talking about supplies for the baseball game I invented. I figure if I can't play real baseball, I might as well play pretend, so I made up my very own baseball league in my head, but I needed to make a playing board and all the game materials so Kenny and I can play it.

"You go clean up and I'll take you downtown," Dad said, and I was about the happiest kid in the world. My pretend baseball game is all I ever think about in springtime.

I had to wash up at the kitchen sink 'cause Mom was in the bathroom taking a shower and singing "Somewhere Over the Rainbow" at the top of her lungs. She's still acting goofy sometimes and I can tell Dad doesn't like it. "Geez Louise, Sadie," he says. "Where's your mind at. We've got no butter in this house," or he reminds her that she left the milk out on the counter. Yesterday she forgot to bring the clothes in from the line and they got soaked in the afternoon rain, and he was some mad about that. "What am I supposed to wear tomorrow?" he kept yelling, but it was like she didn't even notice or care that he was upset. She just kept smiling as she shelled a bowl of peas, like she couldn't even hear him.

At least for a while Dad will be home nights, so I won't have to make sure Kenny does his homework and goes to bed on time. Kenny never listens to me, not even when I holler at him and tell him he's going to be in some trouble if he doesn't mind me and I have to go get Mrs. Fong to make him do what he's supposed to do. He just shrugs and says, "So go get her," then takes out his charcoal and pad and draws long past his bedtime. I think sometimes he's still up when Mom gets home. Not me. I can't stay awake that late. I try to stay up and read, but I always fall asleep and wake up the next day with my book under my arm or sometimes under my face and I have a big red mark across my cheek, which I hate, and that makes me start the day grumpy.

Micky heads back to the mainland soon and I'll be sad to say goodbye to him, but maybe life will get back to more regular with him gone. I like how jealous the kids at school are over me having Micky Byrne as a friend, but maybe Mom will stop forgetting stuff and life won't be so confusing.

Sadira

A white plumeria blossom dropped from the tree. Another followed, and then a handful. Lionel stood beneath the tree, paper bag in hand, trying to catch them before they hit ground.

"You aren't aiming for the bag," he complained, staring up into the tree's core.

I paused in my typing, watching through the kitchen's screen door. The upper leaves trembled. Kenny was climbing higher. I considered reminding him to avoid the smaller, weaker branches but, reluctant to lose my train of thought, I returned to my column.

> *Diners at the Royal last night were treated to the latest in Hollywood fashion, thanks to the lovely Jeanne LeMay who dazzled all with a shimmering gown that left little to the imagination. Color this writer envious not only of the way the frock flattered Miss LeMay's figure, but the way its sparkling baby-blue tones—*

The crack of a branch stopped my fingers. I looked up in time to see Kenny grab a lower branch to break his fall.

He's all right. Keep working. Let them figure it out.

"Mom," Lionel yelled. His slippers slapped against the back steps, and he pulled open the screen door. "Kenny climbed too high and broke a branch."

"Did he hurt himself?"

"Nah."

"Then why are we having this conversation?"

"He broke a branch."

"Better that than breaking his neck. I expect he won't climb that high again."

I let my fingers hover above the keys, Lionel's cue to leave me be. The boys knew the rules. When I was writing, there had to be blood or broken bones before they could interrupt my work.

I reread my last line. *The baby-blue tones did what? Showed off her eyes, her porcelain skin, her platinum-blond hair?* Truth was, I didn't think anyone at the Royal Hawaiian had much noticed Jeanne LeMay, except perhaps for her ridiculous giggle and the way she cupped a hand over her mouth as she ate. Insipid twit. The studio might have shipped her to Waikīkī to drum up publicity for her movie, but they couldn't create charisma where there was none.

"I hate you, I hate you, I hate you." This time it was Kenny screaming.

By the time I reached the door, he had Lionel pinned facedown in the dirt, and was pummeling him. The bag of plumerias lay scattered beside them, trampled. So much for wearing a lei that night. And so much for finishing my column.

I hauled Kenny off his brother.

"One hour," I said as he squirmed. "All I asked you two for was one hour to write my column. Both of you to your room. I don't want to hear a peep from you. March."

"I don't want him anywhere near me," Lionel yelled, his face muddy and tear-streaked.

"Fine. Get a book and go to my room. But I don't want to hear so much as a whisper from either of you. And clean yourselves up."

"It's his fault!" Kenny protested.

"I don't care whose fault it is. It doesn't matter to me whose fault it is. All I want is enough peace and quiet to write. And if either of you had an ounce of brains, you'd want the same. How else do you expect to get shave ice treats or tickets to the movies? You think money grows on trees?"

"You know, it's not too late," Ying said. She sat in her lawn chair watching me as I worked.

I paused in my gleaning of the fallen mangoes scattered beneath the giant tree beside her house. What now? Was this to be another "it's not too late for Kenny to apply to Punahou" reminder or one of her lectures on the boys needing to learn the value of work? I studied her face for clues.

"What is it today? You going to lecture me about why I should have another baby? Why I need a daughter?"

As usual, Ying's expression betrayed nothing. Perfect poker face. She narrowed her eyes, as if willing me to intuit her meaning. Not today. I didn't need another charged moment after the boys' fight. I hadn't heard a peep since I ordered them to their room. At least they were obeying me.

"You haven't made too much pilikia yet," Ying said by way of an answer, assuming, as she always assumed, that I knew what she was talking about.

"I wasn't aware I'd made any trouble. And stop looking at me like that." Ying made me feel guilty even when I had nothing to feel guilty about. "What is it you think you know?"

"What's that boxer man like? He as handsome as everybody says?"

I exhaled. Damn. Was there anything this woman didn't hear about?

"I suppose he's handsome enough. Why? You angling for an introduction?"

"You think you've got troubles now, missy, keep heading down this path and you'll taste plenty of bitterness."

I set down my bag of mangoes and moved closer to the tree trunk to escape the mist moving in. Tantalus's clouds had crept down its slopes and were blanketing the valleys. Ying stayed where she was. She would outlast the rain as she outlasted everything.

"What is it you think you know?" I asked again, kicking aside a rotting mango.

"This look familiar?" She pulled out the tiny bag she kept stuffed in her pocket and drew from it an earring, a rose sculpted from pink coral. The twin to the one in my jewelry box.

"How did you get that?"

"My cousin Loretta. She found it when she was cleaning the boxer's hotel room. Loretta figured it was yours, since she saw you leaving his room."

I leaned my head against the tree trunk and closed my eyes. Sometimes Honolulu felt as small a town as Carlisle.

St. Andrew's cathedral bells began chiming, the sound carrying loud and true up Punchbowl.

"Hah!" Ying laughed. "See! Your God is disappointed. He's warning you to stop all this humbug."

"So now you know what my God thinks, eh? Is there anything you don't know?" I wanted Ying to understand I was angry, warn her she'd gone too far this time by bringing up my private business, but I couldn't help myself. I laughed. "You know you make me crazy."

"You got it all kapakahi. I'm what's saving you from crazy." She held my gaze, refusing to let me look away. "You think you stand on firm ground, your toes dug in, but you're on the edge of one steep cliff. Nothing's going to break that fall."

"Mom," Kenny called through the screen of the boys' bedroom. "May I come out now?"

"Sure. And tell Lionel time's up."

I wanted to move but felt rooted. "He makes me happy." I hated the pathetic whimper in my voice. "Happy like I've never been happy."

Ying nodded and held out my earring. "So keep the memory." She paused. "You don't need that man to be happy. You need to cut out the part in your life that makes you unhappy."

She had brought this up before. She considered Archie more burden than benefit and thought I should rid myself of him.

I shook my head. "Not yet. Not while the boys are so young."

Ying shrugged. "Then learn to live with unhappy. Now go inside. Be useful. Make some chutney with those mangoes."

"Tomorrow," I said, picking up the bag. "I've a cocktail party at the Pacific Club in a bit."

"And he'll be there?"

I nodded. "Then a big dinner at Lau Yee Chai. All the bigwigs. Even Governor Poindexter's coming." It would be my last evening with Micky, and I doubted I'd have a moment alone with him.

"Good. The more people, the less chance you'll slip up."

Lionel emerged from the house and walked slowly to us, his face tense, his eyes wary. I smiled. "Want some sliced fresh mango?" I asked, pulling one from the bag. His face relaxed. Things were right again in his world.

I wished some equally simple gesture could make things right in mine.

Lionel

Most kids don't say their brother is their best friend and Kenny probably wouldn't say I'm his, but he's definitely the best friend I have in the world even though he bugs me something awful sometimes. I don't even mind most of the stuff he does to me and some of it's even funny, like the other night when we were in bed talking about the baseball league game I'm making and I had to use the bathroom. I got back into bed and was still talking about the different players I've made up, and I didn't even notice Kenny wasn't in his bed anymore. All of a sudden he landed right on top of me 'cause he'd climbed onto my headboard and was just waiting to pounce. He scared the bejesus out of me and at first I was hollering something awful at him, until I thought about it a minute and then the two of us were laughing so hard I would have wet my pants if I hadn't just gone to the john.

It's easy to play pranks like that on me 'cause I never notice stuff like whether or not he's in his bed or if the sugar in the sugar bowl doesn't look like it normally does. Kenny likes nothing better than to play a good prank on someone, and it's usually me that he plays them on. They're not bad pranks like some of the ones the kids at school do to me. Kenny's my best friend that way.

Last week he gave me the best present anyone's ever given me. Better even than the bike I got from Mom and Dad last Christmas. He drew pictures of some of the players I created for my baseball league, just made-up faces and bodies for them, then painted them in uniforms that have logos and everything. For the Hilo Sharks, he made a logo of shark faces with lots of teeth showing and for the Maui Mynahs, he made birds that look kinda like the crows with bright yellow beaks. He says he's going to make pictures for every team in our league, so we'll have team colors and team logos and can set up the players' pictures when their teams are playing. Only problem is, we won't be able to play our game for a couple of months, until baseball season has started. Mom says, "What difference does that make? Play your game when you want to play it." She doesn't understand that this is real baseball even if it's pretend. We have to follow the rules. Kenny gets it. He would never say, "Let's play a baseball game in February." That would just be wrong.

Sadira

I twirled my seat around to face the crowd in the rooftop bar. Only the hardiest remained. A tropical storm had blown in the day before, bringing down power lines, toppling trees, and spewing waves across roads. Though subsiding, it was still walloping us with sheets of rain and powerful gusts. Hotel guests and a few brave locals huddled in the covered area close to the band. Charlie, the hotel's permanent resident, was nursing his second manhattan on the stool beside me.

"What's wrong with your wrist?" He picked up my hand and examined it, his finger tracing the red rash around it. "This sting?"

"Some. Mostly it itches. I don't know where it came from."

"This bracelet new?" He fingered the bracelet Micky had given me as a parting gift.

"Yes, as it happens."

"Looks like maybe you're allergic to its metal. That's a mean rash."

Charlie had been a family doc back in Oregon before he retired to the tropics.

"I haven't worn it much." I could only wear it on a night when Archie wasn't around. "I've never had a problem with gold before."

"I hate to tell you, but it's probably got some nickel and other cheap metals mixed in. I'm afraid you're one of those women who has to stick to the quality stuff. No cheap five-and-dime for you."

"But it's not cheap. It came from a fine jewelry shop in Los Angeles. I have the box."

"And the receipt?" He grinned and resumed sipping his manhattan. "Sorry, kid. You can't always trust the packaging."

Jack O'Brien joined us, leaning back against the bar. "We studying anything in particular?"

"Nothing and nobody to study tonight. It's as dead as I've ever seen it. I'm just trying to work up my nerve to go back into the storm. I should have trusted my instincts and stayed home." I twirled the bracelet. "Difficult to believe I once thought this gig was glamorous and exciting."

"Beats a lot of other things you could be stuck doing."

"When did you become Mr. Sunshine?" I swung my purse over my shoulder. "I'm heading home, guys. See ya tomorrow."

"I'd take that bracelet off, if I were you," Charlie said.

"Right. Will do." Only I didn't want to take it off.

As I struggled to open my umbrella beneath the hotel's canopy, the bracelet slipped off and into a murky puddle. The doorman scooped it up.

"Here you go, Mrs. Doyle."

"You keep it, Keona. Your little girl can wear it for dress-up."

"For sure? She goin' love it. Mahalo." He tipped his cap.

I dipped the umbrella, holding it like a shield before me, and pushed into the wind and rain.

Chapter Eight

August 1939 to September 1940

Lionel

We've got a girl named Kaiyo now. Kaiyo Watanabe. She stays in the cottage between ours and Mrs. Fong's and goes to UH. Mrs. Fong lets her live here free except she has to help take care of Kenny if Mom and Dad aren't around. I think I can take care of Kenny fine by myself, but I like having Kaiyo here. She cooks supper and if we've done all our homework, she lets us listen to *The Lone Ranger* or *The Shadow* or *The Green Hornet.* The Lone Ranger is my favorite. He's got a creed I posted by my bed. I read it aloud every night before I go to sleep so I'll remember how to be a good person. I have to whisper it or Kenny tells me to knock it off. Kaiyo thinks I'm smart to follow the Ranger's creed. She says I could do a whole lot worse than listening to his idea of how to live my life. I think the most important thing the Lone Ranger tells us to do is be "prepared physically, mentally, and morally to fight for what is right." After I punched Byron in the nose for teasing one of the little kids at school, I had to go see Father Wilson. I told him I was just doing what the Lone Ranger said to do, but Father Wilson thinks it's better to fight with words than with fists. I'm not so sure that words are going to stop people like Byron, but Kaiyo thinks Father Wilson is giving me good advice, too, so I have to figure out how to listen to him and to the Lone Ranger, even when it seems like they are telling me opposite things.

Kaiyo teaches me lots of stuff I never knew. Last week, she showed me how to make our own vegetable garden. She's growing cabbage and cucumbers and daikon and ginger root and green onion. She built most of the garden one day while I was at school. When I left in the morning, there was still only grass between our houses, but when I got home, she had dug out a big patch of dirt and put up little wood walls around it. I helped her loosen up the soil and mix in some fertilizer her dad brought from his Waialua store. That's where she's from. Waialua's on the whole other side of the island, near Renee and Mr. Bellingham's beach house. Kaiyo's grandparents used to work on the Waialua sugar plantation, but her dad grew up and started a store with his brothers and sisters. If Kaiyo wasn't going to school at UH, she'd be working at the store just like all her aunties and uncles and brothers and cousins.

I think it would be swell to work in a store like that. She says she can eat all the shave ices and *manapuas* and cone sushis she wants. Even crack seed. She says she never eats all that much of any of it, though. "It doesn't seem so great when it's around you all the time," she says, but I think that would make me want it even more.

She says her little brother used to sneak candy, the expensive mainland kind, so her parents locked him in the store one night and told him to eat all he wanted. He was so sick the next day, he didn't eat any more candy after that. That's what Kaiyo says anyway. I'm not sure if I believe her. I don't think any grown-up would let a kid eat all the candy they wanted, even if they did own the store and everything in it. And I'm not sure about a kid ever having so much candy he wouldn't want more. But so far Kaiyo's never steered me wrong, so maybe it's true.

The day we put in the garden was the same day Kenny had to fold origami cranes. His class was making a tree of a thousand gold cranes for good luck. While Kaiyo and I slaved away in the hot sun, Kenny, Mom, and Mrs. Fong sat in cushy chairs on Mrs. Fong's shaded porch. They folded gold paper until four grocery bags were full of them. I don't know why they all wanted to help Kenny out so much when it was me and Kaiyo who really needed the help. Kenny didn't even stick around. He took off for a Boy Scouts meeting and then Mom headed to work, so poor Mrs. Fong got stuck finishing the cranes. For such a grumpy lady, she can be pretty nice about helping out. Most kids are scared of her 'cause she scolds them for being bad, even kids she doesn't know. But I know she's secretly nice underneath her mean voice. When I told her it was rude of Kenny to dump his work on her, she said she didn't mind folding paper, that it relaxed her, and besides, she liked watching me and Kaiyo work hard. She likes hard work. She tells me and Kenny all the time, "Work harder than everybody else, and someday by and by, you'll be the one in charge." I can tell that's why she likes Kaiyo. She wouldn't let just anyone live in the extra house and be almost like one of the family. She told Mom Kaiyo's not like other girls. "No silly boy hooey. She's too akamai for that. You'll see." I don't know if Kaiyo's akamai, but I do know she smells good all the time, like a forest full of white ginger.

Sadira

I paused at the kitchen window, coffee cup in hand, and watched Kaiyo struggle to hang sheets on the line. The wind whipped her dress round her legs and turned the sheets into sails. She stretched an arm as high as she could, grabbed the rope, and pulled it down to her level. Gripping a clothespin with her lips, she wrangled a corner of one sheet and then another without dragging the cloth over the grass. She seemed slender and delicate enough for a man to circle her waist with his hands, but she was no fragile doll. She exuded a substance and determination that gave me pause. Whether tackling her books or scrubbing a floor, she dug in and got the work done.

"You were right," I admitted to Ying the day we watched Kaiyo create an entire vegetable garden. "She's the angel we needed."

"I don't know anything about angels," Ying said. "But she's a good worker and she knows what she wants."

The part of Ying's grand plan that still caused me worry was Elma. She had yet to sell the Carlisle house, but already her letters were a litany of concerns about the move, the most intense ones focused on Kaiyo. Like all Americans, Elma had seen the *Life* magazine photographs of the Japanese invasion of Nanking. Hundreds of thousands were slaughtered, tens of thousands raped. I'd seen the newsreels, but the Japanese army's atrocities were no reflection on Kaiyo or Hawai'i's Japanese American residents.

"The Japanese are a brutal, ruthless people," Elma wrote. "How can it be safe to have her living with us and caring for the boys?"

I had no patience for her nonsense. "Kaiyo is as much a danger to us and America as you are," I wrote back. "Look at the savagery of the Germans. Should your neighbors shun you? Your own mother could barely speak English."

Mocking her was probably not the best way to persuade her, but she would at least arrive knowing I had no sympathy for her ignorant fears.

The odor of burning tobacco drifted in. I spotted Archie seated on a folding chair in the shade of the guava tree, nearly invisible but for the curl of smoke and glow of burning ember.

"Coffee's ready," I called through the window, then poured myself a bowl of cereal.

He pushed open the screen door. "Morning."

"She's hard at work." I nodded in Kaiyo's direction.

"When isn't she? Makes me tired to be around her. Like a damn hummingbird, buzzing every which way."

I poured myself more coffee and held up the pot. "Want some?"

"Not that sludge you brew. I'll get mine downtown." Archie preferred his coffee weak.

I settled at the table. In the humid morning air, my nightgown clung to me. I hiked the skirt up above my knees.

"What do you have planned for today?" I asked.

"Catch up on a few things at the office. Work on setting next week's schedule. Run some errands. You need anything in town?"

"Can't think of anything. I'll be out tonight and most of tomorrow."

"Of course."

"It's work, Arch." I stirred the flakes in my cereal bowl. "Can we please not do this? We're going to Renee's on Sunday. We'll have some family time then."

"Really? You count that as family time?"

I would not be baited. "I hear Bing Crosby may sing tonight at the Royal, if you want to stop by."

"I'll pass. I'd like to spend some time with the boys."

He picked up his keys and wallet from the counter and headed for the front door. I snagged some flakes as I dipped my spoon in the warming milk. The screen door slapped shut.

Lionel

I've got a big red circle round my wrist. Kinda like the one Mom had a while back, only mine's niftier.

"Quit fussing with it," Mom says when I rub it, but I can't stop myself.

It feels like a scar, the kind prisoners get when they've been handcuffed to a dungeon wall. I've got a book all about dungeons. That's what I was reading when one of those big high school girls sat down on my chair. She sat right on the chair's arm, her bathing suit soaking wet from the pool, and she said, "You don't mind if I perch here next to you, do ya?" only she wasn't even looking at me when she said it and she didn't wait for me to answer. I did mind her sitting there, only I knew better than to say so. She and the other girls were in a tizzy over Mom telling their fortunes. They crowded onto the lanai, the place where I like to sit at Renee's beach house. Actually, it's Mr. Bellingham's beach house, but now that he and Renee are married, it's hers, too. Someday, it'll belong to the baby she's going to have any minute now. That baby better like having lots of people around, 'cause Renee sure does. She invites lots and lots of folks over on Sundays. Mostly people I don't know. A lot of the kids go to Punahou 'cause Mr. Bellingham's kids by his other wife, the wife he doesn't want around anymore, those kids go to Punahou. Those kids and the other people she invites like to play volleyball and tennis and water polo. There's always a volleyball game going on. Nobody likes to just sit except me and Renee. She sits even more now that her belly's as big as one of those grinning buddhas on a restaurant counter. Sometimes she'll come over to where I am, plop down in a chair, and say, "What would I do without you, Lionel? These people wear me out," which makes me wonder why she invites them all over. Maybe it's to make Mr. Bellingham happy. He's the busiest one of all. He takes people out on his sailboat till the wind dies down, then he heads straight to the volleyball net or the tennis court.

When that big girl sat down on my chair, Dad said, "Come on, champ, let's you and me go for a swim," so I had to close up my book and go out into the hot sun. I suppose it's not that girl's fault I've got this red welt on my wrist, and maybe it's not even Mom's fault, but I kind of think it is. It's not like she had to read people's fortunes right there beside me. She could have used the inside part of the house.

Kenny was already sand sliding down at the beach. He's not like me and Dad. He likes the sun and water. Mom says he's half fish, but she's just joking 'cause he doesn't have gills or scales, though his skin does fall off after it burns, kinda the way scales fall off a fish.

Dad and I headed straight into the water and out past the crashing surf to where the waves lifted us up and dropped us down. Those waves were so big, my stomach fluttered like on the Ferris wheel. I get scared being out that far by myself 'cause a shark could bite off my leg or arm, but it's OK if Dad's there to protect me, only he didn't protect me from the Portuguese man o' war. When that thing wrapped its blue stinger round my wrist, I started screaming and thrashing so bad, Dad thought for sure I was drowning, at least that's what he told Mom. "Honest to God, Sadie," he said, "I thought he was having a seizure." I couldn't tell him what was wrong 'cause I kept gulping water. Finally, he got hold of me under my arms, pulled me onto the sand, and scraped the blue stinger off with a stick.

"Pee on it," one of the Punahou kids kept saying, "pee on it," only I didn't want anyone peeing on my arm. I was crying and saying, "Don't pee on me," and Dad said, "Calm down, Lionel, no one's going to pee on you," and he made me sit where he could put my hand in the water, then he packed wet sand over where the stinger had been and a grown-up lady said, "Somebody see if Renee's got papaya or meat tenderizer for the poison." A boy ran off to the house, only Renee didn't have any of that stuff, so they just kept putting wet sand on it, which I don't think helped at all 'cause it kept stinging and stinging.

"Let's take a walk," Dad said. I think he was embarrassed I was crying so much. I was plenty glad to leave 'cause I hated all those kids seeing me cry like that, even if they don't go to my school. Someday I might see them again and they'll remember I'm the kid who cried over a jellyfish sting.

At least I've got this great red scar now that will maybe last till tomorrow. I'll let the kids at school think I got kidnapped and put in a dungeon and hung by my wrists. I won't actually lie and tell them that, but maybe they'll use their own imaginations to think of it. I just won't say what really happened. That's not the same thing as lying. At least I don't think it is.

Not lying is one of my best things. "I'll say this for you, Lionel," Mom always says, "you're incapable of lying." I don't think she always thinks that's a good thing. Last week she and I saw Mrs. Cransten from church at the downtown drugstore. Mrs. Cransten was really glad to see us and asked lots of questions. Mom said almost nothing, so I had to do most of the talking. When I told her Mom still worked most nights and Dad was away on the outside islands, Mrs. Cransten's voice got real soft and sad. "You poor darlings. You must miss your mama something awful." I told her no. I said it was good 'cause Kaiyo cooks better than Mom and never yells. That's when Mom said, "We best get a move on, Lionel," and she barely even said goodbye to Mrs. Cransten before she practically shoved me out the door. Driving home, she held on tight to the steering wheel, so tight her knuckles turned white. I think maybe that was a time when I wasn't supposed to tell the truth.

Sadira

"Come through the side yard, not the kitchen door. That'll spare you the nanny army," Renee warned me. I was stopping by to see her and meet the new baby. "Judith's made me a prisoner in my own home. Hired a whole troop of nannies to keep me from harming her precious granddaughter. I swear they'd boil me in hot water if they could, just to be sure I don't give the baby my cooties."

I parked at the end of the long drive, then slipped through a gap in the croton hedge. Renee lay by the pool, stretched out on a chaise lounge, a Waikīkī-to-Pearl Harbor view splayed before her. She leapt up, cried, "Hallelujah!" then galloped across the stone terrace, nearly tackling me in a bear hug.

"Don't run, woman, you just gave birth. Though no one would know it to look at you. I hate you. You've no belly at all."

Renee linked our arms. "Don't hate me. We both know this body's the only thing I've got going for me, and Lord knows, it'll quit on me soon enough. Besides, it's been almost two weeks and my boobies are still sore."

She groaned as she lowered herself onto a stack of cushions. "And my butt still smarts. But I already feel better just seeing you. Now show me what you brought."

I passed over my shopping bag. "Contraband to cheer you up. Don't let the nannies find it all."

She squealed. "I adore you. Everyone else brings fancy little dresses and silver cups and stuffed bunnies. As if it was the little beast and not

me who suffered for hours." She reached a hand in the bag and pulled out
the box of See's chocolates.

"You remembered!" She immediately opened the box and popped one
in her mouth.

"I talked a visiting Hollywood director into sharing his bounty."

"In exchange for what?"

"Let's just say, I'm a real pal."

Her second reach produced a generously sized bottle of Drambuie.

"No! How did you manage it? Harrison hasn't been able to find any
for weeks."

I shrugged. "I know a guy who knows a guy. I also had the good sense
to stockpile it a long time back."

"And Ying's ginger cream!" She dropped the straps of her swimsuit,
scooped out some cream, and rubbed it over her swollen breasts.

"As promised. She made it fresh with roots from Kaiyo's garden."
Though I had no part in the garden work or the blending of the cream, I
was proud of Ying's and Kaiyo's enterprise. "So where's this baby Martha
of yours?"

"Lolly, not Martha. Martha's only the official name to keep Judith
happy. Some dead aunt of hers. I agreed, provided her middle name be
Laura and we call her Lolly. That's what my daddy called me. Short for
Lollipop."

"I don't know. Sounds an awful lot like a Bellingham kind of nickname.
Don't they call Harrison's sister Pepper? And I think one of them's a
Jiggie."

"True, they do specialize in childish nicknames, but at least Lolly
comes from my family." She flipped her suit straps back up and jumped
to her feet. "Time for a swim before the beast starts wailing for more
food. I don't understand why they can't feed her from a bottle like every
other modern child. You got a suit on under that dress?"

I nearly cautioned her it was too soon to swim, but caught myself. She
had enough people worrying over her. I slipped off my cotton shift.

"Last one in's a rotten egg." She cannonballed into the water. We managed a few laps and some time floating around on inflated mattresses before one of the dreaded nannies appeared, baby in arms.

"Mrs. Bellingham, you really mustn't," the young woman cried, pristine in crisp white. "It's not good for you."

"Precisely what about it isn't good for me, Bridget? The sun? The water? A bit of exercise? How can any of it hurt me?"

"Doctor's orders. You really mustn't."

I felt sorry for Bridget. I wouldn't want to be the creature caught between Judith and Renee Bellingham.

"I doubt any doctor would refuse me exercise," Renee said, but she stepped out of the pool. "I assume it's time for the little monster's feeding, so you win this one."

As she rinsed off at the outdoor shower, she called back to Bridget, "You can tell Judith I'm being a good girl—no chlorine will get on the baby." Then, wrapped in a fluffy white robe, she followed the nanny back to the terrace, where began an elaborate construction of pillows to support Renee's arm, and a draping of sheet to hide her breasts.

"Heaven forbid you might glimpse a bit of my nipple." Renee winked at me.

The nanny nestled Lolly in the pile of pillows at Renee's side, then hovered close by until the baby latched on to her breast.

"Well, you're a natural." I was sincerely impressed. I had failed at both of my attempts to nurse.

"I should hope so. I spent enough time attaching babies to my ma's teats. Don't see what all the fuss is about. Babies know what to do." She glared in Bridget's direction. "Do you suppose we could have a little privacy now, Bridget? I promise not to smother or drop her."

"I'll be just inside should you need me, Mrs. Bellingham."

"I'm sure you will be. Now vamoose." Once Bridget was out of sight, Renee nodded at the shopping bag. "Be a love and pour me a nip. Helps the milk flow and the mom glow. Bridget's not the only one who knows a thing or two about babies."

Renee lifted Lolly from the pile of pillows and tucked her in closer beneath the breast, her elbow cradling the baby's head. She cooed softly and ran a finger over Lolly's cheek. The kind of gesture any ordinary mother might make.

"Anyone looking at you would think you've got a soft spot for her." I handed her the glass.

"I know." Renee laughed. "Who'd have thought one of these things could turn me to mush. I used to swear I'd never get saddled with a kid, and now I've gone all goofy over this one." She leaned in close and inhaled. "But then, you really are the sweetest-smelling, loveliest creature ever created, aren't you, my little Lollipop?"

I caught a glimpse of Bridget hovering in the shadows. I often imagined how it would be if it were I and not Renee who had ended up married to Harrison. Difficult not to envy Renee everything she had. The fine homes, the wardrobe, a life of leisure. And I would do so much more than she if I were in the role of Mrs. Bellingham. I could influence elections, improve the city's appearance, cultivate the arts—all things of no interest to Renee. But I would also have to live in a house full of Bridgets, all of them watching and reporting to Judith, who made Arch's mother, Prudence, look as menacing as a gnat.

"So bring me up to speed." Renee turned her attention back to me. "When's that mother of yours getting here?"

"A few more weeks. Early October." I leaned back in my chair. "The closer it gets, the more nervous I am. I already feel myself drowning in disapproval."

"I'd be on a boat to Hong Kong if it was my mother. But then, my ma's never gone further than twenty miles from home, so no danger of her ever showing up." Renee gazed down at Lolly, who was sucking loudly, her little fists kneading Renee's breast. "Slow down, little girl. It's not going away." Suddenly serious, she turned to me. "You think our kids will resent us the way we resent our moms?"

"I'd say one of mine already does." I reached out a finger and Lolly wrapped her fist around it. "But not this one. All she wants in the world is you."

"He's a good kid, you know," Renee said. "Not always easy, but there's not a false bone in his body. I give you credit for raising a kid who's one of a kind. Most people only want their kids to shut up, fit in, and mind their manners."

The topic always came back to Lionel.

"I take no credit for who Lionel is, especially if that means I don't have to take any blame either."

"I say let him be different and to hell with what people think. I'm not going to let anyone make Lolly something she's not."

"And what do I do when he's sobbing himself to sleep at night 'cause some kid stole his lunch or pinched him, passing in the hall? Being different causes him a world of pain."

Renee wouldn't understand, not really, until other kids were calling Lolly a circus freak or a teacher washed her mouth out with soap for asking questions or expressing an opinion.

"You tell him the truth. You tell him he's a damn better person than all of them and a damn sight smarter, too."

Renee shifted Lolly to her other breast, and the infant latched on like a greedy fish, sucking so fiercely my own breasts ached in sympathy.

"Mommy could use a splash more, please." Renee held out her cup to me.

I envied her ignorance of what lay ahead and the simplicity of her present life. Easy to be happy when your child still adores you and an army of nannies spares you sleepless nights and messy diaper changes.

I refilled her cup and poured a splash for myself.

"Here's to babies and mothers," I said, raising my cup. "May we manage somehow to endure one another."

Lionel led Elma down the path to her new home. She walked at a slower pace than I remembered, and with a slight limp. Another troubling sign.

I hadn't recognized her at the pier. From our spot on the terminal deck, I scanned the passengers and skipped right past her. Not because she looked any different—her hair was no whiter than when we left and she stood ramrod straight as she always did. What disguised her was the frantic way she searched the crowd, like a child afraid. My Elma was unflappable. Fearless. Her distress worried me. What if I could no longer depend on her to care for us?

"You can't wear your shoes inside, Gran," Lionel said when they reached the threshold.

Always Mr. Black and White and No Exceptions.

"Of course she can," I said. "Just leave your shoes on, Elma," but she was already slipping out of them. She set them beside the others on the porch.

Once inside, she also removed her leis and jacket and dabbed at her face with a tissue.

"I'm a bit wilted in this heat."

"It does take getting used to," I said. "Do you want to change into something cooler?"

"That would be lovely."

I had little hope that a change of clothes would be of real benefit. Even on sweltering summer days in Carlisle, Elma wore undergarments, including a corset and stockings, beneath long-sleeved dresses.

I sent the boys back to our cottage to do homework until lunch and led Elma to her room. She snapped open one of her suitcases and removed a sleeveless cotton shift, unlike anything I'd seen her wear before.

"That looks a good bit more comfortable."

"I picked this up in Havana. It's a bit daring, but quite a lovely relief in hot climates. I noticed you're not wearing stockings. Do you suppose I could get away with that myself around the house?"

This was unexpected. I'd never seen Elma's bare legs.

"You can do whatever you'd like. Things are far more relaxed here in

Hawai'i. I only wear stockings for work. You could be truly wild and skip the corset as well."

Elma rolled her eyes. "I plan to remain a respectable woman no matter where I am. I won't have all my lady parts jiggling about."

I laughed. "Wear whatever makes you comfortable, Elma. I'll leave you to it. Bathroom's across the hall."

"I won't be long. And thank you for all this."

Her eyes welled up and we both pretended not to notice. With her permission, I'd already unpacked the trunk she sent ahead and tried to make her bedroom inviting. I'd set out her knickknacks, placed family photos on her embroidered doilies, and hung two of her favorite paintings. Even her bed was done up with her own linens and crocheted spread.

"Hello!" Kaiyo called from the front door.

"I'm in the kitchen."

While Elma changed, I was preparing a lunch of egg-salad sandwiches, sliced mango, and a pitcher of lemonade. I was nearly done setting the table.

"Yum," Kaiyo said. "Looks delicious. Where is everyone?"

"Boys are at our place. Elma's changing into something comfortable. Your timing's perfect. I was about to fetch the boys."

A jarring shriek interrupted me.

"Oh Lordy," I said. "I forgot to warn her about geckos."

"And I forgot to tell you I've been having centipede problems."

I found Elma in the hallway, clutching a washcloth.

"There's a monstrous creature in the bathtub."

Kaiyo joined us, butcher knife in hand. "Your resident exterminator to the rescue," she said. With three quick chops, she reduced the centipede to bits, then extended her hand to Elma. "You must be Mrs. Schaeffer."

"Yes, and you apparently are my hero. A pleasure to meet you, Miss Watanabe."

"Call me Kaiyo. I apologize for the rude introduction to your new home. The nasty beasts love to crawl in from the drain pipes. There's nothing for it but to chop them up. I'll clean up this mess."

For two months I'd worried about this moment. They were such an unlikely pair of roommates—one old, one young; one German American, one Japanese American. Elma was bound by a fierce code of courtesy and civility, but I didn't trust her breeding to temper her notions of propriety nor inoculate her to the anti-Japanese sentiments infecting the country. Kaiyo was equally gracious and polite, but young and enjoying her first taste of personal freedom. The most I'd hoped for was a mutual tolerance.

"Put me to work," Elma said. "How can I help?"

"I'll wrap up the remains in some newspaper and dump it outside. The dead parts attract live ones. Perhaps you could set the teakettle boiling? We can wipe the tub with bleach, then douse it with boiling water."

"Perfect. Point me to the kitchen."

Elma followed Kaiyo down the hall, warriors unified in their quest to conquer all manner of germs and pests. All was well.

Chapter Nine

January to December 1941

Lionel

Thanks to good old General Woodruff, we are ready and waiting for the Japanese to attack us. He keeps drilling the troops and even makes the whole island practice. He surprised everyone with what they call a mobilization order, which meant we had to scramble like crazy, the way we would if the Japanese or the Germans attacked us. In two hours every one of the twenty thousand troops on Oʻahu was in place and ready to fight. There was a policeman at almost every intersection, ready to tell drivers what to do.

A couple weeks ago Kenny and I got to help with a practice blackout. They set off all the sirens and the wailing was so bad it hurt my ears. At home they had to shut off all the lights and move around in the dark as if they were blind. We Boy Scouts helped the police at the intersections 'cause of the traffic lights being off and all the cars driving in the dark. We helped keep the cars from hitting each other. Pretend enemy planes filled up the sky and the army tried to find them with its giant searchlights, so the sky was full of fat beams of white light crisscrossing over one another. Most of the time you couldn't see anything in the sky. I saw planes a few times, but it made my neck hurt to look up like that. Mom says we've got nothing to worry about 'cause Japan is so far away they couldn't possibly make it all the way here to attack us. She calls it a "useless exercise in fear-mongering." My Boy Scout leader says we must always be ready to defend our home, so it's good to practice because you never know, and I figure the generals and admirals know a whole lot more about this stuff than Mom does. She also says the best thing about having the fleet in town for maneuvers is having all those handsome boys in white clogging the sidewalks downtown. Personally, I think they're a big nuisance, what with the way they whistle at the local girls and pick fights with the guys, but I do like having the aircraft carriers anchored right off Waikīkī Beach. They're too far out to swim to, but we can see them from the beach.

Mom's friend Jack took me out for a ride on his sailboat 'cause Dad is away on the Big Island and Jack said maybe I'd like to try something new. We couldn't sail too close to the carrier offshore, but we got close enough to watch some of the planes practice takeoffs and landings. I figure those pilots are just about the bravest guys in the whole world. I tried not to think about what would happen if one of the planes fell out of the sky above us and we couldn't sail away fast enough to escape being part of a fiery death ball. Jack didn't look scared at all. I wish I could be brave as he is.

Kenny didn't come along. Mom said it was OK for me to do something special without Kenny.

Jack let me steer for a while and I didn't get seasick at all. Mom told him I have a stomach of iron. "We all learned that," she said, "on the voyage over. Lionel was the only one who never got queasy." It's true. My stomach even feels like iron when you smack it. Jack sailed me way out to sea, so far we could hardly see Oʻahu. He says he likes to do that when life gets too busy and complicated 'cause the sea's the one place where he can find peace and quiet. He's right about it being plenty quiet out there. I got a little nervous about how quiet it was and how tiny Oʻahu got. When he said, "Would you feel better if we sailed back?" I said, "Yeah," so we did.

I hope he asks me to go out again with him sometime and teaches me more about sailing. Mom says she doesn't think she'd like it much, being on a tiny boat in such a big ocean, but I think she might be surprised. Jack makes it feel real safe, and best of all, he doesn't talk a whole lot, so a guy can lie back and not have his head hurt. It was sure a swell day.

The best thing of all that's happened is Gran Schaeffer finally got here. We went to meet her ship and give her a swell aloha welcome. We made so many leis for her, they almost covered her whole neck. "Oh my," she kept saying over and over as she wiped her hankie across all the sweat on her face, "I guess I really am in the tropics now," and I couldn't tell if she was happy or sad about that. Mostly, I think she was some relieved to see Mom, Kenny, and me waving at her from the terminal. I bet she was scared that maybe wires got crossed and she'd landed in the wrong place. Mom got real quiet when we saw her at the ship rail, and I think maybe she was crying a little bit. She told me to stop being ridiculous when I asked her, but her eyes were all wet and she held her whole body still as a statue. I think we're going to be A-OK now that Gran's here.

Sadira

I tapped on Elma's screen door as a courtesy. Unlike my door, this one was newly scrubbed, and I could see Elma at work inside.

"Come in," she called without turning around. She was up on a stool wiping the cabinets.

I lifted my evening gown and stepped into the gleaming space. Open windows and gusting trade winds made it difficult to keep spaces clean in the tropics, but Elma wasn't about to lower her standards.

"You heading off?" Elma asked.

"Yup. Kenny's at Scouts and Lionel's doing his homework. The casserole's in the fridge ready to pop in the oven." Though Elma did most of the cooking, every now and then I made one of the boys' favorite dinners. Elma would gladly have done all the cooking, baking, and cleaning, but I wasn't ready to relinquish full control. I feared soon enough her oversight would reach too deeply into my life.

For the most part, the new arrangement was working out well. Besides keeping her cottage spotless and everyone fed, Elma helped Kaiyo with the boys. Kaiyo did our laundry and ironing and maintained the vegetable garden that fed us all. In lieu of rent, Elma sewed for Ying and her family members, anything from mending a seam to crafting evening wear and daytime ensembles. When Ying needed a letter proofread or ad copy written for herself or family members, she came to me. The scale still tipped heavily to my advantage, but I hoped that over time, it would feel more equitable.

"Whom do you get to meet tonight?" Elma asked, climbing down from her stool. An explosion in the distance rattled the windows. "My Lord, what was that?" She clutched the counter.

"The army practicing. You'll get used to it. A lot of nonsense. As if the Japanese would ever be foolish enough to attack. A lot of wasted worry when there's a real war going on."

"Nothing wrong with being prepared." Elma rinsed her sponge at the sink.

"Well, no one can accuse them of not being prepared. That's all they do—prepare. As for me, I've a rather uninteresting night ahead. Nobody special expected at a cocktail party I'm covering. Only the usual locals, but I shall make them feel quite special for being on the guest list."

"It sounds as absurd as the columns you wrote back home."

I hated conceding the point, but she was right. It turns out the world abounds with social climbers and those who live vicariously.

"After the party," I continued, "I'll stop by the Royal. I want to meet up with a Hollywood producer who's in town." I took a peanut-butter cookie from the platter on the counter. "He's been keeping a low profile so far. There's also some vaguely royal playboy from Eastern Europe here with his playmates, but I'd rather he played privately. He sounds like quite the bad boy and not someone I want to give free press space to."

Elma shook her head. "I do not understand these people you meet. Surely they've been raised to know the difference between proper and improper conduct, and yet they seem to choose to be ill-mannered. And what does it say of you, that you spend your evenings in their company? A married woman alone cavorting with all sorts of disreputable persons."

Elma didn't know the half of it. I knew better than to share most of what I witnessed during my evening patrols. Elma was still grounded in the previous century, expecting everyone to adhere to an outdated code of decorum. Evidence to the contrary wounded her, as if indiscretions were personally directed at her.

"I fear, Elma, there is no antidote for bad behavior. No one is immune— least of all, it seems, the so-called aristocrats. These are delicious, by the way." I took another cookie.

Elma frowned.

"I know, I know. I shouldn't be snacking on cookies, but I might not get a chance to eat while I'm working." Before Elma could advise me to eat something nutritious instead, I blew her a kiss. "I've got to get a move on. Tell Kaiyo I left the ironing pile on the couch."

I trusted we'd soon be an efficient operation. I lifted the skirt of my gown as I crossed the damp lawn. We still had our bumps, but things were smooth enough that I could squeeze in a little ad work for Ying's business friends—work I could bill them for. I enjoyed the work and, it turned out, I was good at it.

I stuck my head in my own kitchen door. Lionel sat at the table, his books spread open before him. "Heading out, love. Your gran will come heat up dinner a little later. Kenny should be home by six."

Lionel threw his pencil on the table. "I can't do it."

He knew how to pick his times.

"I have to get going, Lionel. What is it now?"

"These algebra problems. They're stupid. They make no sense." He picked up the sheet of paper in front of him and tore it to pieces. I willed myself to remain impassive.

"I'm sorry you're struggling. I'm sure Kaiyo will help you when she gets back from classes."

"What am I supposed to do till then?" He crossed his arms and glared at me.

As many times as I reminded myself it was better to throw water rather than gas on any charged encounter with Lionel, it took every bit of self-control to stop myself speaking my mind.

I suggested he work on his other assignments.

"I finished them." He loved egging me on.

"Well, good. Sounds like you deserve a break. You can go visit with Elma till Kaiyo gets here."

He kicked a table leg. "She'll just put me to work."

I slapped my hand against the door frame, my good intentions and patience gone.

"Enough of this. I can't help you if you choose to be miserable. You can sit here and pout, you can go read a book, or you can go help your grandmother. I don't care what you do, but I do not have time for your nonsense."

"You never have time for me," Lionel yelled as I let the screen door slap shut. "You never have time for anything except those stupid fake people who don't even like you."

Lionel, age 13

I always thought it would be scary to be in the middle of a battle, but I wasn't scared at all except for maybe the climbing the tree part. I didn't like it when I got on the first branch and looked down 'cause it felt like I could flip right over and crack my head open on the ground. My brain and blood would be all mixed up with the smushed mangoes rotting under the tree. Dad says, "So don't look down," when I say I'm afraid to climb trees, but I can't help seeing the ground. Kenny climbs nearly to the top of the tree 'cause he's too little and dumb to know how bad it would be if you fell off a branch.

It was Kenny's idea to climb into the tree and to haul up the hose so we could talk through it when the bombs and the planes got too loud.

I called the first branch, which wasn't the best one for seeing the sky and all the way out to the ocean, but it's big and I can wrap my legs around it horsey-style and not feel wobbly. I'd rather be safe than see everything. What I really wanted was to go back inside and sit on my bed, only I knew Kenny would laugh at me if I did.

That's where I was when the bombs first started going off—sitting on my bed, working on the quilt I'm sewing. When Gran Schaeffer started me on it, she made sure I had everything I needed to sew it up. Needles, thread, my own scissors, and a ring to hold the material steady and tight like a drum when I do the final quilting part. I'm still putting all the pieces together. It's called a crazy quilt, which means there's about a gazillion and one separate pieces of cloth of all different sizes and shapes, and I have to sew them all together the way Gran showed me. I'm going to give it to my mom for some Mother's Day or Christmas or birthday, but sometimes when I don't like her so much, I think maybe I'll give it to Kaiyo.

When we heard the planes overhead and the bombs exploding, Kenny, Dad, and me thought it was just another practice. The floorboards shook each time we heard an explosion, but we didn't get scared. The military had been practicing so often and for so long that bombs going off felt normal. At breakfast Gran said, "It's just another drill," but Dad was smart. He said, "Odd to do a drill on a Sunday morning." Still, none of us thought any more about it. I sat on my bed pretending I was in London and in the middle of the blitz with Germans dropping bombs and the English trying to shoot down the planes. It was hard work imagining I was in the middle of a battle 'cause even with all the booming noise, it didn't feel like war. It was sunny outside, the sky super blue like it always is in December. It was nothing like the black-and-white newsreels of bombs falling and people climbing out of heaps of bricks and stones that once were houses. To help pretend, I didn't look out the window. I just looked at the fabric in my hand and told myself, *You are safe inside your brick house as the bombs rain down on London. People are running and screaming and dying, and you are sitting here sewing a quilt.* But hard as I tried, I couldn't make believe it was a real war.

We were sitting in the car, ready to go to church, when Dad switched on the radio. Webley Edwards said, "This is the real McCoy, folks." Soon as we heard Webley say that, we piled out of the car fast. Gran and Dad talked about waking up Mom and Kaiyo but decided not to disturb them yet. We were all going to go inside to listen to the radio, but Kenny said, "I don't want to miss out on seeing all the action. Let's go up the mango tree so we can watch it from up high," which is how come I ended up having to climb the tree.

We couldn't see much 'cause all the good stuff was happening on the other side of Punchbowl. On our side we could only see downtown and to Waikīkī. We did have a good view of Round Top and Tantalus behind us, where some of the planes were coming from. They flew pretty low and we could see the big red circles on their sides. Out in the water, a bunch of them were chasing a destroyer and making it zigzag, trying to get away, and we even saw smoke from a bomb hitting McCully Street. Everything shook, even the branches in our tree.

I kept waiting for our guys to start firing back and for our planes to get up in the air so we could see a real dogfight, but it took forever and ever for our guns to start firing. When they finally did, we had to go inside. Mom was awake by then, and when the shrapnel started falling from the sky, she yelled, "Get inside now, boys!" Getting down out of the tree is the part I hate the most, especially when Kenny is waiting for me to shimmy down first. Mom was yelling, "Now, Lionel," as if I hadn't heard her the first time, and Kenny was pushing on my shoulders like he was going to shove me right off the branch. Sometimes I wish I could switch families and get a better one.

Sadira

When the front door slammed, I pulled the sheet up over my head and burrowed under the covers. Elma, Archie, and the boys were supposed to be on their way to church. I could hear the radio, the volume nearly loud enough for me to distinguish what the announcer was saying. I beat a fist against my pillow. I was never allowed a moment's peace in my own home. Archie knew I needed to sleep in that morning after a late night at the Royal and with the Caldwells' tea coming up that afternoon. Tough enough to sleep with that blasted bombing practice thundering around me. I knew the military meant well, but those constant drills were worse than a nuisance. I rolled over on my back, suddenly aware that something wasn't right. Webley Edwards was talking, and he didn't do Sunday morning shows. His voice was always warm and welcoming, but that morning he spoke with an unfamiliar urgency. I forced myself out of bed, grabbed my robe, and headed to the living room, where I found Elma on the couch beside the radio, her arms wrapped around herself.

"What's going on? Why aren't you at church?"

"It's the Japanese." Her eyes scanned the ceiling as planes passed overhead. "They're attacking. It's a real attack."

"Oh, for goodness sake, Elma. It's a drill. What's gotten into you?" I threw open the front screen door and stormed out to the porch, cupping a hand over my eyes. The planes were flying low and there were far more than usual. I squinted. These weren't like the ones I'd seen in other drills. These had red circles on their wings and bellies. The army was getting too realistic in their war games. No wonder Elma was in a state.

Something exploded downtown near the harbor and I swore the whole porch trembled. I turned back to the house. As I swung open the door, Webley said, "Again, if you've just tuned in, this is not a drill. It's the real McCoy. We are under attack."

"Where's Archie?" I asked Elma, who hadn't moved.

She nodded at the kitchen. I found him in the pantry, frantically pulling canned goods out of the cupboard and stacking them on the counter.

"What are you doing, Arch?"

"Packing up supplies. We have to head into the mountains." Cans toppled as he tried to stack them and missed. Several rolled and fell to the ground.

"Watch out. You're going to ruin this stuff." I grabbed his arms to make him stop. "Calm down. We need to think this through. We don't even know what's happening."

"We know all we need to know. There's no time to wait around. Listen to that racket out there. This is a full-scale invasion. You think it's only planes they've got? They could be landing troops right now, swarming the island. We need to get away while we can."

"And what then? How will we survive up there?" I picked up a can of corned beef hash. "How long will we last with a few cans of this stuff? We've got to keep our heads, Arch, stay calm, and wait till we know more."

"I have to do something, Sadie. I can't just sit here and wait for them to show up on our doorstep."

The house trembled as another bomb exploded.

I disagreed with Archie. The Japanese couldn't possibly launch an invasion from such a distance. But keeping him constructively occupied seemed my best hope.

"Let's do this sensibly," I said. "You start an inventory and I'll get dressed." It occurred to me I hadn't seen or heard the boys. "Where are the kids?"

He looked at me blankly.

"Damn it, Arch. You don't even know where they are?"

"In their room? They were just in the car with us. I figured they followed us inside."

They hadn't been in their room when I got out of bed. I ran out the back door in my bare feet, robe flying, yelling, "Kenny! Lionel!"

"Up here, Mom!" Kenny sat grinning on a high branch of the mango tree, one end of a hose in his hands. Lionel, perched on the lowest limb, held the hose's other end. "We figured out our own way to communicate." Kenny put the hose to his ear and told Lionel to talk into his end.

"Get down from there, both of you. You're going to get yourselves killed."

From where I stood beside the tree, I could see to the Diamond Head side of the city. Puffs of smoke rose from the McCully and Waikīkī neighborhoods.

Before Lionel could drop to the ground, the antiaircraft fire began.

"Into the house. I'll get Ying."

Ying didn't answer when I called at the door. I found her in the kitchen, studying a map of O'ahu. I sat down opposite her, reached a hand across the table, and placed it over hers. She shook it off.

"We need to get into the mountains," she said. "This air attack is just a trick, a diversion. It's the beaches that are dangerous. That's how they'll take us. They'll land on the beaches and sweep up across the island, slaughtering as they go. Just like Nanking."

I shook my head. "No. This is different. Nanking was lost even before the Japanese invaded. Assume you're right. Assume they're landing on our beaches right this minute, how many troops could they transport this far? They can't possibly overwhelm our massive military presence."

"If they want these islands, they will take them. Don't underestimate their capability." Ying stared hard at me, then returned her gaze to the map. "They would be crazy to try and land on the north shore. Surf's too rough. But if we went into the Ko'olaus from the Wahiawā side," Ying pointed to a section of the map, "there's this huge stretch in the Ko'olaus all the way to Kahuku and Waimea."

The house shook with another bomb hit. The sirens continued to wail, the antiaircraft machine-gunfire held steady.

"God." I squeezed my forehead with my fingers. "I can't think with all this noise. Shut the hell up," I screamed at the ceiling.

Ying looked up, smiled, and shook her head, then grew serious again. "Maybe Kaiyo's family knows this area past Waimea Falls."

"Even if you can find your way in, how would you survive?" I slapped the tabletop and stood. "I'm not doing this. I'm not going down this path. This is not Nanking. We are not about to be massacred, not on an island full of soldiers and sailors. We'll be fine. The most important thing is to stay calm and not give in to fear."

I stopped myself saying more. It wasn't like I had any basis for denying the possibility of an invasion. I was the one who kept saying the Japanese could never pull off an air attack, and now hundreds of planes were flying above us and dropping bombs.

"I need to check on Kaiyo and get back to Elma and the kids. Come with me?"

"Harrison," Ying said, staring hard at me. "Harrison has that whole valley up Kahuku way, owns even the slopes behind. Lots of land to disappear into. He knows the terrain."

"And there's no shelter, nothing but bananas and guavas to eat. And how would we get in there? If they're landing on the beaches, they'll cut off the road. Come to my house. Be with us."

Ying lowered her gaze back to the map.

"When you decide what you're going to do, let me know." I paused by the door. I wanted to plead with her, tell her I was terrified, too, that managing Archie, Elma, and the boys was more than I could do alone, that I needed her. "I don't think running away will save us, but if we stick together, support one another, maybe we'll be OK."

She folded up the map. "OK. You win. This time I'll listen to you. You better be right, missy."

Kaiyo was kneeling, her back to us, weeding one of the vegetable gardens, impervious to the noise around her. I motioned for Ying to go on ahead and I ran to Kaiyo.

"It's an attack," I yelled, pointing to more planes overhead. She turned her head to the sky and squinted. I grabbed her arm and tugged her to her feet.

"The wash," she said. "I haven't hung it yet."

"It'll wait. We have to get indoors."

Being in the house offered no protection from bombs, but we weren't their target. The house could at least protect us from the falling shrapnel of our own army.

The kids and Ying were seated around the kitchen table, watching Elma ladle hot chocolate into cups.

"Pass the cookies, Lionel," Elma said as Kaiyo and I entered.

Good, I thought. We were regaining our balance. Archie stood at the window, staring blankly ahead, the canned goods no more in number and no more organized than when I had left him, but Elma was helping to restore some order. A much calmer Ying sat beside Lionel.

"Are those real Japanese planes attacking us?" Kaiyo asked. She held her hands, dirty from the dark soil she'd been weeding, out in front of her as a surgeon might after prepping to operate.

"This time it's not a drill. Those are real bombs," I said. "Now come wash your hands at the sink."

"I need to get home," she said as she lathered and rinsed her hands.

"Don't talk *pupule*. Nobody's leaving," Ying said, a bit harshly in my opinion, given that she had been the one wanting to flee five minutes earlier. Elma ladled a cup of hot chocolate and passed it to Kaiyo.

"We need to figure out together what we're going to do next," I said.

"I've got a suggestion," Lionel offered.

"I know you mean well, Lionel, but this isn't pretend. The grown-ups need to sort out a plan," I said.

"I was just going to say you might want to get dressed." He slammed his chair against the table and headed to his room.

I gripped the table's edge.

Ying collected a notepad and pencil. "I'm going to make a list of everything we can start doing. First, we have to figure out how much food we have between us. Elma, you count all the stuff here and at your cottage. I'll count mine. Kaiyo, you figure out the garden produce— how much we've got, what's coming up soon. When all this humbug bombing stops, the boys can help you weed and gather vegetables. Eh,

Archie? You going to help?"

Arch turned in her direction, still dazed.

"You go find your and the boys' scouting supplies. Sleeping bags, tents, canteens, lanterns. Anything we can use if we need to *hele* on up the mountains. Kenny, you go help him."

"And me?" I asked, somewhat irritated by her presumption in dictating our duties.

"You listen to Lionel and put some clothes on. Then you can stay by the radio and keep track of what's going on."

I headed to the bedroom but didn't dress immediately. I needed time to calm myself.

The thin white cotton curtains were dancing, animated by the trade winds, the sky a vivid blue behind them. How could the world collapse on a day so lovely? I let myself lie down, not to sleep, just to breathe and rest. Not for long. It wouldn't take me long. Ten minutes, maybe just five, and I'd be back out there, doing my part. Pretending it didn't feel like a prison at all to be trapped inside with my calabash clan.

There was always the chance I'd get lucky. Maybe Ben would call. Maybe he'd need more reporters to cover the attack. Maybe I would get a ticket out of the sidelines.

"Damn it." I dropped my bag to the ground after Elma went back in the house. "God, how I hate this." I spoke more to myself than to Kenny, silent beside me.

"It's the law, Mom."

"And it's ridiculous."

I was sick of the way we were forced to live after the attack. The blackouts. The restrictions on travel. The ugly trenches crisscrossing the parks and schoolyards. Barbed wire on the beaches. And then there was the tiresome chore of carrying a gas mask everywhere. All the time. No exceptions. It had been weeks since the attack. The Japanese had not invaded, yet we lived as if an attack were imminent. Worst of all for me was the end of all celebrity travel and nearly all society life in Honolulu. Waikīkī was unrecognizable, with its empty hotels and closed nightclubs. No more stars to write about, only human-interest stories of ordinary people managing in desperate times.

"At least you still have a job," Ying said when I complained about how dreary my life was.

I knew Ying was right, but it didn't make it any easier to smile through afternoons spent with officers' wives volunteering at Tripler Army Hospital, or reporting on the school drills where students filed into trenches. This was not a world I had any interest in writing about.

"I need to get out of here," I'd announced over breakfast that morning. "I will go absolutely stir-crazy if I spend another Saturday pent up in this house."

Kenny, Lionel, and Elma had ignored me. The boys kept eating their cereal. Elma sipped her coffee and read the newspaper.

"I'm serious. We're going out today."

"Where?" Kenny lifted his bowl to drink the remnants of his cereal milk.

Of course, that was the problem. Where could we go? We couldn't drive anywhere. Gas was reserved for essential travel. We could walk down to the Art Academy, but the boys went there weekly for art classes. There was nothing there we hadn't seen dozens of times. Movies cost money.

"Ala Moana Park. We can walk there and have a picnic lunch."

"I don't want to walk that far. Besides, I've got homework to do," Lionel said as he cleared and rinsed his bowl.

"How about you?" I asked Kenny. "Is it too far for you to walk?"

"Nah. I don't mind. But we can't swim, can we?"

I shrugged. "We'll find a place where someone's cut a hole in the barbed wire. I don't think the Japanese will choose today for their invasion." I turned to Elma, who was still engrossed in the paper. "Want a little fresh air and sunshine, Elma?"

Slowly and methodically, she closed and folded the newspaper. "I suppose the exercise would do me good."

Heaven forbid she might do something just for the fun of it. With Elma, everything had to have a value beyond its basic pleasure.

It took nearly an hour to get the three of us ready and our bags packed with towels, mats, and food.

Lionel sulked in his room, angry at being left alone. "You're the one who wanted to study," I said. "Don't complain to me." I let his bedroom door slam shut.

Finally, we were out the door, and then Elma remembered the gas masks.

"What every beach picnic needs. I sure wouldn't want to be jailed for not being vigilant," I said. Elma ignored me and headed back for them.

"You OK, Mom?" Kenny stood in front of me, his arms crossed, taking my measure. "You feeling all right?"

Before I could answer, the screen door slapped shut. I shook my head at the sight of Elma in her cotton dress with three gas masks in hand.

"Just try and get us now, General Tojo," I said, taking my mask from her.

"Is there something wrong with your constitution, Sadira?" Elma picked up one of the bags I had set on the ground.

"No," I sighed, heading off in the direction of Ward Avenue. "I'm quite regular, thank you."

I set off at a fast clip and told myself I loved my mother and was acting like a brat. Yet Elma was driving me batty. Grateful as I was that she had moved thousands of miles to be with us, I was finding her presence a challenge. In the five years we'd lived apart, I had shed her Elma way of doing things, discovered the rest of the world didn't fixate on having a regular digestive tract or insist on ironing sheets and mopping a kitchen floor each morning.

"What's the point," I'd said when she insisted on ironing the sheets. "They won't stay wrinkle free."

"True, but they will remain softer." And so Elma spent every Sunday afternoon in her kitchen ironing the bed linen, dragging every inch of the sheets over her highly sanitized floors.

"I'm sorry, Elma. I didn't mean to snap." I slowed my pace to let her and Kenny catch up.

"It's the war eating at you," Kenny said, repeating the phrase so many used to excuse a whole slew of bad behavior.

"I suppose so." I didn't really agree. It was the war, but it was also Archie and Lionel and a pervasive unease in myself. I had not sat comfortably in my own life for a long time, but work had distracted me. Now, with little work, my life felt unbearable.

I punched Kenny playfully. "I vote that for one day we ignore the war and pretend life is as it was before the bombing."

A passing car honked and the driver, a neighbor, waved. It felt good to be outside, headed somewhere, and for a moment, acting as if we were still alive. I was itching for novelty and amusement. It might be a long time until I was dancing under the stars again, but they couldn't keep me locked up during daylight hours.

"How about we grab a shave ice on our way?" I said to Kenny.

"Yeah. That'd be great."

We were pinching our pennies, but I could still afford to buy my son a cup of ice with syrup.

I knew it was coming before Elma said it.

"I still don't understand why they don't offer maple syrup as a topping."

"Because you aren't in New York anymore, Elma. Now you get to have pineapple-flavored snow cones."

Why do you have to bring out the worst in me, I wanted to scream, exasperated with her and even angrier with myself.

At the top of Ward, before we started the steep descent, I deliberately kept my eyes on the ocean ahead, careful not to turn to the west. Since the day we drove out to Red Hill and gazed down on the destruction at

Pearl Harbor, I had averted my eyes whenever we circled Punchbowl. I knew I couldn't see the devastation from so far away, but the image of the inverted USS *Oklahoma* still haunted me. From where we had stood above the harbor, it glistened like an enormous silver fish flipped over, belly to the sky, desolate in oil-slick water under a setting sun.

"So, Kenny," I said, "tell Gran that joke you heard at school yesterday. The one about the rabbit and the giraffe. I bet she'll like it just fine."

Chapter Ten

March 1942 to December 1943

Lionel, age 14

After the day Kaiyo came home shaking from a shopping trip downtown, I began going with her to run errands. We go to the fish market, the grocery, even the shrine where she prays. I don't go inside with her at the shrine. I sit on a little wood bench they have outside the *torii* gate. She never takes long. It's not like going to our church, where it can go on and on and on, especially on communion Sundays. I don't know what she does in there and it doesn't seem polite to ask. "Never ask a person about their politics, their religion, or how much they make," Gran Schaeffer says.

I go along with Kaiyo because sailors and GIs clog the sidewalks and make it scary for girls to walk around on their own. Especially Japanese girls. The service guys say terrible things to them. They say things to Kaiyo no guy should ever say to any girl, and they still say them even when I'm walking alongside her. They act like she's some kind of animal who can't understand them. But she does understand and I understand, too. At least some of it. They use some words I've never heard before, things that make no sense. The first time I asked my mom about them she told me never to say them again, so I still don't know what they mean exactly and I don't dare ask anyone at school 'cause they might tell a teacher I said them and I'd be in big trouble. Or else they'll think I'm some kind of dopey kid who doesn't know anything. All I know is the stuff they say is bad, things no man should say about any woman.

Kaiyo used to keep her eyes on the ground in front of her and we would walk really, really fast, as fast as we could, only that seemed to make them laugh, like they knew they were scaring her and they liked that. One day she said, "Lionel, we aren't going to act afraid anymore. From now on, we will walk the way we want to walk, slow or fast or in-between, whatever pace feels right for us. And I'm not looking at the ground anymore. From now on, I'm looking them in the eye."

Gran Schaeffer didn't think the looking them in the eye part was such a good idea. "They might get the wrong message," she told Kaiyo. "The opposite idea from what you want them to have."

"What I want is for them to know I will stand up for myself. I won't let them turn me into a frightened ghost."

Only I know she really is frightened when we are walking along like that. Sometimes she holds my hand even though it makes them say more awful stuff, teasing her for having a boyfriend, when anybody looking at us would know she is way older than I am and a girl as pretty as her would never, ever be interested in a goofy-looking kid like me.

Two times a month we do an extra-long walk to visit Kaiyo's uncle at the Sand Island camp where he is locked up like a criminal, only he never did anything bad. Only two days after the attack, FBI men went to her family's store in Waialua, put handcuffs on her uncle, and took him away, just because he published a newspaper about what was going on in Hale'iwa. I don't see what's so bad about giving the score from the high school football game or saying what day they're holding the church bazaar or posting the schedule for the Japanese language school. The generals thought maybe he was a secret agent sending messages by code to the Japanese navy. Her uncle sure doesn't look like a spy to me. He has lots of gray hair and sad eyes and each time we bring him a package of razors and chocolates and toothbrushes, he bows and bows and says, "Arigato gozaimasu," and Kaiyo says, "English, Uncle, English," and he says, "Hai, hai," but he keeps using Japanese words 'cause he can't help himself. Kaiyo worries the generals will think his speaking Japanese proves he is a spy. We can only visit him two times a month, and Kaiyo is the only one who lives close enough to visit, so we make sure we never miss a visitors' day. She and her uncle bow and walk backward when it's time to go, as if neither one of them wants to turn their back on the other, like maybe turning their back would seem like closing their hearts. She cries the whole way home. Not loud. Not so as anyone else would notice. But I can feel her body shiver.

Mom tells me I'm right to be angry at Governor Poindexter, for letting them lock up Japanese who've lived here all their lives. She says locking up our neighbors and friends just because they're Japanese is wrong, and she even said so in one of her newspaper columns. She wrote for all the world to read, *I'm of German descent and you don't hear anyone saying I should be locked up. This is racism pure and simple*, and man oh man, did that get a lot of letters flying to the editor. I asked how come none of her big-deal friends who know all the generals and own things like the pineapple cannery and the sugar plantations can't make them set the people free, and she said, "It doesn't work like that, Lionel. I wish it did, but powerful men don't use their power to help the little guy. They use it to help themselves and their friends."

"Don't go filling the boy's head with angry ideas," Gran Schaeffer said. "Let him be a kid." But when Mom said, "You're one to talk. You had me posting suffragette notices when I was eight years old," Gran laughed and said, "Well, you're right about that. I guess, Lionel," she said to me, "your Gran has become a regular old play-it-safe, white-haired lady. Don't listen to me. Listen to your mom. Speak up for all the people who can't speak up for themselves." Now that was a first. Gran Schaeffer never admits she's wrong and Mom's right. The only one saying nothing angry about it is Kaiyo. She does what Ying told her to do after the bombing: "Keep your mouth shut." Ying thinks it's easy for Mom and Gran to get all riled up, but that folks like her and Kaiyo have to be more careful. She didn't say why, but I think maybe it's because they aren't haoles. There may not be many haoles in Hawai'i, but they sure do get to be in charge of most everything.

I asked Kaiyo once if she ever wanted to take her boyfriend Buster to meet her uncle and she said, "I can't do that, Lionel," and she wouldn't tell me why not. I don't know if she's ashamed her uncle speaks so much Japanese and is afraid Buster will think he's the enemy or if she's worried her uncle might be angry at all the mainland haoles for locking him up. If you ask me, I think she can do a whole lot better than her boyfriend Buster. Driving a cool motorcycle doesn't make him a good guy, and I don't like the way he doesn't come to the door to get her when he picks her up. Like he's not really a gentleman. She doesn't seem to mind, though, and always has her happiest smile for him.

I know I should be grateful to guys like Buster and all the other sailors and soldiers crowding our island who are willing to die for us, but I sure do wish they would learn themselves some manners. I wish even more that Governor Poindexter would come to his senses and grow a heart. I'd like to see how he'd feel if someone he loved got locked up on some island for doing nothing except being born in a different country.

Sadira

Renee disconnected the massive hose that stretched from the farm's milk tank to the truck's, then set it back in place, scrambling up and down the truck's ladder with a confidence and ease that surprised me. She hadn't seen me yet. I didn't want to interrupt her work, so stayed in the shade of the dairy barn's eaves. When she'd finished filling out a clipboard full of paperwork, I stepped out of the shadows.

"Hey there," I called across the expanse of packed dirt that separated the farm buildings from the fields.

She lit up in her usual unaffected way. "What the hell are you doing out here?" Even an ill-fitting white uniform of starched pants and shirt couldn't diminish her beauty. Her mass of blond curls was wound tight in a bun beneath a stiff white cap, the kind soda jerks wore. "Boy, are you a sight for sore eyes." She hugged me close. "But seriously, why are you here?"

"I could ask the same of you. Ben sent me out, only he didn't tell me you were part of my assignment. I'm here to interview women filling in for the men who enlisted."

Renee tossed her clipboard and pen on the truck's passenger seat. "I doubt Ben even knows I'm working here. Harrison isn't exactly thrilled about it."

"You're actually working for the farm?" Despite appearances, I found it a stretch to believe Renee was a dairy truck driver, skilled at operating machinery. "Can you drive this thing?"

She stared at me as if I were daft. "Of course I can. I'm a farm girl, remember? My pop had me driving tractors and trucks soon as my foot could reach the pedals. I'm helping out 'cause it's work I know how to do and I like hanging out here. The crew has always been good to me. They let me ride their horses when I stay at the beach house. Also doesn't hurt that it's one of the family businesses."

I'd wondered if including the Dairyland Farms in the article was due to it being a Bellingham business, but I hadn't raised the question with Ben. It was no secret the Bellinghams owned the farm. The acres and acres of open field had belonged to the family for generations.

"Last I heard, Judith had you serving tea to soldiers at the officers' clubs."

"That lasted about five minutes. What a waste of everyone's time and energy. Last thing I wanted was to wear chiffon and gloves while serving hot tea on a soggy afternoon. The only people more desperate than me to escape were the poor guys in uniform. By comparison, I'm in heaven here."

"The work doesn't scare you?"

"Not for a second. Baking a cake, sewing a dress—those scare me. This is easy work. I pick up a truck in 'Aiea each morning, drive it out here, load up the milk, and head back to the processing plant. Easy-peasy. Plus I get to wear this stylish outfit." She struck a pose. "I'm surprised you haven't commented."

"Trust me. The image is etched in my brain. I'll be sure to describe it in detail, right down to the embroidered red cow above the shirt pocket. In fact"—I pulled my notebook and pencil out of my purse—"let me jot down some details before I forget." I listed specifics I wanted to be sure to include. "Now explain to me how this milk hose works. Make it sound complicated so I can impress the readers with your skills."

Renee gave me the gist of what she did to connect the hose between the two tanks, get the milk moving from one to the other, and keep track of when the truck's tank was full. "Not much to it."

"For you, maybe. I'd be terrified I'd contaminate the tank or spill milk all over the yard. Seems like plenty to keep straight." I scribbled down the specifics as I spoke.

"No more than what you do when you write up a story. People just aren't used to women operating machinery, so they think we can't do it."

Jeff Garcia, the dairy's manager, strolled over to join us. "I see you found one of our angels."

After briefing me on the work women were doing on the farm, Jeff had set me loose to observe on my own. "Go watch the wahines at work," he'd told me. "They know folks from the paper will be looking around."

Renee linked her arm in mine. "Sadie and I are old pals, Jeff. I don't think she has any illusions about me being an angel."

"Not true. After watching you handle that equipment, I get it. You're a pro."

Karen Franzoni, the photographer who'd ridden along with me, was doing her own reconnaissance. She emerged from the milking barn.

"I got some great shots of Della cleaning the machinery," she said as she approached us. "She's a pistol. You'll want to talk to her, Sadira."

"Will do. And this is my friend Renee Bellingham, who drives for the dairy. We'll want shots of her as well."

Karen nodded at Renee. "As in, Mrs. Harrison Bellingham?"

Renee shrugged, clearly uncomfortable. "I keep quiet about that out here. Do you guys have to use me for this story? Plenty of women are working harder than me. Plus, Harrison won't like it."

I knew Karen wouldn't press the point. As a new hire, she couldn't risk trouble with Harrison. It was different for me.

"Harrison will be pleased as punch when he sees the front-page shot of you with the headline: *Mrs. Harrison Bellingham Keeps Milk on Our Tables.*"

Renee actually shuddered. "I hate it. What I do is nothing special. Besides, Judith will blow a gasket if she finds out I'm driving a truck."

I wrapped an arm around her waist and squeezed. "Sorry, kiddo, but there's no way I'm passing up this opportunity. That face of yours sells newspapers and Harrison knows it. He and Judith will put a good face on it and play proud. They're not dummies. It makes the family look good. Now let's get a shot of you climbing into the truck."

"How about I get a shot of both of you," Karen said. "Two strong women doing their part."

I expected Renee to resist, but she grinned. "Why not? It's been you and me from the start when it comes to the *Chronicle.*"

Karen posed us with Renee balancing on the truck runner, a hand on the cab's open door as if she were climbing up to the driver's seat, and me down below, pad and pencil in hand, gazing up as I interviewed her. Soon as the photos were done, Renee slid into the driver's seat.

"I need to get a move on." She closed the door, tore a sheet from the clipboard, and handed it out the window to Jeff. "Your copy, boss."

"Talk later tonight?" I asked. "You can help me fill in some of the blanks."

She rolled her eyes. "OK, but promise me you'll talk to the other women and use their stories. Not just Della. Be sure you meet Sister.

She's out in the pastures right now. They're the ones who'll give you the good stuff." She started the engine, then leaned out again. "Hey, Jeff." She nodded in my direction. "This one really knows her way around a horse. Put her on one with some spirit, then tell me all about it tomorrow." She put the truck in gear, beeped her horn a couple times, and drove off, churning up a cloud of fine red dust.

"OK then. Let's go meet Sister," Jeff said, heading away from the barn. "But we're taking the jeep."

I laughed. "So you don't think I can ride a horse?"

He winked. "I know Renee."

He drove us out on a dirt road that bisected the fenced pasturelands. The fields sloped down from a low mountain ridge to the coastal highway, a strip of asphalt separating the fields from the shoreline. From our vantage point, the north shore waves appeared serene—gentle, undulating swells that crested and dissolved into white foam. Up close, the waves were mountains towering as high as fifty feet.

"This is spectacular. Can we stop a moment so I can get some shots?" Karen asked.

Jeff pulled off to the side. "You been to Makawao?" he asked. "You want a view to knock your socks off, you gotta check out upcountry Maui."

"Trust me, it's on my list." Karen climbed on the jeep's backseat for a better view. "I'd say you're a pretty lucky guy to see this every day."

I could see why Renee didn't mind the daily drive out there. O'ahu offered beauty in abundance—nothing could beat the drama of the Ko'olaus' windward cliffs or Mānoa and Nu'uanu's lush tropical valleys— but this juxtaposition of cow pastures and ocean swells was both unexpected and pleasing.

Karen sat down again.

"Hope you saved some film for the people shots," I said.

"Not to worry. I'm hoping for some action shots with the horses. I trust this Sister person knows how to handle a horse?"

"For sure," Jeff said. "She's a true *paniolo*."

As we bounced down the bumpy road, I raised my face to the sun. The wind whipped back my hair, and I could taste the ocean salt on my lips, smell the sun's heat against my skin. For the first time in a year, the moment felt almost the way life was before Pearl Harbor, that time when worry didn't overwhelm all else.

The bombing had changed everything. I hated life in its aftermath. Martial law meant curfews and rationing, an end to personal freedom and all that gave us joy. The military took over and turned the island into an encampment. They occupied even the Royal Hawaiian Hotel and the University of Hawai'i, where a massive burial pit was dug for the thousands of bodies they expected would fall in a Japanese invasion. Barbed wire lined its campus walls and trenches crisscrossed its campus. It felt beyond endurance and yet, over time, we adapted until it became our normal life, a normal thick with corrosive fear and uncertainty. Every article I wrote for the paper was a story of loss and despair.

For the first time in the months since the attack, I felt a glimmer of hope that sunny morning. In our darkest hour, our island women were stepping forward to pick up the burden as men enlisted. All our lives we'd been told this was work women couldn't do, and yet women were driving trucks, operating family businesses, rounding up cattle. In a myriad of ways, they were proving their capacity. And one of those amazing women was Renee, my silly, outrageous, fabulous Renee who I hadn't thought could so much as change a light bulb. The article I would write was forming in my mind, a story of something hopeful and inspiring. On that dirt road, driving beside green pastures and a rolling sea, happiness seemed possible.

Lionel, age 15

"I remember skating on the lake that year," Miss Eleanor said when Gran started telling stories about the winter of 1893, when all of Lake Ontario froze up solid. "We drove all the way to Oswego and it seemed like half the state was out there skating. Some folks even skated clear across to Canada."

I think the reason Gran and Miss Eleanor were such instant pals is they'd both lived up by Lake Ontario a long time ago. You'd think they'd be glad they aren't there anymore, and I think they do like it here in Hawai'i, but seems like all they talk about is what it was like way back then. I don't know why anyone would miss things like blizzards and dead leaves and spring mud. Besides, it's not like Miss Eleanor lived in New York all that long. She was born and raised right here in Hawai'i, and was only in New York long enough to become a doctor at Syracuse University. Not a fix-you doctor, a study-plants kind of doctor. Plants are what she likes best. She liked them even before she went to study in the ladies' part of Harvard College. Once she became a college student, she kept learning more and more about them. She got so good at botany, she came back and taught it at the university here. Thanks to her, UH has a whole garden of its own, one that's even bigger than the one Miss Eleanor created at her father's house in Manoa. "Nani Lani" is what they call the house. It means "beautiful heaven." Her garden is so big and so thick with trees and bushes, you can't even tell from the road that there's a house in the middle of it. All you see is a black iron fence around what looks like a giant park with huge shower trees and thick walls of croton. It takes two full-time gardeners just to keep it under control.

Gran and Miss Eleanor didn't meet 'cause of plants though. They met at church. On Gran's very first Sunday, Miss Eleanor took her under her wing, and now they're like a pair of mynah birds, chattering nonstop when they're together. Mom says it tickles her pink to see Gran so happy, but she says it with her lips smiling but her eyes not. I'm not all that sure she means it. I am for real happy about it 'cause I'm like Gran. Neither one of us had any real friends in Carlisle, that kind of friend who thinks the same thoughts you think before you even say them out loud. I still don't have a friend like that, but I figure if Gran had to wait till she was a really old lady to find her true friend, then maybe even I will have one someday before I die.

Miss Eleanor invited us all to her place for Thanksgiving this year. It was some feast, I'll tell you. Not that Mom and Gran don't fix up a real tasty dinner, but Miss Eleanor has a cook and a maid and a fancy house with fancy china and crystal and silver. Gran made Kenny and me practice our manners before we went, to be sure we wouldn't embarrass her. I've never been in a house that made me so nervous. Miss Eleanor has giant vases made thousands of years ago in China, and Persian carpets so thick you can't hear a person's footsteps on them. Miss Eleanor's so kind and friendly, you'd never think she had buckets of money and a head stuffed full of more information than most of us will ever come close to knowing in our whole lives.

Kenny likes her whale collection best. Not real live big whales, just small carvings of whales. She lets Kenny take them off the shelves and study the ways people carve wood and stone. He likes the stone ones especially and is trying to make his own stone lions. They don't look nearly so nice as Miss Eleanor's whales.

Miss Eleanor wants Gran to move in to keep her company—"be my companion," is how she says it—and I think Gran wants to, but she keeps saying, "No, no, Sadie and the kids need me," as if we can't all take care of ourselves just fine. Besides, we have Kaiyo around to help, too. Mom gets quiet when they talk like that. I don't understand why. She gets real snippy with Gran all the time, sighing and rolling her eyes at stuff Gran says, so you'd think she would like the idea of her moving out. I would be sad to see Gran move away, even if it's only a few miles. I like her being there when I come home from school. She's the only person except Mom and Dad who's known me from the second I was born, and sometimes I think she likes me better than Mom does. A person needs someone who likes them even when they do stuff wrong, though even Gran tries to fix me sometimes, like I'm a painting or a song she's trying to make just right. But I want her to be happy before she's so old she dies, so I think if she wants to be Miss Eleanor's companion, she should be.

Before we ate our Thanksgiving dinner, Miss Eleanor took me upstairs to show me the huge bedroom she's having fixed over. Her dad used to live in that room. She said his room was nothing but bookshelves and piles of papers and for a long time she couldn't face digging through it all. Finally, though, she got the energy to tackle it, and now the room has fresh wallpaper and carpets and looks like a place for a lady instead of a guy. If Gran decides to take her up on her offer, this is where she'll live, like a grand lady. Standing there, looking at all that fancy stuff, all I could think of was Gran's tiny room with only a single bed pressed up against one wall, a small dresser, and a wood chair. That's all. I think we need to help Gran decide to move in with Miss Eleanor. She's so old she could die any minute now. She's going to turn sixty-five on her next birthday, and I think she should get to be happy, even extra-super-happy, before she kicks the bucket.

Sadira

It was Eleanor's hand on Elma's elbow that first caught my attention during Thanksgiving dinner. Not that it was lingering or caressing, but its very gentleness and the smile it sparked suggested intimacy. Elma never showed me, her own daughter, any kind of affection. If I had placed a hand on her elbow, I expect she'd have swatted it away.

Lionel nudged me, the gravy boat in his hands, and I realized I'd been staring. I ladled gravy liberally over my slices of turkey and potatoes, even over the string beans and stuffing. Across from me, Kenny studied a salt shaker shaped like a whale.

"What kind is this one?" he asked Eleanor, as he had earlier of her many other whale carvings and porcelain pieces.

"Beluga. And the pepper is a killer." Eleanor picked up the shaker. "Doesn't look very ferocious, does he?"

"Have you ever seen one?" Lionel asked. "Killers, I mean." Everyone in Hawai'i had seen humpbacks, they could be seen from shore, but only those on the open waters saw killer whales.

"False killers, yes, but actual ones, no. Archie, you must have seen a lot of whales from the ferry."

I had to admit Eleanor was a flawless hostess, reaching out to each of us in turn. Tuning in to Kenny's interest in whales, guiding Lionel to her collection of old maps, offering me access to her vast personal library of novels. I couldn't tell if this was fine breeding or an effort to win us over. As if we didn't already like and respect her.

Archie beamed under Eleanor's spotlight. "I saw them all the time, but the most memorable was off the Big Island—a sperm and her calf." The only thing Archie liked as much as drinking was telling stories. He launched into this one, and as he spoke, Eleanor gave him her full attention, clapping with delight when he described the calf mimicking its mother. I read nothing false in her response.

I wanted to like her. I did like her. She was one of the few women at church who'd always been kind to me. For that matter, I more than liked her, I admired her, and there was a lot to admire. Her advanced degrees. Her career at the university. Her travels. Her gardens. Her elegant home and manners. I also appreciated Eleanor's generous response to Elma, whom she embraced as a bosom friend despite the disparities in their backgrounds. But that same generosity and all her graciousness made me uneasy. Why such generosity to us? Why such affection for Elma?

Although we had spent the entire Thanksgiving Day at Eleanor's, Elma was heading off again the next morning to see her. She hovered by my front windows, waiting for Mr. Nakamoto, Eleanor's driver.

"What do you two have planned?" I asked.

"We're going to work on the remodel of her father's room. Sorting out what pieces will go where, as well as the bedding and drapes she'll need. I've offered to sew up anything she wants, but she insists on using her decorator, who apparently has her own suppliers. It all seems quite the waste of money to me, but who am I to argue with Eleanor's impeccable taste? I am getting such an education."

"She's certainly having an effect on you. I barely recognize you, what with the places you're going and the foods you're eating. I never thought I'd live to see the day when you'd be wearing sandals and slacks."

"Isn't it grand!" She beamed. "A whole new me in a whole new world." When she caught sight of the black Cadillac pulling up to the curb, she cried out like a kid waiting for the ice cream truck. "He's here."

"I'll come by and get you later," I said. "Say, around two or three?"

"No need." Elma's hand was already on the doorknob. "I promise to call if I need a ride." And she was gone, practically dancing up the walkway.

At two thirty, I pulled into the long driveway that wrapped through Eleanor's property, and parked in the guest area beside the massive garage with its second-level rooms for the staff. I braced myself for Elma's wrath. She would not like me showing up unexpectedly. I didn't care. Besides, I had an errand to run nearby and dishes to return. Eleanor had sent us home with bowls and bowls of Thanksgiving leftovers.

I heard their laughter long before I saw them. They were on the terrace doing something that had them in stitches. "You look like a schoolgirl," Eleanor was saying as I emerged from the tangle of garden that surrounded the terrace and walkway. Elma sat perched on a stool, a towel draped around her shoulders. Her thick beautiful hair littered the terrace stones. A sharp bob cut ran along her chin line, replacing the neat bun she always wore. Eleanor held up a mirror as Elma admired her new look. She nodded and giggled when her hair bounced. "Oh, Sadie," she cried when she saw me. She never called me Sadie. "Look at me. I'm a modern woman, thanks to Eleanor."

"It's quite a change, all right, but I have to agree with Eleanor. You look more like a schoolgirl than a grown woman." I was embarrassed for her.

She lowered the mirror and fixed me with a look so withering, my eyes welled with tears. "That makes sense, seeing as how I feel like a young woman."

She studied herself again in the mirror. "I may just have to get myself a swimsuit. About time I swam in Hawaiian waters."

She squeezed Eleanor's hand. "Thank you, dear friend."

Eleanor pulled the towel off Elma and shook it out. "If anyone can pull off a young look and remain dignified and elegant, it is you, my dear." She offered her hand as Elma stepped off the stool, then, using the towel, brushed the hair residue from Elma's clothes, sweeping the towel over her legs, neck, and chest.

I was desperate to leave.

"You've brought the bowls back," Eleanor said, finally recognizing the containers in my arms and taking them from me. "How thoughtful of you to return them so promptly. Will you join us for a cup of tea?"

"Thanks, no. I have to get to an afternoon reception. I only stopped by to see if Elma needed a ride home."

"We must have crossed wires," Eleanor said. "I believe Elma is staying for tea and perhaps even supper?" She looked to Elma for confirmation.

"Yes. That is the plan. And you needn't worry, Sadira. Mr. Nakamoto will see me home safely later this evening."

The two of them might as well have simply said, "Go away and leave us be," a request I was happy to oblige.

"Then I'll be off."

"Thank you again," Eleanor called. "I promise we'll take good care of your mother."

Since when did Elma need anyone to take care of her, I wanted to know. If this was what she wanted, if she preferred the company of a practical stranger to that of her own family, then so be it. She was free to make an utter fool of herself.

"Come have a look in the full-length mirror upstairs," was the last thing I heard Eleanor say.

I woke to "*junk an'a po, I canna show*" being chanted over and over again outside my window until Kenny finally said, "Scissors. You win," and Ying called from the front yard.

"Coming," Kenny answered, as loud and clear as if he and his friend stood beside my bed, thanks to Hawai'i's damn thin walls. The boys' *zoris* slapped as they ran around to the front. Sleeping in on a weekend morning was never a serious option, but now that the boys were older, I had less patience for their lack of consideration. I drifted back to sleep only to be woken by shouts from the front yard. That was it. I jumped out of bed, grabbed a robe, and headed for the door.

Kenny and Walter Ho stood red-faced and rigid opposite one another.

"*Wop yo jaw,*" Walter shouted. "I beat you again." Marbles lay scattered across the walkway.

Kenny grabbed Walter by the arm and twisted it behind his back. "Only 'cause you cheated."

As I stepped onto the porch, Kenny pushed Walter to the ground and landed a punch to the side of his head. I grabbed Kenny by the armpits and tried to pull him off the boy.

"Kenneth Eugene Doyle, get control of yourself!" Elma yelled, looking more like a tank than a woman as she crossed the lawn with great strides.

As Elma and I struggled to separate the two, Ying arrived with a hose that she turned on Kenny. He released Walter and covered his face. Though I jumped back when Ying began spraying, I got soaked as well.

Elma grabbed the dripping Kenny by the arm and collar, and pulled him in the direction of her cottage. "March yourself straight over to my place, young man."

I started to object. I was standing right there and should be the one disciplining my son, not Elma. He should be heading into our home, not hers. But it was Elma who managed day-to-day life while I worked. Either I granted her license to manage the boys her own way, or I had to devise another plan.

I helped Walter up. He had a small gash above his eye and his lip was bleeding.

"Come on inside and I'll clean you up," I said.

"I'll take care of him," Ying said, reappearing without the hose. "Don't think I don't know your role in this, Walter."

She led the boy away. Whatever had just happened was apparently familiar to Elma and to Ying. I was the visitor in my own household.

"They at it again?" Lionel asked, looking up when I entered the kitchen.

I grabbed a dishtowel and dried off what I could.

"This happen a lot?"

He shrugged. "Nah. Kenny usually only blows up if Walter gives him a hard time about Dad."

"What do you mean?" I sat down at the table opposite him. "What does Walter say?"

"The same old thing everyone says. That Dad's a no-good drunk. But he only says it when Kenny does something to make him mad. Like last week when Kenny threw Walter's Swiss Army knife up on the roof."

"Why'd he do that?"

"'Cause Walter drew a picture of Kenny kissing Cindy Nakamura and said he was going to post it on her locker."

I had no idea who Cindy Nakamura was or that Kenny liked her. Clearly I was losing touch with my sons' lives.

"OK. Thanks."

And of what use was this information to me anyway? I hadn't a clue how to sort out this dispute or change the dynamic of Kenny's relationships. I didn't even know what relationships he had. I had surrendered the parental role to Elma, Kaiyo, and Ying.

I ran a hand through my hair. Life was nothing but drudgery—no music or dancing, not even daytime gatherings with friends. Renee and Harrison didn't bother inviting people to their beach house anymore. The drive ate up too much gas. I ached to be giddy, to dance and laugh and not care about yesterday or tomorrow. I even hated the way I looked. No reason to dress up, no sparkle in my eyes. When I stood before the bathroom mirror, all I saw was a dull, weary woman staring back.

I was flipping through Kenny's sketchbook a couple hours later when Ying rapped on the screen door. I had picked up the book, curious about what held Kenny's attention. Mostly people's faces, as best I could tell.

"Thought you had a luncheon to cover at the Academy?" Ying said, talking to me through the screen.

"I'm playing hooky. I think Honolulu will survive not knowing what the ladies ate and wore. Got a sec?"

We settled in the rattan rockers on my porch, glasses of iced tea in hand.

"I'm losing control, Ying." I spoke softly, not wanting the boys or Elma to hear. "Of myself. Of the boys."

Ying kept rocking.

"This is the part where, as a friend, you reassure me and say, no, Sadie, you're doing fine."

"Except you're not."

"Except I'm not."

"So what are you going to do about it?"

I shrugged. "I don't know. I've no idea how to make things better."

"That part's easy. You need a better job. A better job means more money, more money means more choices."

I laughed. "I'm lucky I even have a job, with the war on. You said so yourself. Who's going to pay me more than what I make right now?"

"You will. It's time to stop thinking like an employee. You need to work for yourself and have other people work for you. That's the way to make money."

"What business do you think I could run that would make any kind of money?"

Often Ying's ideas struck me as either hopelessly naive or delusional, but I had learned not to dismiss them out of hand. Ying hadn't gotten rich by accident, and there was no mistaking, she was a very rich woman who chose to live modestly.

"Advertising. Help people sell things."

"I'm already doing that. For you." I looked at Ying pointedly. "I appreciate the extra money, but it's not exactly a windfall."

Ying stopped rocking. "A few ads here and there? Small potatoes. You have to think big. Why do people read your articles? You think it's for the information? You sell something every day. You know what catches people's attention, what kind of life they want to live, what words and ideas keep them interested. People will pay you to write those words for them."

"Ridiculous," was my first response, but then I thought about how often I commented on how some business needed a better sign out front, a cuter jingle on the radio, a better catchphrase, a more appealing menu.

"You really think I'd be good at that?"

"I pay you to write my ads because they help me sell more. More people—people with bigger businesses—will pay you, too. Pay you even more than I do." Ying set down her glass and stood to go. "You think about it. We'll talk more."

I stayed on the porch, rocking slowly, and tried to imagine how this might work. I was confident I could write ads and, with the help of a designer, make them pleasing to the eye. But maybe I could do more than that. I knew a lot of people in Honolulu, a lot of powerful people. Maybe I could use those connections, get paid to introduce people for their mutual benefit. I thought about how effective the government was at swaying the public's view of the war, convincing people to sacrifice for the sake of the country. Maybe I could create a kind of business propaganda, use the same strategies to sell products.

By late afternoon, I had decided Ying's idea wasn't so harebrained after all. Maybe I could create a whole new kind of business, a service that a developing city like Honolulu needed and no one else was providing. I started a list of all the people I could reach out to, the restaurant owners, the retailers, the political candidates. It was a long and encouraging list, and I knew everyone on it would open their door to me, listen to my pitch. "Thank you, Ying," I said, suddenly hopeful for the first time in a long time.

Seventy-five buttons in all. Seventy-five tiny fake pearls, each with a matching loop of fabric to slip around it. They ran from my neck to below my knees. They cinched tight the cuffs around my wrists. I was fine until I fastened the final buttons at my neck. As if a switch had been thrown, my body went from calm to panicked, my heart sped up, sweat beaded on my forehead. I hadn't realized when Elma suggested this style of dress how confining it would feel, how oppressive to be wrapped so tightly.

Calm down, I told myself. *Close your eyes. Take deep breaths. You are not suffocating.*

But it felt as if I were, as if I were in a cocoon I couldn't escape. I fumbled with the loops at my neck. If I could just undo the top ones, perhaps the feeling would subside, but I couldn't slow or steady my hand enough for the delicate work of sliding off the tight loops. And there were so many. The thought of the sheer number and the time it would take to unfasten each heightened my distress. I scanned the bathroom for shears. If I had to, I would cut the damn thing off me.

My God, this must be what it's like to be buried alive, I thought, as I grabbed either side of the dress's shirtwaist and yanked the blouse open. Buttons popped and skittered across the bathroom floor. I snapped loose the cuff buttons and let the dress drop, a puddle of fabric at my feet. Panting, I soaked a towel with cool water and pressed it to my face.

"Sadira?" Elma stood in the doorway.

I looked up from the sink, my face dripping.

"I went a little batty." I dried my face, then picked the dress up off the floor. "Something about how tight it is." I fluttered a hand across my chest. "The neck so high and the sleeves so long. I've gone and popped the buttons."

"I'd say you more than popped them." Elma examined the bodice.

"At least most of the loops are still intact. Easy enough to sew buttons back on."

"I can't wear it. I'm sorry, Elma. I know it was a lot of work and it's lovely. Really. It's just too constraining."

"I'm sure I can find someone less high-strung to make use of it." She crouched down, running her hand over the floor.

"Stop. I'll do that, Elma. I'll find them and pass them on to you."

"So I can reattach them?"

I wrung out the wet towel and pressed it against my face again. "No, of course not. I did the damage, I'll sew them back on. Leave the dress."

Elma draped it over a towel rack. "I came in to let you know we've got everything packed in the truck. The boys are coming along to help unload it all. I've promised them dinner and a ride home."

"OK. Great. That'll work out just fine. I'm heading out soon myself."

"I assume you've something else to wear."

"You know I do." I kept my face buried in the towel.

"Well, then. I'm off. I told Kaiyo I'd come back Monday to give my room a good final scrubbing."

I couldn't imagine how there was any portion of Elma's room, let alone any part of the entire cottage, that required further cleaning. I leaned back against the sink, my hands gripping its edges.

"I'm sure you'll leave everything fine and dandy."

The front screen door creaked open.

"We're all set, Gran." Kenny appeared in the doorway beside his grandmother, his T-shirt damp with sweat. Nearly thirteen, he was still more boy than man. He caught a glimpse of me and backed into the hall with a "Whoa."

"Sorry," I said. "Bit of a wardrobe problem." I pulled my robe from its hook, wrapped it around myself, and followed them into the living room. "Thank you for helping Gran." I gave him a big hug. "I'll be late tonight, kiddo, so you won't see me till morning."

"Got it." He headed back out, Elma close behind him, but she paused at the door.

"Sadira," she began.

"Don't, Elma. Please, don't. I'm fine. Go. They're waiting. Eleanor will wonder where you all are."

Despite her short hairstyle and stylish slacks, Elma was still the mother I had known all my life. Rigid back, hands folded at her waist, purse in the crook of her arm. A woman of steel. Unflappable. She would never be the one on her knees, retrieving buttons.

"We'll see you and the boys for brunch tomorrow. Eleanor suggested we dine on the terrace."

"Right. Sounds lovely."

She hesitated, as if still deciding something. *Do not come over here and hug me. Do not*, I silently begged her.

"Gran!" This time it was Lionel calling.

"Coming," she answered, and was out the door.

Chapter Eleven

March 1944 to June 1945

Lionel, age 16

One day, Kaiyo stopped talking and singing. Before the not-talking time, she was so in love with her sailor boyfriend Buster that she'd forget people were around. She'd bust out singing "Taking a Chance on Love" or "You'll Never Know" while she did the ironing or sliced vegetables for supper. Then, one day, she stopped. "It's not your concern," she said when I asked. She didn't say she was OK, she just wouldn't tell me what was troubling her.

Turns out it was something. A really big something. A baby-big something. Buster went and got her pregnant, and Mom about blew a gasket when she found out. Ying was the one who guessed it. She knows the signs. Mom's the one who's supposed to have a special gift for knowing what's going to happen to everyone, but Ying's the one who figured things out for real. 'Course she told Mom, and Mom told Kaiyo that Buster would have to marry her. "But I don't want to marry him," Kaiyo said, and Mom said, "How exactly do you plan on surviving, then? You think you can raise a kid by yourself?" Mom said it in her really loud voice that makes me shake inside.

I wasn't supposed to be hearing all of that. Mom, Ying, Gran, and Kaiyo were sitting in the kitchen talking when I got back from my trumpet lesson. They were so busy yakking they didn't even notice I was home.

"I can't marry him, because he doesn't want me," Kaiyo said, and I could tell it shamed her to admit that. I think she really loved Buster and that it hurt her bad when he didn't love her enough to marry her. She sounded like she wasn't just angry with Buster. She sounded like she was angry with Mom, too. I understand that. I'm angry at Mom almost all the time and I raise my voice to her a lot, but Kaiyo doesn't. Normally, Kaiyo acts like Mom is some kind of wonderful and never talks back to her. Though sometimes she listens and acts like she's going to do what Mom says, and then she goes and does what she wants to do. I don't know if Mom ever notices how Kaiyo can be tricky that way.

Anyway, Kaiyo said she couldn't marry him and Mom said, "I don't care what he says or what he wants. He doesn't have a vote in this. He gave up his choices three months ago."

"She can't hold a gun to his head and force him," Gran said, though I think we all know Kaiyo could do that and might do that, or at least I could picture her doing that.

"No one's holding a gun to his head," Mom said. "But a word to the right person and the navy will see to it he does the honorable thing."

They were quiet for a while after that, like their mouths finally got worn out.

"Could you stomach living with this man?" Ying finally asked. "You don't have to stay married to him, just long enough so the baby has a name."

"It's that or give the baby up," Mom said. "We can set you up at the Salvation Army home in Manoa. After you have the baby and it's adopted, you can come back, pick up the pieces, and move on."

"No." I knew Kaiyo's voice and I could tell from the way she said that "no" that there was no way she was changing her mind. "I won't give the baby up to strangers."

After that night, things moved fast 'cause Mom called up some big-deal navy guys she knows and made them tell Buster what's what and then some. Miss Eleanor even helped by calling some important people she knows. Next thing ya know, it was the big day. Kaiyo still wasn't talking or smiling, and she didn't even put on a nice Saturday party dress. I picked a gardenia for her hair but she wouldn't wear it. "I want it to last," she said, putting it in a glass of water. "I'll keep it beside my bed to sweeten my dreams." I don't think that was the reason she wouldn't wear it, but I liked the idea.

I would have offered to help raise Kaiyo's baby so she wouldn't have to marry Buster, but I couldn't 'cause I have other plans. I haven't told anyone yet, but I'm going to enlist in the navy when I graduate in a year and a half, maybe even before I finish high school. Mom always says she hopes the war ends before Kenny and I are old enough to fight, but I want a chance to do my part. Mr. Parker, my trumpet teacher, thinks I'd make a great flag man 'cause of my sharp memory. Waving those flags around on an aircraft carrier sounds pretty swell and important. I made a set of my own flags and got a manual to help me learn the code. I practice out in the back field when no one is around. If I already know everything there is to know about signaling, they'll have to let me in.

Mom keeps talking about the day when I will go to the mainland for college and she never asks if that is what I want to do. If there was a college where I could read all the books I wanted on the Civil War and airplanes and ships, then maybe I would think about going there, but if college is like high school, then all I can say is a big, "NO THANK YOU." I don't want to do any more sitting in classrooms with teachers saying, "Stick to the subject, Lionel," or, "Give someone else a chance to talk, Lionel," or, "You may not raise your voice just because you don't like what someone is saying." I want to do my learning by myself so I can decide what I am going to learn and not have to listen to stupid people talk about things they know nothing about.

Besides, me going to college won't do anybody else any good. I think it's important to be a good citizen and a good man, and good men serve and protect their country. There is no way I am going to end up like my dad, who never did anything to protect us or our country.

We all tried to eat breakfast on the wedding day, but no one was very hungry. Kaiyo didn't even sit down with us, and she nearly didn't get in the car at the last minute. Gran gave her a goodbye hug that made it seem like she was headed for the gallows. I saluted her and reminded her that the Lone Ranger says, "All things change but truth, and truth alone lives on forever," and I told her I was proud of her for speaking the truth and accepting the consequences. I thought it would make her feel better, but that was the only time I ever saw her get weepy.

After they left and Gran went back to Miss Eleanor's, I headed to the kitchen and it was one big mess. All our dirty dishes were just sitting there. Gran hadn't even put away the bread or the jars of jelly. It was like all of them lost their heads over this. I hate it when things aren't the way they're supposed to be. Dirty dishes aren't meant to be sitting out on a table, and if you leave jelly jars open, the roaches and ants will get in them.

Most of the time people make no sense to me, and I don't think I will ever figure them out. But at least things like cleaning dishes and putting things where they belong and doing my homework are part of a system. I like systems and knowing what needs to be done and when and how, so I set to work that morning. I didn't have a whole lot of time 'cause of school. I turned on the hot water full blast and filled up the dishpan with soap and hot water, and I scrubbed those dishes really well. I even washed off all the counters and the table and put everything away.

I couldn't tackle Kaiyo's vegetable garden till after school. With all that was happening, she'd let it go to rack and ruin. Even though it was raining something awful, soon as I got home, I pulled up every single weed and picked all the ripe vegetables. Most things I couldn't fix, but at least I could make those things right. I only wish Mom had let me skip school and go along to the courthouse. I could have stood beside Kaiyo and told her everything was going to be OK. I didn't know if it would be or not, but sometimes you just need someone to say it so you can maybe believe it.

Sadira

It felt good to see the cocky grin gone from Buster's face. I'd never liked that kid, the way he roared up our street on his motorcycle, blasting his horn, commanding Kaiyo to come bouncing out to meet him rather than knocking properly at her door.

If I happened to be outside when he arrived and he was forced to acknowledge me, he'd pile on the fake charm. "Afternoon, ma'am," he'd say in his Southern drawl, his hands clutching the motorcycle handles, his arms tensed to show off his bulging muscles. He wore his T-shirt sleeves rolled up, tucking a pack of Lucky Strikes in the fold. He even hid his eyes under aviator shades to create the illusion of a pilot's courage and ability, as if anyone would ever let him sit in a cockpit.

But it worked. The way Kaiyo melted before him, you'd have thought he was Frank Sinatra. I couldn't fathom how an otherwise intelligent, sensible young woman could be swept up by such a sorry excuse for a man.

His bravado was gone that morning in the courthouse. He looked sharp enough in his dress blues, but a scared little kid stared out from under his cap. He and Kaiyo weren't yet twenty-one, young as Arch and I were the day we wed. That day, Arch probably looked every bit as immature as Buster, but to me he was a fully grown man, handsome and commanding in his brother's suit, a portrait in confidence and capability. I gazed up the aisle at him, certain he was my soul mate, my Heathcliff. I desired nothing in the world except his touch, his adoring eyes, his giddy delight at calling me wife.

The judge looked as if he felt sorry for Buster, like he might intervene to save him, and I suppose I would have understood if he had. No one wanted this. This was no act of love, no cause for celebration, but we grown-ups in the room—the captain, the judge, and me—we knew the hard realities. Marriage was the only honorable option.

As for Kaiyo, she stood expressionless through the entire brief ceremony, then barked out an "I do" that sounded more like a curse than a vow. There was no kiss to seal the deal, not even a hug. Pronounced man and wife, the pair stepped apart and went their separate ways. Might as well have marched down the hall and started the divorce proceedings right then and there, but the agreement was to wait a year.

"You can drop me at the University Street entrance," Kaiyo said as we headed up King Street toward UH. She had classes that afternoon and had brought her textbooks with her.

A heavy March rain enveloped the island. Streams ran down each side of the road. When I pulled up to the curb, Kaiyo swung open the car door and unfurled her umbrella, but before she could step out, I put a hand on her arm. "Wait." The face she turned to me was cold and impatient. "You'll have another chance," I said. "Someday it'll be the right guy and your wedding will be a joyous day. You'll get a happy ending."

"Just like you and Archie?" she said.

She slammed the door and ran, the umbrella tilted into the curtain of rain, her books clutched to her chest.

Lionel

I don't know how come I knew to stay home two days after the wedding. Instead of heading off to church like I do every Sunday, I waited. I practically went and stood on Kaiyo's porch, I could feel it that strong, a notion something huge and terrible was coming our way, coming the way lava pours over a crater's edge and creeps along real slow and steady, burning everything in its path. I felt it, but I couldn't tell how it was coming—if the Japanese army would drop from the skies or a tsunami sweep over us—only that it would crush and pull us under.

Turned out, it arrived in a regular old Ford sedan. Just pulled up at the curb, dull and ordinary as any old car except you could see the two guys in it. Could see their dress uniforms, the caps on their heads. I knew this was trouble.

I don't know what I was expecting. Not that she would scream. Kaiyo wasn't a screamer. I think in my secret heart, I was hoping she'd come running to our place, wanting me in her hour of need. But she didn't.

I didn't knock on her door when they left. I just swung that screen door wide open a few minutes later and went on in. She was sitting there in the big chair Gran left behind, perched at its end like she might shatter in a million little pieces if she moved so much as her tiny finger.

"He shot himself."

She said it soft, said it the same as she might say, "He put on his socks," or, "He ate a piece of toast."

I couldn't make sense of it. Why would a man married to the prettiest girl on the island ever want to leave her or his own kid growing inside her belly? If I were Buster, if I were the luckiest man alive, I'd spend my whole life making sure nothing ever hurt her or the kid we made together. I'd make sure she was happy every single day I woke up beside her.

I don't know if Kaiyo blamed Mom. I don't know if I blamed Mom or what Mom thought in her most secret of secret places. Sometimes I can't sleep for worrying I've done wrong to somebody. One day I spent the whole afternoon kneeling in the back of the school chapel, praying for forgiveness 'cause I said something nasty for no good reason other than to make myself feel better. I think if I were the one who made Buster marry Kaiyo, if I had done something to make someone so miserable he'd rather die, I'd be feeling pretty flat-on-the-ground awful every single day, but Mom was just as ornery and bossy as she ever was. She acted like nothing happened, though I gotta think that at least some part of her is sorry. I don't think she meant for Buster to die.

Sadira

For the first time in my life, I understood what it was to need a drink, which is how I came to be sipping manhattans alone at the Pacific Grill at three in the afternoon. The problem was, drinking changed nothing. Buster was still dead and I felt somehow responsible. It never occurred to me the kid would take the coward's way out. I figured he was just a spineless boy from Kentucky, scared to tell his folks about their half-Japanese grandkid. No one had even asked or expected him to stay married to Kaiyo. Turned out he was the worst kind of coward, the kind that runs. I should have known from the way he was sweating in his dress uniform at the courthouse. When the judge asked if he took Kaiyo to be his wife, he stared down at his gleaming black shoes, never looking her or the judge in the eye. He was a man with no moral compass.

I twirled the cherry in my drink, dipped it up and down in the amber fluid.

"Drowning your sorrows?"

Jack O'Brien was the last person I wanted to see. He had warned me not to get involved. "It's not your problem to fix," he'd said.

"I wish I could drown them," I said. "This stuff's overrated. Two drinks and nothing feels better yet."

Jack signaled the bartender, ordered a burger and beer, then sat down beside me. I braced myself for his "told you so."

"What brings you to the grill at three on a workday?" I said.

"Hunger. And a birdie tipped me off you were here. I thought maybe you could use a friend. Someone to talk to."

"Thanks, but the last thing I want is to talk."

He nodded and we sat in silence until his burger arrived.

"Some fries to help with the bourbon?" he offered. "Those manhattans are pretty strong."

As he ate, I snacked on his fries and weighed ordering a third drink.

"By the way," I said, remembering he'd done me a favor, "thanks for getting Lionel out of the house last week."

Jack had taken Lionel for a sail after we heard about Buster. Lionel, of course, had fallen apart as he always falls apart when life gets rough—even if it has nothing to do with him. I had enough to do helping Kaiyo with the funeral arrangements. I couldn't manage Lionel as well.

"Happy to spend time with him. He's a unique kid. Sees things in surprising ways."

"Unique is a kind way to put it. He has a few other qualities you left out. Overly sensitive. Disrespectful. Know-it-all."

Jack took a pull on his beer. "Maybe it depends on how you look at it. Feeling things deeply and without apology isn't necessarily bad and probably rougher on him than the rest of us. I grant you his lectures can get a bit tedious, but he also speaks uncomfortable truths we probably need to hear."

I laughed. "Or you could call it being rude." I wasn't in the mood for another lecture on Lionel's special gifts.

Jack placed a hand over mine with such tenderness I jerked my hand away.

"Forgive yourself, Sadira. You couldn't know what that kid would do. You tried to make things right for Kaiyo. That wasn't a bad impulse."

I tipped back my glass then tossed some cash on the bar. "I'm done."

My shawl slipped off my shoulders as I turned to stand. Jack scooped it up and draped it over me. "I'll take you home."

"Thanks, but I can get myself home." My legs were wobbly as they hit the ground. Jack steadied me.

"I promise not to say another word." His voice was too soothing and his arm far too comforting as we stepped out the door and into the harsh daylight.

"Sometimes I really hate you," I said, and meant it. I did not need him to set me straight or rescue me. I didn't need anyone.

"I can live with that." He ushered me down the sidewalk, the shower trees arched over us, a canopy of brilliant yellow blossoms. Sometimes I also hated Hawai'i's beauty. It created such dissonance when the world was falling to bits.

As I stepped from the car, one of my heels sank in a crack between the driveway's cobblestones. I caught myself before tumbling to the ground, but still managed to nick my nylons as I extracted the heel.

A swell way to start the afternoon. Not even through the door and I was already a mess.

Harrison's mother, Judith, was honoring a few of the navy's finest young officers—those lucky enough to be assigned to Pearl Harbor. To show her appreciation for their service, she'd invited them to afternoon tea and a chance to meet the young ladies of Honolulu's finest families. Her white stucco villa nestled at the base of Diamond Head shimmered in the hot afternoon sun. I surveyed the scene through the arched colonnade separating the drive from the gardens. Officers in dress whites and girls in linen dresses speckled the lush green lawn. A tableau of money and privilege and stilted conversation. I scooped a glass of iced tea off the tray of a passing waiter and headed for a pool of shade beneath one of the wide-canopied monkeypod trees. We were suffering a spell of Kona weather, which meant that an oppressively humid air mass pungent with the too-sweet fumes of the pineapple cannery enveloped the island. No cooling trade winds swept down the mountain slopes to provide relief. Dressing for the tea had been misery. I was wilted before I pulled on my dress. The humidity frizzed my hair and melted my makeup.

Mrs. Bellingham was receiving guests in the music room, but the music room and Mrs. Bellingham were forbidden to me. The family's matriarch made it clear no reporter was welcome in her home even if it was she who insisted the paper cover the tea. "Be discreet," was how Harrison put it.

It was no simple task juggling a glass of tea and a notepad, but there wasn't any place to set my glass. The only tables and chairs placed out for guests were inhospitably in the open sun, as if to deliberately keep us from being too comfortable or lingering too long. It didn't help to be wearing cumbersome white gloves, which I managed to soil with makeup each time I dabbed at the perspiration on my face.

"To hell with this," I muttered, and pulled them off with my teeth. I stuffed them in my purse and extracted a handkerchief and pen. A giant wet circle now marked the spot on my chest where I'd cradled the glass against me. "Ah geez," I said aloud. "I look like I'm nursing."

"Having a rough day, Doyle?" Jerry Spikes, the photographer sent to assist me, appeared at my side.

"Is anyone having a good time in this beastly heat?"

"The gang up at the pool seems to be managing OK." He gestured to the gardens above us, into which were tucked a tennis court, swimming pool, and pool house. "The younger Mrs. Bellingham is entertaining guests."

"That can't be good. You didn't take any pictures, did you?"

"Right. Because I'm that stupid."

I patted my brow and temples delicately with the hanky, but I was sweating so profusely the cloth was quickly soaked and my face no less wet.

"What I wouldn't give to jump in that water. I don't suppose they're handing out swimsuits?"

Jerry shrugged. "I'm guessing it's swimsuit optional up there."

"Hold this a sec?" I passed him my glass, scanned the crowd, and scribbled names on my pad. "No big surprises so far as I can tell. What does it say about the importance of my work that I actually know the names of all these girls? Not a one of whom's done anything worthy of mention, and yet I'll write about them just because they're privileged. And we will further glorify them with your photos, so other young women can be jealous of their dresses and shoes and perfectly coiffed hair. Some business we're in."

He set my glass on the grass. "Yeah, it's a tough life you have, Doyle. The angels weep." He wandered off.

I knew I was lucky to have a job, but I had no spirit for it anymore, especially when there was nothing to write about except insipid gatherings and spoiled princesses.

I rescued my glass and headed for the hedge-lined path that zigzagged up the crater's slope to the swimming pool.

"Keep it in the air!" a female voice called from above me. I wondered if they'd moved on to the tennis courts, but when I passed through the bougainvillea-laced arbor, I discovered a young woman poolside, her back to me, with a large beach ball in hand. Two young men stood opposite her and a handful of others lounged on chairs poolside. They were tossing the ball back and forth and deliberately aiming to have it fall short of one another's reach. The idea was to make the others fall in. They were, the lot of them, gorgeous—the kind of playmates I'd expect Renee to have, at least the Renee of the past, but she was nowhere to be seen.

"Afternoon, all," I said. "Perfect day to be poolside." I received a few unenthused nods in response. "I'm looking for Renee Bellingham. Do you know if she's around?"

"Over there," an older woman said with a nod of her head to the pool house. She resumed reading her magazine.

I found Renee bent over papers spread out on the dining table the Bellinghams used when entertaining poolside.

"Sadie, you came. I hoped you would."

"You look busy."

"Boring stuff. Reports from the dairy." It turned out Renee could do more than drive a truck. She'd taken on a management role.

"Are you sorry you switched from driving to office work?"

She shrugged. "Not really. I like using my brains. Makes it tougher for Judith to ignore me. Come. I've some fabulous people for you to meet." She took my hand and led me back out to the pool.

"Everyone," she announced, "this is Sadira Doyle, my dearest friend and Honolulu's very own Hedda Hopper. Play it right and you could earn some special press while you're here." She then introduced me to a crowd that was suddenly a good bit friendlier. This was, it turned out, the lead cast of *Bravery in Paradise*, a war film being shot on Oʻahu. Of the bunch, Stella Mason was the only one I'd seen in anything before, but the others were effective at suggesting any failure to recognize them said more of my ignorance than of their fame.

"Judith invited them for lunch and a swim, so I get to play hostess rather than make small talk with the officers. Aren't I a lucky girl?" Renee had linked arms with Hugh, the film's handsome young lead. "Join us later, why don't you, Sadie. We're getting drinks at the Banyan Court at four."

That was an easy yes. I couldn't remember when I'd last had real Hollywood celebrities to write about, let alone sipped cocktails at the Moana.

"So?" Jerry asked when I rejoined him. "Anything of interest?"

"As it turns out, yes. We've some Hollywood swells in town. Been a long time since I've had a little glamour to talk up. Got plans for later this afternoon?"

"Just on standby."

"Swing by the Moana around four," I said. "They're a gorgeous bunch and eager for publicity. I expect they'll cooperate for some good shots. Head up to the pool now and you might even get some bathing suit action."

"Will do. Unless there's someone in particular you want me to catch down here, I'll take off after that."

I scanned the crowd. To me, the princesses, like the officers, were nearly indistinguishable from one another. There wasn't a one I wanted to glorify above the others. "If you've got some good shots of the officers, we'll be fine."

With my face and scalp now drenched and my dress damp against my back, I approached one of the young men close by. I needed to chat with a least one of America's heroes. "Good afternoon, I'm Sadira Doyle, a reporter with the Bellinghams' newspaper, the *Honolulu Chronicle*. I was wondering if I could speak to you about this lovely party and get your thoughts on Hawai'i's fair young women?" I wiped my hand on the skirt of my dress before extending it.

"Lieutenant Ethan Miller, ma'am."

The poor guy was sweating even more than I. I signaled a waitress, unloaded my empty glass on a tray, and took a fresh one for him. "You look as though you could use something cool," I said, certain this sweet-faced man-child before me had not yet seen combat. "Where do you hail from?"

"Rhode Island, ma'am."

"So you are a man well acquainted with the sea. Welcome to our slice of heaven. Tell me, Lieutenant Miller, what was your first thought when you saw this exquisite home?"

The earnest Lieutenant Miller thought the Bellingham home magnificent and his hostess most generous. As for the young ladies scattered across the lawn, he had never seen a lovelier group.

"Particularly the Polynesians," he added as he gave an appreciative eye to a passing waitress of Japanese descent, decidedly not among the blond women handpicked to meet him, and definitely not Polynesian. "They are such an exotic and attractive people."

"And what do you have to say about our local foods? Any particular favorites?"

A smile plastered in place, I diligently recorded his response. After all, macaroni salad was a popular island staple.

I waved the article in my hand at Harrison and Jack. "Drumroll, please. I'm dropping off my final article for the *Chronicle*." I tossed it in Ben's inbox. Judith Bellingham's tea party had given me the motivation needed to launch my own agency.

Harrison clapped and Jack whistled, but neither got out of their seats.

"So, what are you two doing here on a Sunday afternoon? Tojo about to surrender?"

They were seated by the news desks, their feet propped up, tumblers in hand. A bottle of Glenlivet rested between them.

"We're discussing the great questions of the universe," Harrison said.

"Maybe you'd like to weigh in?"

"Try me."

I pulled up a chair.

"Join us?" Jack held up an empty glass.

"Just a splash."

I gave Harrison my full attention. Shafts of rosy sunlight, the last of the day, haloed the top of his head and shadowed his features. The trade winds rocked the blinds against the sills in an annoying arrhythmic beat.

"Why is it, do you suppose," he said, "that a man smart enough, and certainly old enough to know better, keeps repeating the same mistakes? Goes and does something self-destructive, knowing"—he paused and slapped the desk on the word "knowing"—"that whatever momentary happiness he may experience will be overwhelmed by inevitable misery."

He took a sip of his whiskey. "Thoughts?"

"Because hope springs eternal?" I offered, then braved a sip from my glass. I liked being treated as one of the guys.

"Ah, Pope. I suppose there's truth there," he said. "This soul was uneasy and believed there might be solace elsewhere, and yet"—he leaned forward and I could see that his face was flushed—"that soul knew"— he slapped the desk again—"no true home awaited him in that female breast." I wondered how many glasses he'd consumed.

"So what did Renee do?" I asked.

"Flew off to Los Angeles and left Lolly and me behind. You know anything about this, Doyle?"

"Not a thing."

Which was the truth. I hadn't seen or heard from Renee since I'd joined her party of actors for drinks at the Moana. She had been the old Renee that evening, dressed to kill and playing the sun around which we all orbited—but without a whiff of romance or attention paid to one man in particular.

"They gave her a small part in that silly film. Did she tell you that?"

"The only thing she talked to me about was doing more at the dairy, learning about its management, taking on a bigger role. She seemed excited." I didn't add that Renee feared Judith would block any possibility of her running the dairy.

"Know anything about a movie producer named Max?"

"You know I do. He was part of the first story I wrote for you. I didn't name him, but you knew he was the producer who promised to make her a star. Renee hasn't mentioned him since I wrote the story. Not a word."

"It seems he's connected to the movie they filmed here. He's the one who got her a role. Sounds like he even offered her a contract."

"I'm sorry, Harrison. I thought all of that was in the past."

Harrison leaned back in his chair, his eyes glazed and unfocused. For the first time in all the time I'd known him, he was a man diminished.

The three of us sat in silence.

"Enough of this," I finally said. "This is Renee we're talking about. This is what she does, who she is. She charms and seduces, she makes us feel we're the most special people in the world to her and in that moment, we are, at least until someone with more to offer comes along. I believe she loves us, to the degree she loves anyone. Most of all, she loves her freedom and ambition. She's hungry. She needs to show what she can do and be."

Harrison scoffed. "What a pair we are. You're as bad as me. We're a couple of romantics conned by a tough broad."

"No. That's wrong and you know it." I wasn't going to let him destroy Renee for me. "She didn't con us. She was never fake. We wanted her to be small, to be only the parts we liked. Except she isn't small. She's a huge, messy, complicated being. I hate her for leaving, but I won't pretend she betrayed me or set out to hurt me. Any more than she wanted to hurt you or Lolly."

I could see Harrison tune me out. He needed Renee to be the evil woman who deserted her husband and child.

"So I guess I should make it official." I placed the envelope with my resignation on the desk beside Harrison. "I've leased office space across the street and will open the ad agency next week. The furnishings are minimal, but it'll do for now. Helen Lau's agreed to moonlight and cover the design side. Leo Klein will do my voice work for radio bits. I'm now chief of my own company, with the debt to prove it."

Harrison raised his glass. "Congratulations, Sadie."

"I wouldn't be here without you, Harrison. You took a big chance hiring me."

"I like to think I've an eye for talent, but we can both thank Renee for making this happen."

I finished off my drink. "Time I got a move on. Thanks for the drink and I'm sorry about Renee. Truly."

"I'll walk you out," Jack said.

He pulled wide the heavy front door. "I'd offer a celebratory dinner, but I need to get Harrison home safe. I'm glad for you, Sadie. Really. Soon enough, you'll be running this city."

"Thanks. I'm not feeling all that celebratory, with the news about Renee." I gave him a tight hug. "I'll miss working with you, even if you are a lousy reporter."

"I'll be right across the street if you need me."

I had the impulse to suggest he stop by for supper after dropping Harrison off, but decided no. I'd sent Lionel off to the Big Island with Archie the day before, pretending it was a gift, a chance for them to spend time together, but I wanted someone keeping an eye on Arch. His drinking was worse and his sales dropping. He needed a profitable trip.

I didn't need more complications, and Jack was a complication waiting to happen.

Lionel

I don't know what I was thinking. Why did I expect a trip to the Big Island with Dad would be any different from how things usually are? As if Dad would be somebody better on another island and we'd have a fine time just us guys. Soon as Dad took me to the first plantation and I saw those giant roaches running over the floorboards and got a whiff of the stinky oil used to tamp down the dust, I knew the trip wasn't going to be like I imagined. The place was crawling with roaches—the big flying kind— and me with nothing to do except try to ignore them in that empty store while Dad and the manager, a guy named Gus, laughed it up in the back room. They were supposed to be working on the next month's order, only it sounded more like they were having a party. I should have known that was how Dad did business. "They love me on those outside islands," he told us back home. I didn't have enough imagination to figure out why his stories made folks laugh so much.

The plantation people were burning cane nearby that day, stuffing the air with a disgusting sweetness that clogs up your nose and stinks up your hair and clothes. After Pearl Harbor we aren't supposed to complain about the smell of burning cane or the syrupy pineapple stink from the cannery. "At least they're cutting down the cane," the grown-ups say, or, "You'll never hear me complain again when Kona winds blanket us with cannery steam." They say that 'cause so many field and cannery workers have signed up as soldiers. There's practically no one left to do the sugar and pineapple work. A lot of kids' moms do night shifts at the cannery, and we high school kids are bused out to the fields to pick pineapples. I hate working bent over in the hot sun, all covered up so the prickly pineapple leaves won't hurt me, my eyes stinging from the clouds of red dirt that cover us each time the wind blows.

At least they sold lots of good stuff at that plantation store. Japanese pickled ginger and radish, cuttlefish and salty plums—and jars and jars and jars of *sei moi*. The huge glass jars lined shelves that covered a whole wall, floor to ceiling. Salty *li hing mui* strips, sliced wet mango, cherry bits, salty lemon peel, red-hot ginger, and lots more. My favorite kind is crack seed 'cause it takes so long to eat. I didn't bother asking if I could have some, seeing as how the prices were about twice what they are on O'ahu and 'cause Dad told me, "One Coke, that's all," when we got to the store. No way he was paying those jacked-up prices. My mouth watered for lemon peel, but mostly I wanted one of the manapuas set out on a platter with a plastic dome on top to keep away the flies and roaches. They were the big fat Chinese buns made of sweet, stretchy bread with fatty bright-pink pork in their middles, not the dinky pork hash kind that you can eat in one bite. I thought about taking one and not telling. Figured Gus probably didn't keep count, but that would be stealing, so I didn't. I just walked on by and told my stomach it would get some of Gran's peanut-butter sandwiches soon enough.

I circled the whole store, then headed out to the porch to watch the smoke rising in pillars from the fields. It was like standing on a little red dirt island in a sea of green sugarcane, the sky so blue and bright overhead it hurt my eyes. I like cane. It sways like a hula dancer. What I don't like is pineapple, with its daggers that slice your hand. It even looks mean growing in the fields, what with the blood-red dirt running along its rows. I don't get why people make such a fuss about them. Folks from the mainland are always wanting to stop by a field and pick their very own, which is actually stealing, but they still go ahead and do it anyway. Maybe that's why it's good the pineapples have prickly tops. Sometimes grown-ups break the rules and the laws, only I can't say anything because that's being disrespectful. If I was going to go grab something without asking permission or paying for it, I'd choose a manapua any day over one of those stinky pineapples.

I was plenty bored by the time Dad came looking for me. He pushed open the screen door and handed me a paper sack. He was smiling like it was Christmas. Inside were a couple manapuas, a couple Cokes, and a bag of wet li hing mui. "When it's just us guys, we can splurge now and then," he said. Which was exactly opposite to what he'd said when we got there. Then I got a whiff of him, saw how red his cheeks were, and knew how come he was being all of a sudden so generous. "Don't tell your mom," he said, like I ever would. I never tell anybody, least of all Mom, some of the stuff he does.

Before I could take anything out of the bag, he reached in, pulled out a manapua and Coke for himself, then said his goodbyes to Gus, who'd followed him out. Gus looked plenty pleased with himself. My dad was supposed to be the one making money off of Gus and instead he got my dad to pay double for that sack of food. I bet my dad was even the one who brought the booze, like a kind of bribe to make Gus like him better.

"What we do this week will be our little secret, OK, champ?" Dad said when I got in the car. I stuck the paper bag between us and rolled down my window. I wasn't feeling so great.

As we pulled out onto the road, I rested my arm on the window frame and lay my head down on top of it. The air rushing over my face felt good and helped calm my stomach. I wanted to be back home in my own room, even if it meant Mom would be squawking at me to mow the lawn or take out the garbage.

"Mind if I eat this other one?" Dad's hand was in the bag before I could say yes.

"Makes no difference to me," I told him, and it didn't. Much as I wanted one of those manapuas, I knew I'd be sick if I tried to eat it.

Bits of pork and bread crumbs went flying as Dad took a big bite. "You can see why I love this job so much," he mumbled, his mouth stuffed. "I got it made in the shade."

Made in the shade? I wanted to yell. *You can't even do your job without drinking. You can't even stop yourself from throwing money away. You're nothing but a big fake. A liar and a loser*, is what I wanted to say, but I kept my mouth zipped 'cause nothing I said was going to make it any better.

To calm down, I did what I always do when things get scary. I tested myself. I tested myself first on the names of all the American battleships, then all the destroyers and all the aircraft carriers. After that, I ran through the names of the navy and army bases and moved on to the names of every baseball team's players, and then the baseball players on the teams Kenny and I made up. When I'm working hard to remember so much information, I don't have space in my brain for anything else. And that can be a good thing.

Gran says I should go see Dad in the hospital. I told her I didn't care if he was hurting and lonely 'cause he deserved to feel bad, but she said I should go see him not for his sake but for mine. She said I'd feel better if I see him and forgive him. I'm not ready to forgive him. I'm still crazy mad at him. We were supposed to be having a special trip, just me and him. It was finally my turn after all the times Mom made Kenny go with him.

Only the trip didn't get any better after the first awful plantation visit. The only thing that changed was I knew not to go out with him when he visited the stores. I just hung out at the hotel in Hilo, reading my books. When I got bored, I walked around the town a bit, but there's not a whole lot to do or see in Hilo. When he hadn't gotten back by seven o'clock the night before we were supposed to leave and I was about starved, I asked Mrs. Hayashi, the lady at the front desk, if there was some place I could eat and have Dad pay for it later. She was nice and got me some noodles from the Chinese place down the block and said she would put it on Dad's bill. I ate my noodles in the little lobby area and played solitaire and tried not to stare at her as she worked on her books at the big old wooden desk she uses instead of a counter for checking people in. Around nine o'clock she asked me if there was someone I could call to see if Dad was OK, only I couldn't think of anyone to call except Gran Schaeffer or Mom, and that would have meant making a long-distance call all the way to Honolulu. Mrs. Hayashi was looking almost angry, her face all tight the way Mom's gets when she's not pleased, and I couldn't tell if she was angry with me or with Dad. At around eleven she said she had to go to bed and I might as well go to bed, too, and get some rest, so I was asleep when a policeman knocked on the door. He came to tell me Dad was in a car accident and they'd taken him to the hospital, which wasn't much of a hospital.

I hardly slept at all the rest of the night worrying about Dad and whether he'd live and how we'd get back to Honolulu. In the morning, another police officer came and said they were going to put Dad in an ambulance that would drive right onto the ferry and take him to Queen's Hospital in Honolulu. The officer gave me a ride to the dock and I had to sit in the back, so I imagined I'd been arrested and was headed to jail for pulling off the biggest heist ever. The ambulance people wouldn't let me be in the ambulance with Dad, which was OK by me, so I stayed by myself in the passenger part of the ferry. I stood in the wayback of the open space part, facing the rear so no one could see me if I cried, which I didn't want to do, but I couldn't help it, mostly 'cause I was so angry at Dad for messing up again. I tried doing what Mom and Gran always tell me to do—burn off that steam before you explode. I pounded the railing till my fist was sore, and yelled all my bad thoughts at the white water of the boat's wake, and maybe it helped some. I don't know. I don't think anyone could hear over the ferry's engines, and right then I didn't really care if they did.

Mom, Kenny, and Gran were waiting at the dock when the ferry arrived, and Miss Eleanor's driver took us to Queen's Hospital, where they had to operate on Dad to fix his broken leg and arm. Mom was shaking real bad in the car and Gran sat beside her, saying everything would be OK, and Mom kept saying, "No it won't be, not this time, Elma, not this time," and Kenny was real quiet beside the driver up front.

Now Dad's lost his job again and I heard Mom tell Gran she has to borrow more money from Ying to tide us over till the new business makes enough money, and Gran said, "It's OK, Sadira. Ying wants to help. She believes in you," and Mom said, "It's too much, Elma. Sometimes it's just too much." Then Gran said what she always says to her when Mom gets like that. She said, "Sadira Schaeffer, you are not a quitter and you are not weak. You will manage this as you have managed every trial in your life. With courage and determination." I don't know if Mom believed her, 'cause she sounded real tired when she said, "I don't really have any other option, do I?"

They say Dad has to stay in the hospital another week, maybe two, so his injuries can heal. Kenny goes by to see him every day since it's not that long a walk from here, but I don't go over. Dad wrote me a note that Mom brought home. It said: "Please forgive me, Lionel. I know I let you down. I am very sorry. Your loving Dad." Only I don't think he's such a loving dad, not when he thinks only about having a good time and doesn't care anything about what happens to me and Kenny. Gran said that's not true, that he loves us very much and only drinks because he's sad and the alcohol makes him forget he's sad, but it seems to me the alcohol only makes him sadder.

At least Kaiyo understands how I feel. Her dad drinks too much sometimes, and that's one of the reasons she wanted to move into town and live in somebody else's house, only now she has to be around my dad who drinks too much.

This afternoon I'm playing my trumpet at a special Scouts ceremony up at Punchbowl in honor of the fallen. Mom says she'll try her very best to be there, and Gran Schaeffer says she'll be there for sure, but the only person I hope shows up to hear me play is Kaiyo. Maybe if his hospital window is open, Dad will hear the trumpet sounding over the crater's rim, but I don't really care if he listens or not.

Sadira

I plopped down at the waterline and stuck my legs straight out in front of me. I didn't care that I wasn't in a swimsuit. The waves could go ahead and soak me. I wanted to feel the rush of water on my legs, the sand molding itself around them. The sun, setting on O'ahu's leeward side, had rinsed the sky pink and the evening trade winds were quickening. I closed my eyes and lifted my face to the breeze.

I was supposed to be hanging pictures in the office and setting up tables for the next day's opening, but I had to get out. And I couldn't go home. It was equally frantic there. Ying had started the boys picking plumeria blossoms at dawn. She and Elma had spent the entire day stringing leis for the noteworthy guests at the opening. Every bucket and vessel big enough was filled with floating leis.

I was just getting a bit of fresh air and had meant to go back, but once I was in the car and moving, I couldn't stop. I drove through and past Kāhala, then around Koko Head and Makapuʻu, until I was on Waimānalo's straight stretch of road. I pulled off and followed a path to the water.

Focus on all you've accomplished, I told myself as my legs sank in the wet sand, the shrinking sun warm on the back of my neck. *Stay optimistic.* But it was difficult to remain positive when I felt so overwhelmed. So much was happening so quickly, and I hadn't had a moment to reflect on it all, let alone feel I had some control over the moving pieces.

Archie was still at Queen's Hospital but would come home in three days and need help as he healed. One more demand on everyone's limited time. Lionel refused to visit the hospital or speak to his father on the phone. He would not forgive Archie and refused to talk to me about it.

I tried to remain patient, sympathetic about what he'd gone through, but he was nearly an adult. He had to cope better on his own. I understood it distressed him to see Arch such a mess in the ambulance, but he wasn't the first kid to face a tough situation. It certainly never occurred to him how difficult my burden was in all this or that he should be helping me rather than adding more to my load.

Typical Archie to sabotage my attempt to create a better life for us all. As soon as my focus shifted to starting up the ad business, he had to make himself the center of attention and cripple us financially. I was sick of it. And exhausted. It was too much for one person to carry. When the police called from Hilo, I have to admit I was for one fleeting moment disappointed when they said he would survive.

"What kind of a monster have I become?" I had asked Ying. "That I should even for a moment wish my husband dead?"

"We all have terrible thoughts in our darkest moments. You need to listen to that feeling. What does it tell you?"

"That I hate my life."

"So maybe you need to make changes."

As if I weren't already changing my whole life.

"What other changes do you suggest? I already quit my job."

"I mean divorce Archie. It's time." For the first time, my response to the idea was pure relief. I could rid myself of him. "Your job is to live your life as best you can," Ying added, "and Archie has to live his. You can't fix him."

"He wouldn't survive on his own. He'd end up dead in some alley."

"Maybe. Or maybe he would realize he has to get control of himself. This isn't working for either of you."

Wings fluttered nearby, but the sky above was clear.

"That you, Pueo?" I scanned the area around me, hoping to sight one of Hawai'i's sacred owls, but saw nothing. My sensitivity to the universe's energy continued to fade. I no longer intuited emotional undertones in people's homes, I discerned no images when I read people's cards or tea leaves. It was as if life had muffled my senses right when I most needed the spirits to guide me. I ached for rescue.

Guide me, Pueo, I prayed. *Guide me, Jehovah. Guide me, universe. Guide me, someone. Anyone.*

No flutter of wings answered. No shadow fell over the sand. A lone sailboat appeared from the Lanikai side, its sails pink in the last of the failing light. The boat was at such a distance, I couldn't make out a human form at the rudder. Was solitude Pueo's answer?

I wrapped my arms around my knees, the rising wind sharp against my bare skin. There was nothing for it but to head home and do what had to be done.

Chapter Twelve

August 1945 to June 1946

Sadira

I focused on the legal pad before me, ignoring the outside commotion. Big news, yes, the biggest, but I didn't have the luxury of celebrating. Not with an ad due in the morning and me with no copy written. I blocked the outside noise from my mind and sharpened my attention.

Nothing was singing to me yet. I read through my list of words and phrases meant to conjure the magic of the Halekūlani. *Enchanted isles, fragrant blossoms, caressing wind, thundering warriors, sheltering* kiawe, *melodious ukuleles, sun-washed sea, waves kissing sand.* All of them tired clichés. I lacked an anchor for the campaign, the fresh phrase or image that would evoke a grand romantic notion of this hotel beside the sea.

Jack tapped on my door. "I figured as much. You have to be the only person in Honolulu working right now."

"I doubt it. Lots of people have to work."

"Work can wait." He grabbed my hand and pulled me to my feet. "I won't let you ignore history."

"What difference does it make if I'm in here or out there? History does not depend on me whooping and hollering."

He pulled me down the hallway of my small agency. "You're not allowed to ignore the moment a war ends."

He pushed open the building's glass front doors. Cheering people packed the sidewalk. Passing vehicles dragged garbage cans and blasted horns. Church bells rang. Young women ran into the street and climbed aboard truck beds packed with sailors and soldiers. The mob roared its approval.

Jack pushed forward through the wall of people, hauling me behind him across Kapiʻolani Boulevard. At the curb fronting the *Chronicle*, he directed me to look up, and I gazed into a snowstorm of paper bits drifting slowly, soundlessly to earth. "It's over, Sadie. We are done with war." He lifted me off the ground and spun me around.

"See!" he said, setting me down. "I got a smile out of you."

He took my hand and started for the *Chronicle*'s front doors, only I stayed rooted.

"What?" He looked genuinely puzzled, as if of course I would go wherever he led. "Our buddies are up there celebrating. It's a time to be with friends."

I hadn't the time for this conversation. Not there on the sidewalk. Not with cars honking and people crowding around us. Not when I had so much to do. It was absolutely clear we were at a pivotal moment in Hawaiʻi. Everything would be different now, and the astute could profit. I planned on being one of those smart enough to take advantage of the moment.

"I can't, Jack. There's too much to do."

"Seriously? Writing an ad for the Halekūlani is what matters most to you?"

"It's not about writing an ad. It's about creating a whole new kind of ad campaign, and not just for the Halekūlani. I need new campaigns for every client I have. Look at these people. The relief and hope on their faces. It's a new era, and I have to be ready to market products for what's coming. The time of sacrifice and frugality is over."

"You can't turn it off, can you? You're always working the angles."

"I'll take that as a compliment."

"Of course you will. Someday you and Ying will probably be running the whole damn state. Just remember every choice comes with a price, Doyle."

"Schaeffer. The name's Schaeffer. And trust me, no one knows more than I do about the cost of choices." I flashed him my best smile. "Go celebrate. I'll catch up to you later."

I returned to my empty office. I'd need my small staff soon enough to help me with the details, but at that moment, I needed quiet and time to map out a strategy.

I had four major clients and several smaller ones. My idea was to create for each of them some variation on the same basic pitch. After years of war, peace and prosperity were at hand. It was time to celebrate, give thanks, and be proud of our country. Accordingly, we would thank our heroes. Free thank-you cups of coffee for every guy in uniform having breakfast at the Kaimukī Diner. Free beer with every pūpū ordered at the Polynesian Tiki Lounge. A quart of Dairyland's milk for every family welcoming home a GI. The bigger clients could run contests: dinner and a night at the Royal Hawaiian Hotel for the person with the best homecoming story. A second honeymoon on Kauaʻi for the couple who'd endured the longest, most difficult separation. The kid with the best "I'm Proud of My Dad" drawing would star in the next Dairyland milk ad. The smaller businesses, like Ying's, could do victory sales events, tributes to the 442nd. I rattled away on my typewriter as I pushed to get ideas on paper. We would sell patriotism, wrap every product and service in the flag. And when the time came to move beyond celebrating and applauding victory, we would promise customers times of abundance ahead, a chance for everyone to be part of the modern era. We'd dictate what it meant to be a successful American. Washers and dryers in every home. More efficiently designed homes. More fashionably attired families. Healthier packaged foods. Whatever the product, whatever the service, we'd make buying it proof of success and character, and even loyalty.

Let the rest of Hawai'i party. Let them relax in the glory of the day's moment. I would win by staying ahead of the others, anticipating and promoting the new, and never resort to old strategies designed for a bygone era. Tradition was done. New was everything. And I was aiming high.

Lionel, age 17

It was a day to remember and then some. Soon as they said on the radio that the Japanese had surrendered, the church bells started ringing like crazy and people ran out of their houses and whooped and hollered and then kinda just stood there on the sidewalks like they expected something else to happen only they didn't know what exactly. My buddy Rodney from up the street came by with his pickup, and me, Kenny, and a bunch of the neighborhood kids piled in the back. I brought my horn along and Stan had a big flag he waved, and we drove down Ward and then along Kapi'olani to Kalākaua and right through Waikīkī, me blasting my trumpet and everyone hooting and hollering loud as they could. Truckloads of service guys jammed the roads and all along the way people stood waving and yelling from the sidewalks. Near Fort DeRussy, we saw a whole band of army guys in uniform marching in formation and a crowd of kids following behind them, making like they were soldiers, too. I've never seen the whole city happy like that before in my whole life. It was better than any New Year's or Fourth of July.

Kaiyo was weeding in the garden when we heard the news, and she cried, too, but I don't think her tears were all happy ones. Ying gave her a big hug and took her back inside the house. Maybe it made her sad to think that Buster wasn't alive to see us win the war. Or maybe she's sad for her family back in Japan. None of her family lives in Nagasaki or Hiroshima, but it made us all hang our heads when we heard what the bombs did to those people.

I didn't expect the war to end so soon. I got cheated out of my chance to help the cause. Mom says she won't listen to any talk of my enlisting.

She still wants me to go to college, but my trigonometry teacher, Mrs. Riley, says that maybe I need to accept my limitations and not try to be something I'm not meant to be, 'cause she thinks I'm not smart. Mom says not to pay her any attention 'cause she knows nothing about anything but math. Mom said, "It's up to you, Lionel. You were put here on God's earth for a reason, and soon enough you'll figure out what that is. What matters is work and grit. Toughen up and stop indulging your feelings, and you'll be OK." Mom believes that we all have possibility and can make something of ourselves if we just try hard enough. "Look at me!" she says. "I was a nobody housewife in Carlisle, New York, and now I've got my own business, and someday I'll buy myself a house. Anything's possible, Lionel, if you just believe in yourself." I don't know if I believe in myself 'cause I don't even know what that means exactly. But I know something about working hard and sitting on my feelings so they don't show so much.

Mom doesn't know it, but I still plan on joining the navy's signal corps, and I practice with my flags every chance I get. Kenny thinks I'm stupid. "You're only going to confuse yourself when you have to learn with the real flags," he told me, but I'm smart enough to keep it all straight. I missed out on being a war hero, but I can still do my part. Someday soon I'll tell Mom I do have a purpose in life. It's just not the purpose she wants me to have.

A long time ago, Ying taught me how to keep from exploding when everything's pressing in on me. I close my eyes and pretend I'm underwater and it's just me and the fish and no one can find me or bother me and I can stay there forever if I want, hiding in the water. Then everything feels quieter and calmer and I stop wanting to punch a wall or jump off a cliff.

But the day the war ended, I only felt happy. I think the world and I are going to turn out A-OK.

Sadira

"We meet again beneath the mighty banyan tree beside the sea, the great panorama of Waikīkī Beach before us, old Diamond Head at one end, surfboards and outrigger canoes catching the waves. This is Webley Edwards speaking for all the islanders and all these mainlanders, most of them members of our armed forces, whose voices now rise with us in that traditional shout that begins our songs from the islands, our aloha, as Hawai'i calls."

As many times as I had watched Webley do his intro to the show before the war, I never tired of that moment when he cried out, "Hawai'i calls," and the music swelled. To hear him share those lines once again, after all those years of radio silence, stirred me deeply. I imagined the mothers and fathers, the sisters and wives, the children of servicemen listening from thousands of miles away to the sound of waves breaking and the steel guitars strumming. Did those tropical sounds bring their loved ones closer to them? Give them hope they would see them again soon, now that the war was ended?

And for the young people, restless as I once was, did the romantic music stir them? I still could not listen to "Aloha 'Oe" or "Song of the Islands" without tearing up. The music evoked so much more than a sense of place; it conjured a yearning for possibility and hope. Out here in the Pacific was a tiny dot of land where dreams could come true. I had recreated myself in Hawai'i and still trusted its magic. Staring out to the horizon line, the ocean vast and sparkling before me, I could believe all doors remained open.

"You on air today?" June Breen asked, sitting down beside me. June managed the Moana's main dining room.

"Doing a tidbit about a soldier who rescued a kid's cat in Wahiawā. That is, I'm on if the guy doesn't fall apart on me. He's got a serious case of nerves." I nodded in the direction of a young private in full dress uniform. He sat at attention in his chair, sweat pouring down his face as he cracked his knuckles.

"Anyone tell him no one will see him on the radio? He's going to pass out if he keeps that jacket on."

"I tried. He said, 'Thank you, ma'am, I'm fine,' and kept it on. All I need is for him to swoon midway through the interview."

"Poor kid. Bet everybody in his town back home will be listening." June leaned forward and lowered her voice. "I've been wanting to talk to you about an idea I have. Any chance we can meet sometime next week for lunch?"

I pulled out my date book. "Absolutely." I always made space for potential new clients. "How's Tuesday?"

"That works. Noon at the Halekūlani?"

"Perfect. You going to give me a hint what you want to talk about?"

"I've got an idea for a restaurant."

"Excellent. I can't wait to hear about it." Restaurant promotion was becoming a kind of specialty for me, and June was someone who knew plenty about the business.

Demand for my services already exceeded my ability to provide them. I couldn't keep up. Ying had been right. This business was going to thrive if I could keep adapting quickly.

A production assistant tapped me on the shoulder to signal my segment was coming up. I walked over to the young soldier, a glass of ice water in hand.

"Please take off your jacket now." I decided no more questions and suggestions, only orders.

He dutifully removed the jacket, then downed nearly the entire glass of water.

"You're going to do great," I assured him. "Pretend I'm your mom and you're telling me what happened. It'll be over before you can blink."

And it was. Even for me, who'd been doing these bits for years, my segments went by in a snap of the finger. One minute I was walking to the microphone and the next I was done and back in my seat. If it weren't for the show's recordings, I wouldn't quite believe I'd even been on the air. I always deliberately pushed out of my mind the idea of friends and family members listening back in Carlisle. Speak to the audience in front of you, I always told myself, but that day it had been more difficult to pull off.

That day I imagined Prudence, Ben, and others of the Doyle clan clustered around their living room radios, hurling invectives at the sound of my voice, saying aloud the things Prudence had written in letters after she heard I was divorcing Archie. Even Elma disapproved, but at least she understood. After all these years of covering for Archie, of telling people he was doing fine when they assumed the worst, I couldn't now persuade them I had no choice left but to kick him out. It seemed it didn't matter what harm Archie caused the boys and me. We were supposed to endure it all.

"In sickness and in health," Prudence wrote, "that's the promise you made."

I resisted pointing out to her that for all these years she had wished Archie would leave me. She had finally gotten that wish. I was out of his life and hers.

I wondered, too, if Renee ever listened to the show. I hadn't heard a word since she left. Her divorce from Harrison was not yet final, and she was living with Max in LA, but I knew nothing more. "She'll be back," Ying kept saying, and I supposed she was right. She might not return for me and Harrison, but there was always Lolly to draw her back.

"You were terrific," I told the young man when we finished, and he had been. Once I got him talking about the rescue, his self-consciousness disappeared and he was a kid from Tennessee telling a good story.

"You made my mama a proud lady today, ma'am."

"Not me, Private Carson, you. You made your mama proud. Thanks for being on the show."

What next, I thought as I sat back down at my table. I still had a chunk of time to myself. The boys were bowling with Archie during his weekly visit. Lionel's resentment had softened enough that he endured the occasional outing. Eleanor, Elma, and Ying were going to a late afternoon showing of *Meet Me in St. Louis*, and Kaiyo was home preparing the nursery.

Jack O'Brien, beer in hand, pulled out a chair and sat down beside me.

"Any chance I can lure you away from here? I know I'm asking the impossible. You are such a busy woman."

"I am indeed a busy woman. A busy and important woman, but I'm intrigued. Lure me with what? The chance to help you write a story that passes for adequate?"

"You keep telling yourself you're a better writer than I, Sadie. We both know I taught you everything you know. I was going to offer cocktails on my boat as the sun sets, but now I'm rethinking the idea." He pretended to scan the courtyard. "Maybe there's another woman here who appreciates a good man."

"I don't think the problem's my not appreciating a good man. The problem is I'm not sure such a beast exists." I smiled. "You know, sometimes I miss seeing you at work, then I remember what that was like."

"Of course you miss me. I'm habit-forming. So what do you say about a sail?"

"You're actually proposing taking me on the never-seen sailboat?"

"Hey, I've taken your kid out for rides."

"Maybe you rented a boat."

"You know damn well I wouldn't go to that much trouble to do something nice for you, Sadira."

"OK, Jack. I'll let you take me out on this boat of yours. Some fresh air would do me good. I just better not get sick."

"No guarantees." He looked out at the water. "But I do believe it's your lucky day. The beach boys would say there's no action out there."

As he paid his bill, I made the rounds of the room, saying goodbye and touching base with those I hadn't yet spoken with that afternoon.

"Always working it, aren't you?" Jack said as we headed for the lobby.

"That's how I pay the bills, O'Brien. Schmoozing and boozing. Gotta keep everybody happy."

As we climbed the stairs, he lightly pressed his hand to my back in a protective gesture. I knew he could not have caught me if I tumbled backward, but it was a comfort all the same.

"Here you go, Mom." Lionel handed me a mai tai and a small plate of crispy *gau gee*. "Miss Eleanor's party chef made the gau gee special for your birthday," he added. "I told him they're your favorite."

"You sure they aren't your favorite?" I teased.

"That's not why I told him to make them. You always order gau gee at Wo Fat. I was not being selfish."

"I know. I know. I was teasing, Lionel. It was thoughtful of you."

"You sure can make a guy sorry he even tried." His body was stiff with fury. Eighteen years and I couldn't get it right.

Eleanor had seated me at the largest of the tables circling her massive terrace. As no other guests had yet arrived, I felt ridiculous sitting there alone with Elma. The terrace was done up with colorful lanterns and elaborate floral displays. It was not the quiet family gathering I had expected.

"Who all did you invite?" I asked Elma.

"It wouldn't be much of a birthday surprise if I told you that."

Lionel reemerged with Eleanor beside him, her arm protectively tight around his shoulders.

This time he carried a plate of steamed buns. A young woman in a white uniform followed with platters of crab crostini and sashimi.

"This is quite the banquet, isn't it?" I said. "Thank you so much, Lionel and Eleanor. All my favorites." Lionel avoided looking at me. His sulking was my familiar punishment.

He took Elma and Eleanor's drink orders and headed to one of the two bars set up for the evening.

Eleanor patted my hand. "He seems to have gotten the impression you thought he requested the gau gee for himself."

"I know," I said. "A poor attempt at humor on my part. I forget that humor's wasted on him."

"Yes, he can be quite literal." Eleanor spoke in a soft, tutorial way as she explained my own son to me.

Kenny emerged from the garden path, a giant double plumeria lei in hand. Ying and Kaiyo, Buster Junior in her arms, trailed behind.

"Happy birthday, Mom." Kenny draped the lei over me. Ying did the same with five strands of *pīkake*.

Kaiyo held back a bit, but called out a soft, "Happy birthday."

"I was hoping you'd bring the baby." Eleanor lifted Buster from Kaiyo's arms. "Aren't you just the most adorable thing that ever was?" she cooed.

A few of my newspaper colleagues appeared next, and then began the steady stream of friends and acquaintances.

"Good Lord, Elma, how many guests are you expecting?" I said. "I barely know some of these people."

"Everyone made their suggestions, and Ying was adamant we include some good business prospects for you. She's learned a few of your tricks. Never miss a public relations opportunity."

Within a half hour, a crowd packed the terrace, a Hawaiian trio was serenading us, and both bars had lines. The pūpūs flowed from the kitchen. I circulated as best I could.

"Are we eating dinner as well?" I asked Kenny. "I won't have any room if I keep eating all these appetizers."

"They're grilling teriyaki beef sticks and 'ahi out back, and I think they've got a bunch of other stuff. Miss Eleanor sure knows how to throw a swell party."

"Apparently, she knows how to do most everything."

After years of minimal food supplies and muted celebrations, we were finally enjoying a raucous outdoor party, lights blazing and musicians playing as loud as they wanted. I indulged the wistful hope that Renee might magically appear, having realized what a mistake she'd made, but Harrison arrived alone and hung back in the shadows with Jack and Ben.

"Kaiyo's doing quite well, don't you think?" Eleanor said when she finally had a drink in hand and joined the festivities.

"I guess, but she's exhausted. I don't know why she tried to go back to classes so early. Even with help, she rarely gets enough sleep." Kaiyo's unmarried older sister stayed with her on weekends to help with Buster.

"I expect school's a good distraction. She needs something to give her hope and purpose." Eleanor's quiet tone suggested this was another observation meant to enlighten me. "Not all women are cut out for child rearing." She nibbled on the pineapple spear from her drink. "The good news is she's talking about going to medical school. She's always wanted to be a doctor. She certainly has the mind for it."

This was news to me. Kaiyo had never mentioned any graduate school ambitions, let alone an interest in medicine. "That's absurd," I said. "She might as well say she wants to be Queen of England."

"You underestimate her. It won't be easy, but she's bright and isn't afraid of hard work. She can do it."

Of course Eleanor believed that. She, who had never had a moment's financial worry, couldn't imagine what obstacles a woman, especially a single woman with a baby, might face in pursuing that dream. The whole idea was ridiculous.

I waved to Harrison, who was now parked at a table with Jack. I needed to be rescued. "If you'll excuse me, I need to check in with some friends." Even Harrison at his grimmest was easier company than a preaching Eleanor.

Irritating as the woman was, I couldn't fault a single thing about her party. The food was glorious, the music perfect, and I was being celebrated as the lady of the hour. By evening's end—with the help of three or four mai tais—all irritation was gone and I was sloppy with gratitude. When Jack proposed a toast, and people lifted their glasses to shout together, "To Sadira," I was on top of the world, my eyes teary and my heart overflowing with goodwill. All resentments and hostilities melted away and I counted myself blessed. Eleanor took the microphone.

"Elma and I are so very pleased you could all join us in celebrating

Sadira tonight. What spirit she brings to our lives. Happy, happy birthday, dear girl. Before I hand this microphone back to our musicians, we've a bit of a surprise. Kenneth, will you do the honors?"

For a moment, I imagined Renee might really be there.

Kenny took the mic. "Mom, I know you've always wished I could go to Punahou, and felt bad you couldn't afford it. The good news is that, with Miss Eleanor's help, they've accepted me and I'll start my sophomore year in September. You won't even have to pay a dime. To make it easier, I'm going to live here with Gran and Miss Eleanor, so I can just walk down the street to school. Your dream for me has come true at last. Happy birthday, Mom!"

He hugged me tight and the crowd applauded and cheered. Tears streamed down my face and I couldn't stop trembling. Kenny handed me the mic and someone yelled, "Speech, speech!" Before I could even try to say a word, Jack slipped the microphone from my hand. "I think you've managed to overwhelm your mother, Kenny." He handed me a handkerchief. "I propose we give her a moment to digest this wonderful news, and serenade her instead." He led the crowd in a boisterous round of "Happy Birthday to You," and then led me to a pocket of quiet at the terrace's edge. I was furious.

"You cut me off. I don't need you speaking for me."

"You'll thank me in the morning. You're not that good an actress. Your rage was leaking."

"You don't think I've got the right to be angry and let her know how I feel?" Jack's arrogance was galling.

"Not at all. It was rotten of Eleanor to go behind your back, but you don't want to ruin this for Kenny. Think about it."

The benefits of the arrangement were obvious. One less kid to keep track of and feed. More breathing space for Lionel and me. And, of course, Kenny would get the education he deserved. It was never fair that only Lionel got to attend a private school. Yet none of that erased my rage at Eleanor's audacity. She and Elma had conspired to steal my son from me, and then pretended it was a gift.

"I'm supposed to shut up and act like this isn't wrong?"

"Yup, for now. Because you'll only make yourself look bad and spoil the evening for Kenny. Talk about it later with Elma. Let her know you appreciate the generosity, but that you should have been consulted. Tell her that when it comes to your kids, she and Eleanor cannot make major decisions without consulting you."

"I'd rather scream at them in front of everyone."

"Suit yourself. But count yourself warned." He leaned over and kissed me on the cheek. "Happy birthday, Sadie. I'm sorry it ended on a sour note. I promise no more interference. I'll take off now."

He circled the crowd and disappeared down the path to the driveway. I stayed in my dark corner and studied the guests, their gestures and expressions relaxed by food and drink, their spirits high.

"You OK, Mom?" Lionel asked. "I couldn't tell if you were crying happy or crying angry. That was a mean thing Miss Eleanor did, going behind your back."

Dear Lionel, so often clueless about social expectations, and yet he could also be the most intuitive and discerning person in the room.

"It's going to be OK, lamb. It's all going to be OK. But thank you." I squeezed his hand. "I love you to pieces, you know. All I've ever wanted is for you boys to be happy."

He patted my hand as if he were the adult comforting the child. "I know, Mom. You don't have to worry, 'cause sometimes we really are."

Despite the dark, I could make out the mass that was Archie slumped over on the front steps of the cottage. Dealing with him was the last thing I needed after a long, intense workday. I jiggled the car keys as I approached, meaning to alert him, give him a chance to sit up, assume some scrap of dignity, but he stayed as he was.

He had been missing for days. "Disappeared," his YMCA buddy Carter told me when Arch failed to meet up with Kenny and Lionel for their weekly lunch. None of the Thomas Square regulars had seen him. The Hotel Street crowd couldn't recall when he'd last come by.

"Hey, Arch." I shook his shoulder gently.

Startled by my touch, he recoiled and raised an arm in defense, then groaned and settled back, resting his head on the step. "Sadie? That you, old girl?"

"Yup, it's me, Arch." I sat on the step below him, steadying myself in the murky darkness, willing myself into the role I had to play once again.

"They got me good this time."

"Who got you, Arch? Are you badly hurt?"

He raised his head a bit. "The kids. The ones that come round the park. They took my bag and roughed me up some."

I couldn't see enough in the dark to know how bad it was.

"I hate to be a bother, old girl. Didn't know where else to go. And when some sailors offered me a lift, I told them to bring me here."

I wished I could harden myself against him. I wanted to hate or even just resent him enough to turn him away and spare myself his dramas, but I couldn't do it. He was still family and, except for the boys and me, completely alone.

"Let's get you up." I grabbed him under one arm and nudged him to his feet, letting him take it slow. "We best get you cleaned and bandaged."

Blood caked his face and hair. He had cuts across his face, a gash in his scalp. I assessed the lacerations as best I could under the bathroom's single bulb.

"I don't think you'll need stitches." Not that I had much chance of getting him to the hospital if he did.

I helped him out of clothes so grimy I couldn't imagine ever getting them clean again, then supported him in the shower as I washed his hair and body, scouring him with a washcloth. To think I once loved that flesh, merged with it to create new flesh. The running water and scrubbing reopened the wounds. Fresh blood circled the drain and soiled the towel I used to dry him.

"Sit here on the john while I get you something to wear." I kept spare clothes for times like this. "Press the washcloth against your head to stop the bleeding."

Once I had him dressed, I set him in a chair at the kitchen table and set to work cleansing the bigger wounds more thoroughly and applying bandages.

"You should be checked for broken bones and internal injuries," I warned as I cut the tape securing gauze to his head. "I'd like to take you to the hospital."

He shook his head. "No. This is fine. All I need."

He was ashen in the harsh kitchen light. Everything about him seemed smaller, as if he were shrinking into himself.

"Hey, Dad." Lionel appeared in the doorway. "You OK?"

"Sure thing, champ! Your old pop's just dandy. Mom patched me up good as new." Archie reached out an arm as if to wrap it around my hips as he might have in better times, but I stepped away.

"I'm going to make your dad some breakfast, then take him back to the Y."

"OK."

"Give us a hug, sport." Archie reached out an arm. Lionel offered his hand.

"Too grown up for hugs, eh? Well, then, a handshake it is. Good to see you, buddy."

"Right. You, too, Dad. Guess I better head back to bed."

"Sleep well," I called as I pulled out the skillet.

I collected a carton of eggs from the fridge. "What'll it be, Arch? Scrambled or fried?"

"Whatever's easiest, love. And maybe some coffee? I could sure use a cup of your good coffee."

I lit a flame beneath the frying pan, prepped the coffeepot, and set three eggs to sputtering.

"I've been thinking, Sadie."

"Yeah, Arch?"

"Thinking maybe I'll move back to Carlisle. My folks offered me a plane ticket. Even said they'd send my cousin Pete out to get me. You know how much Pete's always wanted to see Hawai'i. Then the two of us could fly back to California together. Maybe take the train from there. Wouldn't that be a swell adventure? I could start over again, old girl. Clean slate and all that. What do you think?"

I slid the spatula under the eggs and flipped them, pressed down hard on the yolks, cooking them firm the way Archie liked them.

"I think a fresh start might be just the answer, Arch."

When I placed his eggs and toast before him, he looked up at me with such gratitude and trust, I had to turn away.

"Well, then, it's a plan. And maybe you and the boys could come visit me now and then."

"That sure sounds great, Archie." I placed a hand on his shoulder. "Now eat your breakfast before it gets cold. We want you healthy and strong for a big trip like that."

While he ate, I took a hard brush to the skillet, bearing down with all my weight to scrub off the burnt bits and grease, the steam rising, shrouding my face, clouding my vision.

Lionel, age 18

The mynahs were squawking something awful the afternoon I saw my dad for what might have been the last time ever. Gran says not to think like that. She says you never know what the future holds and maybe he'll sort himself out.

She could be right, but right now my head and stomach hurt and I feel like a lousy son. I may have seen my dad for the last time ever and I didn't say one nice thing to him. Not once the whole time.

He was waiting for me on the front steps of the main library downtown, sitting there with his arms crossed in front of him and his hands under his pits, like he was worried or cold. He stood up soon as he saw me get off the bus. Didn't walk toward me or wave, just stood there under the shower trees, staring as I crossed the lawn. When I reached him, he acted like he was ready to hug me, only I didn't get close enough to let him. He didn't say anything at first, just kept grinning at me like some kind of idiot. The mynahs were screeching and I didn't know where to look. I didn't want to look at him 'cause I could tell, even out of the corner of my eye, that he wasn't doing so great. He was wearing a stretched-out T-shirt and faded shorts and only had zoris on his feet. He looked like he was going to go mow a lawn, not like he was one of the grown-up men downtown on a weekday. His face was all busted up like someone had kicked it. Not once, but a lot.

"Some kids beat you up again?" I asked.

He waved his hand like it was nothing. "Don't worry about me, kiddo. I'm a tough old guy."

We stood there not talking or looking at one another for a while.

"So where we going?" I finally said, 'cause somebody had to say something. "Inside?"

I nodded at the library's entrance. I love it inside the library. It's one of my favorite places, especially the back courtyard where I can sit in a big armchair and read for as long as I want without anyone bothering me. I could stay there all day, except until I have to go use the bathroom, and then, if I'm not fast enough, people move my books and steal my chair and the librarians won't do anything about it. "First come, first served," they say, ignoring the fact that I was the first one there.

"We can't talk if we go inside," Dad said. "Maybe we should find ourselves a bench and sit out here."

Not talking sounded OK by me, but the whole point was to talk. We were there to say our goodbyes.

I shrugged and followed him to a stone bench under one of the shower trees, right underneath the branches lined with mynah birds. He was going to sit right down, not even look to see what was there first, but I said, "Watch the shit," and he stopped just short of touching the bench.

He stood back up and frowned at me, like he was angry, like he thought I was saying he was shit. I pointed at the bench covered in bird crap and he said, "Oh, right," then grabbed a stick and started scraping it across the bench. Like that would make it clean. And the mynahs were still up there waiting to dump more on us. No way I was going to sit there and be a target.

"Can we go someplace else?" I asked. "Maybe just walk?"

"Sure thing, great idea. Why, we can just head on over to the palace and have ourselves a good stroll around the grounds." He patted me on the shoulder like I'd hit a home run or something.

"School going OK?" he asked as we walked along King Street. He put his hands back up under his armpits and was grinning too much again.

"I guess." I was hauling a big Liberty House shopping bag that bumped against my leg and dragged on the sidewalk as I walked. I was beginning to be sorry I'd suggested we walk around.

"Well, will ya look at that." He stopped and stared down at the ground. "A lucky penny. How's about that for a good sign?" He held it up in the light, the same stupid grin on his face, like he'd found a ten-dollar bill or something. He rubbed both sides against his shorts to make it shine, then held it out to me.

"There ya go. A lucky penny to help you remember your old dad."

"You keep it. I got plenty of pennies."

It was mean of me to say that. He stuck the penny in his pocket and his stupid grin was finally gone. He didn't say anything more as we walked along the 'Iolani Palace fence, just shuffled along. He looked old, what with his white beard stubble and his veins standing out ugly and blue on his hands.

"Where you staying these days?" I asked him, finally figuring out that maybe he had no place to go, that maybe he got kicked out of the Y and couldn't take a shower or change his clothes. Maybe that's how come he looked like a bum.

"Don't you worry about me, champ. Your old dad's doing just fine.

Your Uncle Pete's picking me up around five today. I get to stay at his hotel tonight. Make myself presentable before I board that plane tomorrow." He pretend-punched me in the arm. "Ya don't have to worry. I won't show up for my flight looking like a tramp."

"That's great, Dad. I bet it'll be swell staying in a hotel." My arm was tired from holding the shopping bag. "Think we could sit down for a bit now?" I found us a bench in the shade. My plan was to tell him I was enlisting in the navy, but it felt mean to brag when his life was so sad and messed up. We just sat and said nothing.

"Here," I said when I couldn't take the silence anymore. I handed him the shopping bag, trying to act like it was no big deal, like I was just passing along some old shirt for him to wear or maybe a jacket he left behind at the house.

"What's this?" He opened it up and pulled out the quilt. He knew right away what it was. He couldn't help but know, seeing as how he'd only seen it about a billion times over all the years I worked on it. Bits of his own shirts were sewn right into it along with pieces from all our clothes. All these years, I've been cutting up the things in our lives, the shirts and the pants, the curtains and the aprons. I even put in parts of our old Carlisle kitchen tablecloth and some satin Renee let me have from a gown she was going to toss out. It's like our whole life was sewn up in that one big blanket.

"Well, will you look at that," he said, holding it up in front of him.

"Thought you could maybe use something to keep you warm on those cold winter nights back in Carlisle. It's OK, though, if you don't want it. I know it's kind of kapakahi. Mom says the colors and patterns clash so bad it makes her queasy just looking at it."

"Well, it doesn't make me feel sick. No sirree, Bob. I like it just fine." He opened it up wide, then wrapped it around himself even though it was blazing hot, even though sweat was dripping off his face. He stroked it like it was a cat or made of mink, like he couldn't get enough of its soft feel.

"It's swell, kiddo. Just swell." He looked ready to burst, he was so happy wrapped up in that crazy old quilt. I could tell he really did think it was swell just the way it was.

He looked so small under that quilt. A big gust of wind could have blown him clear out to sea. He was a whole other person from the guy I used to pal around with. His eyes watered and his neck drooped like a turkey's. When I was a little guy, he seemed so big and strong. Back then I thought he could do anything. I turned away from him and pinched my nose. It's a trick I use to keep from crying. I tried to make it look like I was shielding my eyes from the sun. As bad a dad as he's been, I didn't want him to know he looked like a sorry sack to me.

"Darn that blinding sun," he said and walked a bit away along the palace lawn, like maybe he knew it wasn't really the sun bothering me. "Won't be missing all this squinting when I'm back on the mainland," he called back. "No sirree, Bob."

That's how I'm going to remember him. Not the way he looked later, standing by the bus sign watching after I climbed on board. Not how he held his hand up like he wasn't sure whether to salute or wave. I'm going to remember him walking away from me, wrapped in the quilt, looking from the back nearly the same as he did when I was a kid. Looking almost like he was still my dad.

Sadira

The rain drummed hard on our tin roof. A gust of wind swept through, slapping the blinds against the panes. A door slammed. This was looking more like a March rain than a June one—the kind that obliterates color and definition. I switched on lights, grateful I'd made it home before the worst of it. I'd spent my Sunday catching up at the office, oblivious to the shift in the weather.

As I feared, the front windowsills were soaked. I lowered the sashes and sopped up the puddles. We were lucky to have celebrated Lionel and Kaiyo's graduations and departures the day before, when the skies were clear and the trade winds steady.

I grabbed an unopened bottle of Drambuie, a graduation gift for me from Renee. "So you can properly celebrate your new life," her note said. Leave it to her to be the person who grasped what Lionel's graduation meant for my life. I dug out a snifter from the back of a cupboard and poured myself a healthy portion.

Fixing dinner was a snap. Elma had stuffed the fridge with party leftovers. I made a plate of dumplings, noodles, and chicken *katsu*. I finally had the house to myself, could do whatever I wanted, and there I was, sitting in my "Mom" spot at the kitchen table, the seat closest to the stove, and facing the pair of windows through which, for so many years, I had watched the boys playing in the backyard. There would be time enough in the days ahead to let go of old habits.

I pinched a pork dumpling with my chopsticks and took a bite. The greasy juice ran down my chin. I reached for a napkin, but there were none. Every one of mine, Ying's, and, I expect, a good portion of Eleanor's, sat soiled in a basket of laundry—laundry Kaiyo would have washed already, but she was spending a week with her sister's family before heading to medical school in San Francisco. As if one week helping Buster adapt to life with her sister would compensate for leaving him behind. I would never understand her prioritizing an education over her child. Ying had laughed at me when I criticized Kaiyo's decision. "You're one to talk," was all she said, implying I'd put my happiness above my boys'. My whole life was a sacrifice. I wiped my face with a dishtowel and added *wash napkins* to my to-do list.

A clap of thunder, rare during Hawai'i storms, rumbled in the distance. I looked into my reflection floating transparent and untethered in the window opposite me. How apt, I thought. A woman unmoored.

At the party the day before, Jack had noted how happy I seemed.

"No tears?" he asked, as if every mother must grieve her children leaving home. I hated Lionel's choice of the navy instead of college, but I was past ready for him to move on.

"Are you kidding?" I'd said. "It's finally my turn. I'm a free woman."

"No tug of the heart? No worries?"

I shook my head. "Not a one. I'm making the most of this."

"Well then," he'd said, pinging his bottle of beer against my soda. "Here's to you, Sadie."

I raised my snifter and saluted the wobbly reflection staring back at me. It was my turn to soar. I wouldn't let any of them take that from me.

I dug into my food and ate slowly, savoring the noodles' spice and the crunch of the chicken. I even read some of my library book, Agatha Christie's latest—*The Hollow*. For dessert, I downed a generous slice of dobash cake and the final drops of my Drambuie.

Before calling it a night, I stood on the threshold of the kitchen door, staring out through the thick curtain of rain, reveling in the night's fierce energy. Somewhere in the yard, metal clanged against metal as the wind tossed loose objects about. The splash back from the rain hitting the top of the steps drenched my trousers, but I didn't mind. If it was pouring this hard on our brown slopes, water had to be barreling over the Koʻolau cliffs, swelling the streams and rivers. How green Punchbowl would soon be—a rare gift in the dry months of summer.

A light glowed from Ying's kitchen, but not from the cottage between us. Kaiyo had always kept the lamp on above her back door. I was in no hurry to gain a new neighbor, but on that stormy night, the expanse between my home and Ying's felt vast and empty.

I latched the door tight against the wind and switched off the kitchen lights. I would run a bath, set a candle burning beside the tub, just in case the wind took down the lines, and soak for as long as I liked. If I had the impulse, I could blast music from the radio and sing along, loud as I wanted. No one would hear me above the deluge. Anything was possible now, and all the choices were mine to make.

Acknowledgments

Hawaiʻi Calls would not exist without the enduring support of my family and friends, the insights of my fellow writers, and the skill of professional editors.

I extend a huge thank you to the many writers, most of whom I met at the Writer's Center in White River Junction, Vermont, who provided feedback on my earliest scenes and, eventually, on my full manuscripts. They include the members of a writing group spun out from the Writer's Center—Gretchen Cherington, Jennifer Duby, Jessica Eakin, and Laura Nagy—as well as other writers whose insights also served the novel's development—Meg Brazill, Suzanne Cote, Laura Foley, Deb Franzoni, Colleen Marshall, and Meg Noonan. Fellow writers and instructors at the Green Mountain Writers Conferences also offered valuable feedback. And while they did not contribute directly to this prose project, I thank as well the members of my poetry group who for so long nurtured my writing and my spirit—Ina Anderson, Doreen Ballard, Bev Barton, Deb Franzoni, and Hatsy McGraw. Special gratitude goes as well to poet friend and teacher Cynthia Huntington for her encouragement and counsel along the way.

Insightful friends also generously read the full manuscript (in some cases, multiple versions) and helped me identify what was and wasn't working. They also boosted my spirits when I felt overwhelmed. Thank you, Linda Doss, Lani Leary Houck, Kathy Kimball, Sue Stritter, and Marice Ann Woodruff.

I thank Sarah Stewart Taylor for her professional assistance with the novel's development and Deborah Heimann for copyediting the manuscript before I began submissions.

A special mahalo goes to Rootstock publisher Stephen McArthur for the honor of including *Hawai'i Calls* on Rootstock's list, to marketing director Samantha Kolber for her guidance and expertise, and to the book's editor and production coordinator Marisa Keller. Marisa's editorial skills exceeded my expectations and I am in awe of her knowledge, insights, research skills, and meticulous attention to detail.

I do not exaggerate when I say this novel would not exist without my treasured friend, mentor, and writing partner Joni B. Cole who, in her workshops and with her feedback, taught me most of what I know about the writing process. More than that, her unwavering belief in this novel's potential and my capacity to create it sustained me through the tough stretches. I could not ask for a truer friend and writing companion. I encourage aspiring writers and avid readers to check out her workshops, books on writing, essay collections, and most excellent podcast, *Author, Can I Ask You?*

My final thank-yous and boundless love go to my family. While this is a work of fiction, it is grounded in my paternal family's narrative. I thank my father, Richard L. Nelson, who wanted this story told, shared his memories of Hawai'i during this era, and trusted me to convey the family narrative's essential truth using fictional characters and plot. He even provided the artwork that graces the book's cover. My husband Jim Matthews, my essential partner in all things, provided unending emotional and technical support and the gift of time enough to write the book; my son Astro Dan Matthews has been my most excellent promoter; and son Dylan Matthews and his wife Hannah Groch-Begley have showered me with their infectious enthusiasm. I am among the luckiest of women.

About the Author

Born and raised in Honolulu, Marjorie Nelson Matthews attended Punahou School, Occidental College, and the University of Hawai'i, Manoa. Her work experience includes writing for U.S. Senator Spark M. Matsunaga (D-Hawai'i), editing for Houghton Mifflin's software division, and managing the Journals Division for the University Press of New England. Her poetry has been published in *Rainbird, Across Borders, Bloodroot Literary Magazine*, and the New Hampshire Writers' Project's Poetry in the Windows event. *Hawai'i Calls* is her first novel.

Also Available from Rootstock Publishing:

CPSIA information can be obtained
at www.ICGtesting.com
Printed in the USA
BVHW070017130622
639633BV00002B/168